The Immortals of Co
Part 1

With Thanks

To Helen and Emma, who both helped in the process of this publication.

To Cath Burge, for her insightful and invaluable assistance in helping edit this book and providing me with ways to improve on the mistakes I made (and still make!).

To Kelly, who fell in love with the characters I spent my life creating and for her endless support and enthusiasm for the story.

To my parents, who supported me even when the story is not the genre of their preference and gave constructive feedback.

To Rose, for the first fan art; for her continued personal support and deep understanding of my universe and the characters within it; for her invaluable friendship and for her faith in the story itself – I cannot thank you enough.

To Andi Cahyo W, the cover-work artist as part of Unreal Studio, https://unrealstudioworks.com/ for bringing Cinthia visually to life.

Map of Mainland by Llykaell Dert-Ethrae with "Wonderdraft" software (Created by Megasploot).

'Song of the Acar Vanta' designed and drawn by Llykaell Dert-Ethrae

Contents

- Blue Horizon
- [Redacted]
- [Redacted]
- Festival

Note from the author

This book is an artsy-fartsy collection of short stories revolving around many characters and serves as a beginning, and prelude, to the series of Covyn. This is a work of sci-fi/fantasy, however, as I don't like to be tied down to any one genre, style, or form, I decided why not add in as many styles as I feel like. And so, this is a unique beginning.

As I do in all things with my writing, I have done so only when I felt it served a direct purpose. This book took over two years to complete, though truth be told I've been working on the characters, world-building and lore for twenty-eight years. This is, quite literally, my life's work.

After decades spent dreaming of sharing my characters and world with you all, I finally get to do just that. I couldn't be more excited to start this journey with you!

Welcome to Covyn, readers.

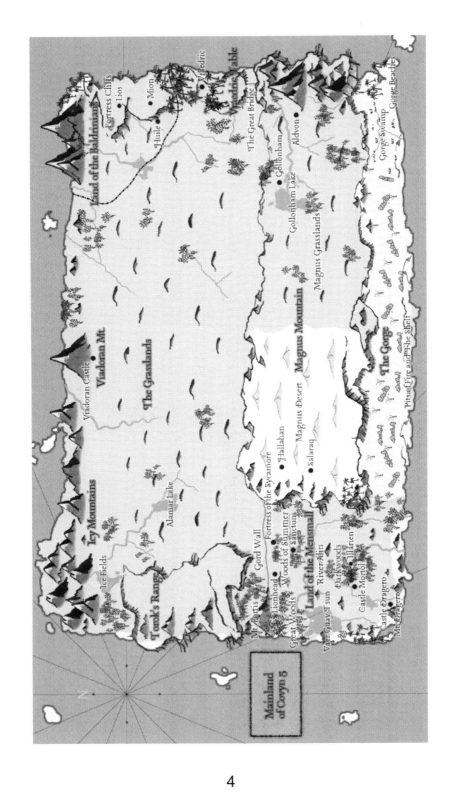

Oh the pendulum weeps for thee
That measure of eternity
Hear its call
Beyond the wall
Heralding toll
Within your soul
Ceaseless knells only to send
All unto its final end.

Must we, the Children of Death, hold this Power?

Our origins? Our origins are… fraught with distress. Savagery. Doubt. And most of all fear. For it is by our very nature that we are deemed above all other kinds. We are perceived as the emissaries of God, and whilst that part is at least true, to place us upon a towering pedestal and garland us with the admiration and awe of all mortal kind is a mishap. We are but people. People making our way through the endless corridors of existence alongside everyone else. Yes, within ourselves we have been gifted a series of powerful birthrights. Powers that seemingly cast a shadow upon the ageing races far beneath us as we stand silhouetted by the ascending half crescent moon of God. Of Inter.

    Yet these 'Powers', the *Cors*, do not and should not raise us to loftier heights. They are merely tools presented to us by the Divine, to be used as we please, for good or otherwise. Should we be feared for the vast and ever amplifying gifts we possess? I, for one, do not fear power in and of itself. No, instead I fear the will behind those who wield it and as such I do tremble at what may come as a consequence of our unpredictable potential. Whether that consequence be as a result of our actions… or others'. And that is why my sister and I are here. That is why we have the Elder Council.

    Whilst the precise nature of our origin is known to one alone, the general history is there for those wishing to delve into its murky and religious-politically dangerous depths. And I do not speak of our exact nature per se, but more of the events that preceded our kind being born into the world of Covyn 5.

    We are the Vampires of Inter, the Ambassadors of Death and all Its Will upon the realm of mortal kind. My sister and I, 'The Twins' as we are referred to colloquially, are the direct descendants of God. We were born into Death together in the year 382 in the Old Times in the city of Illarien, the birthplace of us all. Our purpose: to safeguard the will of Vertio, the first of our kind, and the Vampiric Laws he set out in the years before our creation, as well as those following it. Into us alone, Inter poured a unique gift – the power of bestowing lineage. Through us, all those whom we birth into Death will possess eyes holding all the colours we can imagine, yet none will hold the pure darkness of Vertio's and thus no-one shall inherit the Law unless made by his blood alone.

After his departure to parts as yet unknown, my sister and I stand in his place upon the Council. Together, we hold our, at times, unruly children at bay as best we can. Eternel is, well, Eternel about it, but I wish to take a more personal role in matters and desire greatly to be as involved in their lives as they desire. They are our children after all, our Fledglings, and thus I deeply concern myself with their wellbeing.

A question one never asks another Vampire is *why* – why they converted another to our ranks. It is considered bad taste and a presumption of ill-judgement. That being said, whilst it is generally impolite to pose such a query, I confess I am inwardly tormented over many of my choices. Eternel shares this. It seems we are still young in many ways and our assessments of those we forever altered were not as wise as we at first assumed. Yet, for all their faults, they are still our offspring. Never will it come to pass that I shall abandon them. I am, however, grateful for our position of authority. We would never be able to maintain relations with the other races without the Elder Council. There is some level of redemption in this I suppose, yet ultimately I do not place blame upon myself or other Makers for the choices of our Fledglings. Still, it is hard to avoid wondering if the ills that come to pass as a result of granting them such power are not in some ways our fault. As I admitted, I am conflicted on the matter.

It is worth noting the nature of our birthrights in order to lend perspective on the weight of our decisions. Power comes in many forms. Authority to govern; knowledge and wisdom over how the world works; physical prowess and skill in survival. And magick, which some would call the true power.

Within every Vampire courses the Blood of Inter and with it the potency to enact great feats upon Covyn. We can never become ill or age, yet neither can we set foot within the golden glory of the sunrise. We are able to run at vastly increased speeds and strike with gigantic force, summon stakes, regenerate our wounds as well as heal the minor injuries of others, and see and hear with greatly enhanced senses. Yet these are merely the most basic of the abilities we command. The Sen allows us to speak to and read from the minds of others; The Seer enables the future to be seen; The Shield is a magickal barrier used to deflect dangers both physical and magickal and, through clever manipulation, can be used to form around objects and move them as if through telekinesis; The Black Flames are the flames of Death, and destroy all they touch with a potency greater than that of ordinary fire; and the Cloak and Shadow Cors are those that we use to hide from others. Whilst the Cloak alters the perception of others, Vampires and mortals alike, to not see the caster or whatever the caster wishes, the Shadow changes the Vampire's skin to adapt to its surroundings. Doubtless there are others, yet I imagine we shall discover them in time. I retract that – if they do exist, it is inevitable we shall find them.

Such power within all of us. Merely possessing such power can alter the course of one's very perception of life. There are those even now who have come to believe themselves above not just the mortals we live alongside, but also the High Priests of Inter. The command of those six individuals over the religion of Interism is highly coveted by several of our number and I therefore fear the days ahead.

Must we have this power?
We do.

This is Our Home

We have seen many catastrophes in our lives. The Civil War that annihilated two thirds of our solar System, the rise and fall of the Jameson Regime, the extinction of the Ancients and the despair that followed the loss of their technological and political guidance. Yet here, nestled within the Land of the Mensmall, we have remained, for the most part, unscathed by the tragic losses suffered in the nations of the other races. However, to say we were unscathed is not to say we have not borne our marks from the fallout of those terrible years. As it was, before even my time, the upheaval in the regions beyond our isolation shaped us into the divided peoples we are today. I do not care to recount every detail, for even if I knew them all, I would not have the heart to tell the story. At least not at this time.

For now, all I can say is that we are Mensmall, the proportionally smaller offshoot to Humanity and our race, long since divided as I mentioned, remains in its own lands and lives here in a tenuous peace with one another. I, however, am no longer truly among the handful of groups that populate these lush rolling green lands and neither are my children. Verily, in time it may come to pass that even my children may not originally be Mensmall.

My twin sister and I were once mortal and in our thirty-sixth year we became the second and third Vampires, forsaking our born status in the Bavillion nobility. It was the highest of honours and we graciously accepted without hesitation. To serve Inter forever was a gift we could not refuse.

Upon our change of state, our duties to the Bavillion people were not so much over as altered. We therefore relinquished our positions in the monarch's Court and became permanent residents of the heart of all Interism in Covyn – the forest City of Illarien.

Illarien... Our home, the birthplace of the Vampires, the holiest of locations to all who worship Death and, in my humble opinion, one of the most beautiful places in the world. Situated in the centre of the Darkwoods, it is a place of purest and peaceful darkness, enveloped on all sides by a magick known as the Evernight. This spell encompasses not only the city, but also a vast swathe of the surrounding trees for miles in every direction, shrouding all in permanent blackness. Throughout Illarien, the heavy scent of ancient oaks, firs and ashes floats about the damp air accompanied by the aromas of ferns, the dew upon mosses and the curtains of ever-winding ivy. This heady air, scarcely touched by even the faintest of breezes, is blanketed with the only illumination to dispel the absolute dark. Ever glowing through the trees, these watery ripples originate from singular orbs of glass. They are called Souls, and aptly so, for the light within them comes from the dead. Contained in each crystalline shell is a veritable horde of spirits. Each spirit gives off a minute indigo-white emanation and so, when accompanied by hundreds of thousands of other souls, their combined shine is as the moon spilling into the ocean: brilliant white, azure and deep blue cascades that undulate through the gnarled trunks of ancient trees and billow up to caress the high boughs. Yet even their brilliance cannot undo the midnight that is Illarien's canopy. Vaulted branches knot so tightly that not a speck of sunlight can ever penetrate its dense embrace.

Running through the centre of the Darkwoods is the River Alin and its winding path passes to the West of Illarien, with a number of tributaries snaking into the city itself. One such minuscule trickle pours down into a hole in Illarien. This hole, seemingly bottomless and no wider than a few feet, is the Nightpool. Forbidden to all save the Highest High Priest of the time, it is the direct portal to the Pits of the Dead, where Inter Itself resides with the souls of all who have passed on. Its smooth surface reflects nothing. Indeed it appears to absorb all light. I have only seen it from above – even I, with all my authority upon the Elder Council, do not have permission to descend the winding stone steps down to its mossy banks. Yet to merely stand at a distance is enough, for the overwhelming sense of Its presence below is gloriously tranquil. This pool is why Illarien was created. To protect the sacred doorway to the realm of the dead and to bask in the aura of Death.

Beyond the Nightpool sits the main road trailing through the city. It is a simple dirt path that winds like an adder through the towering conifers and twisted trunks of age-old oaks. Following this street, there are many chambers of residence and religious significance and more are being added as time goes on. There is very little masonry in the city, with most rooms and the furniture being formed from the trees themselves. They will move aside as doors, uprooting and walking aside on roiling limbs before shutting, sealing all in complete privacy, for the winding ivy and smothering mosses upon their trunks work alongside their weaving boughs to fill the gaps. It is like one's own world within a single room. Such is my chamber, simple, yet quiet and peaceful, with the spongy greenery as a rest for my head. Not that Vampires require sleep in the conventional way, but even we tire and embrace a state of dreams from time to time.

As the nature of Illarien is a holy site, it is protected by the soldiers of the Captain, our monarch, as well as a large quantity of high ranking Priests and of course, the six High Priests of the time. It is worth noting that the High Priests and their subordinates possess authority to command the military in times of war and it was this way long before the Vampires came to exist. Now we too defend it, though a militaristic approach is simply the last line of safeguarding this place. The first line is a very basic, but ingenious creation where the trees themselves shift to shroud the city from the view of any passers-by. The next set of defences are the sentries and, of course, us.

Lastly, though not quite as I could recall the details of this hidden site for days, is the Elder Council Chamber. It sits directly next to the High Priest's equivalent and contains a single large oaken table. Upon its centre sits a lone Soul, its luminosity penetrating the darkness within. Currently… my sister and I sit at its head in twin thrones. Around are a number of chairs… the number keeps changing… I confess we will need to discuss this matter at a later stage: the matter of defining an Elder.

I confess it is not a topic of particular import, as for now things have taken a turn for the worse. There is increased tension between the High Priests, their seconds the Intra Vanta

Priests and a few of my more... recalcitrant children. Relations between us are beginning to sour over a conflict of ideologies. Having been born into the world of politics, I am all too familiar with its ever swaying nuances, yet I fear in time my influence will be suppressed. Several of our Fledglings, led by a recent convert of mine, Ulaq, believe it is our birthright as Death's Ambassadors to control the direction of Interism, overruling the authority of the High Priests and whilst this concept is hardly new, the influence Ulaq seems to hold... it is unsettling and cause for great concern. Now more than ever I am afraid of what the future holds for it is clear to me his ambitions go beyond simply taking command of our faith. His distaste, put simply, for the Varndicco people, their worship of the Goddess of Life, Saraanjova, and for Her Daughters, the Sarains, is painfully apparent. If he manages to garner enough support in the Bavillion Courts and amongst the Priesthood and obtain his wish for control over Interism, he would also have authority over the military. Granted, only in a time of war... but that is what I fear he desires.

In addition to this, Eternel is now considering leaving Illarien. She has become fatigued of the politics and this current dark transition and although I understand and will always support my sister... I know I cannot follow her if she goes through with it. I must remain. I have to stay and protect my children. My people. My home.

'Song of the Acar Vanta'
(title unknown)

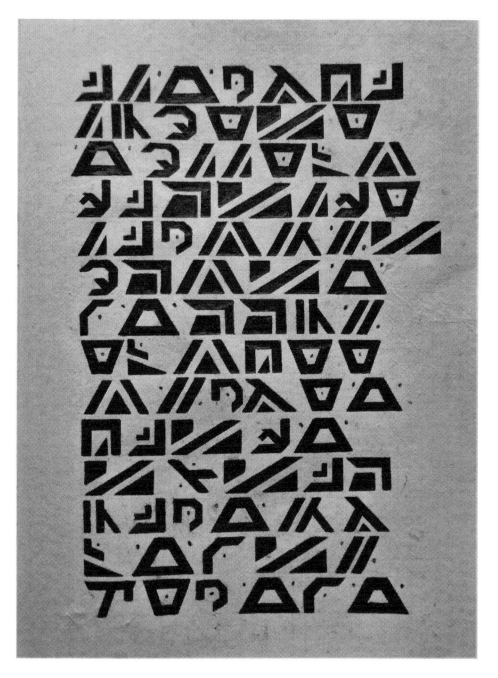

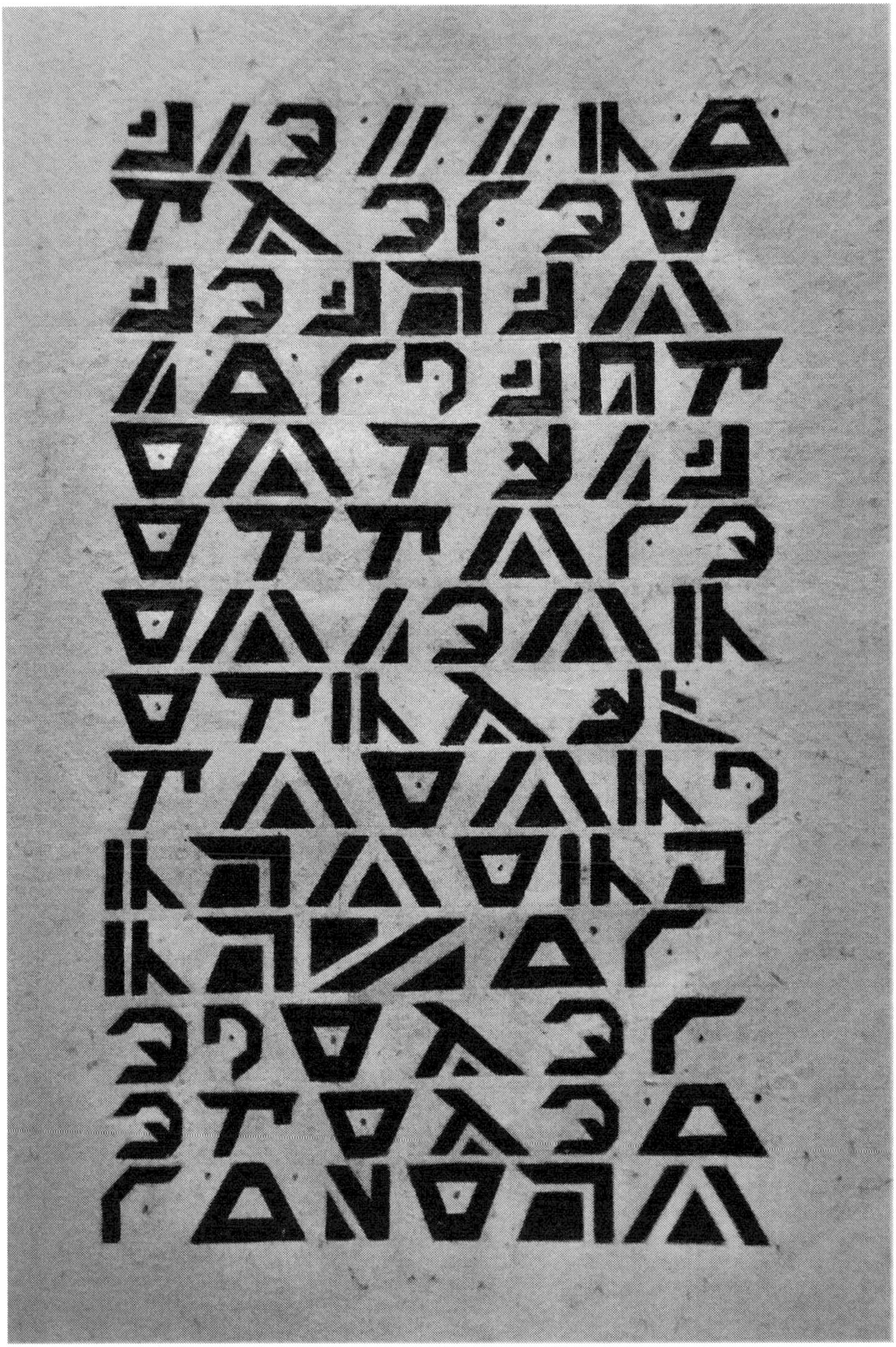

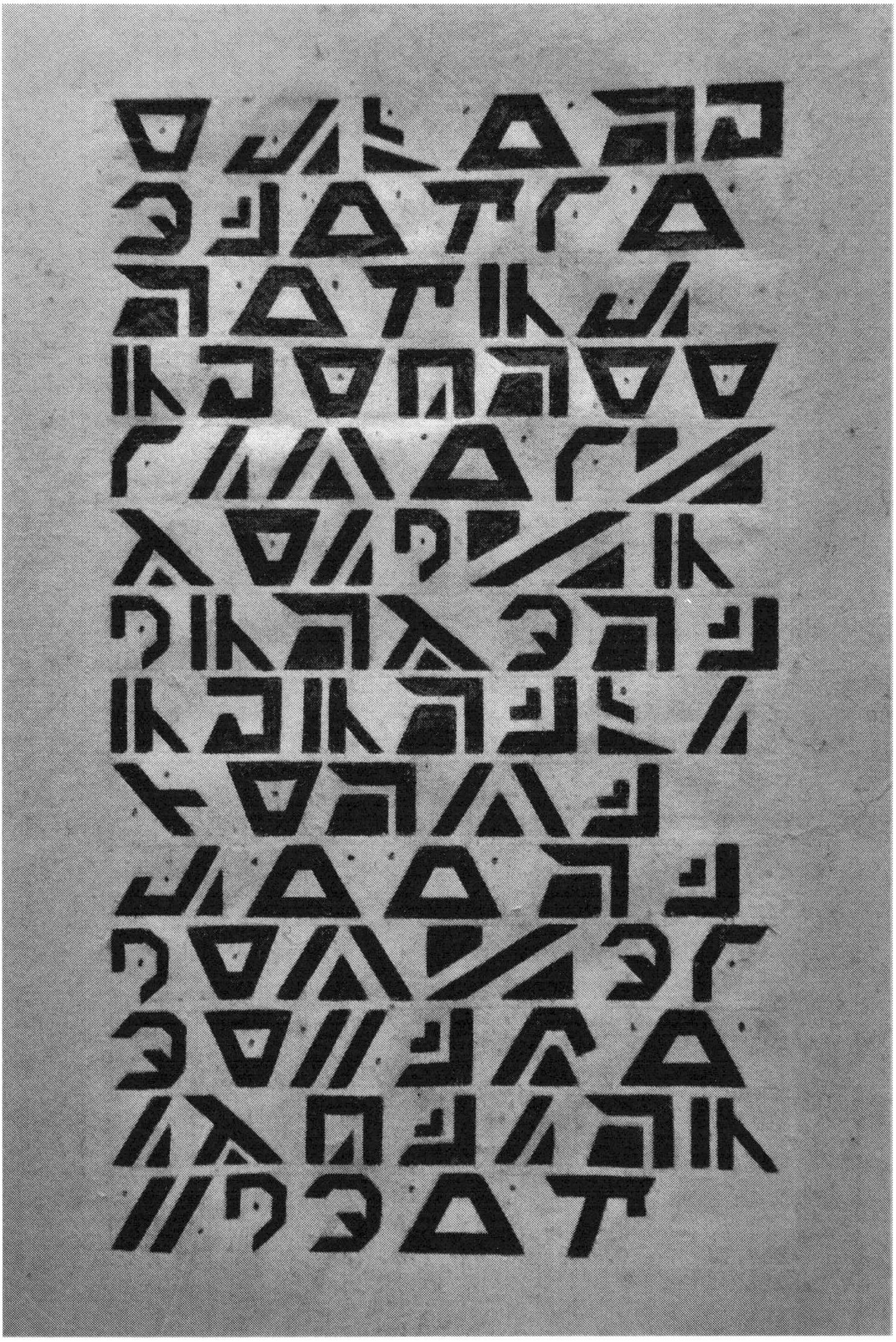

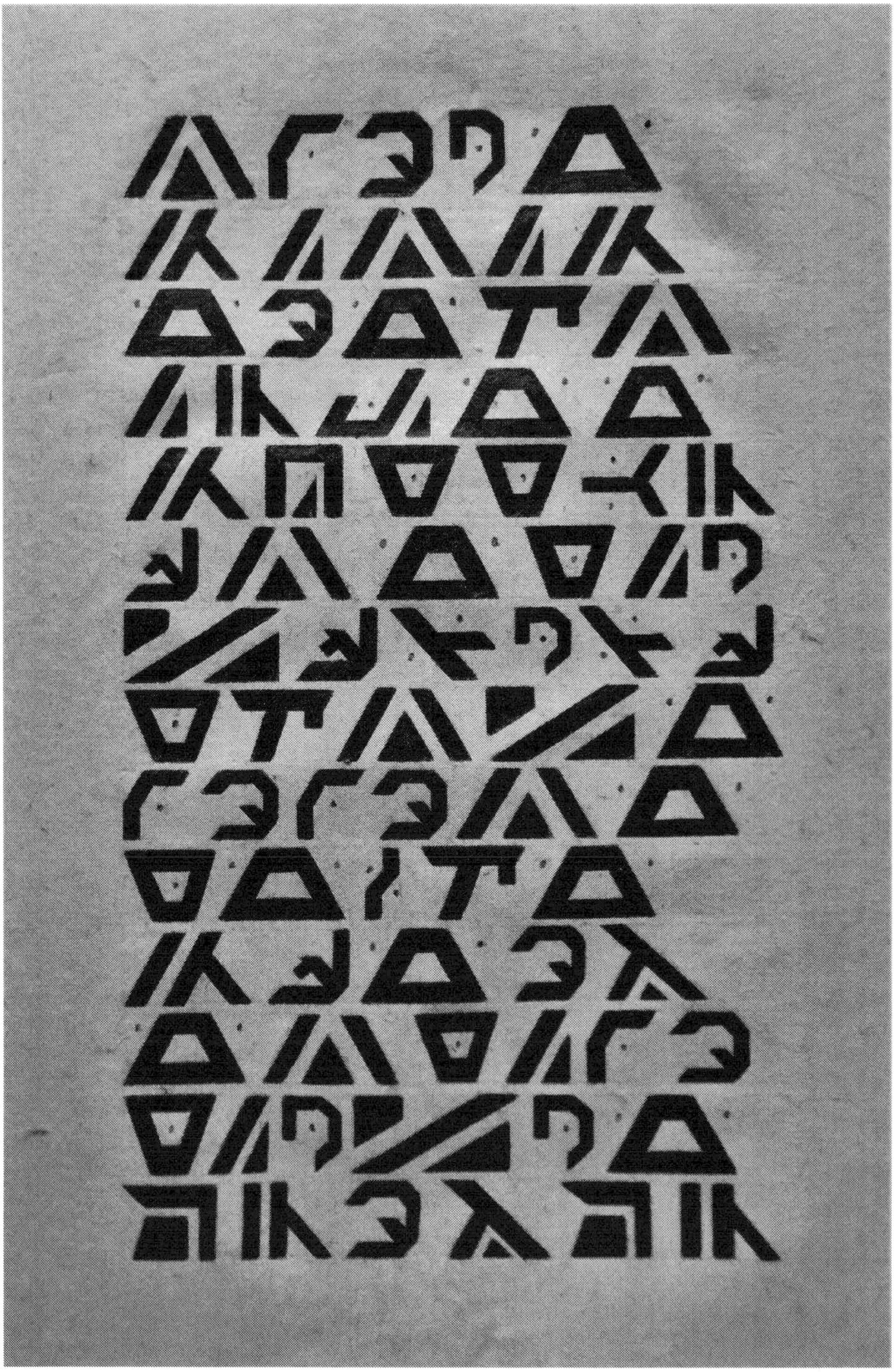

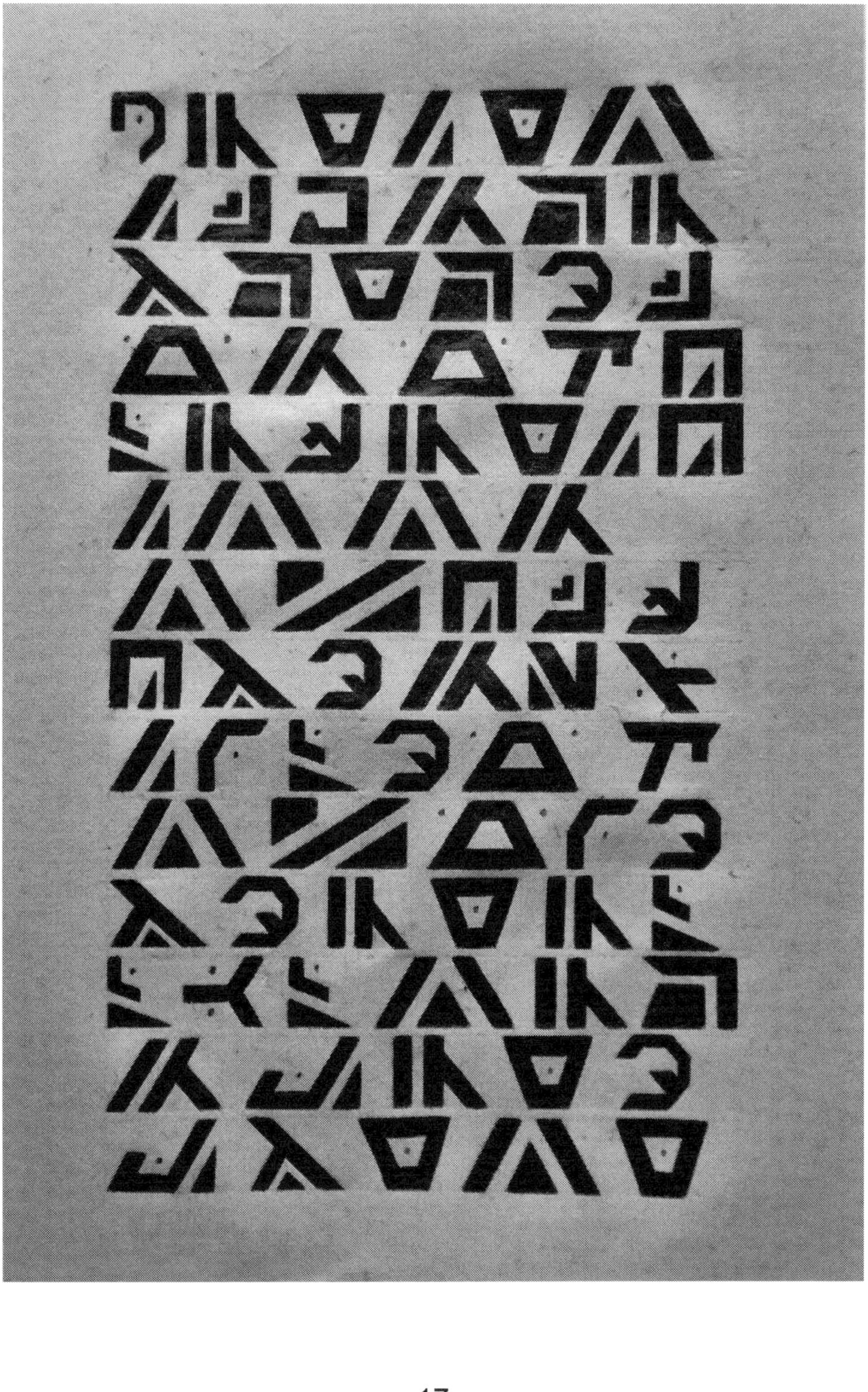

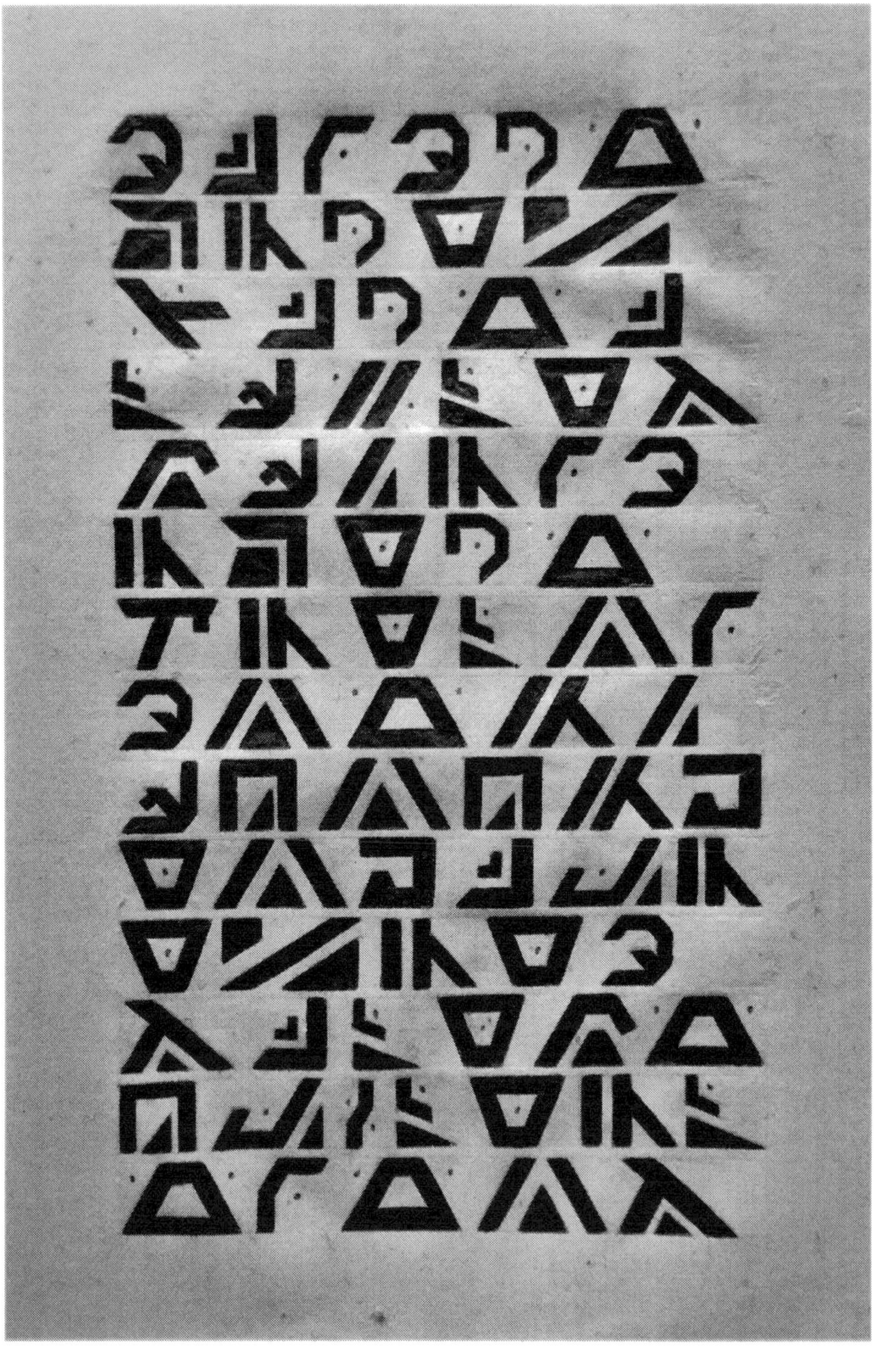

19

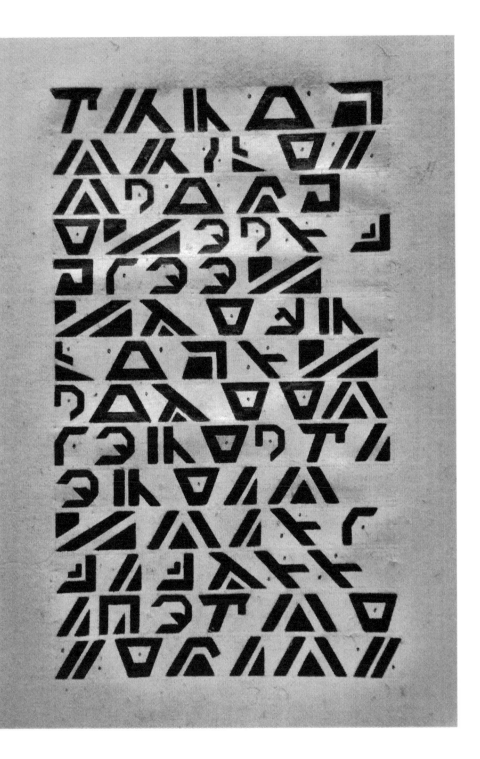

Eternel's Vigil

Harsh winds again.
And dark clouds gather.
Yet she stands, detached, gazing into the grey expanse.

One.

Two.

Three.

Then more raindrops fall upon her cold white cheeks, her cold red lips, her cold shimmering eyes. Her golden hair blusters wetly behind her, as does her damp white dress. As the sea upon the shore below, the water flows down her arms to cascade from her fingertips to the grass beneath her mud-stained feet. Drums of rain pound behind her and lash the sharp rocks upon the shore far below. The grey curtain is eternal, and the sea rushes up to meet it.

Her eyes close.

Her ears open.

The dead drift by, their whispers the wind. She hears all. And comfort does she bestow to the air. Roars of the storm echo into peace. The music of their voices fills her head: A chorus of nature.

The sea gives up its dead.

She gives them rest.

The living of the ocean beckon now. Violent waves crash and ebb, willing her in. Wind turns toward the unknown expanse ahead.

As with all things, there is a beginning and therefore also an end.

She remains, as all passes about her. She stands upon the edge, alone, the undead Ferrier of Inter. She gives the souls sleep everlasting. She jumps into the rush, caretaker of the cycle, and rests in the centre. A solitary being, unshackled from all.

Willow's Wonderland

She dances among the flowers as the butterflies and moths flit through the night. She plants seeds here and prunes branches there. Always moving, always dancing, always enjoying the beauty of twilight. Her feet brush the soft earth and her swaying, daisy-studded ashen hair strokes the lowest leaves. Her smile never fades. Its radiance is matched only by the warm glow of her eyes: twin beacons of bright green, their brilliant hue that of the new-born leaves about her.

Twinkling stars shine amiably through the canopy alongside the spill of moonlight that douses the undergrowth. A breath of wind lets the foliage speak to the dark and the trees sigh in restful slumber. No crackling of twigs; no snapping of branches; no crunch of shrivelled leaves; no footprints in the mud – she passes through the woods without disturbance.

Flower heads turn and trees ruffle in peace as she goes by, saying goodnight to all. Birds and beasts flock to see her and she blesses each and every one.

Nearby, the river flows, its music adding to the surrounding tranquillity, the water moving to her beat. The forest is happy with her. And she is happy with the forest.

The forest keeps her. And she keeps the forest.

She bids all the creatures and plants of the woods to "sleep well" and vanishes with the dark.

Uncommon Fledgling
Illarien, Year 734

"Regarding my reasons for choosing to give this gift… Well, for one, you're uncommonly intelligent. Another is your drive to achieve your passions. I also admire your strength of character. The most important one is not something I can adequately put into words..."

Ah, that last part really did sound like I don't know why I chose her. To some degree, this is true, yet from the moment I noticed her, sitting in the library doing what she does best, I could tell she was special. Hard to think all that was just a few weeks ago. So much has happened since then. I'd like to think it has all turned out for the best. As it is with us, time will undoubtedly tell.

I had certainly not intended upon converting anyone at the time I passed through Salaraq, nor had I ever before, for that matter. After my loss, it was hardly on my list of things to even ponder, let alone carry out, despite numerous, and often obnoxious, requests. However, there was something about Cinthia that I could not help but feel intrigued by. Well, several things in point of fact. Upon her request to know why I chose her, I was more than happy to respond in full.

As Cinthia was understandably cautious of me and my motives, I was as open and honest with her as possible. I told my Fledgling-to-be that I found her a beautiful individual, full of passion, confidence, compassion, and just the right amount of fire in her veins to make her… well, rather a lot more exciting than myself, that's for sure. And her forthright demeanour towards… all things physical, now that is something I certainly admire in her. I don't normally desire to partake in such things and so, as she's more brave than I in those matters, I am in awe of her sheer confidence. Cinthia's a wholly dedicated young lady, throwing herself with every effort at all things pertaining to her chosen subject of archaeology. I recall her almost pouncing on me when I told her I lived at the time of the Ancients! Ha! Her enthusiasm is invigorating. Contagious even. Which is why I entrusted her with one of my many great secrets. I'd been carrying that one around for centuries – it was time it fell into better and more appreciative hands.

I also explained to Cinthia that I was choosing her for the very reason she is not an Interist. Every other Vampire thus far has been devoted to our god, but not Cinthia. She acknowledges Its existence, but holds no opinion one way or another about It. She was therefore chosen because I feel the very fact she is external to the rest of us will lend a singular perspective on not just the Elders but the entire Vampire species. In short, I believe she will become an invaluable asset in balancing the Council's decisions.

Cinthia was – I should say *is* – determined to use her new powers to pursue her career as a discoverer of lost history. This was not just fascinating from the point of view of watching her so heartily discuss her passion, but also for the fact she was not interested in the slightest in possessing or utilising her Cors for any other path than her vocation. I must admit this was deeply touching and refreshing to see and was yet another reason I desired to convert her. That has not altered and I hold no regrets on making her, however… I do regret not informing her more on her Cors and how to control and hone them. I taught her a few briefly, such as how to run, feed, form a Shield and forge a Black Flame, but all with limited success – admittedly at her newborn stage this is not outside recognised norms. However, I failed to even mention the future-telling Seer Cor and offensive summoning of stakes and I know she would have appreciated more time going over both the Cloak Cor and how to feed! She was ired about that. I… am *truly* sorry I didn't have more time. Additionally, in retrospect, I realise just how inconsiderate it was to convert and not warn someone who has faced adversity and discrimination their entire life of the enormous level of negativity many members of the public hold against our kind. I admit, that is partially because I was aware that she is clever and so I assumed she already knew… but I feel I should have done more - I should have told her anyway. Dammit! There is so much more I could have done for her if only I'd *had more time*. Surely I could have waited and gone back at some point, though there's no way of truly knowing if my Ambassadorial duties would have even allowed for it. I am uncomfortable using that as an excuse. At least she knows this and we parted on rather amiable terms. I am not ashamed to confess that I really hope to see her again. And if *anyone* fucks with my Fledgling, I *swear*…! Wait! Is *this* what being a mother is like? I never saw this for myself. Never did I even think I would… not after what happened all those years ago. Still, I am glad I made her, even though my decision was rushed. She is truly unique. And I know she is more than capable of taking care of herself. Even so, I should have done more.

I'm also immensely relieved I didn't kill her! Damn… when her eyes glazed over after I drained her and fed her my own blood - I was terrified I'd botched the conversion! Yet just when panic was about to set in, she came back and bolted upright so fast she broke my nose. Ha! Had I not been overwhelmed with relief over her being 'alive', I doubtlessly would have burst out laughing! Cinthia then took to her new gifts with a thrill I'd not seen in another individual in decades. Her face… it was so beautiful how it glowed with delight at how freeing the experience was for her – to be able to run so fast and see things in all their heightened detail. Granted she tripped, fell and set herself on fire, but she loved every moment!… with the exception of the involuntary immolation of course – she was somewhat irked by that but she dealt with the knowledge that she would have to be careful with her velocities surprisingly well. When I told Cinthia there was so much more to learn, she just said, "Bring it on". Damn… she is really something. I *truly* cannot wait to see what kind of Vampire she becomes.

Rose's Secrets

Down the veiled winding stairs
A cold door of stone
Its weighty charge behind its gaze
Opened by gold flame.
A sombre rose treads down the path
Wise to the danger
Her guiding hand on a shoulder
Last in a long line.
Dispersal of an ancient lock
In a flash of heat
Scribe unto eternity
Hasty whilst it's fresh.
Upon aged vellum fearfully scrawled:
Throes, swamp and shadow
Dire reflections wait for us
Shattering of glass.
Bewildered by their own bad dreams
All guests are silenced
The rose and key alone know all
Burdens they abide.
Arcane presages yellow
Sealed deep within
Every last light will be snuffed out
Back the way they came.

An early visit from the bloom
No shoulder to guide
Her own scrap she would place inside
One among the hoard.
Turning her back upon the key
Shielding her mind
This one would be hers alone
Future child's gift.
Some secrets are meant to be shared
Purpose for their life

Her Fledgling's first adventure
First of lots to come.

Cinthia's Curiosity

Fendivra 12th 735

A diary entry about myself is not something I normally do, but in this case I feel an exception has to be made due to the fucking incredulity of what's occurred since I came to discover this remarkable place!

Immediately after my graduation from the University of Salaraaq as valedictorian (from which I was immensely relieved they omitted my surname, LeRavier, during the ceremony) and after my temporary goodbyes to my only two friends there, I set off into the desert to search for the lost Ancient fortress of Hallahan. It took several weeks of trekking across seemingly identical dunes for miles in every direction. I obviously had to travel mostly at night, for despite the fact I do have a heavy canvas hood and scarf to wrap around my head and face, I learned the hard way it's not always practical. As much as I'm one to prefer using analogue devices if possible, I fucking would have loved some Agungdrian power armour or something to block out the damn sun! I swear they make some great tech – yes, I know I am biased because it's based on, and reverse engineered from, Ancient designs but I don't give a flying fuck. I need a daysuit dammit! I can use my sundials and shit for all other purposes, but an outfit for daytime travel is definitely on my list of things to acquire. Shame they live so far away... and under water.

I've digressed. So after about a month traipsing about the desert fruitlessly and using only the stars and the Ancient Map – which I obtained thanks to Rose - I finally spotted this crumbling ruin just barely jutting out of the landscape. I swear my heart almost stopped. I ran the rest of the distance, unable to contain myself. The part sticking out of the sands is what's left of part of the roof. There was no door so I just ducked under its arch and what I saw then... let's just say it definitely did more than take my breath away.

The interior is in a remarkable state of preservation despite centuries lying amid ever shifting sands, most notably the fountain, still filled with water, standing about ten feet tall in the centre of the elaborately decorated hall. I've since determined the source of this bizarre occurrence as a mixture of ingenious Ancient design and it being fed from a deep underground water source (lake or river? Remains to be seen). Along all the walls are high rounded archways leading into adjacent passages, chambers – including the one I'm writing in at this very moment – and one very large kitchen. OK, so everything is large here because it was built for the Ancients. I've examined all the rooms since then and they too are all in dusty, but otherwise pristine, condition. Also of immense note is the fucking floor of this place – it's one giant mosaic in near perfect shape! Which brings me onto the most amazing fact of all – the mosaics depict the War of Drachir! It's proof of all my theories! The academic community will explode over this find! The Ancients had truly gone to war with the Demons in the Old Times. It's also fascinating because it puts the construction of Hallahan sometime shortly after the war's conclusion, which I'd wager was sometime in the 320's, and was likely used during the Civil War that took place only a few years or so after. This is the most exciting find ever! I cannot wait to tell Bethany and Aaron I found it and that we were right! Well, OK, we were wrong on one count, as one thing I did immediately notice was that this was no fortress – it was a palatial establishment, something of a safe zone command centre for the highest ranking of Ancient military officers to relax and strategise. This was made clear from not just the architectural style but also many leftover documents and books holding accounts of the War of Drachir and the political shifts leading into the Civil War. I have to handle them very carefully, but the history is there!

It was beyond my highest expectations to discover such a find here! Which is the funny part. Or at least we laugh about it now. I certainly felt… *differently* at the time. For the most surprising thing about this amazing place was that I was not the one to discover it.

So at the same time as I was taking in all these incredible details, my attention was drawn to the very different details of two olive-skinned young men – one about my age and the other just younger – completely naked and fucking each other over the fountain. I had to remove my, hood, scarf and goggles from my face to make sure I wasn't seeing things. They stopped buggering the moment I walked in and we just stared wide eyed at each other for a while. Ha! That was a long awkward moment, though they showed no shame at having been caught copulating – I personally wouldn't either but I know that's unusual.

I have to admit, I did also think it was pretty damn hot.

None of us spoke a word and so I eventually asked what they were doing out here. They did not answer, though I found out later it's because they failed to understand me, so I just started my examination of the site. After initially following me around at a distance, which felt rather creepy, I glared at them and bared my fangs. After that they kept to themselves, only watching me from a distance as I went about my work.

It sure was fucking weird at the time. At least we laugh about it now, though I still struggle at times to interpret their bizarre dialect – having been here for years on their own they've developed a unique offshoot to Lingualis. I'm slowly re-teaching the universal form of it to them but it's difficult. I'm actually beginning to pick up their words, but it's slow going. Because of that, I found out they're actually brothers, which at first took me by surprise but it doesn't bother me in the slightest. I've established they cannot read either, so they watch me work with an avidity I find all but distracting. And that's not all about them I find distracting either.

For a fortnight the status quo held, with them respecting my space and us all keeping to our respective rooms during the daylight hours. I quickly became used to their fornicating in the main hall, having had upon more than one occasion accidentally walked in on them. Each time I noticed them looking at me more and I glared back to keep them at a distance. They may not have understood my words but they got what I meant and would lower their gaze and continue to allow me my space. At the very least I did not truly feel threatened by them for I not only had my Cors (which I've never had to use against them), but I also read from their body language they were more curious than anything and they were not aggressive in their attempts to satisfy it. Despite having not seen another person in years – I came to learn later - they made no attempts to break the unspoken boundaries I'd established for myself at any rate. Yet even as I desired to keep these strange men at bay, I caught myself gazing at their muscular arms and backs. I tried my best to ignore it, however, for I had a job to do.

That failed miserably one early morning when I was trying to document my findings from the night. I could hear them in the hall from my room and I could not stop thinking about how much I had been desiring to get fucked myself – it had been a while since Bethany, Aaron and I had our fun in the ruins of Salaraaq. I tried so hard to keep my mind on my work but in the end I couldn't hold back any more.

I barged out and, much to their pleasant shock, began to strip off and joined them. I stood above them, allowing them the option to say no (and to show I was there on my terms) and as they gawked at my body – I don't think they'd ever seen a woman naked before - I noticed for the first time they were not short Humans like I first thought but they were Mensmall like myself. Which worked out well as they were a damn perfect fit. So began our lusty escapades. And damn… they are *good*. I don't know how they learned – they must just have good fucking instincts.

And yes, that was intended.

We still keep our spaces but congregate in the hall at specific times to enjoy one another. They are gorgeous and I fucking love having them both inside me at once! Lucky for me, they're skilled at anal. As we've kept our fun to certain hours I've managed to, for the most part, keep my distraction in check and get on with my excavation of this place. The more I've worked on it, the longer I want to spend here analysing every square inch of it! To make living here easier, we've worked together to dust things off a bit and make it more… well liveable, duh. They're really supportive in their teamwork, often offering to help with heavy lifting, even though I've amply demonstrated I'm far stronger than either of them (where did their social skills come from or were they like this on their own as well?). Upon one such occasion whilst moving a broken appliance out of the way, I found out how they managed to survive out here for so long on something other than water – behind the kitchen is a fully functional terrarium! How the fuck it's still working is still unknown to me but it's truly inspiring to see just how advanced Ancient architects and technology were. Our next plan as a trio is to get the fountain working – not just for aesthetic value, but we all want to fuck in a shower. I'm going to make absolutely sure it's safe to do so first though as I *don't* want that artefact damaged!

I'm not getting distracted again. I'm not.

It's been a few months since I first arrived. I've gotten to know both this place and its inhabitants quite well now, even with the language barrier, although that is a fun thing to work on with them – we have quite a few laughs over our mistakes and misunderstandings... I don't think I want to leave. I mean, of course I'll set out to discover more places and to share my findings with the world but... I want to keep this place as my home. I like it here – I've always loved the desert and it's peaceful and quiet here, aside from the sounds of them buggering each other on occasion, which is actually pretty nice to hear now. I'll keep out the details of the location of this place from my reports – I'll say it would get swallowed by the shifting dunes by the time they found it again. Oddly enough, I think that will be true! We installed a door to stop more sand coming through the roof arch entrance, but it's a constant fucking battle to hold it back! At least the room I've chosen to inhabit is sand-free now. Yet something else beyond the damn amazing finds here and the attrition of its upkeep is bothering me.

The longer we fumble through conversations, the more we make this place comfortable to live in and enjoy each other's company, the more I find myself... my chest feels tight around them. I don't know what it is about them. Is it that they're just another fascinating find to me or...? I don't want to write about this anymore.

Sarahessieth's Art

The night air was always warm in midsummer and that evening was no different than any other before it. A lone man, dressed in a fresh suit and hauling a large wheeled case behind him, strode up to the Fayre grounds that were lit up with bright torches in brackets all around wooden posts between giant elaborate tents dotting the grassy field. A great bustling of Mensmall stretched out before him, the sounds and smells of celebration and open-air cooking swarming his senses, though he intentionally drowned them out. The smaller peoples moved around him paying him no heed either, for strangers in their lands were common at that time of year, visiting from all over to join in the Midsummer festivities. Through the vibrant atmosphere and the array of brightly coloured canvas tents, the man's sight became solely fixed upon a poster of a painting depicting a large older woman hunched over a giant crystal. Below were directions to her tent. He stared at her eyes and grunted to himself before setting off through the throng.

Towards the far end of the grounds, past jugglers, minstrels, tinkers and vendors of myriad delicacies, an aged crimson pavilion squatted. It was adorned with all manner of magical symbols the man did not recognise made from sticks, corn husks and bone. Without looking back at the effervescent crowds behind, he narrowed his eyes and shifted aside the musty front covering.

His pupils dilated and his nostrils were overwhelmed. A dim light from two giant candles on either side of a low table illuminated a deeply smoky atmosphere. Heavy incense burned all around the perimeter of the interior and in the centre, waiting beside the table and a giant crystal, was the older lady from the painting. Her yellow eyes glowed out from the gloom and a smile widened upon her wrinkled features, revealing a pair of pearly fangs.

"Ah, welcome Human traveller!" she said with a slight cackle. "What is it you've come to seek?"

The man sat down on a worn cushion which smelled of ages

of incense. Looking at her, he got straight to the point.

"I seek a poison," he said.

The old woman sighed and gave a wry smile, "Ah, another one. I'm afraid you want to see Sarahessieth, my Daughter."

The man stiffened, though he otherwise did not move. Before he could reply, the lady continued.

"I am Mellacass, her Maker. My dear, you aren't the first to make the mistake thinking I am her, nor will you be the last."

The man nodded, and leaned forward, "I was told she lived in the southernmost village at the feet of the Magnus Cliffs?"

"Correct. This is not said village. This is the one just before it."

He rose to his feet, his voice cold yet civil, "Sorry for the mistake, ma'am."

Leaning back, her eyes narrowing at him, she gave a dry laugh before speaking softly, "Minds, as well as the veil, can be read by me, you know. And I am quite the seer on top of just being wise in my years." The man's face made no change as he continued to stare and listen. Hers did not alter either. She continued, "You fear my knowing of your purpose makes me a threat to your secrecy." She laughed. "No, dear, I am not. Although I do not approve of your life choice, and neither do I approve of my Daughter's in aiding such people as you, she is my Daughter. I will have no harm come to her. And your discovery would lead to hers. It is not in my interest to betray you, for it would mean losing her too. Not to mention that you would be a special type of fool if you thought yourself a threat to an Elder Vampire, regardless of whatever... *accomplishments* you possess."

The man said nothing, but nodded.

"Good," she said, her demeanour warming. "Now that that's out of the way, perhaps you've time for your fortune to be read anyway? But I give to you my usual disclaimer – prophecy only shows what could be – not what will, or should, be. I am more accurate than most, but even the tiniest of things can alter the course of times yet to be. What would you like to know about?"

The man's mouth slid upwards and he dropped ten gold pieces next to the crystal.

"Tell me about my job," he said. "And take the extra money for your helpful information regarding your Daughter."

Mellacass smiled wide and drew the crystal close to her, "Thank you for your generosity. Now prepare."

Only a few miles further south lay the last village attached to the Magnus Cliffs. A small but dense woodland surrounded it, offering little daylight to the moss encrusted houses and shops on its only two streets. Between each of these overgrown buildings thrived writhing masses of ivy that barred windows shut and choked their already twisted chimneys. Ferns grew over everything else and bordered the vanishing dirt roads through the village. At the very end of the second street lay a dark black crooked doorway set into the rock of the cliff alongside several other shops, though these were painted in peeling hues of greens and browns. Above the door in faded gold were written the words: *The Serpents' Draught*. He pushed down the stiff handle and opened the creaking door.

Inside was a dusty chamber lit only through the grimy windows and by several alchemical burners dotted about the front of house workspace. The store was very small so the Human had to bow upon entry and there was very little room for moving about. An unlit grotty chandelier hung lopsided from the ceiling, covered in cobwebs that threatened to tangle in the man's hair as he entered and stared about in awe.

The shop was lined with aged oak shelves hoarding masses of opaque and translucent vials and jars of an unknowable variety of concoctions in all shapes and sizes. Some were as small as his fingers and others were large and twisted in upon themselves, mixing more than one liquid within together in helix shapes only master glass-makers could form. Others were simple jars of circles, cones and oblongs and more still were flasks of silver and emerald. The contents all glistened in the dim light, casting dim hues upon the backs of the shelves. Just across from him squatted a dark oak desk that ran almost the entire length of the shop, attached to the left wall and jutting out two thirds of the way to the opposite one. Upon it were gathered many more phials and flasks of small sizes, arrayed for the customers to get a closer look before buying – a place for the most common of potions to be displayed.

Behind the desk was a small walkway then the far wall where another desk sat littered with an array of bizarre ingredients. Leaves, crushed and fresh, mortars and pestles clean and dirty, the remains of small animals and bugs piled and crushed, and bubbling conical glasses overflowing with steam and oozing mixtures all dotted its gouged surface. Knives and ladles were strewn all over, some sticking out of the wood itself, the rest being hung from what few leftover spaces on the walls there were. Amongst all the clutter, much to the man's surprise, a terrifying array of creatures still moved.

The whole shop slithered with snakes, most known to him to be of lethal status, that roved between all the various vials and jars without moving them. Many more were upon the floor and glided at different speeds through the room.

In the far right hand corner of the store was a tiny crooked doorway leading to the back, through which no light came. Before the wonky frame stood a striking young woman clad in a beige knee-length sleeveless dress that was stained with years worth of spills. Her jet black hair was tied back, revealing her pale neck and her shoulders were adorned with the coils of a venomous bright yellow Cynt adder. Mimicking the snake at her neck, leather straps from her otherwise ordinary shoes wrapped themselves up her bare legs to just below her knees. She was avidly focused on her work, grinding some unknown items in a pestle and pinching them into a heated flask with a satisfying sizzle.

Before the man could open his mouth, she threw up a hand without looking at him.

"Silence! I'll be with you in a minute."

Her eyes narrowed at the ingredients in her fingers as she added the tiniest fraction to the boiling concoction. The mixture gave off a minuscule hiss and she snorted in satisfaction before turning down the heat and washing her hands clean in a nearby basin. Turning at last to face him and folding her arms, she frowned and asked, "What is it that you're after?"

The man, taken by her beauty though not stunned by it and

not fazed by her demeanour, again got right to the point.

"I'm here for poison, Ma'am, and I've been told you're the best in the Land of the Mensmall."

Her stare hardened. "No."

The man also began to frown. "Are you not Sarahessieth?"

"I am she," she replied, not moving or taking her pale yellow eyes off him.

"I was informed you deal in poisons – some of the most deadly in the world."

"That I do."

He frowned more, though was calm in his response, "Then why did you say no?"

"I am not the best in the Land of the Mensmall," she spoke swiftly, tickling the chin of the adder at her shoulder before returning her gaze to him. "I am the best in the world."

The man smiled and she returned the gesture, albeit with an ambiguous quality to it.

"What kind are you after?" she asked after a moment.

"Atrophy's Kiss," he answered. Looking about him at all the vials he took in a sharp breath of air. "Do you have any, ma'am?"

She gave a small snort of laughter and sighed, removing the snake to place it upon the ground with the others.

"Of course I do," she replied. "The question is, do you have the money to pay for such a thing?"

The man brought forth the case which made a deep thud on the floor. "I came prepared for a significant investment."

Sarahessieth looked from the case to the man and stared for a short time before finally nodding. "Wait here," she said.

A short while later she returned from the black recesses of the store holding the tiniest vial in the menagerie of glassware on display. She made as if to give it over, but flicked it back into the palm of her hand.

"But first, I have a reputation to uphold," she said. "I don't care for the details of your job, but tell me at least in part what you intend to do with this. I never sell to people who don't know what to do with my art. Not for any price. You're an assassin, which is perfectly clear from your demeanour. But just how many people do you intend on killing with this? You do know what Atrophy's Kiss does, right?"

"It causes instant rot upon contact either external or internal, literally eating away at the flesh of animals or vegetation," he replied. "It can travel along the body via either the dermal layer or the bloodstream. Also, it is considered one of the most dangerous and feared poisons in the world, for it has no cure nor balm to halt its degenerative progress."

"Very good," she spoke with a hint of sarcasm, her eyebrow rising. "But you've not answered my second question and there's so much more about it you've not mentioned. Go on..."

"I intend on killing perhaps up to fifty people over the course of many years with this."

Her eyelids fell halfway down her eyes. "And *how* do you intend on doing this?"

"By installing a fraction of the quantity contained in the vial within each specialised poison-delivery bullet I use in my rifle."

A genuine sliver of pleasure passed across her lips, "A clever usage of my art! And a sniper too?" A dreamy look permeated her features and she lowered her voice. "Strikes of surgical precision – delightful! So removed from the bludgeoning swordsmen to oft visit my shop. I truly respect that." But then her expression once more turned sour. "But how do you intend to install it in each bullet?"

"I have a small syringe for such occasions-"

"No!" she threw up a hand. "I knew it. Another one who doesn't grasp the severity of what they're dealing with!"

She grabbed a small stool from the front right corner of the shop. "Sit down." she ordered, then returned behind the first desk and leant over it, holding the vial between her fingers.

"In the interests of keeping a customer alive who isn't *totally* ignorant of the substance they are intending to purchase," she began. "And because I believe you're intelligent enough to appreciate my wisdom and art, right here in this vial -" She shook it so it caught in the fires of the burners behind her. "- is the concentrated poison of the flower Viliphae Orpha." She drew out a heavy book from under the desk and flipped it open to a page with a painted picture of the flower upon it. It had seven petals of the deepest purple, it was nearly black, with a set of blood red stamen in the centre. "It is not *one* of the most deadly poisons in the world – like me, it's at the top of the list. A single touch of its petals causes instant rotting of the skin that will result in the loss of digits, even limbs depending upon the level of exposure. Consuming it will cause death. You therefore need to handle it with great care. And that's only the basic flower." She shook the vial again. "For this you need to take even greater care. One single drop is enough to kill a *minimum* of twenty healthy men when added to a shared beverage for example. You would never require that much for a single bullet."

She stood up straight and retrieved four items from a drawer behind her: a syringe, a brush, a wooden splint and a steel scalpel.

"You suggested using a syringe to apply the poison to a bullet, but never even mentioned gloves! Firstly, only synthetic gloves will do as leather will just be eaten away. For me, it's a little easier as I can get away with my bare hands as I'm a Vampire, but it's bad practice in general, same as using a syringe or even a small brush, because both methods can lead to cross contamination." She tossed the brush and syringe behind her back into the drawer. "Any poison can remain present in bristles or a needle for a long time, even after you think you've thoroughly cleaned them, yet that of the Viliphae Orpha is far harder to remove. It can then mix with other poisons and ruin your artistic moment of a specific kill type, and you would not want that. Not to mention that due to liquid tension, bristles will soak up more than you require thus wasting your supply. Same holds true for a syringe." She held up the wooden splint. "Equally, using a wooden implement for Atrophy's Kiss is unwise. Being formed from a biological lifeform, it will seep into the wood and cause it to rot away. If the wood has been treated with a sealant, it will still seep into the grains and cause cross-contamination with other substances. In other words-" She glared hard at him. "- it will either ruin other poisons or you may touch it yourself accidentally." She threw the splint behind her as well and flourished the scalpel. "Metal; solid and not a needle. This is your main way to handle it. Glass is acceptable too. Both can be sterilised thoroughly and retain no residues upon their surfaces. Basic soap and water can be used to remove it, but afterwards, always place it in fire for a good minute to make sure any remaining quantities are burned off. Now as for how much you need for a single job..." She retrieved a jar from one of the many shelves and uncorked it, then dipped the scalpel inside. The substance, a kind of oil, dripped off the blade back into the container and she left it there until only a smear remained.

"This is an example using a substance of similar viscosity," she explained, holding it out in the dim light for him to see. He leaned forward and nodded. "Barely any. Even then it will be enough to kill several people. By using such small amounts on each of your shots, you should make it spread to easily seventy five or a hundred targets."

As Sarahessieth cleaned the scalpel and returned the jar to its place on the shelf, the man frowned and asked, "With all due respect, is it not in your interest for me to use more of it then have to return to you sooner?"

She stiffened, her back to him, then turned her head. "Financially perhaps. But my art is not to be squandered. You do know why this costs as much as it does?"

"The risks of its creation. Therefore also the skill in its making."

She snorted and toyed with one of her many snakes as it made its way across the table towards her. After a brief moment of silence with the snake licking her fingertips, she turned back to face him. "Indeed. The flower itself is also extremely rare, growing only in the most ancient of meadows and forests. Finding, obtaining, refining and perfecting – not an easy process and one which I alone have mastered. You're paying for the creation of one of the hardest things to forge – what you see here is but the store front for basic creations. I have to cook this up-" She shook the vial again. "-over the course of two months using my most prized equipment that are housed in the back, most of which was custom made by myself over centuries. You're paying for hundreds of years of expertise and the artistry of potion making. And as much as I love money, I love my art infinitely more and as such I will not sell to just anyone."

Lifting her dress, she slid one of her legs onto the desk to sit sideways upon it and leant over towards him.

"So, do you have what it takes to own this beautiful creation?"

The man raised an eyebrow at this, though said nothing of it and instead opened up his case upon the floor, careful to avoid iring the slithering occupants of the shop. Inside were scores of rows of gold coins gleaming out in the firelight.

"For the vial," he said, lifting out two thirds of the contents. "Twenty thousand gold units."

Sarahessieth said nothing and straightened her back, staring down at the gold through half-closed eyes. The man gave a small smile.

"For the imparted wisdom of ages," he continued, lifting out a quarter of what was left. "Two thousand five hundred gold units."

A satisfied smile rose on her mouth and she slipped off the table to stand up in front of him. With a flick of her fingers, she flourished the vial.

"It's all yours," she said. "For being so attentive and polite."

"The pleasure was all mine," he said, taking the vial and placing it in a steel seal in his case. He locked the case, stood up and looked at her. "I hope to do business with you again soon."

"No."

He looked at her confusedly.

"Ma'am?" he asked.

"The pleasure was *not* all yours," she replied with a sly smile.

The man stiffened as her hand reached out to gently touch his chest and stroke down his white shirt. He grunted as her fingertips delved lower.

"I like a man who's civil, efficient and can keep up with me in… *conversation*." Her eyes blazed into his and she bared her fangs in a widening grin. "And when that man is also a precise, artistic killer… well..." She drew back her hand and beckoned him into the rear of the shop. "We should exchange stories."

"By all means," he nodded with a smile and followed her. "Though I have a lot of them."

"Then we'll be busy for a while."

She walked out to the front of the shop and flipped her 'open' sign to 'closed'.

Blasphemy's Baptism

Her eyes darted about the darkened passage. The blinding murk broke with the orange glow of passing torches along stone walls. She caught glimpses of bloodstained flesh, powerful arms clad in bones and sinews and the cackling faces of those who held her lithe form so fiercely in their grip. Throbbing pain pulsed in her head and along her scuffed legs as their paces quickened. She stumbled and yelped. They yanked up her ankles and continued soaring through the shadows.

Hot air surged past and billowed her matted blond locks, bringing with it the pungent aroma of rot. The malodour clung to the inside of her recoiling nostrils and along every inch of her exposed and already soiled body. As the familiar sensation of dread wakened once again, streaks of lachryma cleared the dirt down her paling face and her heart pounded ever more madly in her chest. Suddenly, the shade was clearing. She gave a hoarse plea, yet it fell upon the deaf ears of her lurid captors.

A cavernous chamber gaped ahead, its maw causing her irises to contract from its belched firelight. Massive bowls of flames lined the walls, casting nightmarish dancing shadows upon the arched ceiling far above and illuminating blood-painted, heretical symbols along every surface. Between the vats were platforms holding gargantuan drums that stood being pounded in unified rhythm. The young woman's bones shook from their tremors. Even the jeers of the growing crowd were drowned by their thunder. Long lines of oaken tables stretched through the cave, decked with intoxicants and delicacies fit for a royal banquet. Platters of silver, decanters of crystal and sculptures of bronze reflected the fire's brilliance into her soaking eyes as she was hauled past them.

As she neared the tables' end, hundreds of men and women around her began to chant. Their songs were as indiscernible as their motives for her. Whenever she had tried to communicate with them, they would ignore her and laugh like rabid animals. Still, she screamed for her release.

For six days she had screamed. And for these six days, the only communication from them had been the language of suffering. Without proper rest, she had been dragged from her cell to the cavern and been used by men and women alike in every way imaginable and then in ways she could never have conceived. In desperation, she had prayed to her god for help. No answer came.

Her prayers in those six days were always quiet, for she did not wish to be heard. Yet, upon the sixth, they had become barely a whisper. And now, as she was knelt onto the cold stone floor, she cried only to her captors.

Her hair was pulled from behind her, forcing her to look up. Her stomach churned and she struggled to look away as the person behind her held her fast. Yet more tears flowed and she panted the moment her focus was placed upon a new sight she would not forget.

Lying just before the far curved edge of the cave was an oblong pool many metres in length and raised up from the floor. Black stone steps lined its edges and led up to its surface. The trembling woman did not have to see its contents to know what filled it, for the suffocating stench of blood flowed down from above to her repulsed nose. As nausea started to take over, her shaking became weaker and she swallowed hard in an effort to abate the sensation. Yet her attention was stolen once again.

The heaving masses behind her sank to their knees before the pool and their chanting became quieter. Turning her terrified eyes to her side, she could just make out countless bowed heads with expressions of fearful respect etched upon them. Meanwhile, the cacophonous drum beats had begun to slow and hammered instead in twinned strikes. The noise was so loud, it reverberated the ground underneath her legs to connect with the pool above. Down the steps pulsed waves of crimson that soon lapped at her cringing knees.

She had never understood the language the crowd intoned, but this time, her brows furrowed in wariness over two new words she found she recognised. They were ones she had not heard in years. Gulping, she remembered them clearly.

"Acar Vanta!"

A fairy tale of yore. An ancient fable admonishing the trappings of doubt, estrangement from god and everlasting damnation. The Unholy Amen of Inter. Fraction by fraction, her sights travelled back up to the pool's surface.

Its surface had begun to stir.

Out from the palpitating vermilion waters ascended the head of a woman, crowned with a circlet forged from Human bones and crenelated with the skulls of seven small animals. As she arose, the firelight of the cave glistened off her statuesque nakedness, her perfect olive skin dripping with red rain. Adorning her shoulders were elaborate twin pauldrons crafted from carved Human skulls and running down the length of her elegant back curved a long spine. Within her left hand she wielded an inverted scythe and above her head hovered the top-halves of seven Mensmall corpses, their entrails dangling out.

The chanting in the cavern had grown in volume the more the object of their reverence came forth, once again nearly matching the beats of the drums around them. This had only served to further chill the ice running through the young captive's veins as she beheld the spectacle and as both the lady and their song reached their full height, she screamed in an ear-piercing note for what came next.

Harrowing screeches rent the air mixed with agonised gargles. Several bony, blood-stained hands grasped the edge of the pool and dragged forth their hewn bodies. The young woman's eyes roved over them as they hauled themselves over the side and grappled each stone down with excruciating desperation. A single chain was attached to each of their trailing spines and led back to two ankle bracelets shackled to the lady towering above them.

The captive struggled to escape the clutches of those restraining her limbs, yet their grip could not come undone. With sickened fear strangling her every nerve, she found even her gaze was unable to avert from the clawing advance. Their sepulchral howls, sanguine vomit and imploring expressions seared the deepest recesses of her soul. As a haze began to cloud her vision, she realised that the wailing aberrations possessed fangs in their gaping mouths. Violent trembles coursed through her and, through a wave of fresh tears, her sight slowly lifted to stare at the holder of their leashes.

She had not moved. The genuflecting congregation raised their voices and heads to gaze upon her and chant "Acar Vanta!", whilst the drums pounded harder than ever before. Suddenly, the being's head and shoulders ignited in roaring flames of pitch. The chanting ceased and became a single large cheer. The echoes vibrated through the blond woman, indistinguishable from her own shivering. With the clink of the chains all but fading into the background, her attention remained riveted and as the lady opened her eyes at last, the captive found herself ossified.

Twin voids of flawless night regarded her with an unknowable will. Within their abyssal bastille, the young woman's gaze, alongside all the light in the cavern, was held fast and the only evidence of her own existence was reflected in the minuscule strands of purest silver that slithered and writhed in the onyx oceans. There were no whites to her eyes, and these perfect, obsidian and argent depths haunted the soul of the restrained female.

The longer she stared into them, the more she could feel them penetrate her body, pierce into her mind and expose every last recess of her spirit. She tried to back away, but the iron grips upon her arms and legs pushed her forwards again. Her shudders intensified as the crowned woman began to take the first steps towards her, descending the stones and pulling her ruined prisoners aside. Neither the deafening crowd nor the aria of the tortured could divert the frozen captive's focus away from the blood-soaked lady as she made her way down. She could no longer scream. Her throat seized shut and her breathing had stopped. Through blurry streams, she witnessed their arm reach towards her face. Long, graceful fingers, still dripping with life, caressed her pale cheek and stroked it with a thumb. The captive's skin quaked under the soft touch and her jaw clenched so hard it sent pangs all through her neck and face. The being before her then smiled. It was unfathomable in nature, made worse only with the revealing of fangs. At this point, amidst the whirlwind of nightmares and screams rendering her thoughts all but unintelligible, a solitary question stood out and without making the conscious effort to think it, she did.

Who is this?

The smile on the lady widened. Leaning down further, her eyes bored deeper into the tormented girl's, holding her still. Unable to give even the slightest twitch, the mortal felt her hair stroked and the velvety press of lips upon her own. In the very next instant, she felt a booming crack echo in her mind, hammer through her flesh and shake the very foundations of the chamber.

God.

Blood spilled from above and the fires all around fluttered until the air-rending reply ceased its tremors. The masses roared in the wake of its fading resonance and, in perfect uniformity, they addressed the Vampire.

"Acar Vanta!"

"Mother of Whores!"

"Icon of Sin!"

"Unholy Amen!"

"God!"

Their reverent calls, freezing her sobbing form, stormed the miasma of her mind as its focus became bound within the two black holes assaying her soul. Her stiffened body made the instinctive effort to retreat, but her muscles did not answer. Instead, they jerked in the tightening hands of those behind her and had she been more aware of herself, she would have sensed her limbs beginning to numb. She whimpered as the Vampire bored further and further into her. At the moment when all within her had been breached, the immortal moved back to once more tower above her and shift her gaze out over the now cheering congregation.

"Here lies a nameless wretch..." the Acar Vanta boomed in a voice so loud and deep the cavern again vibrated to each

49

syllable. The blond woman flinched in pain from the power of it and did not notice as the Unholy Amen pointed down at her with the scythe. "Full of... *modesty*... *doubt*... and *misguided ideals*: weaknesses that cannot be abided." She slammed the weapon so hard into the stone floor its surface shattered like glass. The captive gave a small shriek. "Her blessed purification, bestowed by my hand and at my will, begins now!" Turning her sight from the crowds, the Acar Vanta leaned down and brought her lips besides the mortal's earlobe.

"Be reborn, My Child," she whispered passionately.

Wide, wet eyes regarded the Mother of Whores with terror as the kneeling woman remained frozen in place. Without looking at her, the immortal gave a casual wave to the frenzied mob. Immediately, they yanked the young woman backwards. In an instant, her petrification melted and she kicked, flailed and screamed as scores of grisly-clad cultists piled around her with groping hands stretched out and ravenous glints in their insatiable eyes. In a swift motion, glass and metal crashed to the floor and, giving a loud cry of pain, she felt her back slammed into the heavy oak of one of the banquet tables. Revulsion and fear surged through her as she uttered what she knew inside to be hopeless cries of protest. Even had they listened, their lecherous yells would have drowned them out. Hyperventilating, she shut her eyes as tightly as possible as the first of the eager participants clambered onto the table, damp and stiffened genitals in hand.

"Tonight!" declared the Acar Vanta. "She shall achieve my Mark. Envy her, for you are but churls before me and she shall ascend to a far loftier position to serve at my feet!"

Nearly an hour passed. It did not feel like such a time had progressed to her, for she had done her best to drown in her inner turbulence. Amidst the whirlwind of blind agony, she felt the heat and throbs of dozens of men and women. The taste of putrid salt, the repugnant stickiness upon her bare flesh and the vibrations of cold metal between her legs left her retching and in a nightmarish stupor. When all went suddenly quiet after this time, she felt sweaty limbs detach themselves and heard the rapid scuffling of feet as they moved away. She slowly opened her eyes.

The cold blackness of the Unholy Amen's gaze stared down into her. Her stomach lurched and her throat seized to compensate. A single finger outstretched and lay upon the mortal's lips. The young woman could feel her whole head held completely still from the gentle touch and she trembled against the wood as the haunting smile from earlier formed upon the face of the Acar Vanta.

"It is good you know better than to reject that which they have gifted unto you," she spoke.

Nauseated waves of repulsion flooded the captive and her eyes wept anew. They flowed faster as she witnessed the seven chained Vampires float high into the air above her. A fresh spasm from her gut hurled a quantity of her stomach's contents into her mouth. An eyebrow flickered upon the visage of the Mother of Whores, causing an icy lancet to pierce the girl's heart. She then felt the tiniest increase in the pressure holding her quivering lips shut. She swallowed hard, trying to divert her focus onto anything else.

Crimson rain had begun to drip onto her already soiled skin and as much as she wanted to turn her head from the grim precipitation, she could not. Her whole body was stricken still via unknown means and the removal of the immortal's finger did nothing to allay this.

The Acar Vanta started to lead the congregation in a low, melodious chant. The drums died down at last and all in the chamber returned to positions of supplication. A cold, feathery touch burned upon the young woman's neck and chest as the Unholy Amen drew her finger down from her chin, across her throat and settled between her breasts. Underneath its unyielding caress, the girl's heart fluttered in panic then, without warning, a thick black liquid splashed down, coating her body. She gasped and some of it dropped into her open mouth. Spitting out the vile swill, her attention shot upwards. The bound immortals hung garrotted, the remaining contents of their half-bodies emptied upon her. In her revulsion, she almost failed to notice the frigid sensation that scorched its way up from her chest to settle at the base of her jaw. She stopped spitting and tried her best to look away from the form of the Acar Vanta as she leant over her. It was no use. Her sight blurry from her tears and a state of frightened delirium, her focus became dominated by the instigator of her misery as she closed in.

A gentle, passionate kiss was laid upon her trembling lips.

"Don't forget to breathe," the Acar Vanta whispered in her ear.

The young woman's heart raced faster and she gave a shriek of pain as she felt her hair yanked upward by the Acar Vanta. Her body collided with the ground and its stones scratched her skin as she was dragged across it. The cacophonous cheers rang out once again, masking her cries. She then looked ahead. Her legs kicked out and she clawed at the floor to stop herself going further.

The pool was growing larger in her darting field of view. She struck out at the hand gripping her hair, but the grasp of the Vampire was absolute. From the surging crowd behind them, several of the cultists seized her struggling feet and arms. Amidst her agonising screeches of protest, she felt the coldness of iron clamped around her wrists and ankles and her limbs were wrested together behind her. The chains about the feet of the Unholy Amen were gone. Several now held her fast.

They reached the dark steps. The captive howled from the pangs shooting through her limbs as the Vampire hauled her up by the fetters binding her. Her lungs pumped so hard with every inch forward she began to see stars in her stricken eyes, but this did not stop her from perceiving the crimson mirror coming closer. The room span around and she gave a final squeak of terror just before she was cast into the pool.

Pure panic set in as she did her utmost not to breathe in the suffocating liquid around her. The heavy iron restraints were pulling her deeper down. The loud cries of the crowd became something of the past as the only sounds she paid any attention to were her own internal cries. However, amidst the dread, a voice, soft and sultry, passed through the hurricane in her head to strike like a javelin through to her core.

Fall...

Yet, just as suddenly as she had heard it, she felt the refreshing cold of air once again as the immortal lifted her out of the blood by her restraints. A massive, desperate gulp of air entered the girl's lungs and she was turned around to face the hungry smiles of the Acar Vanta's followers.

"Behold her baptism in the First Severeds' blood!" boomed the Icon of Sin, holding her up for all to see. The metal bit into the young woman's flesh and her arms felt like they would pop out from her shoulders. The Mother of Whores continued, "She is blessed to be covered from head to cunt in the precious life that was removed by MY WILL!"

The shivering girl's knees collided with the edge of the pool so she could see the heaving masses bearing jubilant cheers at her misery. Spluttering still, she realised another dousing was coming and took in another large breath right before her head and shoulders were forced back under. The celebratory cries from the crowd were deafening, but through them, again, there came the voice inside her. It was unfamiliar.

Addiction...

Whilst it faded, the roars and moans of the cultists took to the fore and the echoes of their inability to hold back their desire any longer rang in her ears.

The young women's life-soaked head was brought up again by the Acar Vanta. Another large gasp of air filled her chest and the Vampires' voice yet again shook the very walls.

"MY WILL! NOT INTER'S! I am the *Breaker* of the First Tenet! The Unholy Amen of that false god! And SHE-" She undid the shackles holding the girl in an instant and brought her to her unsteady feet. "-SHE will become the embodiment of MY WILL! BLESSED in this unholy union beyond her understanding! Look upon her with jealousy – this is her beginning – her new life as the Word of the Acar Vanta! MY *BLASPHEMY* UNTO THE WRETCHED INTER!"

An explosion of applause accompanied the already raucous cheering of the crowd to overwhelm the senses of the young lady. Unable to move from dismay, she barely noticed the

Vampire once again lean towards her ear and so she started upon feeling the air from her voice tickling her lobe.

"They're here for you, my Blasphemy," came the calm and reassuring whisper. "They're all yours. How lucky you are to have so many admirers desiring you and wishing they *were* you."

The Blasphemy of Inter was swivelled around until her back bent over the crimson pool. The tips of her long, sullied hair brushed with its surface, rippling it out beneath her. She dare not move. Yet when she looked up at the embodiment of all her fears, her breath caught in her throat. A smooth smile was crossing the Acar Vanta's features, instilling in Blasphemy a nonsensical sense of serenity. The Vampire's gaze deepened as she inched closer to the woman, each moment feeling like an eternity. The Acar Vanta's eyes shone and, for the first time, the girl felt able to speak.

"P-please," she muttered. "S-stop this! Please don't hurt me."

The Unholy Amen's expression altered not a single iota, and as the crowds came upon the plinth to surround them - some dancing in the blood, others standing and readying themselves for the next assault - her loving reply came to echo in Blasphemy's ears.

"We won't hurt you..."

The immortal lowered the young woman backwards into the liquid life. Blasphemy's breathing hastened as panic went into overdrive once more, and her eyes pleaded with the woman she could not overcome.

"But, this is just the beginning..."

The blood rose to her neck and she shook her head in terror, fresh tears mixing with the crimson underneath. The familiar smothering flooded the nerves in her flesh. Her heavy sobs seemed to reverberate in time with the calls of the congregation and with each rise and fall of her chest, she felt the all-powerful touch of the Acar Vanta's tender fingertips forcing her under.

"And we will give you pleasure beyond imagination..."

As the red reached her ears and cheeks, her panting deepened and accelerated. At last, she closed her soaking eyes and took one final despairing gasp of precious air just as her entirety was enveloped by the wretched waters about her.

"Just forgo your inhibitions, My Child. Surrender to me and my will."

The following hours were a noxious trance. The moment her baptism was complete, the Mother of Whores left her to the devices of her devotees and Blasphemy was once more subjugated to their carnal whims. In abject despair, she willed herself to fall into unconsciousness. Such mercy was not forthcoming, however she ended up in a daze where she managed to take very little of what happened to her in. What minimal conversation there was amongst the cultists beyond the unfamiliar language of the rituals was comprised of perverted comments regarding the young woman's dishevelled appearance, her lacking sexual abilities and the attractive, albeit somewhat emaciated, nature of her body. Few of their words sank in, and those that managed to permeate her despondent haze she abhorred.

Eventually, beyond tears and the effort of screams, the young woman collapsed in sheer prostration onto the heavy oak table, its cool damp surface being the only source of comfort for her. Soon, the icy soft touch of the immortal's fingers slid under her armpits and hoisted her to her lifeless feet. Unable to resist from complete exhaustion and terror, Blasphemy allowed herself to be placed face down upon the table. She barely noticed the cold of metal against her skin as her ankles and wrists were chained to each other under the table. Inaudible and inane murmurs of desperation were all she could manage. Some semblance of reality managed to return to her as the crowd's laughter turned once more to a uniform chanting. The Acar Vanta then sat by her side and pressed on her lower back.

"Everyone rejoice! For now is the moment! I give her the first Mark of my Will!"

A sudden sharp pain shot through her shoulders as a needle pierced her skin. She jerked to get away, but between the restraints and the Acar Vanta's grip, her muscles were unable to respond to her deepest wishes of escape. Then through her hazy panic, she swore she could hear another voice in her head. A profound sense of violation poured over her as she recognised it as that of the Icon of Sin.

Remain still, My darling Child. I do not want to hurt you. Soon you will realise that you are blessed beyond all others and my choosing of you is the greatest gift you've ever received. Relax, my beautiful girl, and place your faith in Me.

Leave me alone, please! I beg you, ma'am! Blasphemy replied.

Sssh, relax and let go. You will know Me and My Will and know that all I do now is to perfect you. I will always take care of you, my Child. Place your faith in Me and receive My Blessing.

The Acar Vanta suddenly spoke out with her voice to the ravenous onlookers.

"Do you not wish to be in her place?! Are you not poisonously envious of her fortunate place at MY feet?!"

The roar of agreement from the crowd shocked Blasphemy into opening her tired eyes. She witnessed with a fresh onset of nausea the genuine attitudes of envy and reverence they held in their features.

"Did you not come here for her?! To give *her* pleasure and to enjoy the pleasure I offer through her?!"

The congregation repeated their agreeing yells and Blasphemy closed her eyes once more, attempting to re-enter the dream space that, whilst still being a living nightmare, was a marginal relief from her waking reality.

It must have worked, because the next thing she knew she was waking up in mid air, her limbs outstretched and chained to a square metal frame just in front of the pool steps. The deafening jubilant screams of the masses startled her conscious and the first thing she witnessed was a reflected image of her back from a giant mirror in front of her.

It was inked with a symbol depicting the Acar Vanta herself. Seven inverted septagrams rose in an arc above the naked form of the Unholy Amen who was adorned with a crown crenelated with seven finger bones and her body was wreathed in black fire. Just above the crown rose a reversed crescent moon that fitted perfectly beneath the stars. In her left hand was an upside-down scythe and in her right she bore a chain that bound the kneeling form of Death Itself as They were forced to pleasure her. Beneath her feet lay a pile of crushed skulls that tumbled down almost to the small of Blasphemy's back.

Blasphemy wept, repelled by this permanent addition, yet anguish was drowned by fear as she saw the Acar Vanta take to the top of the vat and address her subjects.

"Behold! This is the first of days! Her beginning as MY BLESSED BLASPHEMY! HERALD OF DAMNATION! This marks the start of her ascension to sit at MY FEET!"

The air was rent with an ear-splitting roar that stumbled the congregation and left Blasphemy screaming in pain. Squinting, she witnessed the pool behind her was pulled, crumbled and shattered as if by an unimaginable gale until all the stones were torn apart and sent spinning at blurring speed around the Icon of Sin. The blood from within floated amongst the maelstrom before forming gigantic vermilion wings upon the Vampire, who now hovered above Blasphemy. Outstretching her elegant arms to her sides, the immortal arched her back, and the wings unfurled, their tips spearing into the walls either side of the enormous cavern and sending the flying masonry aside. The eyes of the Acar Vanta then blazed with midnight fury as she bellowed out to the cult.

"REJOICE ON THIS UNHOLY DAY, my heretics, and WATCH HER RISE!"

Natalie's Stains

I don't feel that... I don't feel it's wise to be talking about this. You *know* she's always listening! She hears all! I can't... I couldn't help you survive even if I wanted to. You know her power. And don't call it 'winning' again! There is no *winner*. You think I *won* in my time? No-one does. Only *she* ever does. She takes the best of us and turns it into her own twisted ideals.

Look... No you listen! I wouldn't even know where to start. I *know* you're scared. I was... I still am. I live in constant fear. No!... Will you just listen!? I know things are worse for you than me, but we aren't allowed to help students 'graduate' the year. What?... I... I don't know... I think... maybe... Look... I *can't* help you survive this nightmare, but I can tell you my story. She teaches our stories in class anyway. She damn well boasts of Equinn's achievements all the time... Teach you how to fend for yourself? I can't. No. No! Shut up and calm down! Sorry... just... please stop crying and I'll... I'll explain how I did it... Then I will tell you the one thing that matters more here than surviving. Don't fail this one thing... not like I have.

When I first arrived at this... 'school', all I could do was think about my sister. Whilst I desperately desired to see my parents as well, I had always been especially close to my little sister and I sat in terror over the potential of never seeing her again. Of never holding her again. She was my best friend and I hers. I had no idea where I was and neither did anyone else around me. We all assumed we were going to die. As it so happens, that was closer to the truth than we knew at the time... No... I don't believe I'll ever see her again. Even if I did... I don't know if... I don't want to talk about it anymore. When I arrived, I had the same assembly you had a few days ago. The Head Mistress gives the same speech more or less every year: That there are one hundred of us, all locked in a fortress surrounded by a forest full of ravenous aberrations, and only one student will 'graduate' into her alumni of immortals. The rest die, killed off, as you know, by the other students to prize strength of mind, spirit and/or body. The power of the 'self'. It's... beyond evil.

Sickening. I can't find the words to appropriately convey my disgust for her. Like everyone else, I was horrified upon hearing this. The others around me suddenly had gone from fellow abduction victims to my enemies. Glances were exchanged. Teeth ground. Nerves ignited. You saw it for yourself with your peers. What semblance of friendships may have been made during our transportation evaporated in the blink of an eye. I trusted no-one, for she prescribed a situation that discouraged it. I went solo. Some went into groups. It became tribal outside the neutral times and zones of this inescapable place. I knew full well that groups only encouraged the use of shorter knives down the line, so I kept my distance.

No killing is allowed for the first twenty-four hours. As it's doubtless designed to do, the first meal that evening resulted in alliances and groups formulating from strangers. Everyone tried to make themselves seem useful to others. Natural leaders stood out. We divided. Many, like myself as previously stated, stayed solo. It's… regretfully the wise choice. This is a large castle and there are lots of hiding places during the daylight hours for someone to sleep in without high risk of discovery… No, I can't tell you where I hid. I can tell you I moved about, never staying anywhere too long. I know the layout of this place probably better than most students who went into groups – they tended to sleep in the dormitories together – safety in numbers. Often, several people would go in at sunrise and only one would emerge at dusk. Yet there were some who stayed as a group for most of the year. We all had a year to… be the last one standing after all. After that time was up… well… you know what she said and it's no bluff. One or none. There were a few years that had no graduates. Students apparently had banded together and stood up to her, saying they'd all rather die than kill their friends… to die rather than give her the satisfaction of a graduate. It's a rare sight and it's not worth pursuing. The vast majority of the time, they'll turn on each other as the second hand counts down the final minute anyway. In the end, if you come to know her as I do, you'll know those displays of defiance mean nothing to her. To her, they're just dust in the wind. They thought they'd make her angry. A vain hope. She doesn't care what happens or how we do things. She only cares about watching us suffer in this… shithole of perpetual agony. I cannot possibly imagine a worse fate than being taken here and forced to do the things we do… I know, sorry…I've digressed. I'll continue…

So aside from hiding between lessons and in order to sleep (which I didn't always manage to do), I attended her teachings. There's no bluff here either. Attendance *is* mandatory. Most were given by her, especially those focused on her self-serving philosophies, but some were given by her other students. No doubt you've heard of Equinn already… You've not? I mentioned her briefly, but I'm surprised our Head Mistress hasn't mentioned her by now. Equinn is her prize pupil – the only student to single handedly massacre all ninety-nine of their peers. She broke the rules to do it, killing them all within the first twenty-four hours, but our repugnant Head Mistress was so *damn* impressed with her survival instincts and cold selfishness, she allowed it and so that year lasted less than a day and she's been rewarded with teaching classes in addition to the usual Vampiricity, like myself… No, I'm not a teacher, thank fuck for that… I… I didn't make the cut… Some small compensation for my sins… How did she do it? Equinn used the catering to poison everyone… I don't care to relate the exact details. Point is, impress the Head Mistress enough and she'll let you teach the new students. Back to my story: I'd attend the classes, keeping close to an exit of any kind – a vent, a window, the door (but only if desperate as that's the bloodiest place to be). I'd spend most of it planning my escape as opposed to paying attention to her insane philosophies about true power being obtained only through serving oneself. The worst ones… were the sex lessons. Some students liked them, but I think they were all fucked in the head to begin with. I could barely handle listening to how to kill someone effectively, how to steal and be stealthy – yet those lessons are regrettably why… why I'm still… *alive* – but… but the sex ones… I felt rotten doing them. She ruined sex for me forever. I loved it before, but putting a bunch of people who are on constant edge over everyone there trying to murder them and forcing them to fuck one another is just… I was sick many times… What?! You're a… Really?… I'm so very, *very* sorry… I don't know what to say… No-one deserves this kind of introduction to it… Sorry… Anyway, people had their possessions stolen… I had that happen to me so I stole things back, which was the only good to come of those times. One item I stole stood out. It was a climbing hook. Using rope I'd obtained on my own, I fashioned an effective grappling hook. In terms of escaping lessons alive, I used it to scale the walls outside the windows. To my knowledge, no-one else had ever used such a tactic. Far below I'd see those hungry, black and olive skinned horrors prowling the woods… I therefore didn't take long learning how to master using my tool.

Now, not every lesson will result in a bloodbath right outside the classroom, and whilst I'd never say you can relax in this tormenting place, you will have some measure of relief… Yes, if you live long enough… I'm sorry... Most of the time, groups let each other pass by, knowing they've got a whole year to do the deed and they'd prefer to live as long as possible before committing to a likely fatal engagement. Due to this, there's some reprieve in the middle months where not much happens. People actually have made friendships and even engaged in art (I didn't because I was too busy focusing on keeping my eyes on everyone else). We've apparently even had a few bands, with the Head Mistress providing all musical equipment – she loves all forms of art, if you couldn't tell already from her theatrical nature. Which brings me to perhaps the second most discomforting aspect of living here and whilst not related to my personal story as a student, I still feel that you should know because if you've not yet learned of this, then you at least won't be as shocked as I was when I saw the full extent of her evil.

I remember them all as if they were still happening. It's burned upon my very retinas and stalks my every nightmare. In the main assembly hall, she holds the most abhorrent rituals a few times a year. All graduates take part without exception. I've… I have… I hope you never have to do what I've done… What I was made to do… Perhaps… Perhaps death is better?

The Head Mistress has another name… Well, a title actually, given to her by one of the three High Priestesses of Inter she holds… captive here. Our Head Mistress hates Interism above all other things – I don't know fully why – and she… she abducted three of the most famous and powerful of their order and… converted them into Vampires… No – Shut-!… You don't understand what she did before converting them! Whilst some Bavillions do desire to be closer to their deity by being Vampires, these three *clearly* aren't like them and were… stripped of their mortality against their will…Don't think they wanted what's happened to them! Our Head Mistress gave each one of them a different… ritually significant disability. One cannot see, another cannot hear and the last cannot speak… Exactly, that's exactly what it represents with the evil in question being Interism. She has them chained apart and crucified. There's a dungeon underneath the stage and they're lifted out from it, blood-starved and… the looks in the eyes of the two with them… I cannot even imagine their acute suffering. As bad as it sounds, I'm immeasurably relieved it's not my sister up there. I just kept imagining it was…One of them… reminds me of her... It also made me feel grateful for the first time that I was only a student – at least I stood some chance of getting out of my predicament. They have no such hope. Every ritual involves a lot of blood, painting it upon their… the three of them are always naked and… we are forced to paint their skin with blood – I dare not know whose or what – into magical seals and other blasphemous symbols. Afterwards, the Head Mistress leads us graduates in some sort of prayer-like chant… I don't know the language or what I'm saying most of time, but one thing does repeat and I now know what it means. Apparently, a long time ago, in one of the first rituals, the youngest of their number, the blonde one, called the Head Mistress by an ancient title of absolute perversion in their religion. A name from folklore so old the origins are completely lost to time: The Acar Vanta… 'The Unholy Amen'… It's the Anti-Inter, an all-powerful entity of damnation… I don't know… I know she is incredibly old and by extension extremely powerful. According to her, she's the second eldest of all the Vampires, born centuries ago from the first Vampire, so as far as I know, the stories could have originated around her. Either way, I don't care. She's unimaginably strong and infinitely cruel. That's all you need to know... After we paint the High Priestesses, we unchain them and... I... The Head Mistress makes us... have sex with them... I... I... I had no choice... We're threatened with... I *can't* go through what they have... I would never do this willingly!... I'm sorry... Thank you... But I still *do* it... like I... Ok... I'll focus... Dammit! She then has us toss them to the students to... do the same thing if they want. We, as graduates, 'lead by example' to encourage the students to follow suit. A lot refuse, though some enjoy it and they sicken me. If some of us have to die, then... I don't know if I mean that but it sure goes through my head... I know I deserve that too...

Which leads me onto the worst part, at least for me. I cannot rid myself of their faces... contorted, pained, terrified faces of the twelve people I... killed. Half were in the first two months, which tend to be the bloodiest times as groups establish themselves and settle into a sort of understanding. It's not always the case, but it happens fairly often. Whenever I slept, I'd have to tape my mouth shut for fear of screaming from anguished dreams and giving away my location. Fortunately, these stone walls are high and echo well so others couldn't pinpoint my location. That saved me a few times. Throughout everything, I felt myself die each time I took away a life. Their terrified and... *helpless* eyes seared into my memories... I cannot forget it... My first kill was a strangulation... I will never do that again. His... purple... I... can't say it... he haunts my dreams more than most but... my final kill... I'm sorry...

He had been a leader of a group determined to stick together, but after they took out the last opposing packs, he knew what would happen next and struck his companions first. That left myself, somewhere hidden in the castle, and him. I had successfully out waited everyone else, killing only when I absolutely had to, running and hiding the rest of the time. Since I was known to be the last individual student, all remaining parties ignored me, too focused on their bigger threats. It made life a little easier towards the end. I was roused from my current hiding spot by his voice on the internal radio challenging me to a duel in the assembly hall. Of course, I knew full well it could be a trap, having become too used to that sort of thing over the months. Instead of going directly there, I took my time searching the rest of the castle for any possible remaining students. I cannot express just how terrified I was – I was drenched in sweat, trembling with every step and peering around every corner in fear that an ambush was awaiting me. I traversed the many stairways, corridors and passages in this manner. I wore no shoes to dampen the echoes of my footfalls, keeping the only weapon I had left, which was my grappling hook, clenched in my sweaty hands. After what felt like a lifetime, I made it to the hall. He stood there pacing back and forth in front of the Head Mistress and the other graduates. They hadn't noticed me yet, or at least they didn't acknowledge my arrival, not wishing to aid him in any way. Knowing the Head Mistress, she knew where I was at all times, but still. It was disgustingly the only time I've been thankful of her – she allowed my element of surprise and if it weren't for that, I might not be… *alive*… Nevermind. I peeked around one of the entrances to the hall and waited until he had turned to walk in the opposite direction before swiftly turning the corner, swinging my hook above my head and casting it at his neck. He heard the motion of the rope in the air and turned faster than I hoped, but the rope and hook caught about his throat… I… I moved quickly and… pulled him by the rope to the ground and jumped on top of him… I… partially unravelled the hook… tightened… the rope… and I… I plunged the hook's teeth into his throat like… like… I wasn't thinking. I just acted on instinct. I shook violently and uncontrollably, but I didn't cry. I had cried before, but this time… I had become more used to it. Adrenaline was… My hands, arms, legs and face were coated in his gushing blood. I looked up to see the graduates staring at him… I shot to one side as they swooped like a wave onto him and… I think you can imagine what immortals did to someone choking on their own blood. I desperately wanted to crawl away, but lay petrified a short distance from them… She then glided over to me with a smile… I will never forget it… I still cannot fathom the exact expression, but if I had to guess it felt like pride… It keeps me awake at night to this day… I couldn't move for fear and she lifted me into her arms… Before I could do anything, all became a haze. She stripped me… groomed me… drained me…

All the blood upon my hands are as stains upon my soul. Forever marred and never pure. And that is my message to you. No matter what happens… No matter what ills befall you… No matter how much agony you face or how many people you're forced to kill… No matter if you survive this unending nightmare or not… Do not let her win by changing who you are. I am a failure. I commit terrible acts in her name because I am too afraid to say no. I am not a winner. I am not a graduate. I'm not even a survivor. And I will never be able to face my sister again after all I've done. There are worse fates than death. Never compromise who you are to simply survive.

Willow's Puzzlement

"I mean, it's always been there, but I'm sure it's been getting worse over the last couple centuries! Ever since the Holy War ended, really. I just don't understand it."

Willow's bright verdant eyes glanced up at Amakay, who stood there, her brow and jaw tensed. The younger of the Elders, though rather older in physical appearance than the woman perched opposite her, opened her mouth as if to speak, but managed only to utter an apprehensive sigh. Willow, sitting on a moss covered boulder with her knees up to her chest looked down at the ground, her long white locks shielding her face from view.

"Why do they treat me so bad? Glaring at me. Whispering behind my back. Averting their gaze whenever I enter their vicinity. I've done nothing to them! I swear!" Willow leaned back against the oak behind her, wrung her hands and her lips began to tremble. "I've only ever tried to be kind, right from the start and welcome them into the Council upon their conversion. You remember, right? I gave you a huge hug as soon as the trees parted and you entered."

Amakay smiled, her pure black eyes reflecting the faint blue light illuminating the surrounding darkness of the forest and nodded. "Yes, I do remember. It was nice for me to feel wanted on the Council at the time."

Willow beamed up at her. "I know! I'm thrilled Vertio converted you, by the way! You didn't deserve how you were treated at the time either." Her face became etched with concern before adding, "If you ever want to talk about how things are going with her, I'm happy to listen."

"The less you know, the better, Willow," she responded, shifting position. "But yes, you have always been congenial."

Willow nodded. "I've also tried to be as helpful around here as possible! I aid in everyday rituals with the Priests and Priestesses, I attend every Council meeting early, I've saved so many lives by helping Ellandu'el tend to our wounded soldiers both in and outside of war and I help every living plant in Illarien to grow." Amakay took in a sharp breath as she finished her sentence, but Willow did not notice and carried on, "Even after all they've done by talking down to me and treating me like an outsider, I still smile and try to help them in all Elder matters!" The first drops of black tears began to well in her eyes. "What have I done wrong? Why do they treat me like this? Is there something wrong with me?"

An uneasy countenance upon her, Amakay paused for several moments before answering.

"There's nothing wrong with you, Willow," she reassured, shifting once more. Several seconds passed before she continued. "It's just... many of the Elders... they're not too keen on certain... aspects of your personality."

The youthful immortal stared out across the leaf strewn ground to the gargantuan trunks opposite, her vision clouded by lachryma. She shook her head.

"Bu-but I always try my best to be nice! I'm always happy to see everyone, even when they don't like to see me. I give everything to the other Elders, the Council and Illarien!"

"No, I mean-"

"I gave them all hugs too when they first arrived! I never left anyone out. And I always try to keep a positive feeling going in Council meetings, even when things are at the worst. I help and listen and give support to everyone!"

"It's not that!" gently interjected Amakay, gesturing with her hands for Willow to stop. She tensed and took a deep breath. "It's... to do with your... attitude... towards certain things."

Wide eyed with surprise, she mumbled, "My... attitude?" Willow's gaze grew unfocused. For a while she sat staring into space, oblivious to her friend and the forest around her, tears threatening to spill down and stain her alabaster cheeks. Eventually she blinked and came back.

"Oh," she muttered. "I understand."

Amakay brushed her brown and silvery hair out from her face as she knelt beside Willow, grasping hold of her shoulder in one hand. Willow clung to her own legs, bringing them in as close as possible. Sobs echoed closely in the dense wood. Some time passed before she wiped her tears away and loosened her grip on herself.

"I love *everyone*," she whispered in a voice so quiet Amakay had trouble discerning what she said. "And that is good. I won't change. I have no reason to. But-" Her volume returned to normal and she glanced up through her hair at the opaque canopy. "-I get that not everyone enjoys how… how I do it."

Amakay's grip eased and she looked away, closing her lips tight. Willow intensified her stare at the darkness as she spoke on, "I just tried to be nice. I only want to make others happy and what better way is there to do this than by showing them love?" Squeezing her friend's hand, she removed it from her shoulder and stood up, smiling once again, albeit a weak one.

"I'm not changing. I'm not hurting anyone after all. Maybe they're just not used to someone caring about them? After all, some of them are not very nice. Ulaq, Sylvia and Karalenn for example. Maybe they're just lonely inside and don't like to show it?"

Amakay's expression fell and she closed her eyes. She took a deep breath and then stood up next to her. Willow did not stop talking.

"Or maybe they're in pain and need someone to show them love? We immortals do carry around a lot of pain at times. Whatever their reasons, I'll be sure to continue to show them kindness anyway so that they know I mean them no ill and only warmth!" She gestured outward with her hands. "I'll just be less… boisterous about it this time, since that's what must be getting on their nerves." She turned with renewed energy to her friend, eyes shimmering and threw her arms about her.

"Thank you, Amakay!" she exclaimed, sniffing a little in the process. Amakay held her close and feebly returned her smile. Pulling back, Willow straightened up and bounced on the balls of her bare feet. "Thanks for helping! I'm off to tell Daddy Pantheon about this! I feel better!"

Without a second's hesitation, Willow shot off in a blur into the enveloping shade of the forest, no branch nor twig cracking to echo the sound of her departure. Amakay took in a long, deep breath and looked in the direction Willow had flown.

"I hope he can tell you what I could not," she muttered to

herself and the green around her.

Cinthia's Meeting
Illarien, Year 1093

The last beams of moonlight kissed the earth beneath Cinthia's light tread as she crossed into the newly familiar edges of the Evernight. She melted into its welcoming shadow, owing mainly to her midnight hue garb. The spider silk clinging to her body absorbed the shade, merging every inch of her body with the surrounding murk save for her head. It was exposed, goggles atop her forehead, the face wraps and hood draping down her shoulders and back, revealing the only exceptions to the gloom around them. Her vibrant ginger locks were in their usual parallel pigtails behind her head and her pink eyes, though only dimly glowing, in such an encompassing darkness as the Evernight they appeared much brighter than they were and glinted off the dew soaked mosses as she passed by.

Ducking under the nearest coniferous and oaken boughs, taking care not to have them catch on her bag containing her various notebooks and archaeological gear slung over her shoulder, she felt the long dulled pangs of anticipation kindle within her chest. A rare, minuscule smile flashed across her features. The darkness ahead held an allure she had been unable to appreciate on her initial visit as the experience had been an overwhelming one and consequently her time there had been short lived. She had not even attended the Elder Council. She intended to rectify both, having come prepared for a lengthy stay.

The blanketing shroud of the woodland stretched out for as far as she could see, unbroken from the totality of the opaqueness of the vaulted canopy sprawling for miles high overhead. Cinthia, her knee-high boots making very little noise as she passed over the leafy ground, made her way in deeper, relieved to be privileged with not only permission to enter, as was registered by the magic of the city recognising her, but also the knowledge of Illarien's precise location. It was hidden somewhere far within and its borders shifted, hiding itself from sight. According to the legends, which she had briefly studied centuries ago prior to her first visit, one could walk through the very heart of the city and never even know it was there, as the trees would shift to conceal it. Cinthia, however, had debunked this when she first visited, finding that only the ever altering borders acted in this manner to lead people on meanders out around the city. Seeing as Illarien itself was almost entirely comprised of trees to begin with, this was doubly effective at keeping its exact location a secret. Having ones identity magically imprinted upon the immortal memories of the forest city was only half the security measures for preserving its secrecy. Yet it had been this very privilege that had made her leave as soon as she had done.

Three hundred and fifty-two years ago, Cinthia had spent just two days in Illarien before turning back round and returning to Hallahan and the comfort of her boys. The archaeologist had been welcomed with such attention, awe and idolisation from the mortals who viewed her with utter reverence for just being what she was that she could not explore anywhere in the city without Priests, Priestesses and soldiers flocking to her with praise and questions about herself. A new Elder in their midst, a celebrity for the religious community had come home. Unable to Cloak properly at her young age, Cinthia, feeling anything but peaceful in the place that felt nothing like home, bade her farewells to the few Elders she had managed to meet and made her way back to the centre of the Magnus Desert. Yet this time things were different. She was well into the process of having specialised her Cloak Cor and could remain hidden not only for longer but also from the younger, and less perceptive Vampires and as fascinating for her as it would be to learn about her species' birthplace, it was not her sole motive for returning. In fact, it was simply a bonus.

Fifteen major publication successes under various pen names and hundreds of artefact contributions to the many museums of the Humans saw her rise to become one of the foremost and respected experts on Ancient history, yet despite all that the remaining pickings for undiscovered city ruins and new leads on other fascinating finds had become rather slim. As a result, restlessness and discontentment began to rear their heads. She found herself going over the same old manuscripts, digital data archives and relics in search of answers and hints of new discoveries, yet to no avail. Consequently, Cinthia, feeling her life was slowing down, was all too happy to be given an excuse to return to the home of Interism.

It had only been a few days prior to her arrival at Illarien's borders that Cinthia had been in Hallahan, poring over Ancient documents she had memorized, when she had heard the summons. The dulcet voice of Lady Ellandu'el echoed in her mind, albeit marred by a somewhat uncharacteristic urgency. This raised the archaeologist's eyebrow. Without having delved into details, Ellandu'el urged every Elder to attend an absolute emergency session of their Council and the High Priest Council in three days time. Cinthia's gut had twisted, knowing something dire must have occurred, but she ignored it, deciding in the end that whatever happened was not only out of her control but was also highly likely not her business as she was not an Interist. The very fact the High Priests had been called for suggested this to be a religious matter and so her presence was neither essential nor significant. Despite this and despite the fact that attendance was never mandatory, Cinthia still felt a mixture of concern and responsibility due to the urgency in her associate's voice, however ultimately assuming that whatever crisis would be discussed was out of her scope to help in, her curiosity won out and she packed her bags. Her boys opted not to attend, as they had every time a summons had been called, and so Cinthia explained why she was going and that she would likely stay for a while after the meeting to research Illarien. Used to her wont for lengthy and often solitary exploration, they wished her all the best in her endeavour, teasing her by requesting that she retrieve some valuable relics as gifts for them. Laughing at their attempts to provoke her, Cinthia playfully punched them whilst explaining that they knew she couldn't as that went against her archaeological code. She then bid them goodbye for the duration, her smile fading as she left.

After about an hour of her traipsing deeper into the thick forest, the first hints of deep indigo glowed at random intervals through the branch-woven horizon and the air grew more still and quiet. Cinthia gave a small satisfied snort of air whilst hurdling over a fallen tree, knowing the borders of Illarien were near. Her heart felt lighter and accelerated as the anticipation grew. She unstrapped her flask from the utility belt on her hips and took a deep draught of the thick warm liquid within. Belting it back into its holster, Cinthia de-Cloaked as she continued to move forward through the dark.

It was only a couple minutes later when she heard the far off rustle of leaves in the undergrowth. She halted and her eyes shot to the spot where the sound originated. Through the dense shade and between myriad boughs and greenery, she spotted several heavily armoured, spear-wielding Bavillion soldiers attempting to encircle her, yet they stopped the moment her gaze met their own. Surprised they were not the lightly equipped sentries she had encountered on her previous visit, her brows furrowed. Cinthia's ears picked up one asking another if she was Lady Rose and a tiny twitch of an amused smile passed across her face.

"I am Elder Cinthia, *Fledgling* of Lady Rose," she declared across the wooded expanse, standing upright and still. "I'm here answering the summons of Lady Ellandu'el."

She continued to hold her position as they moved towards her, their garb making little noise for its hefty nature. Once they had come within ten feet, spears still brandished, Cinthia saw one of them was a Priest, wearing a traditional pitch black robe. Embroidered upon its left breast was a simple silver, left-facing crescent moon. Her gaze rose to meet his. From under his thick hood, she could see the Priest's dark eyes squinting hard at her and roving all up and down her form. Her stomach squirmed but she made no show of it and stood her ground. She watched as he wove an invisible shape in the air with a single hand, muttering under his breath. After a moment, the shape glowed silvery white in the form of the waning moon of Inter before altering to a vivid rosy pink colour and then melting into the air. He gave a short grunt of approval and gestured for the soldiers to relax.

"Welcome home, Elder Cinthia," he spoke, bowing. The other men followed suit. Cinthia, observing their reverence, did not

73

move but took a deep breath to counter the twinge in her chest.

"Come, my lady, we will escort you to the Elder Council Chamber at once," the Priest said, his voice polite, yet firm.

Cinthia nodded and followed him into the forest depths. Three soldiers strode behind her whilst the rest re-dispersed into the Evernight. As curious as Cinthia was becoming about how these mortals managed to see so well in the dark, a far greater query made her gut begin to twist.

"You're very well armoured for sentries," she probed the Priest in front of her. "And is it normal for sentries to be accompanied by a Priest?"

Another grunt issued from his throat, however this one sounded heavier than the last. Following a few moments of silence, Cinthia continued.

"And if my memory serves me, not just any Priest, but an Intra Vanta."

A brief quiet passed, the only sound being the needles and leaves crunching underfoot. Without turning or slowing pace, he replied in a sombre tone, "Your memory serves you well, my lady. The situation that has brought you here is more dire than has been conveyed. A great deal of secrecy surrounds the issue, though myself, others of my rank, the High Priests and some of the Elders know what has occurred." He made as if to finish, yet as if he could hear Cinthia's whirling thoughts, he added, "And no, I cannot elaborate. Just know your presence is required most urgently to resolve the matter."

"Thank you, Priest," she said, the anticipation from earlier dissipating. Indeed, the closer they moved to Illarien, the more her jaw clenched.

Eventually they came to an area where the trees had become much thicker and the soothing rush of water echoed in from the right. The group passed by a Soul perched on its carved stone platform in a bush, its white-blue brilliance illuminating Cinthia's near translucent skin as gently as the moon had done before she entered the Evernight. Cinthia's eyes locked on to it, staring through its delicate glass surface and into the swirling clouds of spirits swimming within. Her mouth opened as she made out faces of all sizes and species pressing their bulging, inquisitive eyes against the surface, watching the party go past. She swallowed hard and forced herself to look ahead.

The forest opened itself up and the main dirt street of Illarien stretched out in front of them. Small Souls dangled from the trees whilst the larger brighter ones squatted in random locations around the forest floor, shining out indigo and white waves that danced on and between the giant trunks like water and sunlight. Although brighter than the rest of the Evernight, Illarien was still dimly illuminated. Cinthia, having no trouble seeing in even the darkest of places, wondered again how the mortals coped with it. She could only assume the same magic used to hide Illarien from the rest of the world allowed for its denizens to see in the dark. Through the deep blue, she could spot the dense carpets of moss, lush curtains of ivy and indomitable conifers and deciduous sprawling and thriving in a vast and colossal display of life, which she found to be all too ironic. The canopy towered like a cathedral above them and was so black that Cinthia presumed only other Vampires like herself could make out the arched branches. Despite her tension from moments ago, Cinthia's chest felt alight as she drank in the sights all around, a wide smile crossing over her face. The Vampire hadn't realised she had slowed her pace until the soldier behind her stepped on the back of her boot. Apologising, she shook herself and caught up to the Priest.

As they turned down the road, the River Alin rushed by more quietly than before, its pace slowing as it entered the holy city of Death. Cinthia took note of the masses of soldiers loudly marching ahead, Priests and Priestesses, who conversed in urgent tones, going in and out of rooms comprised from the forest itself, tree trunks uprooting themselves and walking aside to let occupants past before resuming their original positions and a general air of extreme disquiet clinging to the entire bustle. The Intra Vanta began to pick up his pace and requested Cinthia keep close to him. She did, her awe now faded and a stern countenance replacing it. Cinthia noticed without joy how most people this time went about their jobs, paying her no heed, however this did not last long. Small groups of Intra Vanta Priests and Priestesses caught sight of Cinthia's eyes and leery shadows fell over their faces. Cinthia's mouth shut tight and she frowned, her heart beginning to pound harder. The temptation to read their minds tantalised her, but the Elder shook her head and avoided their gawking.

Fighting their way through heaving crowds of military and civilian personnel alike, the small group arrived in front of a heavily guarded segment of forest, behind which nothing could be seen. The trees were sealed tight, with woven ivy and thick moss filling in the gaps between the monolithic pillars. Though this level of privacy was typical for all of Illarien, the royal elite guard was not. Cinthia took a deep breath as she saw the almost humanly tall women, their elaborate silver and obsidian spears grasped in expert hands. Their light, embroidered spider-silk armour, greaves and split battle skirts were remarkably manoeuvrable and their height proved intimidating on any battlefield. As much as Cinthia appreciated the inclusion of women in the highest echelons of Bavillion military service, something Humans had rarely done, she was paying uncomfortable attention to the fact that their presence cemented just how serious the situation must be: it was well known they only left Castle Mortol, the Bavillion capital city, in times of war.

The Intra Vanta signalled for the guards to let Cinthia into the Council Chamber. In unison, the two closest soldiers looked at her then stood to one side.

"With Inter's Blessing," he said, gesturing for her to enter the parting trees. "May this all be over soon."

Cinthia nodded at him in farewell as she stepped over the threshold into the Elder Council Chamber. The moment she did, the trees resealed themselves behind her and the cacophony from the outside faded.

Cinthia froze.

Several Elders, who stood and sat at various intervals around a giant oval table, had ceased talking the moment she entered. They regarded her with mild confusion, with several more peering around those standing to catch a glimpse at what caused the hush. Some looked down their noses at her whilst others held an air of indifference. Cinthia cloaked her mind harder than normal and her face grew hard. Many of their expressions quickly mimicked her own, with a couple narrowing their eyes. After a few moments of intense staring, the others returned to their whispered conversations and the rest reclined in their seats.

Cinthia, brushing off their cool welcome, strode over to one of the large throne-like chairs sat opposite most of the Elders present. Dropping down into it and placing her bag underneath, she stretched out her legs under the table and folded her arms, frowning at the grains of the wood in front of her. It took several long moments of her wondering just what kind of situation she had chosen to involve herself in before she regained an interest to take in her surroundings.

It was obvious that she had arrived alongside the rest of the early attendees for, by her count, there were several Elders besides her boys that were not yet present. Coincidentally enough, she overheard two Elders discussing the matter.

"...Athed, Nightgale and the other one won't be joining us. And of course Eternel won't be gracing us with her presence either..."

Upon hearing that there were other Elders besides her partners that were not going to be in attendance, Cinthia felt her chest tighten. Whatever was going on, she was glad her boys were not going to be part of it. If there was a serious danger on the horizon, which, given the mobilisation of the Bavillion Army outside, seemed certain, she wished for her lovers to stay as far away from it as possible. Her heart pounding, she continued to ponder what it was she had stumbled into. The room around her lost focus as Cinthia started analysing all she saw on her way in. Her biggest clue was the posting of the royal elites. Next was the involvement of the High Priests and then the Intra Vanta Priests, renowned for their military service and lethality on any battlefield. She tried to push the thoughts of that outcome from her. Cinthia refused to engage in a second Holy War, not just for the acute terror of the senseless devastation it would unleash, but also since it had nothing to do with her in the first place. It would be a religious matter, and therefore she had no connection to it. She had come to study Illarien and its history after all and nothing more. A marble hard expression once more dominated her face. That was not entirely true. She had also come because she was concerned for the welfare of the few Elders she knew, mainly Lady Rose and her loose associate, Lady Ellandu'el. Yet already the situation seemed far graver than Cinthia had anticipated and she felt foolish for assuming that it would have been any different. As likely the only non-Interist present, Cinthia felt whatever the matter turned out to be, it was none of her business and her input was not essential. She would help those two if possible, but she concluded that the matter would be out of her hands anyway. Sighing, she realised her thoughts on the matter had gone in a circle since the summons.

Cinthia took in a slow deep breath, the leaves on the trees and the winding grains in the oak becoming clearer again. She unfurled her fingers then proceeded to crack her knuckles to loosen them up. Likewise, she then cracked her neck from side to side but as soon as she finished, her breath caught in her throat as she spied someone in her periphery watching her.

Without moving her head, Cinthia's eyes roved upward and across the large table. A young looking Vampire, not much older than Cinthia had been when she had been converted, sat glaring at her through a thick black fringe that framed her face. The woman's arms were folded so tight her muscles looked like they would burst. She was sitting far forward in her seat, sneering with such poisonous contempt that Cinthia could not help but raise an intrigued eyebrow. However, it did not take Cinthia long to deduce, at least in part, the motive for this stranger's unprovoked ire, for she possessed the very same tinted eyes as her.

Rosy-pink met rosy-pink. The archaeologist cracked a smile at just how incensed this person appeared. Cinthia rolled her eyes, looking away at last, which seemed to stoke the fires opposite her. Having no sure idea what the issue she took with her was, nor giving even a mote of a care for why, Cinthia could only assume it had something to do with Lady Rose having made them both. Down the years, Cinthia had heard rumours Lady Rose had converted one other, but she had never concerned herself with the details. The same could obviously not be said for said other. After several long moments in which she felt her glare upon her still, Cinthia half closed her eyes and exhaled tiredly, turning her gaze further along the table.

Immediately she wished she hadn't. A couple stood hungrily examining her which unnerved her to the point she attempted to look away once more, yet her attention upon them became arrested. They were clearly twins and at first glance Cinthia had assumed them to be identical like Eternel and Ellandu'el, though upon closer inspection it became clear one was female and the other male and each possessed a physical beauty unlike anything she had ever witnessed in another person. They seemed to radiate pure fairness and if it weren't for the desiring glints in their deep rose-red eyes as they drank in Cinthia's appearance, she would have felt drawn to them. Instead, as stunning as they were, she could only feel a distinct urge to recoil deeper into her chair. Despite this, she felt it hard to avert her gaze, and her breath became shallower. The lady's perfect mouth snaked upwards in response and without taking her edacious gaze from Cinthia, she leant over to her brother's ear and whispered to him until he too possessed the same uncanny smirk. Cinthia then rolled her eyes again and chose to stare at the oak in front of her. This fed their amusement and they gave a few short giggles. In an attempt to block out all around her, she tried to refocus her thoughts on what was to come, yet before they could formulate, she was startled by the chair next to hers becoming occupied by someone jumping into it.

Cinthia's temper flared at this sudden shock and for the fact yet another person was now ogling her. Cursing in her mind and with eyes glowing hotter, she glared upward, opening her mouth to demand to be left in peace.

All words froze on their way from her throat. The warmest of countenances and jovial beams shone out in front of her, causing her to hesitate in her confrontation. Another immortal converted at the same age as Cinthia sat riveted to her with large vivid green eyes, long flowing hair the colour of purest snow and possessing the widest and most elated of smiles. She was clad in a simple dress that matched her hair, save for the bottom which was frayed and stained green and brown just like her bare feet and knees. Like the twins on the other side of the chamber, she too was astoundingly radiant though this was also amplified by her buoyant demeanour, giving her such an air of positivity Cinthia felt herself swept up in it and so all she could do was stare dumbfounded as the Vampire's lithe hand shot out to her.

"Hi!" the ashen-haired immortal exclaimed. "I'm Willow!"

Cinthia still could not speak. All she could do was stare. After several moments of them exchanging glances and with Willow giving the occasional giggle, Cinthia managed to mumble out the words, "Ummm… hi."

"Hi!" Willow repeated with a light laugh and bobbing her head from side to side.

"Hi..." Cinthia muttered, taking her hand at last.

Willow, clasping her and shaking, gave several more delighted giggles before saying, "Sorry, I've kind of put you on the spot there, haven't I?"

"Yeah..." admitted Cinthia, retracting her hand.

Willow folded her legs in the chair, grasped her ankles and leaned into them.

"Sorry, I just get really excited when new Elders come to Illarien! I've never seen you before, so I wanted to make you feel welcome! You must be Lady Rose's Fledgling, Cinthia, right?"

A twitch at the edge of Cinthia's eye flickered for the tiniest of seconds. "Yes, I am."

Willow's smile became even broader and she bounced up and down in her chair. "Oh sweet! I was hoping we'd meet someday! Lady Rose has told me all about you!"

"Ok…?" replied Cinthia, her brow furrowing. As she spoke, she noticed out of the corner of her eye Rose's other Fledgling intensifying her glower. A flash of insight came through the archaeologist's mind, though she pushed it aside for now.

Observing Cinthia tense over her revelation, Willow shook her head. "Oh, nothing bad, don't worry. Only good things! She thinks very highly of you and so it's a very great pleasure to meet you!"

"Thanks," replied Cinthia with a little more life. "And likewise."

"Aw, thank you!" she exclaimed. Willow's eyes suddenly shot behind Cinthia to the doors. Cinthia heard the roots unlatch themselves from the soil and turned to follow Willow's line of sight. There were three mortals dressed in the black cloaks of Priests, each embroidered with unique insignias unfamiliar to Cinthia, followed by the three final attending Elders of whom two she recognised. Lady Rose, clothed in what appeared to be the same red dress she had converted Cinthia in, entered just after the last Priest and ahead of an unknown male Elder. Bringing up the rear, Lady Ellandu'el flowed in and gestured for the three mortals to take positions at the table.

"Well, I hope to speak to you again soon!" whispered Willow, swirling around in her chair to lean into the burly chest of a very tall Vampire sat on her right. Cinthia looked over her shoulder at her to see Willow grinning at her. "Don't be a stranger!"

Turning back to the newcomers, Cinthia witnessed the mortals, whom she assumed to be the High Priests, take their seats, though she frowned as she observed them. Famously, there were always six High Priests at any given point in time, including the Highest High Priest or Priestess. For such a paramount meeting of both Councils, Cinthia wondered with a growing weight on her chest, where then were the other three? Cinthia then caught the gaze of her Maker who was sat toward the top of the table near Ellandu'el. Despite immortals never truly requiring sleep in the conventional sense, Rose seemed as if she had not rested in days, her perturbed eyes telling more than her body could and her hair, although being tied back, had the occasional wandering strand as if her fingers had continuously run through it and dislodged them. The Vampire Ambassador only gave a single, solemn nod to Cinthia. Cinthia returned the gesture. Rose's attention turned to her right where the unknown Elder beside Ellandu'el, who was sat at the head of the table, was still standing. The already quiet chamber grew silent and the air held a tension that infected every part of Cinthia's being. As he composed himself and a series of papers he had brought with him into the room, Cinthia turned to the current Head of the Elder Council. Ellandu'el bore the same shadowy countenance as Rose and looked to be even worse for wear, her white dress having several lengths of string trailing from it and it being covered in leaf and mud stains. Likewise, her face was coated in a light dust of dirt as were the entire lengths of her arms. She spotted the top of Ellandu'el's dress was blackened with large blotches. Her gaze went to the Elder's eyes. They were on the verge of tears, and previous trails of obsidian that had since been wiped off stained faint meanders down through the dust on her cheeks. Cinthia's jaw now hurting, she returned her attention to the standing Vampire.

His head rose up from the papers to address all those attending. As he opened his mouth to speak, Cinthia's demeanour soured as she saw his eyes for the first time. They were all too familiar to her from the records of the Holy War and her upper lip curled in revulsion, though he did not notice and opened the proceedings.

"Welcome my brothers and sisters," spoke Ulaq, his voice slow and solemn. "Tonight is the night of the 12th of Ravenaar, 1093, and we have all been summoned to hold emergency council not only as Elders, but as Interists. It is with a heavy heart that I confess this may be the worst occurrence since the Holy War." Cinthia glared at him as he said this and noticed through the corner of her eye that she was not the only one. Ulaq didn't pause. "Some of you are already abreast of the details of why we are all here. As you can plainly see, this is no ordinary Elder Council meeting." He gestured over to his left along the table. "In an historic merging of the two Councils, we have with us today the most esteemed guests of the High Priest Council, the Highest High Priest Puln -" Ulaq gave a small bow of his head to a middle aged man sat between the other two mortals opposite Cinthia. This man returned the gesture. "- High Priest Varill and High Priest Asra." Ulaq motioned to the men on Puln's right and left respectively. "I'm sure most, if not all of you, have noticed as well the security around our beloved home has been tripled and the military has been running routine drills and sweeps of the woodland for the past 72 hours. His royal majesty, The Captain himself, has also graciously deployed his elite guard to patrol our most sacred locations. Needless to say, the situation is indeed a grave one. To elaborate on what has transpired in Illarien over the past three nights, I give the floor over to Highest High Priest Puln."

Ulaq took his seat beside Lady Rose and Cinthia's sneer faded as her rapt attention shifted from him to the religious leader. Her breathing was shallow as Puln stood up, cleared his throat and placed a single hand upon the table as if to steady himself.

"Thank you, Elder Ulaq," he spoke in a grave tone, his expression dour. "And thank you Lady Elder Ellandu'el for calling together the largest gathering of Elders in history." Cinthia blinked a little at this detail, though quickly dismissed it as she felt she should have surmised that earlier. "I speak for… us, when I say that we are grateful for the Elders' assistance in this disturbing matter." He glanced around the silent-stricken Vampires, his eyes wielding what Cinthia felt was wariness, before he swallowed hard and spoke out a little louder. "Three nights ago, three of the High Priest Council vanished without any signs of their departure. High Priestesses Sara, Janic and Gwendolyn were last seen in the early evening by many witnesses before failing to show up for midnight prayers. The three of us -" He pointed to the two men sat either side of him. "- and many other Priests went to their quarters to check on them, but found no sign. We then searched the other major sites in the city but they were not to be found. As we knew the three had no real connection with one another save for their rank, suspicions began to rise at this time." Puln let his gaze fall to the table. "I went to the chambers of Lady Elder Ellandu'el and requested for her to locate them using her Sen Cor. However -" Puln looked up once again, this time with a bitter glance, at all the Elders present. "- she could not locate them."

The archaeologist glanced around. Various looks of consternation and fearful murmurs circulated the oval table. A shuddered inhale came from her right and she saw Willow clasp her mouth in her hands, her face fraught with shock. Cinthia's attention then roved over to Ellandu'el. Glistening tears rimmed her shimmering eyes as they bored hard into the space in front of her, though otherwise she remained quite still. In the chamber, an uneasy quiet once again strained the air until Amakay sat forward in her chair.

"But that's *impossible*," she said. "Any one of us could have found them."

"That is what we thought too," replied Puln with a sombre nod. "So I immediately requested Lady Elder Ellandu'el contact her sister to use her Sen Cor. Yet even the Ferrier of Inter could not sense their presence anywhere in Mainland."

Cinthia's thoughts suddenly centred around an uneasy knowing dread. Just as Puln before her, her eyes roved over the other Elders in the room, her insides wrenching a little tighter.

"What?!" blurted Willow tearfully through her hands. "What happened to them?!"

"That is precisely what we are all here to discern," Puln answered. "There is no power on Covyn capable of hiding from the great sight of Lady Elder Eternel. Or at least there isn't supposed to be..." He paused for a moment before continuing. "We have kept a constant check upon the Pits of the Dead, via regular Communisars with its inhabitants, inquiring if their souls have joined Inter's ranks, yet there is no sign. We therefore know they are not yet dead. Just in case their presence was somehow overlooked by Lady Elder Eternel, we immediately organised a massive search of Illarien and the surrounding area without informing the soldiers or lower Priests of the precise nature of the situation in order to prevent panic. They were told to look for three missing female Officials from Mortol who got lost on their way here. Ladies Elder Ellandu'el and Elder Rose were of paramount assistance in the search. We have only tonight given up scouring these lands. To go over the implications that arise from neither of the Twins being able to see the High Priestesses, I now give the floor over to the one present, Lady Elder Ellandu'el."

Cinthia looked to the Head of the Elder Council. Lady Ellandu'el stood up from her throne, her gaze not rising to meet the others in the room and as she began to address them, Cinthia's ears fixed upon her every word.

"Thank you, Highest High Priest Puln," she spoke with the faintest of wobbles in her voice. "Though I must correct you on a minor point. My sister's Sen Cor does indeed have limits, at least at present, for it has a limited range which is currently fixed to the Land of the Baldrinians far to the East and there is one who could Cloak from her should he wish," she paused, now looking at her audience. An insightful silence hung in the air around them as small nods of agreement and muted grunts murmured around the table. Cinthia frowned knowingly, yet her intensifying nerves were anticipating the ancient immortal to make another point entirely. Ellandu'el continued, "Elder Vertio, the true Head of our Council, is the one Vampire capable of Cloaking from my sister, however I am not here to accuse him of abducting them. He has been missing for centuries and harming the religious order of Inter would be akin to him killing a part of himself. That being said, whilst I do not believe him responsible, it is technically feasible for him to have done this, and so that is the first implication."

Stunned silence filled the chamber. Across the table, Cinthia caught Ulaq nodding contently alongside several other Elders. Cinthia squinted as she observed this, but her mind was intently elsewhere and she had become very uneasy at the prospect of locking eyes with most of the other immortals. Ellandu'el continued to speak.

"Though, admittedly, I do also feel it is the weakest point to discuss."

"Me too!"

Willow's hand shot into the hair as she piped up. Cinthia, jogged from her ruminations, prised her head around to face her. Several Elders sent Willow chastising glowers. Eyebrows arching, Willow added, "He might always be a grouchy old man, but he's not the kind to kidnap anyone."

Cinthia managed to crack a fraction of a smile. Ellandu'el, pausing for the briefest of moments, nodded then continued addressing her points to the group, several of whom Cinthia now sensed to be as on edge as she was.

"The second implication is that the three High Priestesses simply left Illarien and all its lands together of their own volition as swiftly as possible as to go beyond our sensory ranges before we noticed them missing. However, the first problem with this is, as Highest High Priest Puln pointed out, they had no real outside connection with one another, only knowing each other through their spiritual duties. Although we cannot presently prove this, it is highly likely to be true and therefore they would have no reason to leave together. They would also had to have known the precise location of every Elder and our respective sensory ranges to get out undetected for, as Elder Amakay correctly stated, any one of us could have found them by accident, and at any time, before they had time to make it past the borders of the Darkwoods, even if they were on horseback. Secondly, knowing my sister's Sen is mainly restricted to her present location on the Fortress Cliffs, and I say mainly as we are always able to connect telepathically wherever we are on Mainland, I asked instead for her to use me, her Twin, as a conduit, thus extending her great range to scour these lands for them, yet she could see nothing that way either. This, as many of you can surmise, leaves us with but one probable scenario." Ellandu'el's face fell even further and she stared hard at the immortals sat expectantly before her. Cinthia, her eyes widening and the breath catching in her throat, realised the time had come for the conclusion she knew to be revealed. Once again, all other sensory input drowned as she clung to Ellandu'el's every word. The Head of the Elder Council sighed then continued in a heavy tone, "Since none of us, nor Lady Elder Eternel, sensed their presence the most likely explanation is that they were abducted by another Elder whose Cloak Cor is beyond anything we possess or can penetrate."

Cinthia's heart stopped, her face blanched and her fingernails dug deep into her palms. There it was. Although she knew her own innocence could be established as her mastery of the Cloak did not yet allow her anywhere near such potency as Ellandu'el described, what she had said confirmed the conclusion the archaeologist had already reached: the danger had not passed. Indeed, it was almost certainly amongst them now. Cinthia swallowed hard in an effort to contain her rising nausea, though it proved little help. The only measures of relief came from the knowledge that her boys were not present nor were any three of them a target to anyone there. Using that reprieve, Cinthia raised her eyes to scan the chamber to study the reactions of the others.

What became immediately apparent were the looks of contentment upon the faces of the three mortals. For a brief moment, she was as confused as the other Elders present, yet Cinthia recalled Puln's attitude that he adopted during his talk. She then noticed that whilst the others also regarded the trio with suspicion, they did so amongst themselves as well. There were mutters of disbelief, concern and conjecture and from Cinthia's right she could hear Willow burst into tears. Before the tension could escalate to spoken volumes, Ellandu'el concluded her speech.

"As a consequence of this terrible and grave possibility," spoke Ellandu'el, raising her despondent voice a little to be heard over the murmurs. "The investigation will be handed fully over to the High Priest Council with no further deductive input from us, effective immediately."

Ellandu'el resumed sitting in her throne to a smattering of protests that turned into louder calls of disagreement. As Highest High Priest Puln stood up once again to lead the meeting, he could not speak over the rising clamour and vainly tried holding up his hands to signal for quiet. Shouts went out declaring the theory as nonsense as no-one there had the kind of power that could have escaped the Ferrier's sight. Others railed that they had been sold out to the High Priests and that their fates should only be decided amongst themselves. Regardless of what was said, the majority of them shot cautious glances at one another and the entire atmosphere of the chamber soured. After a quick couple of moments where the noise mounted into a deafening roar, the rosy-eyed Vampire sat opposite Cinthia stood up and screeched across the table at Ellandu'el.

"Is this why were we fuckin' escorted!?" she cried, slamming her palms into the wood. "You had already decided this, didn't you?! It wasn't because of a possible 'security threat' – it's because you moronically suspect us! US! And now you betray us to these fuckin' idiots?! You *stupid* bitch!"

Cinthia's whole body gave a sudden start as Lady Rose launched from her chair and boomed down the table at the younger woman.

"*Natalia!*" Rose exploded, her voice as thunderous as her expression.

Natalia screeched, shaking her head and spitting on the table before making as if to leave the chamber. Cinthia's nerve-racked attention locked onto Rose as she moved to block Natalia's way and commanded her to retake her place, the Ambassador's face so stormy it send a chill through the archaeologist. Natalia swore, turned back around and slammed her chair into the oak before shoving her back against one of the scores of trees walling them in. Lady Rose glared at her before returning to her post. Cinthia then looked about the rest of the chamber to see with little surprise that no-one had taken any notice for they were embroiled in shouting matches of their own, their anger and alarm signalled upon their contorted faces. She folded her arms about her, the gloomy whirlwind that was her mind considering if things were always like this here but also racing over the fear that her fate, and inextricably that of her boys, would end up in the hands of these three men whose agenda she could not discern, though guessed it was to do with some inner religious power struggle she had no interest nor stake in. The prospect made a lump develop at the back of her throat. Her gaze then returned to her Maker's whose dark shadow had not yet diffused. Cinthia's heart ached as she beheld Rose in her dishevelled state, though she was at a loss on how to help even herself at this time, let alone her Maker. Sensing her Fledgling's gaze upon her, Rose's tension eased as she looked across at her. As Rose took notice of Cinthia's demeanour, her face molded into one of concern and mouthed to her, '*Are you alright?*' Cinthia gave a single unconvincing nod, the weight in her chest becoming heavier, before averting her gaze once again to the wood in front of her. After several moments where Cinthia felt her Maker's attention on her still, she was jolted from her spiralling worries from an ear-splitting shriek from her right.

"*JUST STOP!*"

Infuriated and frightened gazes turned, becoming stunned upon seeing Willow standing atop the oak, face strewn with tears, breast heaving and fingers toying with the frayed edges of her dress.

"Please!" she pleaded through loud sobs, her face racked with grief. "Please just stop arguing like this! I know this isn't a nice time for any of us -" She looked around the table at everyone who now stood quiet, with many narrowing their eyes at her. "- and I don't believe for one minute that anyone here has done this. But we all have to co-operate so we can prove our innocence and not let fear and unfair suspicion get the better of us! Otherwise, we just look more guilty and we waste time on ourselves when we could be looking for the lost High Priestesses!"

Cinthia's eyebrow raised at Willow's singular fervour, though at the same time she gave a small sigh of relief.

"Oh will you just shut the FUCK UP, Willow?!" screamed Sylvia back at her. Willow recoiled as if she'd been physically struck by the words. At the same time, Ulaq gave a short chuckle. The violet-eyed Elder continued, "We are sick to DEATH of your naive ignorance! Like always, you have no idea what's really going on."

Willow's knees collided with the table, her hands burying her head and tears gushing between her fingers. Cinthia glowered over in the direction of the dark-haired Vampire alongside about half of the other individuals in the room, including the High Priests, though Sylvia continued to shout down the weeping Elder.

"With us under their investigation, it means they have authority over us! It means, you ignorant child, that they can subdue our authority in the faith for as long as they decide this investigation needs to take! This is not about the High Priestesses at all – it's a political coup to stifle our God-given right to wield more power over the direction of Interism!"

Cinthia sneered and looked away, disgusted whilst also amused at the irony that it was Sylvia who seemed to have no idea what was actually going on. However, Cinthia assumed her argument to be a conscious distraction from the bitter knowledge one of them was guilty. Yet having her previous assumptions about there being tension between the Councils confirmed only served to feed the muscles tensing her stomach. She tried her best to shut out the clamour of supportive and dissenting yells, but her sight was caught by a very tall man leaning over the table to extricate Willow from the eye of the furore. This Human-sized immortal picked her up in his arms and brought her frail sobbing form into his giant muscular chest. Cinthia, feeling a small surge of warmth in her at this sight, briefly exchanged a respectful glance with him as he retook his large seat and stroked Willow's ashen head.

The moment her gaze left his, everyone in the room fell silent at once. Some held the temples of their skulls, others grimaced and the rest backed down from their arguments, their sights falling from one another as they sat back down. Cinthia's eyes widened and she bared her fangs as she heard it alongside the rest. A deep, melodic tone, much darker, more remote and commanding than Ellandu'el's voice, seeped into her mind until her entire brain seemed soaked with its every word.

Heed our Willow's words, it said. *And take heed of how dire things are. None can ignore the fact the guilty is among us. Not with clever words. Not with diverting claims of imagined conspiracy. Not even with baseless assumptions of an external culpable force. For it is clear to all that if neither my sister nor I could see them, then either an Elder or a Wizard is responsible. The latter lacks motive and so we look to our own, regardless of how disturbing this implication may be. Now desist your prattling and commit to the investigation. I will remain here, awaiting my part.*

Cinthia's grimace faded with every word and her breath caught in her throat. Her eyes shot to the top of the table. Ellandu'el had remained standing and once the voice had finished, she sighed and addressed both Councils once more.

"I am agreed with my sister," she declared. "And I will initiate article twenty-one of the Council Charter if I have to. Now, acknowledge the authority of the High Priest Council in this investigation. We will now, *finally*, listen to their decision on what is to be done and we will *all* commit to it in the *shared* interests of our Interist brethren to find and hopefully save our missing High Priestesses."

As Ellandu'el sat down, Cinthia's nerves flooded with tension once again. Puln stood and cleared his throat.

"Thank you, Lady Elder Ellandu'el," he said, his throat weakened from the shouting match. "And I pass on my thanks to your Twin, Lady Elder Eternel for her *timely* intervention. Our plan is simple. We will continue to search for them over the next two weeks in the outlying settlements and beyond using the full garrison here in Illarien and the majority of our Priests. If no sign of them has been found in that time, we will have no choice but to abandon our search and promote replacements. In the meantime -" He cleared his throat once more. "- we will be summoning and holding all Vampire Elders in Illarien until such a time as their innocence has been established. If the guilty party is found, we can promise swift justice will be meted out."

Cinthia's gut knotted as she found herself failing to dismiss her deepest fears, despite the fact she had expected them. The irrational should have been easy, such as if her boys were accused: they were both specialising in the Velo Cor so their innocence was easily proven. However, knowing the agendas of the High Priests, there stood a high probability of them colouring their conclusions. Given her choice in specialisation, it would be only too easy for them to use her as the easy way out and then punish her boys as accomplices. Her skin shivered beneath her day suit as an unnerving wave of vulnerability washed over her and she shut her eyes, trying her best not to let anything show to the others. The moment her lids shut, another unsettling train of thought dawned on her – how many of the Elders present were aware of her own choice of specialisation? How many of them could use this to cast suspicion upon her? The fact she was the odd one out was enough of a reason to target her. Cinthia's upper lip curled into a sneer.

"Just how long are we talking?" she heard Ulaq ask.

"As long as is necessary," replied Puln. "The only exceptions are the Lady Elder Rose and Lady Elder Eternel as their duties are of major and divine import. As is plain to see, we are missing several Elders here today – they will need to be brought in immediately. Questioning will begin once all are present. In the meantime, all Elders must remain within the borders of the

Evernight at all times. If anyone leaves without the unanimous decision of the High Priest Council, they will be held in contempt and arrested without question. At the same time as your questioning, we will question the mortals of Illarien as well for any witnesses – guards, Priests and anyone else who may know anything. After this meeting, we will officially release to the public the true nature of our investigation and that this is a time of great sorrow for our people. If there are any questions you may have, now is the time to ask them and afterwards, this meeting will come to a close."

Cinthia forced her eyes open and glared at each Vampire in turn. Almost every one of them was a potential threat to her and her boys. All she wanted to do was run into the Evernight and Cloak as heavily as possible until they arrived, though she realised how unsafe that would be given how the skilful the scum responsible was at wielding of the Cloak Cor. As uncomfortable and mad as it was, staying in the Council chamber amongst everyone, including the potential guilty party, seemed like the safest option. Her eyes blazed at the very notion.

"I have one," said the Elder next to Sylvia. "Why did we just forget the most obvious suspects? Why aren't we accusing the White Witches of this!? They're the only ones with any motive!"

"Elder Cantel," Puln answered. "The only thing that's obvious here is that the White Witches cannot Cloak. Whilst they possess many horrific Gifts, that, thankfully, is not among them. They were my first assumption too, until the Twins could not find the High Priestesses."

"That does not mean one of us isn't helping them." he retorted.

"We will investigate *all* avenues," pressed Puln.

"What about those of us who don't own lodgings here?" shot Natalia.

"Accommodation will be provided as usual. You are an Elder after all," replied Puln in an irritated tone. Cinthia, who before would have been comfortable having a private area to herself, felt nothing but rage at the threat of her personal space being violated, yet neither did she relish the prospect of camping out in the open at this time.

"Is that all?" Puln asked.

Cinthia swept the room once again with her eyes. The air was electrified with indignation, mock patience and fear, with almost every Elder present exhibiting at least one of these. Rose and Ellandu'el both sat looking into space and Willow appeared agitated in the giant Vampire's arms as she continued to shake and weep. Cinthia's own features displayed a sour discomfort and she felt the urge again to flee through the forest to wash clean the events of the meeting.

Puln nodded and coughed again. "In that case, this meeting is adjourned. Lady Elder Ellandu'el, if you could stay behind for a few minutes, I would be grateful."

As if every Elder in the chamber shared Cinthia's will, they all dispersed through the opening trees into the city, with Willow sending her a feeble smile over the man's shoulder whilst he carried her out. Cinthia got to her feet and slung her bag across her back, nodding at Willow but otherwise ignoring the others. Making her way to the exit, she overheard Puln asking Ellandu'el to summon all the other Elders to Illarien. This was drowned by the marching and hubbub coming from the bustle of the city outside. Cinthia Cloaked without thinking and strode out without any idea of where she was going. She had just turned the corner out of the entrance when she heard her name called from directly behind her. Glowering at first over being seen, Cinthia eased up upon recognising the voice as one of the few people in Illarien she was able to trust and she turned to see Lady Rose smiling and weaving through the elite guards towards her.

"Hello Cinthia," she spoke upon catching up to Cinthia, her face falling somewhat when she saw how tense she still was. "I'm sorry for intruding. Don't worry, I'm Cloaking us right now. Would you... like me to escort you to a more quiet location so we can talk?"

Cinthia nodded, unusually grateful for the company and proceeded to follow her Maker through the teeming people. It did not take long for Rose to lose them and wander off into the close darkness. For a short while, the echoes of the masses rang out into the night and then fell quiet as the forest shut off behind them. The duo were alone in the Evernight, with only the faint indigo light shimmering in the distance and Cinthia gave a small snort of relief.

"I'm glad you know Illarien so well," she said to Rose, facing the trees stretching out in front of them. "Useful to know secret paths and exits. Especially now."

"Indeed it is," Rose answered, her voice strained. After a brief moment of scanning their surroundings, she asked, "Are you ok?"

Cinthia slowly shook her head. "You?"

Rose returned the gesture. "No, but I've been through worse. I just wanted to..." She made as if to reach out to touch Cinthia, but retracted her hand before it neared her. "To make sure you're alright. There's still a danger whoever is guilty may strike again. Naturally, some of the Elders presume themselves immune to this threat, though most either try to ignore this fear or mask it by dodging the issue. We are not like them. I... am worried for you. I... know all this can't have been easy on you, and I just want..." she broke off and breathed heavily. Cinthia, stomach churning from the reiteration of her fears, finally faced her and saw the etchings of concern woven deeply into her features. Her heart gave a small leap. She nodded.

"I know," she whispered. "Thank you."

Lady Rose clasped her hands over her abdomen and smiled. Silence rolled by. Eventually, the Ambassador nodded and said, "Despite everything, it is good to see you."

Cinthia, whose sights had since flicked downward, murmured in acknowledgement, "Same."

Another minute of stillness went by where Rose studied her demeanour before speaking up once again, "I hope you know... no-one can suspect you. It is impossible for you to be considered responsible. You're only over a century into your specialisation. You will be ok." She reached out and grasped Cinthia's arm so gently, the archaeologist barely felt her touch. Cinthia still stiffened a little. Rose took in a short breath and pulled back her hand.

"If it comes down to it," her Maker said. "I'll testify on your behalf. As will the Twins."

Cinthia remained silent, staring at the ground. Rose, her face falling further, knelt down to put herself in Cinthia's line of sight and she looked up at her with mournful fire in her eyes.

"I won't let them take you."

Cinthia's heart quivered. Straining to stay as rigid as the trees around them, she eventually nodded.

"Thank you, Rose."

The Ambassador smiled now and resumed standing opposite her. Several silent moments trailed by before Cinthia raised her eyes to look at her Maker. Lady Rose was once again holding her hands together in front of her and her lips were parted, clearly on the verge of asking something. Her gaze regarded Cinthia's with acute concern and she inhaled before inquiring, "You're deeply worried for them, aren't you?"

Cinthia, a sharp twinge jolting her heart, shrugged her shoulders to hide the shiver that ran up her back, "Of course! That goes without saying. They're..." she trailed off, her throat seizing up and lowering her gaze.

Rose nodded and spoke with a steadier tone than before, "I promise I will not let anything happen to them either."

A tear fell from Cinthia's tensed cheek, her teeth grinding in the close darkness. Her fists clenched so tightly that her fingers glistened and the occasional drip collected upon her white knuckles before dashing the needles on the floor below.

"Thank you," Cinthia choked.

Rose took a step towards her and opened her arms. Cinthia shook her head and continued glaring downwards. Resuming her previous position, her Maker nodded once more.

"You will all be under our protection. Neither myself nor the Twins will let anything happen to any of you."

"The investigation is under the High Priest's authority. What if they decide we're guilty?"

Rose did not miss a beat before replying in a chilling tone, "I will *never* let them take you."

The haunting resonance in her voice made Cinthia look up at Rose. As she stared into the fiery eyes of her Maker, she found it hard to breathe.

"You..." she managed to get out. "Would defy them... for us?"

A tender smile melted the hardened countenance of Rose, "Always. You are my..." she broke off. Rose's throat closed and her eyes shot to the canopy. She then sharply inhaled, looked back at her and continued, "Yes. I would always defy them to keep you safe."

Cinthia stared at Rose before her damp gaze fell and she shook her head. "No," she whispered. "I should be the one to..."

"There's nothing wrong with having a little help from those who care about you," Rose countered, her voice growing concerned.

The archaeologist slammed her eyes shut and spoke again through gritted teeth, another trail of onyx dripping down her face. "I can handle this on my own."

Rose reached out to touch Cinthia's arm, but her Fledgling flinched and took a step back. In a whisper as soft as it was sincere, Rose passionately replied, "But you don't need to."

Cinthia shook her head, taking several deep breaths as she did so, "I *have* to. I have to be *able* to. On my own."

Rose's brow arched and her features grew troubled, "Why?"

Opening her sodden eyes, Cinthia replied, "You know why. Most of the time we're nowhere near here! They are my *partners*. *I* have to protect them!"

Rose gave a small nod and a knowing smile. "And who protects you?"

Cinthia stared up at the pitch vaulted boughs high above, "I can look after myself. I'm the stronger of us. It's my duty."

"And we're stronger than you," replied Rose. "And whilst you're right that we'll not always be near you, we are now. Let us – let *me* – protect you."

Cinthia cursed and streams of tears poured down to drip off her chin. Shaking, she stared hard at her Maker. Her heart leapt in her breast and her knees threatened to give way at the sight of her reassuring demeanour. She shook her head and once again averted her gaze. Crystalline droplets mixed with coal rivers to clear up the stains upon her face. Shuddering all over as she took in a steady breath, Cinthia forced herself to stand upright and look at Lady Rose.

"Ok," she muttered.

Rose closed the distance between them and at last embraced her Fledgling in her arms. Cinthia twitched, but did not attempt to break contact, not even as she felt her Maker place a soft kiss upon her head. After a few minutes of being held and stroked, she pulled back and looked firmly at Rose.

"But if you can't see through their Cloak, how do you protect yourself?"

"We stick together," came the swift reply. "The High Priestesses were likely separated when taken. And they were not Elders."

There was a pause when Cinthia looked quizzically at her, whilst sniffing and wiping her face dry. Eventually, her features bared resignation and she admitted, "It's a long shot, but it's better than being on one's own..."

"I know that's not easy for you," responded Rose. "But I'll do my best to give you as much space as is wise."

"Yeah..." Cinthia said, her breaths still shaking. "Thanks. I appreciate it." Several moments of silence passed between them where Cinthia folded and rubbed her arms whilst gazing at the fallen leaves beneath her feet. After a while, her normal voice had recovered and she asked, "But... can you please do me a favour?"

Rose smiled and nodded. "Of course. What is it?"

"Just," Cinthia spoke, standing very still. "Keep it amicable, not familial. Please?"

There was no reply. Following a few seconds where the only sound to be heard was the minute breaths of air whispering through the trees, Cinthia's gaze met her Makers'. Rose's mouth was open, but no words issued forth and her eyes glanced away. After another brief moment, Lady Rose spoke at last.

"Of course."

A pang hit Cinthia's heart as she saw Rose smile uncomfortably back at her and she once more looked at the forest floor. The next couple moments saw Cinthia's unease return and she nodded.

"You know, Rose," she began. "I didn't just come here because I was summoned. I came here mainly to study Illarien.

Now that that option's fucking shot I'm only really here for one reason." She looked into the eyes of her Maker who returned the gaze with curiousity. "I came here... because I wanted to make sure you were alright."

The bottom of Lady Rose's lip trembled and she replied, "Thank you, Cinthia. That means a lot to me."

Cinthia nodded. "No problem."

The two stood once again in the perfect quiet of the Evernight, with Cinthia turning her sights outwards into the undulating blue light that filtered through the blanketing darkness. The ripples of indigo that stroked the giant trunks and caressed the shade itself tantalised the archaeologist's vision and soothed her racing mind. Yet a weight soon fell upon her chest and she sighed in an attempt to dismiss the thought. However, it came back to her in the form of a question.

"Would you consider visiting Illarien again, once this is all over?" asked Rose from behind her.

Cinthia frowned and lightly shook her head. "Rose... I am not sure. What is painfully obvious is that I don't really belong here. On top of which I don't care for the fucking politics. I don't want to get involved in this shit again. I am fully aware of this being an anomaly among meetings, but the agendas, the posturing and the bullshit will always be there. This is your domain, not mine. I dig holes and carbon-date dead people. I run around ruins and take pictures of things most people assume are just rocks. I'm not a politician and I really would rather not get involved."

Rose remained quiet for a time until she nodded and replied, "You could do more good than you know. Besides," she added with an encouraging smile. "You saw the others in there. It's never exactly a truly formal, or even professional, affair. Whilst we technically have our protocols, we almost invariably end up in some juvenile shouting match."

"Which is another reason why I'd never want to be involved," Cinthia spoke.

Rose gave a short laugh. "Fair enough. Though my original question was more to do with you studying Illarien."

"I don't know..." mused Cinthia. "Maybe in a long time. Maybe if things improve here soon? I just don't know..."

They stood deep in thought for a few minutes, watching the waves of light rove across the blackness and the occasional leaf fall through it, casting large and bizarre shadows over the trees and undergrowth. Following the cascading trails of blue-white illumination across the woodland, Cinthia felt the cool tides of calm start to rise within her. The call to explore, though normally running free within her when faced with the unknown, remained fully suppressed, yet in the hypnotic fluctuations shimmering before her she could at least experience some measure of relief.

"Shall we head back?" asked Rose, jerking Cinthia out of her reverie. "I'll show you around my quarters. As I'm the Elder Ambassador they're rather lavish so there's plenty of space. You can make yourself at home as best you can."

"No," replied Cinthia. "Thank you. Not yet. I just need a few minutes on my own, if that's alright?"

Rose nodded, scanning the horizon, "Very well. I'll wait for you back on the main street. Please don't take too long."

"I won't."

Cinthia heard the retreating footsteps of her Maker behind her followed by the uprooting and shuffling of the trees and then nothing. Cinthia inhaled deeply, allowing the fresh scents of pine and leaves to fill her up and relieve her aching muscles. Her eyes fixated upon each rise and fall of the watery shimmers that slowly washed her burning nerves. The utter quiet whispered to her like an old friend and her ears and skull tingled from its smooth caress. The sinking of her feet through the decaying foliage sent up flashes of memory and soon, with the light of spirits shining in the sea of black and her boots below ground level, Cinthia was home amidst the endless sands beneath a clear and infinite starry sky. A flicker of a smile played on the corner of her mouth as she pictured herself standing outside Hallahan with its entrance hopelessly covered in the dust of the dunes and her boys welcoming her back from a long and fruitful expedition.

A new sound ripped her from her dream. Immediately, she dropped beneath the undergrowth, her every sense trained on the location ahead and her body tensing all over again. Cloaking even harder than before, she strained her ears to listen for it. In the far distance, she could just hear a shrill, pained cry coming nearer that echoed through the trees towards her. Her heart pounded so hard in her chest she could barely make it out. Every instinct told her to run back to the main street, but Cinthia could not flee. Concern held her fast. Against her better judgement, she edged back towards the trees she had come through earlier. Brushing fern stems aside with her boots, she perched defensively amongst them. No sooner had she done this, a louder sob shuddered over the expanse to meet her, sending a paralysing chill up her spine. Forcing herself to take slower breaths so as to keep herself from being noticed, she cupped a hand against her ear and leaned towards where she assumed the noise originated. For a while there was nothing, and she had lowered her hand when through the leafy bushes, she spotted the nearest Soul. It sat in its stand several metres away, but even from there her eyes depicted the swirling spirits inside with ease.

She froze.

Another howling wail pierced the encompassing night, but this time a lot closer and seemed to be emitted from every direction. Cinthia wildly turned her head, but the cries refused to be pinpointed. Her fingers gripped her thighs as she crouched in cover and her breathing hastened despite her best efforts. Then an idea struck. Her desperate sights swerved to lock onto the foggy souls trapped within the glass orb, hoping they might have been able to locate the source of the wailing. The mad scouring of their bulging eyes however made it clear that they knew no more than she. Her breathing ceased altogether as another petrifying lament reverberated loudly and caused her heart to skip a beat. She cursed in her mind, regretting her stupidity, and tried to make her way to the doorway. Suddenly a cry of shock came from behind the tree with the Soul in front of it. Cinthia positioned herself defensively and the spirits turned to where her eyes now stared. A dry branch cracked. She bared her fangs and formed a Shield in front of her.

A tiny, pale, grime-coated hand slid its way round the rough bark of the trunk followed by twin lanterns of something that was neither the indigo of the Souls nor the last purple of a sunset.

Cinthia flinched in pain as her eyes and skin were scorched and she fell back into the undergrowth that had once concealed her. Launching herself upward in terror, she pulled her goggles, facewraps and hood over her healing face then glared over to where the searing lights had been.

They had vanished.

Shaking, Cinthia searched in every direction for a sign, but there was nothing but the close and silent Evernight. Swearing out loud now, she felt the chill of panic settle in and a lump developed in her throat.

Then a soft sound came from behind her. Cinthia shrieked, leapt forwards and swerved to face whatever made it. It then came again, softer still. It almost sounded meek. Cinthia's terror turned to confusion, her features plastered with shock and bewilderment.

"Hello?" she hesitantly asked to the dark.

As Witnessed Through Shimmering Portals

Tides of water and time lashing upon a monument of eternity
A maelstrom murk, a crushing chill, a drowning
No mortal treads this path
In the deep
In the dark.

Currents of merciless black within a crevasse in the abyss
An intimate surround, a haunt where twin prisms pierce the
gloom.
Strands of primal gold billowing in the obscure swirling drink
A mesmerising dance, a deceptive calm, belonging to
An infinite well of knowing.
Such a perilous hoard comes at a perilous price.
Vastness of wealth and potency amongst an empty and ignorant
world
A painful omnipotence, an envious insight, a charge
That cannot be forsaken or forgot.
Where shimmering portals perceive all
Thoughts and memories laid bare
Solitude is sought
Solitude is cherished.

Sunlight fades and starlight roams upon a battered shore
Lungs strain to heave out their murky icy haul
A routine purge, a typical climb, an ascent
To watch over the seas
Upon the brink
Upon the way.
Merging of sky and sea into an eternal shining void
A border vanishes, an absolute night, a portal
At the opening of her soul.
The Blue Horizon dawns
Reflected in her shimmering tranquil gaze.
Once more they come unto her over the waters
Tiny indigo lights

The stars in the sky that only she can see.
They wash over her as rain upon the rocks far below
She listens to their thanks, their laments, their tales
As they pass between her golden strands and marble flesh
Around her heart
And beyond.

It is endless
It is joy.

And she hears
Everything
Across mountains, hillocks and plains
Throughout time
Throughout space
Rushing thoughts, beating hearts
Entire ages of conflicting emotions
Of bursting love, of rising hate
Of every concept born to creation
All living minds are hers to perceive.

The Ferrier of Inter, upon her cliff of stone
The great listener
Perception unparalleled
From the opening within her soul
The loquacious deceased
And her unrestrained Sen
Acquires without end and more than she ever desired.

Every day of every year she dives into the engulfing cold
Then ascends to blue starlight
Carrying the weights of the living and the dead.

So much time
So very much time
To see all.

Is this a pattern? Has this been seen before?

Is this all there is?

No.
There is more.

Beyond the incessant thoughts of mortals
There, buried beneath the stone
Behind all concepts and wisps of memory
Within deepest black
A dim glow.

Upon her aged bluff, staring out to sea
Her pale features darken like that of the heavens above
Her eyes narrow, peering harder at what lies
In that most tenebrous of places.

In all her ages
In all of time
Never had such a thing nor thought
Chilled her ancient blood as thoroughly as that.
Yet there it lies,
Undeniable in its malevolence
A mere perception, unbound by form or name
A force beyond imagining
Shrouded in emerald flame.

This was no surprise
Not to her
For she had long suspected such a presence
Yet knowing it was there changed everything
For her perspective of all the ages was forever altered
Now she knew of a greater game
The only game
Her place within nothing more than a mere speck
In an infinite war
Far grander than even her imagining.

She sighs calmly in the cool night air

Knowing there is much to think about.

Willow Learns to Ride a Dragon

Upon a dragon
She is flying
Against the skyline
She is soaring
Catching the gales
She is sailing

Up
and
up
and
up
and
up
and
round
and
round
up in the clouds
and now she's flying
upside-down!

Against the clouds she is flying on high
Soaring through her hair as she sails the sky
Far beneath her are all the towns they pass by
To say she's not happy would be a great lie.

Spitting a fireball out with a cry
Willow's dragon sets all the night-life awry
Running round screaming in fear that they'll die
Villagers leave their own homes in a sty.

Willow's dad stands below with stomach awhirl
At the sight of the beast his toes start to curl.
Afeared for his daughter he threatens to hurl

As the dragon flips through the air with a twirl.

Looking at its wings their nerves mount and churn
Yet all in the village do not come to burn;
Neither grown-ups, children, forest nor fern
Would ever have to end up stuck in an urn.

For a greater delight she never could yearn
Grinning so widely her head swerves astern
At the sight of her dad her ride does she turn
And lands not expecting a lesson to learn.

A fretful expression etches his face,
Yet fades upon Willow's joyous embrace.
Her arms tightly wrapped makes all fears erase
Squeezing her firmly they leave with no trace.

Having no clue she had caused such a stir -
All below had passed by in a very swift blur -
Her heart now pounded with a powerful whir
As folk viewed her as nothing more than a cur.

Standing in-between the townsfolk and her
Willow's dad addresses their leader as 'Sir,
No hair on the people nor leaf on a fir
Were singed whenever the dragon did purr'.

Saying they were fully just in their rants,
Willow speaks of her love for people and plants
Repenting for scaring them out of their pants
And making them scatter all over like ants.

Accepting their speech the folk say no more,
And whilst giving out an elated roar
The pair saddle up on the dragon to soar
Up high and on towards the home they adore.

Up

and
up
and
up
and
up
and
round
and
round
Joy has been found
As now they're heading
Homeward bound!

Sarahessieth's Visitor

One of the many small windows at the front of her store sat angled open, fingerprints marking parallel trails through the darkened stains upon its exterior. Through this gap wound her pets as they all made their way in, the warm night air no longer beckoning their hunt and the familiar odours of the store enticing them home. A slight breeze breathed past carrying the scent of trees and the damp undergrowth, though neither this nor her slithering friends distracted Sarahessieth from the bubbling pot before her. Into its watery contents she scraped a series of finely chopped stems and petals and stirred thoroughly for several silent moments, her eyes never leaving its surface. Once it had started to give off a foul smelling steam, she turned down the heat and placed a lid over it, leaving it to simmer as she turned to clean her knife in the basin.

A large number of the snakes climbed onto the desk and came up to the Vampire, first eyeing her task then glancing up at her. She raised an eyebrow at them all, hands still working the vegetation off the blade.

"Hunting not go well tonight?" she asked.

Their tongues slid in and out in response.

"I see."

The knife now clean, Sarahessieth hooked it onto the wall and entered into the gloom at the back of the store. After a couple moments, the potion master returned from her private chamber brandishing a batch of preserved mice.

"Here," she stated. "But you really ought to try harder. The night is still young."

The snakes took their meals away to a corner of the store. It was only a moment later however, whilst Sarahessieth busied herself clearing up the rest of the desk that she felt something was off. Her nostrils widened and her head turned to her right. The air entering her shop had changed.

Sarahessieth stiffened. Her focus shot towards the open window. There was nothing to be seen, yet that did not ease her irritation.

She took a few steps forward, wondering what could have interrupted the nocturnal hunt of her snakes, yet before she could reach her door to see off whatever was there, a scent, peculiar and heady, wound its way through the gap and into her nose. Sarahessieth stopped in her tracks, and all the snakes about her store ceased moving. It was familiar, that of blood and bodily fluids yet unlike anything she had encountered before and as it filled the room, her body was caressed by it until she felt a rush of heat throughout her. The Vampire's heart throbbed. Suddenly, her eyes shifted to the door for behind it she sensed a great presence.

A pulsing energy emanated from beyond. Her heart pounded all the more as the force took hold and coursed through every part of her. It blanketed the Vampire in sweltering waves that grew in intensity until her skin felt like it was on fire. Just as Sarahessieth began to feel threatened and formed a Shield around herself, her mind was penetrated and flooded with a vast crimson vision. The Vampire gasped as her own sight was lost and all she could see were blissful endless tidal waves of blood stretching outwards into the blackest of nights. There were no stars, but silver did appear in the dark heavens in slivers that writhed with minds of their own.

Sarahessieth's body felt light and as awe and curiosity mingled with fear, her feet, now coated in the life of countless fallen, floated through the searing winds that tore at every inch of her flesh. A deep thunder hurtled across the midnight horizon to drown her ears in a deafening cacophony of chants and incantations she could not comprehend. Flying in dumbfounded yet wary fascination, she ground her teeth and threw her hands to her ears though this did nothing to silence the guttural chorus. The vision then changed from the boiling ocean to a rapid series of crystal clear images wrapped in airs of absolute rage and maleficence.

Sarahesseith's entire body suddenly ignited with an almighty euphoria as scenes of suffering and the cries of mortals and immortals alike spilled into every corner of her mind. Her ears began to bleed from the screams, her skin burned hotter from the ire and a chill gripped her spine, but she shook them off, enticed by all she was shown. There was a fortress of students put to death, the most lavish of brothels hosting the grandest of orgies and masses of dark writhing lascivious limbs that glinted in the night. Blood and the mangled remains of countless people poured over Sarahessieth until she could no longer breathe. She was thrown into visions depicting a trio of women tortured and ruined, a blanket of stone encasing the broken, and a cathedral of bones and hunger that rose so high into night she could not see its peak. Throughout all, a hatred, ancient and unquenchable, scorched through to Sarahessieth's very soul filling her with adoration and dread, its focus on the unworthy. The imbecilic. The compassionate.

The more images flashed across her wide blood-stained eyes, the faster they passed by and the rising of acute joy and terror threatened to explode the Vampire's heart. They held her fast, and as they accelerated by, she discerned the patterns, the designs and, at last, the final intent.

The chaotic fleeting visions culminated upon a singular being, one that sent torrents of icy veneration cascading throughout the potion master. A tall figure, wrapped in utter rancour and swirling waves of rage, stood upon a mountain of bones wielding with an iron grip an inverted scythe in their left hand and a chain in their right. The chain led down to a collar shackled about the pitiable form of a hooded and robed skeleton who was forced into pleasing this statuesque being. Upon their majestic head sat a crown of seven bones and flying high above them rose the seven desecrated remains of mortals. Sarahessieth could not breathe. She was frozen in place, drowning in blood, her entirety captivated. As the immortal stared with ever widening eyes at the glory before her, she noticed it was the most beautiful woman she had ever seen. This embodiment of beauty and malevolence stood perfect and absolute and the harder Sarahessieth's heart began to pound in her frozen chest, the louder the thunders in her mind bellowed and the eyes of this divinity blazed into her. Their infinite darkness tore away all light and only the slithering streaks of silver within them reflected the Vampire's dumbfounded visage.

As flames of purest pitch exploded from behind this dominion of fury, Sarahessieth knew then that she looked upon the face of god and choked out the only query in her mind.

"Who are you?"

The thunders ceased their chanting and silence blanketed the furore of darkness and flame. Sarahessieth felt every crevice of her being penetrated and perceived by the almighty stare of the woman. Her body stiffened, yet she repressed the urge to resist, fully aware she hadn't the power even if she wanted to. After an age where the Vampire sensed each segment of her personality scoured and understood, the woman hooked the chain to the scythe and held out her right hand. Sarahessieth, trembling from a surge of elation, reached out to take the hand of god.

ACAR VANTA.

Suddenly, Sarahessieth was launched back to her shop. She was standing in the same place just before the door and her snakes slithered about as if nothing had happened. She gulped in air, catching her breath after holding it for so long and she swerved about, searching for any signs of the lady. There were none. Sarahessieth swung open the door to her shop and ran outside.

There was nothing to be found. No footprints. No disturbance in the air. Not even a remnant wisp of her intoxicating scent. Sarahessieth swore and frowned, rubbing her sore arms. After another brief glance for any clues she may have missed, she returned inside and shut the door.

"I will find you," she whispered. "*God.*"

Cinthia's Horizon
Hallahan, Year 1176

The moon shone aloft in the blackening sky as the last tinges of violet faded from the heavens. Hundreds of stars held their candlelight in the clear air, not a wisp of cloud floating to dull their vigil. Their gentle glow illuminated the endless sands around Hallahan that rolled off further than even Cinthia's preternatural eyes could see as she sat atop a dune outside her home, leaning back on her hands as they sank into the coarse grains behind her. With her knees bent, the soles of her worn boots dipped beneath the surface of the dry ocean as she sat alone, staring into the empty expanse. Only the slightest of breezes disturbed the silence, brushing the ends of her askew pigtails as it passed by. The air was still warm, but would soon cool off as the night drew on, though this change would not affect her.

Firelight spilled on the ground. The sound of a door opening and closing could be heard just behind and soft footsteps padded through the sand. The desert floor next to Cinthia then shifted as the space next to her became occupied. She did not move and for a time there was silence as the pair stared out across the dry sea. Eventually, Cinthia felt fingers intertwine with her own. She squeezed them.

"I know that look," came a comforting voice.

She glanced down at her legs and gave a small smile. "You know me too well."

His hand moved into hers and held tighter. Cinthia let go and placed her arm around their shoulders, bringing him in close to her.

"We're here for you," he whispered, leaning his head against her shoulder.

Cinthia stared out across the sands again. After a brief moment, she replied, "I know."

The man shifted closer in to her and she stroked his upper arm as he did so, her cheek leaning into the top of his head. She slowly inhaled, taking in his every scent and a warmth filled her chest, though it came with a great weight that seemed to pull her further into the sands around them.

"There's always more out there," he said, putting his arm around her waist.

She made no reply, a small frown etching her otherwise blank features as she scoured the horizon.

"Maybe..."

The man held her tighter.

"So, what's the plan this time?" he asked.

Cinthia's frown deepened as her focus upon the vast sands continued. Her eyes picked up on the smallest grains far away being toyed with by the meagre breeze. Her gaze followed as each mote of stone fell over one another down the cooling hills.

"I dunno..." she mused in a whisper.

They sat for a several moments before the man looked up at her with an understanding expression.

"Want some space?" he asked.

Cinthia broke her attention on the far off dunes.

"No," she whispered a little sharply. Pulling him closer, she added in a softer tone, "I want you here."

He nuzzled into her neck. Cinthia sighed and squeezed his shoulder. Closing her eyes, she asked, "Where's-?"

"He's showering. He'll be out soon I bet."

"Good. I want you both here."

"So, you've got an idea?"

"No. I just want you here."

The next several minutes passed in thoughtful quiet, with Cinthia feeling the gentle rise and fall of his chest and seeing the stars begin their nocturnal journey across the sky. They reflected in the dulled irises of her eyes as she stared upward, her brow furrowing more with each passing moment. After a while, however, the light in her eyes shone a little brighter. The corner of her mouth curved upward and, looking down once again at the desert before them, she nodded.

"I have an idea."

The man gave a quiet chuckle. "Never doubted you for a second. What is it this time?"

Cinthia removed her arm from around him and leant back into

her original position.

"I'm going to do something I've never done before. Something..." She glanced down and around, searching for the right word. The light grew brighter in her eyes. "*Exhilarating.*"

"Not to spoil your fun or anything, but you've done plenty of 'exhilarating' things before."

"Not *quite* like this," she laughed, standing up and brushing the sand off of her.

"Then," he started as he got to his feet, "is it really worth it? I wouldn't want you to be in any danger-"

"-I said exhilarating, not dangerous," she retorted, mock punching his biceps and smiling at him. "Don't worry – you know I'm not really one for danger. But what I have in mind to do is..." She gave a small laugh. "Illegal."

She drew his face to hers and kissed him. After a few moments, she pulled back and looked him in the eyes.

"This will be frigging awesome!" she declared.

"You've still not mentioned what it is..." he reminded her with an amused smile.

A smirk plastered Cinthia's features before she leaned in to whisper in his ear. His eyes widened and he let out an impressed chuckle.

"Fuck, Cinthia! Are you serious?"

"You can fuck me anytime, anywhere and yes, I am serious. They'll never see me coming after all. So no danger."

"Fair point," he admitted. "And... how about *now*?"

She cocked an eyebrow at him and folded her arms. "You heard me. Going to make good on my offer?"

He held out his hands to his side. "Do I ever turn you down?"

Cinthia grinned and laughed as he came over. She gave him another kiss before she shoved him to his knees and tore off his shirt.

"Shouldn't we wait for-?"

"He's miles ahead of you," Cinthia stated matter-of-factly, not stopping in her task. "He's already naked from the shower. You're the one who has to play catch up. He'll be here by the time you're ready."

As she continued to remove her partner's clothes, Cinthia

glanced out to the endless expanse on the horizon. Once again, a weight fell upon her chest and the brightness in her eyes dimmed. Shaking her head, she returned her focus to him just as her other partner stepped into the darkness of the night to join them.

Much later, as the moon began to sink and the first hint of blue arose in the distance, Cinthia donned her day suit, making sure it was sealed. Fastening her thigh bag to her, she glanced behind at her archaeological gear sack that sat propped against her desk. It would remain there for the first time in centuries. Cinthia then looked into her mirror. The pink glow was dimmer, but began to revive as she made the final preparations to leave. Not least was one particular detail. She reset her pigtails to their parallel positions behind her head. Then, donning her hood, positioning her goggles and raising her face mask, she set off.

Unruly Children
Vampire Hunter Headquarters in Aldvon, Year 1176

Lady Rose gently brushed the long folds of her crimson spider-silk dress out from under her as she took her appointed seat around the giant circular table. Its darkened glass surface reflected the high ivory and green marble of the hall as well as the other significant persons present: Officials and experienced soldiers from every sector on the continent gathered in the chamber and took their places around the table with quieting murmurs of concern. Across from Rose, bathed in the brilliance of the electric lights overhead, sat her very old friend, Talin Kvacha, who had donned her pure white ceremonial dress adorned with embroidered golden leaves. Her posture mimicked that of Rose and she flashed her a warm smile. The Elder acknowledged her whilst pondering her suspicion of why the meeting was called. She had heard rumours of Vampire related crimes being on the rise, however, such normal incidents would not require the turnout of not only herself, but also The White Witch and what appeared to be every last Admiral, Colonel and Sarain in the Vampire Hunter's ranks. Folding one leg over the other and moving a few strands of her auburn hair behind her ear, Rose shifted her attention to the woman taking to the podium above the table. She wore a pristine, and highly decorated, white and gold uniform, and, as she switched on the microphone, all the remaining hubbub died down.

"Ladies and Gentlemen," she addressed the group, echoing loudly about the stone room. "As Chief Admiral of the Vampire Hunter order, I, Sister Fey Mahel, hereby am calling into session the organisation's expert Hunters and investigative Officials as well as the The White Witch, Talin Kvacha -" She gestured below. "- and the Vampire Ambassador, the Elder Lady Rose." She signalled across the room. Rose nodded, paying no heed to the heads that turned to face her. Sister Fey continued, "All of you are here as this is an emergency session. As some of you are already aware, a large string of horrific and gruesome Vampire attacks have occurred over the past fortnight."

A screen descended from the ceiling behind Fey, with a digital representation of a map of the Fortress Cliffs. Upon it were a series of red circles representing attack sites, next to which were written the dates upon which they occurred. Rose absorbed the details.

"Normally, the Vampire Hunter order would handle such matters on its own," Fey explained, pointing to the screen. "However, since the reports from a score of witnesses state that these attacks were done by a whole host of individuals, as opposed to a single person, the matter is far more grave than usual. The findings of our forensic pathologists corroborate the accounts of multiple perpetrators. The witnesses provided further information, describing all members of the group to possess yellow irises."

Her suspicions confirmed, Lady Rose's stern gaze shifted to Talin, who gave a simple supportive nod.

"According to the records of lineage provided to our order by Elder Lady Rose," said Fey, turning to face them all once again. "And from our own intimate knowledge of the Vampires, it is clear these homicidal immortals are from Elder Ulaq's bloodline."

Rose's brows furrowed, but she otherwise did not move. She could feel the eyes of all around her begin to rove in her direction. Ignoring the others, Rose redirected her focus to Sister Fey.

"Now, we have no reason at this time to think there is a link between Maker and Fledglings, however I feel given his nefarious past and his ongoing outspoken ideologies, it would be wise to investigate all possible angles. Furthermore -" Sister Fey's tone grew heavy and slowed. "- as these attacks have not been contained and are of a particularly brutal nature, they have attracted the attentions of not just the Baldrinian Emperor, but also the Covyn Law Enforcement. Both are calling for harsher sanctions against the Vampires. This very morning I was in communication with Human General Gabel and they are demanding answers as to how these homicides were allowed to take place."

Sister Fey took a deep uncomfortable breath and then looked

at Lady Rose. "It is to my regret that I was asked to summon you, Elder Lady Rose under such dire circumstances. The General especially wished for me to demand a statement from you in regard to these murders."

Rose sat forward in her chair. "I'll be more than happy to assist in any way possible. What would you specifically like to know?"

"I think giving your insight on Ulaq would be best for now," carefully replied the Chief Admiral and for the briefest moment she paused before adding, "Though if you cannot, we will have further things to discuss."

An expectant discomfort settled in Rose at the mention of 'further things to discuss'. After respectfully gazing at each member of the group, she opened her mouth to speak in a steady and deliberate tone. "I do not know if he is involved in this. I, myself, have no evidence to submit on either his innocence or guilt, yet I agree with your stance on the matter – that we should not leave any stone unturned so to speak and look into his possible involvement."

"Are you *sure* that is the statement you wish to provide the General with, Elder Lady Rose?" replied Fey. Rose leaned back into her chair, folding her fingers across her lap as she did so, saying nothing. The Chief Admiral continued, "I think it is safe for me to assume I speak for everyone at this session that your record as the Vampire Ambassador is nigh impeccable and you are held in high regard by us. However -" Fey's eyes stared into Rose's. "- I hope for all our sakes you are able to provide us with *something*."

Lady Rose, gaze falling to her hands, nodded. "The Daylight Contingency?"

There were hushed whispers and grumbles of disquiet from around the entire table. Looking over at Talin, Rose saw The White Witch confirm her suspicions with a single cheerless nod. Rose's face hardened. The Elder's attention was then caught by the woman sitting on Talin's right hand side. This one was much younger and was obviously a Hunter from the Agungdrian power-armour she wore. The woman gave Talin a quizzical glance to which The White Witch leaned over and quietly relieved her of confusion. The short distance across the glass was child's play for the Vampire to hear over and she picked up the ancient woman explaining to the younger lady what Rose had referred to. Talin had just finished when Fey cut across the mumblings of the others.

"That is what we're all hoping to avoid, Lady Rose," she said in a heavy tone. "General Gabel was very clear that if you could not inform us immediately if Ulaq is involved or not in any way, then he would demand authority over the investigation. The CLE would then undoubtedly take steps to overrule us. We've long maintained our independence from them as it's in all our interests to do so. Therefore, if you do not do something on your end, Rose -" Her voice was steady though the underlying concern in it was obvious to all. "- I'm afraid their faith in your ability to contain such occurrences will be broken. You know what this means for your kind and ours."

"I am aware of the stakes and more than thankful for matters to be in your hands," agreed Rose.

"I am glad. At this time I only ask you do not give them an excuse," emphasised the Chief Admiral, holding up her hand. "I am merely warning you of which way the winds are blowing at this time."

Lady Rose bowed her head in response. "In that case, allow me to revise my previous statement regarding Ulaq's potential involvement."

The silence around the table was palpable and all eyes were once more upon the Elder. Rose reclined in her chair without expression, her body still as she stared at the screen behind Sister Fey with mock interest. After a few moments of peering at it amidst the pressuring quiet, Rose sat up straight and addressed the Chief Admiral.

"You can tell the General that it's not him," she declared. "He has not left Illarien in months. Additionally, his style has always been to convert then set loose Fledglings to act upon their own will. Those guilty are most certainly acting on their own. Regardless, tell the General I'll still return to Illarien at the earliest possible opportunity and bring Ulaq in for questioning by both the Elder Council and the Vampire Hunters just to be sure."

"Thank you, Elder Lady Rose," replied Sister Fey. "For your wise and insightful assessment of the situation. I'm sure he'll be satisfied with your judgement and, with your continued help, we can now continue our investigation into the matter."

"I am more than happy to be of service," Lady Rose declared, a hint of a smile playing about her red lips.

The rest of the meeting passed by smoothly and without further words from Lady Rose. She watched and listened to several members of the group take to the podium to provide further details regarding the investigation. Most interesting to Rose was the presentation given by the Hunter at Talin's right, though not just for its informative content. Another White Witch, Second Lieutenant Raelya not only represented the very best the Hunters had to offer judging from the various medals attached to her armour, but also demonstrated her skilful deductive reasoning and in depth knowledge of psychology, yet despite these she showed clear discomfort throughout her talk. Avoiding the eyes of everyone in the Headquarters but Talin, Raelya shakily relayed the accounts given by the many witnesses to the attacks. Even with her unsteadiness, however, she managed to get through it and recount the finest details of the perpetrators' appearances and behaviours. As she concluded her section of the meeting, Rose once more exchanged a glance with her old friend.

At the meeting's end, when all the members of the group began to either disperse or talk amongst themselves in smaller parties, Lady Rose vacated her seat and made her way around the table to greet her friend, but was stopped halfway by a very nervous looking Raelya, whose chunky armour moved surprisingly quiet upon the stone flooring.

"Elder Lady Rose, right?" she asked with a tiny tremble in her voice and holding out a gauntleted hand. The Vampire smiled and shook it. Even through the armour Rose could feel it was quivering.

"That is correct," she replied, gazing into Raelya's eyes. "And you are Second Lieutenant White Witch Raelya, yes?"

The Hunter nodded. A silent moment passed before she spoke again, "I hope… I hope you are alright."

"I am," Rose stated. "This is not my first time in difficult politics."

"I'm relieved to hear it, though I really should have expected that, given… well, everything that I know of you," the Hunter said. Her eyes grew alarmed at her own words and she added, "From your reputation, I mean. You… you handled yourself very well out there."

"It was nothing I haven't gone through before," Rose replied. "For someone wholly used to fieldwork, you did very well yourself."

"How did-?" Raelya asked a bit taken aback, but then she shook her head and a look of realisation passed over her face. "Ah, you read my mind."

"Not at all," the Elder replied with a smile, holding up her hands. "I never do that in places such as this – it's professional courtesy. It's just clear to me from how you were on the podium that you're not used to public speaking. Which is very understandable, by the way."

Raelya's cheeks turned a redder shade and she placed her hands behind her back. "No ma'am, I am not used to that. I am a White Witch first, a Hunter second and a soldier in both instances. This was my first major meeting where I was asked to speak."

"This was your first time?" asked Rose, catching Raelya's gaze with a reassuring smile. "Believe me, I know how hard it can be. You did very well for someone who's never done it before. My first time was a great deal worse, so please don't feel bad."

"I appreciate that, ma'am," Raelya stated, relaxing. Returning Rose's bright expression, she added, "But I defer to your expertise on this matter. I confess that I am jealous of you, ma'am."

"Please, call me Rose," requested the Vampire. "And there's no need to feel jealous. I'm just very practised."

"Thank you… Rose." she mumbled.

"Oh, Rose? Yes, she is assuredly a savant of articulating her way out of the most arduous of quandaries."

The two of them turned to face Talin Kvacha who glided

barefoot towards them across the marble floor. Raelya bowed to her and Rose smiled in response to her display of reverence. The Elder and ancient White Witch then embraced before standing back into their social triangle.

"As I was saying," continued Talin, clasping her hands together in front of her. "Rose is all too familiar with navigating bureaucratic pressure. Out of the two of us, I would always admit it is she who is the expert dance partner in the ballroom of politics."

"That's about the only place I *can* ever dance," joked the Vampire.

"As if I require reminding," teased Talin. "May your two left feet live on in infamy."

Raelya's tension eased at their exchange, however Rose noticed she still wished to ask something and so gave her an encouraging glance.

"My apologies, ma-, uh, Rose. I just... wanted to make sure you were all right," she started, her voice rocky, looking at both Talin and the Vampire. "Though I confess I am curious... so please forgive me for backtracking… but did you not feel helpless, having to give in to the General's demands? To be, more or less, forced to lie? I guess… I'm asking two things: How do you cope under those circumstances and what more can you tell me about The Daylight Contingency?"

Rose replied, "Thank you, Second Lieutenant. I really do appreciate your concern. Yes, I am doing just fine." There was then a momentary lull in the conversation as the Elder gathered her thoughts. "Now, to answer your first question… well, to begin with, this was not that difficult of a situation," explained Lady Rose, gesturing to the table nearby. "It was just everyday work to me, though I am concerned for the outcome. And as for your second inquiry," she paused, looking at Talin. "That is a big question, so I'll try to be as succinct as I can. The Daylight Contingency was created by Humans many centuries ago, who knew Vampires grew in power over the years, to counter their potential threat, but it hasn't had much traction in all that time. Simply, this is because down the ages each generation of mortals has decided that since the oldest Elders were not yet powerful enough to be considered 'weapons of mass destruction' – as is quoted from the Contingency – then they would not invest the immense sums of money required into developing weapons specifically to combat our kind. It's not financially worth making something they will likely never use and would only ever use on very few individuals if the need arose. They therefore leave the job to future generations and the Vampire Hunters to deal with. At this current moment in time, there appear to be members of the CLE who are more invested, if you pardon the pun, in pursuing the Contingency than in previous years. This happens from time to time – normal fluctuations."

"Ah... I see. Thank you... But... if you don't mind me asking, how does that impact both Sarains and Vampires, like the Chief Admiral stated?" asked Raelya.

"In short-" Talin Kvacha took over from Rose. "- it possesses the capability of igniting another Holy War. As an organisation comprised of mostly Sarains, the Vampire Hunters are more aware of our holy counterparts, and as such we are more accommodating of their wishes and needs. With us, as Rose well knows -" She waved a hand in her direction and Rose nodded in response. "- we always collaborate with transparency to devise anti-Vampire weapons, and only request conversion records and lineage histories, but never more invasive information unless lives are in peril. Conversely, the CLE would not be so respectful. Since our establishment, we have retained independence from them, yet if they were to attempt to take command, they will press for strident sanctions against Vampires. The kind that will include the disclosure of deeply intimate information regarding them, as well as further, off the records, advancements of countermeasures. As Rose remarked, they do not have a lofty sentiment of the Vampires. If I recall correctly, the whole quote from the Contingency characterising their kind is: 'Weapons of mass destruction, disasters waiting to happen, capable only of becoming more dangerous over the centuries'."

"This could then lead to another religious conflict," concluded Rose. "As the Daughters of Saraanjova, the Sarains and White

Witches are still the most effective weapons against Vampires. The CLE would use you against us both in terms of pure magick and in terms of developing new weapons inspired by your Gifts. So my report designed to maintain the Alliance between our peoples."

The young White Witch stood in silence for the whole explanation, and seemed to grow more tense with each new bit of information. When they both had finished talking, Raelya blew out her cheeks and sighed. "I'm glad I don't have your jobs."

"It can certainly be an ugly position to be in," mused Rose. "Though it has its perks."

"Oh? Such as?"

"Well, for one," the Vampire answered. "It enables me to keep one hand on the wheel so I can help direct things in the way they need to go. And secondly -" She smiled at two White Witches. "- I get the pleasure of meeting such fine people!"

"And uphold amicable connections," prompted Talin.

"Too true."

A few moments passed in quiet, but Rose saw that Raelya wished to say something. The Elder went ahead and spoke up for her.

"What's on your mind, Second Lieutenant?" Rose asked.

"Umm... nothing really, I'm just curious," she replied, not taking her eyes off of the pair of them. "I'm just wondering... how long *have* you known each other?"

Lady Rose and Talin Kvacha exchanged sly smiles with each other.

"I met Rose for the first time amidst the peace treaty deliberations at the conclusion of the Holy War in 704," recounted Talin. "It was shortly before I became The White Witch. Myself, several Sarain Mothers and the Lady Rose united to establish not just the Varndicco-Bavillion Alliance but also the Vampire Hunters."

"I wasn't the only Elder to help with those, I'd like to point out," said Rose. "Ellandu'el, Amakay and others were of great significance as well during those days."

"Together we toiled to forge a lasting Alliance concurrently with developing contingencies of our own for conceivable future

Vampire attacks. It was not facile to marry those points at a time as delicate as that, but after the unimaginable ruination precipitated by Vampires, Sarains and Ishteieen alike, the general populace was thankfully more invested in fostering peace. Rose aided in the design of the very first weapons for the Vampire Hunters. Her actions, accompanied by our own transparency, assisted in cementing trust. We have kept this old-fashioned method going ever since. It has always benefited more than it has hindered. And through those shared efforts, we became very close friends."

Raelya, much to Lady Rose's surprise, stood to attention and saluted her. It was the Vampire's turn to have her cheeks flush with colour at the unexpected tribute. Flustered, Rose did her best to hide this by bowing of her head.

"Elder Lady Rose," spoke the Second Lieutenant. "It has been an honour to meet you. Your work, your life – you are truly a hero. I know I could never dart through the miasma of politics like you. And through all that time, to still be here fighting the good fight – I am proud to work alongside you."

The flattering and sudden statement took Lady Rose by surprise. Uncertain how to react, Rose worked a simple smile onto her flushing features. "Well... thank you. I do my best."

Lowering her arm, Raelya took note of Rose's blush and looked at the floor. "Sorry, ma'am – Rose! It's just the... uh, last of the nerves from earlier... and... um... Anyway..." she stared hard at the ground and swallowed. "Ummm... thank you for indulging my many questions and thank you for your advice earlier." The Hunter's face had become redder than Rose's and it took all the Elder had to stifle a grin. Straightening her back, Raelya cleared her throat and continued. "I really must be going now to get on with my share of the investigation and I'm sure you two have some catching up to do anyway, so -" She offered her hand to Rose once again. "- I'll say goodbye for now."

Rose, feeling her own face burning, shook Raelya's hand, taking note that it was quivering more than when they first met, and bade her farewell. Raelya took one last respectful look at Talin before turning to vacate the hall. As soon as she did, Talin shifted to face the Elder, her face aglow.

"You must excuse Raelya's timidity," she began. "She has desired to meet you for as long as I can recall. Your famous, and at times, infamous, tenacity has been an instrumental inspiration to her."

Lady Rose breathed out and mimicked her friend's expression. "That explains much. And here I thought she was just jittery from the presentation."

"She most certainly was," conceded The White Witch. "Yet there is a fire in her heart that gives her strength to overcome adversity. I am proud of her for her efforts during the meeting as well as summoning the courage to introduce herself to her childhood idol."

"I thought there was something I liked about her," teased Rose before she added, "Seriously though, she did a good job today. Public speaking is not easy."

"Verily," replied Talin. "And she managed to execute it without incident. She is a most capable person."

A cheeky grin slunk onto Rose's face. "Most assuredly so, though it has not escaped my notice that you were a significant part of her ability to carry on. The way she only looked at you during her talk, and how she behaved when you joined our conversation. Forgive me, my friend, but I feel there is something... familial between you two. Am I correct?"

Talin raised a smug eyebrow, "It takes one to know one, Rose."

The pair laughed for another moment and the Vampire folded her arms before speaking again.

"Your behaviours are not unlike a Maker and Fledgling," mused the Elder. "At least in some instances."

"The comparison is an apt one. Raelya is my White Witch in training. I specifically chose her from over three hundred potential Sarains to tutor."

Lady Rose gave a small gasp. "That is an immense honour. Actually, I cannot draw an appropriate equivalent honour in our own ranks. The closest would be being converted by the oldest amongst us, but even that's not quite the same as being picked to study under. I understand why she looks up to you as she does."

"Raelya was the obvious choice," Talin explained, a far-off look entering her eyes. "Indeed, I would go so far as to say she was the only choice. She had not only shown valour and mercy in combat – rare traits to be sure – but she also demonstrated she possesses an abyssal well of compassion for others. Vampires, Sarains, Humans, Baldrinians – even Dragerians. Others held too much resentment. She is a rarity and thus a credit to our people."

A warmth ascended through Lady Rose's chest and it must have shown in some fashion as the next thing she felt was her friend's gentle hand upon her shoulder. The Elder sighed and acknowledged gratefully.

"What of your children, Rose?" Talin inquired, squeezing the Vampires' arm.

Rose's eyes grew unfocused as she stared across the hall towards nothing in particular. As memories played across her mind, her fingers began to dig into her arm and a tired smile flashed across her face.

"Now, that is a question," she replied. There was another moment of her losing herself in recollections before she spoke again. "Which one would you like to hear about?"

The White Witch said nothing. After several moments of having her question go unanswered, Rose was stirred back to reality and looked up at her friend. Talin held a vague expression, one that she could only assume to be a mixture of playful curiousity and comforting empathy. As Rose analysed her confusing visage, Talin raised an eyebrow prompting the Elder to answer her own query.

"Well," she began, swallowing hard as she brought her focus back. "My second Fledgling, Natalia, is being as obstreperous, disobedient and disrespectful as ever. She's proving to be quite the handful on the Council at the moment, which is causing me all manner of grief." Rose frowned and snorted. "I honestly don't know what to do with her. Ellandu'el has tried helping, but Natalia's even less likely to listen to her than she is to me as she is the head of the Elder Council. Sometimes I just think she desires to be an irresponsible child forever."

"Perhaps she is having difficulty adapting to eternity?"

suggested Talin.

"No, she's always been a rebellious one, despising any and all authority figures without exception." The Elder shook her head. "I have given up trying to reason with her and steer her toward a better path."

"And what of your first? Cinthia, isn't it?"

Rose's face shone, yet her eyes glowed with hint of sadness, "Yes... Cinthia," she breathed. "She is truly an amazing and unique individual. Sadly, I've not seen or heard from her in years, though I admit this is hardly unusual for her. I do keep track of her when I can though via my usual channels. She is quite the accomplished woman now, having published multiple books on Ancient culture and is renowned in archaeological circles. I am very proud of her and wish her all best in her continued endeavours, but..." She glanced over at Talin with a sad smile. "I miss her a very great deal. I hope she is OK." Brightening, she let her arms fall to her sides. "Now *her* I hope you get to meet someday."

"How *amusing* you should mention that..." said Talin with a wide smirk.

Lady Rose gave a tiny quizzical frown and asked "What do you mean?"

"I can most certainly attest to your brief summary of her," answered The White Witch. "For she leaves an indelible impression. I have something of a confession to make, my friend. I have very recently had the pleasure of meeting her, albeit under circumstances most irregular. She is indubitably a talented, beautiful and fascinating individual."

The Elder's frown deepened with suspicion and she asked, "She definitely is as you described, but what do you mean, 'circumstances most irregular'?"

"Oh... nothing..." said Talin. "Nothing crucial anyway."

Whilst a hint of a smile threatened to crack upon her face, Rose's gut twisted and she did her best to maintain her composure as she pressed for an answer. "Talin... what aren't you telling me?"

With a stifled snicker, Talin leaned in close to her and whispered in her ear. The Elder's face blanched to match the white marble around them and her jaw fell open. In the very next instant, Rose burst out yelling in a voice so loud it didn't cease echoing for several moments.

"She did WHAT?!"

Blasphemy's Choice

You know me. You all know who I am. You've penetrated my thoughts, my memories and have seen how I came to be. Yet did you, you moronic prudes, see *that* moment, when I *chose* Them, realising Their great truth?! Let me enlighten you then, you fucks.

At first I couldn't understand why it happened: I couldn't fathom Their Will. All I did was suffer. From one unholy ritual to another I was tossed from one depraved cultist to another all in Their Name: Unholy Amen. **_GOD_**. I can't fucking remember exactly for how long. Point is, it took me *forever* to get it through my thick skull just why They were doing this to me. I mean, *They* told me *constantly* – it was Their Blessing and that I was to become the vessel of Their blasphemy against the false god Inter. But I was revoltingly blind to what that actually meant.

All I saw were people raping me and using me for their twisted pleasures, whilst being used as a blood-covered symbol of power in every sinful ceremony. For every sacrilege, sexual feat and act of submission to Their Will I was marked with Their Word in profane arcane glyphs and symbols until now, today as I stand caged before you, nearly every inch of my naked flesh is covered in beautiful treachery. I was strapped down and made to come repeatedly over The Icons of Sin, to repeat the Seven Sacred Sins whilst covered in the crimson life of the Seven Severed Corpses. And all I could do was weep, like a pathetic whimpering child.

I slept originally in a damp cell. That changed after my baptism in the Severed's blood, where I'd first witnessed Their almighty power. My God moved me to a lavish bedroom full of comforts fit for royalty. After every session, God would hold my broken, sex-stained body to Them and gently stroke my sticky hair, whispering words of comfort and repeating this was for my benefit. That I was the envy of Their subjects – for no-one else was deemed worthy of serving at Their feet. Indeed I witnessed their envy for I had God's favour. Their slavering jaws and aching stares seared the proof of their appetites and hopeless ambitions into my mind.

One evening, I realised my door hadn't been locked. I ran as quietly as possible through the vacant stone hallways, past the stately ballroom and the lavish whores' quarters to the surface entrance and opened the door. The night air kissed my face, beckoning. Yet I couldn't move. As freedom stretched before me, I couldn't ignore the tingling between my legs and the teachings in my head. In *that* moment, it dawned on me how foolish I'd been — everything they did was truly for me. They'd desired *me*, pleasured *me* and granted me *great* authority! They'd always taken *care* of me! My groin was wet and I purged the final remnants of shame from my mind. **They** were truly more a God than Inter ever was. I ran immediately to Their chamber and prostrated myself. Without hesitation, I gave Them my body, mind and soul, embracing Their hatred of your fucking counterfeit deity! And They officially named me ***Blasphemy***.

Natalie's Inferno

Amber sparks drifted with ash along the midnight air to land upon the still scorching rubble. They were joined by a cascade of smothering smoke that blanketed the burning masonry, distorting the dancing glow of the flames through the dark. The faint hiss of sizzling flesh and muttering drops of rain could be heard across the quiet of the aftermath accompanied only by the smallest dripping of life as it trickled over the debris. The fallen and burnt stones that had once been the fortress now lay in utter chaos, scattered and rendered undone, searing the cadavers held fast beneath them. The reek of the corpses permeated the heavy cloud and wound through the dust and debris until it came to penetrate the bleeding, soot coated nostrils of the broken immortal. Entombed within the collapsed structure, Natalie's still and oozing body jerked into consciousness at the stink invading her nose, shaking loose the cinders atop her head to partially unveil her raven hair. Her eyes roved as she observed her predicament with rising panic. Her chest heaved in terror and she wailed, becoming aware of the crushing weight of the rocks and smouldering oaken beams atop her regenerating body. Natalie's reawakening nerves shot forth waves of agony through her, her bare flesh burning against the encasing sepulchre and the bones in her legs reattaching themselves to each other. In a desperate bid to lift herself out of the sweltering mess, she pushed her bare hands against the fallen stones on the ground before her with as much strength as she could muster. It was a mistake. Screaming, her throat hoarse from smoke, she recoiled from the scalding rocks, her palms blistering and unable to curl into fists. She tried using her elbows to lift herself instead. Crying in despair, Natalie gritted her teeth and cursed the air, tears streaming down her soot-stained cheeks as she shoved downward with all her remaining might. The rubble wouldn't budge and she sobbed as the flesh on her elbows peeled from the heat. Her arms fell limp against the dampening ash around her, hopelessness settling in her breast. Natalie, unable to cease coughing, scoured for anything she could use to aid her escape. With the Vampire's bid to find something bearing no result, Natalie let her gaze become arrested by the raging glow to her left. The flames in the distance pranced in her damp eyes and, in the following moments where Natalie stared forlornly at them, her face contorted until her expression mimicked the fires themselves. Her fangs bared and ground against her jaw and tears of anguish gave way to ones of ire. A boiling maelstrom of thoughts whirled about her mind, yet there was only one question and one alone that mattered amongst the storm. *Why? Why* did that twisted evil bitch do it? After everything they went through! After all their trials and suffering for her to just end it all? What was the point?

That evening had marked the end of the school's planned one hundred-year run. As such, the Acar Vanta threw her most lavish party to date, sparing no expense on elaborate décor, various blood fountains, tailored ball gowns, live music and delicacies for the mortal staff members. Had it not been an occasion celebrating the culmination of the Acar Vanta's and graduates' sinister artistry, Natalie would have likely enjoyed herself. Instead, she chose to sit alone in a corner of the assembly hall, doing her best to avoid the company of her peers and scarcely hoping that this finale would result in their freedom.

The crimson and gold embroidered dress she had been measured for, whilst fitting to her like a glove, left a swirling nausea in her gut. She felt more akin to a puppet than a person. The long silk red gloves only served to sicken her further as a terrible reminder of her innumerable sins. Thankfully, she was allowed to take them off, though the dress, like so many other aspects of the school, was mandatory unless removed for carnal reasons. This revolted her. Conversely, the vast majority of the other young immortals took to their new garments and the celebration as a whole in high spirits. None more so than Equinn. She was clad in a gown made from the purest white fabrics and sauntered about with such pride that Natalie thought the others would trip over her ego. Although the Acar Vanta had often made it clear that all graduates were considered equal, it had not gone unnoticed she clearly had her favourite. Natalie assumed this was reflected in the fact only Equinn wore all white, taking it as a repulsive reference to her purity.

As the evening drew on and the festivities got into in full swing, with graduates gorging themselves on the fountains' bounty and removing their clothes to partake of altogether different pleasures, the Acar Vanta dismissed the faculty from the hall and took to the stage. Upon the wooden platform sat three identical black chests, all locked. The Unholy Amen, attired only in a thin coal and silver robe, stood in front of them and addressed the Vampires.

"All good things *die*," she boomed, emphasising each word. She then smiled, "I'm sorry, I meant 'All good things come to an *end*'." A roar of laughter echoed from the crowd throughout the chamber. Only a few, Natalie included, remained silent. "Which I suppose amounts to the same thing. This school of mine which I have devotedly watched over and guided now for precisely one hundred years has blossomed and borne such rich fruit. And oh, my Fledgling graduates, how you have grown. You have sprung up to embody true strength in this world. You rose above the chaff of your peers and struck them down in service to yourselves to reap the rewards of life eternal. Whatever motives you may feel you have acted upon to get to this point are irrelevant. It was your strength, your will to survive alone that won through. Along the way, there were those who believed they might achieve some measure of victory through defiance." There was a smattering of sarcastic applause and torrents of ridicule from the graduates. Natalie turned her gaze to the floor, her stomach churning. The Acar Vanta gestured to the audience, her features freezing over. "They have passed on like pestilence in the wind leaving you, my children, to inherit the earth. *Victory*... Indeed. Like I said... ALL... GOOD... THINGS... DIE!" The deafening celebratory screams of her peers shook Natalie to the core and she closed her dampening eyes. With a resonance far deeper than before, the Acar Vanta continued, "And here, at the end, with all you vanquishers gathered, will we bear witness to an end so very... long... awaited!"

Shedding her gown to stand naked before them all, the Head

Mistress stood to one side and curled her left arm up to her ear. At the familiar cranking of mechanical cogs, Natalie's eyes shot open and she could not help but turn her attention to the stage to witness the end of three poor souls she had aided in torturing.

The Unholy Amen summoned from the depths of the castle the rusting iron bars that held the trio of High Priestesses cruciform. Wooden panels shifted aside and from beneath them arose the bound, bare Interists, their obsidian and silver eyes glazed over in age-old capitulation save for the youngest, whose eyes had been torn out. Their bodies had been washed and what physical harm had befallen them in prior rituals had healed, their regenerative flesh unable to convey the horror of their recurring tortures. Natalie shook her head and wept, doing her best to cover her face so her peers would not bear witness. The bars ascended higher until the toes of the hanging immortals were a short distance above the floor, all the while the excited cheers from the more twisted graduates echoed in the hall. The stage shut, the Acar Vanta took to the fore and the sacrilegious ceremony commenced to the rowdy ovation of her Fledglings.

"Perversion!" The Head Mistress screamed, raising her arms above her head, her eyes blazing. "Lubricity! Free Will! Urges dictated by the natural law! These are violations of the highest order in their eyes!" She jabbed at the crucified trio. "Sins of the flesh, mind and soul! *These* aberrations, fettered by their wilful ignorance, are the true violation! A mark against nature, natural selection - the entire evolutionary process! Cretins of the highest calibre! Their putrid ideology cannot be allowed to persist! Interism states that the embracing of our sexuality is abhorrent. A great sin! Their penance must reflect their transgressions!"

Natalie sat frozen to her chair, unable to avert her frightened eyes, as the Acar Vanta unshackled the mute trio, letting them collapse unceremoniously to the stage floor. Some instinct must have still lingered within their broken souls, because as soon as they crashed to the planks, they clawed their way to the edges of the platform to get away from their scourge. This amused the jeering masses and the Unholy Amen's eyes burned as she circled around them. Natalie's mind was a whirlwind, hoping that their ending would at least come swiftly but the rising sick in her throat betrayed the fact she knew better than to wish for such a thing. With unimaginable speed, the Anti-Inter descended upon the youngest Vampire and yanked her head backwards until it could be heard to snap. Natalie recoiled, shuddering and covering her ears but could not avert her gaze. Blood dribbled out of the poor girl's mouth onto the rabid onlookers below who lapped it up and the Acar Vanta, straddling her, plunged her fangs into her pale shoulder. The blind immortal screeched an unearthly howl of agony that quickly turned to muted gurgles. One of the other Priestesses reached out to her with a trembling arm, but before her fingers made contact the girl was hoisted up by the jaws of their nightmare and spat out onto the ravenous graduates. They swooped down on her to feed, molest and beat the long-since defeated young woman, much to the suppressed anguish of her fellow believers. Black blood coated the front of the Head Mistress and she observed her frantic children with the same minuscule smile that haunted Natalie's dreams. Even then she still could not discern if it were pride or some other revolting emotion. All she knew was that it petrified her.

After a brief moment taking in their revelry, the Acar Vanta dragged the other two Priestesses back towards her then turned to unlock the first of the black boxes. Without effort, she lifted it down to the group and spoke.

"Here are the instruments best suited for the Blind One's punishment!"

She unveiled the contents. Within were all manner of sexual instruments, ranging from simple dildos to erogenous torture devices, various restraints and at the bottom lay two pokers.

"She came here a virgin," spat the Unholy Amen. "I rid her of that regrettable state and you will now prepare her for the end in the same manner. Take your fill of her in whatever way your loins most desire, but do not kill her. Yet."

Just as the twisted group started to inflict all manner of agonies upon the girl, the entire hall shook like an earthquake had struck and a thunderous crack reverberated through the chamber up to the rafters. The glass fountains of blood rattled on their pedestals, decanters shattered on the floor and the whole flock of graduates gasped and looked up from their disgusting acts. Silence fell. Natalie had squeezed her eyes shut at the commotion, but opened them again at the sound of nothingness. Her blood froze solid. Every graduate in the hall stared at her, mouths agape and not moving an inch. The two High Priestesses that still possessed eyes wore the same expressions. Natalie's breathing stopped as she scanned their shocked faces, their stiffened limbs and at long last, the vacant space upon the stage. Tears of jet spilled forth from her to dash upon her paling quivering cheeks and her every muscle seemed go limp. A cold trickle ran down from her groin to her thighs and shins, staining her crimson dress and pooling at her feet. Natalie felt the gentle, icy touch of fingers upon her bare shoulders. They stroked up her skin to caress her exposed nape and her heart near exploded in her chest. Her neck hairs stood on end as blood gushed forth from her eyes as sobs burst uncontrollably from her. She dared not turn her head and as she felt the coldness of breath upon her left ear she made every effort not to scream.

"That means *everyone*," came the caressing whisper. Natalie choked as her ear was penetrated by a long wet tongue exploring it. Slamming her eyes closed, Natalie gritted her teeth in unfettered terror as she attempted to fall into a dark abyss. Yet before she could escape into herself, she felt an almighty pinch at the back of her neck. The faces of the graduates were now a cocktail of smug satisfaction, derision and mockery. Natalie's mind was in chaos with spiralling feelings of utter humiliation, repulsion and dread. She felt herself lifted up by the vice upon her and her every muscle stiffened as the Acar Vanta softly pushed herself up against her back. More liquid trickled down her legs to dribble across her shoes to the floor and she tried to avoid the eyes of the group. She began to move forward. With every step the Head Mistress made her take, Natalie felt her spirit die and the closer they came to the blind Vampire's twitching body, the more she was consumed by despair. They stopped in front of the poor broken girl and Natalie felt the Acar Vanta grasp her left arm to outstretch it towards her. Her sister's visage suddenly flashed before her eyes. Natalie, screaming inside her mind and face soaked in black lachryma, shook her head and mumbled pleas for it to cease. They were met with the laughs, jeers and screams of animosity of her peers. As her hand was forced to make contact with the young woman's vulva, she then heard a soft snort of satisfaction in her ear.

FRIG HER, came the command in her head. **Or take her place**.

Natalie's sobs were her only comfort. Numbly, she obeyed and to her shame she continued to do as she was told even after the Acar Vanta had left to start preparations on the second Priestess. Abject terror ran through Natalie and as she witnessed the new and inventive tortures her peers and Head Mistress unveiled for the three unfortunates, she hatred herself for her own cowardly part in the putrid carnal display. Looking up from her insufferable burden, she was met by the bitter stares of the others, many grumbling insults as well as taunts over her weakness - her inability to stomach such pleasures. What few allies she might have thought she had amongst them at one time were silent and offered no support for fear of their own lives. One person did ask why she was bothered by it when she had done all this before. Natalie did not respond. She had always been repulsed, but this time… they were to end them. Natalie shook with grief and ground her teeth, forcing herself to continue her repulsive work and trying her hardest to repress the image of her sister's face.

"She came here a fool," roared the Acar Vanta, holding up the deaf Interist by her throat. A bolt of fear struck Natalie, thinking at first the insult was intended for her. The Unholy Amen continued, "She actually believed me when I promised to take her instead of the Blind One. I swiftly showed her the error of trust – a crutch for the weak. Now take your fill of her as well, forcing her to watch everything you devise for the young one she cares so much for."

The graduates exploded with gibes as they surfed her body overhead to kneel her before the youngest. Natalie took the opportunity to stop her repugnant act and move to the back of the crowd in the hope she'd be ignored once again. Her peers would not allow it. They formed a semi-circle around her and pushed her toward the Deaf One. Hyperventilating, she turned to face the woman she was chosen to punish, but her path was blocked. Equinn stood between them, her glare piercing into Natalie and brandishing one of the pokers.

"You disgrace us," she spat, her voice dripping with disdain. Without warning she brought the bar up to connect with Natalie's temple. A heavy crunch echoed alongside the startled gasps of the crowd followed by the gushing of blood onto the wooden floor. Natalie dropped instantly, twitching before them. Stars wheeled in her eyes against a curtain of black. Immense agony pounded in her skull, blocking out all thoughts save for instinct and she grasped her wound in her hands, moaning out loud. The graduates all gave Equinn a wide berth as she circled the wounded Natalie, twirling the poker in her hands. Natalie, desperate to heal, crawled blindly toward the nearest blood fountain but felt the ground in front of her splinter with the forceful descent of the rod.

"It's a wonder you managed to graduate at all," Equinn hissed, spitting in the face of the downed immortal. Crouching before her, she hiked up her robes to avoid the life pooling around Natalie and leaned in close.

"And you'll get what's coming to you," Equinn finished, sneering. She wildly kicked Natalie in the torso over and over before turning her back on her to focus upon the second Priestess. The rest of the graduates followed suit and left Natalie to bleed out.

Gurgling blood and unable to stand, Natalie looked up through blood-coated eyes to see the table before her. Atop flashed her salvation. Flowing crimson tantalised her vision and she forced herself to crawl forward, putting all her focus and energy into making the distance. Terrified the others would stop her if they could, she made every effort to quiet her moans of pain and the scuff of her ruined dress as she dragged herself onward. The screams of the woman that held their attention masked her approach and Natalie bit her lip to stop herself from weeping over the prospect of being thankful for it. Every inch forward sent new waves of crippling pain and fear through her body and mind, and she dared not look back, clinging to the hope they would not see her. The tiny pattering of the dripping blood resounded just above. A single mouthful would surely be enough?

At last she arrived, her life-stained hand stretching up the table leg, but it proved too high. Swallowing her own sable waters, she ground her teeth and stretched upward with every ounce of strength left she could muster. Her hand just slipped over the edge and felt the cold relief of a glass. Curling a finger to draw it closer to her palm, she managed to grab a hold of it. In a darkening haze, she strained upward as far as she could manage to victoriously dip it into the beautiful red stream. She cracked a smile as the blood poured into her cup and then she brought it at long last to her failing lips.

The rejuvenation was immediate and overwhelming. Natalie shook her head to clear it from the retreating pain and managed to stand. Without hesitation, she refilled her glass and drank deeply once more. It wasn't enough. Putting it to one side, the Vampire dunked her head into the fountain's stream itself and partook of the life force of the fallen. It gushed down her throat in revitalising waves, its power allowing her body to mend itself and the more she gulped in, the more she could feel her wound's flesh sewing itself up. Her head and shoulders coated in vibrant red, she shivered with new-found strength and, turning back to the crowd of deplorable creatures, she felt something deep within her soul snap. Without thinking, and her eyes ablaze, she took up the poker from the floorboard and stormed her way through the crowd to Equinn. The girl's eyes widened with shock right before Natalie unleashed all her rage onto her. The rod cracked Equinn's head, torso and limbs, splattering her pure white garments and blonde hair in her ebony life. With every crunch of broken flesh and bone, Natalie felt a sliver of satisfaction course through her veins, spurring her to strike with increased fury. Yet before she could do further damage, an invisible force slammed into her chest, winding her and sending her careening back into the fountain. Glass and blood sprayed in all directions, covering the nearest onlookers in shards and drops. Natalie rose to her feet, shaking in fear and anger, to look at the smug grin upon Equinn's distorted, yet regenerating, face.

"I'm older than you, bitch," she shouted, licking her own blood from her healing lips. "You don't stand a chance."

Natalie's fingers tightened their grip on the metal rod, all reason leaving her. The pair stared each other down as their peers cleared a circle around them. Equinn's smirk stung her nerves and she poised herself to attack, yet it was in the very next moment that her rage would be entirely snuffed out.

The Acar Vanta, having witnessed events unfold without a word, glided down from the stage to stand between them. In an instant, Natalie blanched, her anger drowned. Equinn, almost fully restored to her natural beauty, laughed and walked to one side but Natalie barely noticed, for every mote of her soul was focused on the Unholy Amen. A suffocating silence filled the assembly hall as the hater of Inter encroached upon Natalie until she stood just a foot from her. Natalie's tears returned in full and she could no longer hold the poker. It fell with a clang to the floor and she backed away into one of the other tables. The Acar Vanta closed the gap once more.

"*Vengeance*," she whispered in a voice that seemed to repeat itself over and over in the terrified girl's head, "is a powerful thing. *You* are *proof* of my Word. For you have found strength because of it. Remember that. *Always*."

In a movement so swift Natalie could not see even with her enhanced reflexes, the Anti-Inter slapped Natalie so hard she saw only blackness.

An unknown length of time had passed by the time Natalie at last came to. She was stirred from merciful unconsciousness by a series of blood-curdling screams and explosions. Jolting awake, she assessed her situation. Her face paled and she stifled a horrified shriek by squeezing her hand to her mouth at the scene of slaughter in the hall.

The walls were painted black with immortal blood. Not an inch had been left untainted by the events that took place whilst Natalie had laid stunned. The furniture was all but destroyed and the fine décor ruined, drenched in a harrowing mix of running crimson and obsidian. The three chests were open, their instruments sodden with the remains of their respective Priestess. Coated from head to toe in sticky onyx, the Acar

Vanta stood upon the ash-strewn stage feeding off of one of the graduates, their confused cries for mercy going unheeded and growing weaker by the second. At the feet of the Unholy Amen lay the decaying corpses of Natalie's peers, piled, draped and twisted together against the stage, tables and floor. One by one they were turning to ash. Between the Acar Vanta's legs was Equinn. She knelt naked, also anointed in the life of the former immortals and lapped at the vulva of the Head Mistress. Her clothing had been folded and placed to one side, stained by the blood of the dead around them. Natalie tried with all she had to not vomit. Her gaze bolted around the rest of the room, searching for a way out. In the corner adjacent to where she sat in silent fright, were stacked the mutilated bodies of the former faculty members, their life having been drained dry and through the many sets of doors lay yet more cadavers of graduates. Some had been torn in half, their legs tossed several feet from their torsos. All were disintegrating to fine dust before her eyes. There were no other exits, so her only chance to escape was as slim as it had been for the others. Natalie shook her head in panic and her body shivered all over. She would have to try to make the run. Taking several deep breaths, she readied herself to stand and bolt for the nearest door. She took one last look at the couple on the stage and as soon as she did so, her heart stopped.

The Acar Vanta stood up straight, her blood-laden hair sticking to her flesh and her abyssal stare penetrating through Natalie's retinas to pierce into the deepest recesses of her soul. Natalie, feeling her violate her mind, backed into the corner as far as she could manage, clawing at the wall behind her. Equinn irritably turned from her task, her mouth and chin soaked in the ebony vaginal juices of the Unholy Amen and upon seeing Natalie's frightened display, a victorious expression formed upon her features. Natalie was unable to take notice, her attention riveted upon her greatest fear. Her legs buckling under their own trembling, she steadied herself between the adjoining walls. Casting aside the deceased husk, the Acar Vanta moved like water down the stage steps, crushing the dissolving cadavers beneath her feet to stand in the pools of blood at the base of the platform. Equinn followed suit, grasping up her robe and standing just behind her. She flashed another vainglorious grin at Natalie. Neither said a word. For several moments, the trio exchanged glances before Natalie could take it no longer. In a fit of hysterical panic she managed to blurt out, "WHY!? Why are you doing this?!"

Equinn's face fell, her eyes rolling and she turned away. The Acar Vanta continued to bore into Natalie, but she too remained mute. Natalie's breathing hastened and she screamed at them, "WHY?! What was the *point*!? You made us all immortal, let us live because *we passed your tests*! We were meant to go on with our lives afterwards! WHY DID YOU KILL EVERYONE?!"

The expression of the Unholy Amen altered not a single iota. Equinn sniggered then exited through the door. Natalie's brows furrowed and she opened her mouth as if to shout once more but nothing uttered forth. Her sobs were the only thing to be heard in the assembly hall and fell only upon the ears of the dead. Eventually, after several agonising moments of waiting, the Acar Vanta's mouth curved into a small, enigmatic smile. Natalie felt her spine freeze and shook her head in desperation. Her nightmare cocked her head to one side and the smile broadened. Tears poured forth from Natalie's eyes as she shook her head all the more, crying out.

"No! Please NO!"

In an effortless gesture, the Acar Vanta cast a gargantuan obsidian fireball into the structure above and behind Natalie. Natalie launched forward, giving one last yelp of terror before the scorching masonry crashed down, burying her.

The memories of that night flashed across Natalie's wet eyes like the taunting flames in the distance, sparking an unmitigated rage within her. This fire merged with disgust at her own weakness, feeding the flames of loathing. She had played the role of the coward for too long, committing unforgivable acts just to save herself. How many lives had she witnessed ruined and done nothing? No more! Ignoring the agony in her throat, she screamed at the top of her lungs. It echoed through the haze, frightening off the voracious monstrosities that dwelt in the woods. The ire within her built and flooded her every vein with a boiling heat. Slamming her palms once more against the scalding rocks, she pushed upwards with all her fury, her wrathful wails like a wild animal's. The rubble budged and shifted above her, cascading dust down upon her head and shoulders, but she ignored it. Continuing to scream at full force, she summoned all her Vampiric strength to hoist the debris on her back. It lifted slowly and once it had risen enough, she shot out from under it. It crashed back down and reverberated the air in harmony with her perfect rage. As her body repaired itself, Natalie breathed heavily and stared out into the night, eyes blazing with purest hate. Bearing her fangs, she screamed out at the forest.

"I will stop you! No more will I cower as you bring utter *ruin* to others! I won't *let you*! I swear on my *sister's name* I will stop your sickness! It was a mistake leaving me alive! And it will be your last! For the sake of future people, and people like her, I *swear* to you, as long as I have breath left in me, *I will do everything in my power to kill you*!"

A Light on the Shore

A lone man tussles upon a boat. He is drenched in the rains that have been hammering the oak planks beneath his sodden feet and the darkening shoreline for the past hour. His net is empty. The sails strain against their pulleys, buffeted by merciless gales. The man wipes his brow of spray and deluge alike as he struggles to maintain in charge of the possessed canvas. A heavy boot squelches as it slams into the mast and the determined groan of the sailor as he grapples with the ropes in his pulsing arms is lost to the cracks of lightning and the deepest rumbles of thunder that split the ever blackening sky in twain. He cannot seem to make the distance. Just over the nearest roiling crests protrude teeth of stone so tall they seem to have belonged to the Giants of yore, yet through the lashing downpour he finds it hard to judge the gap betwixt his vessel and the ravenous maw before him. He quickly leaps, ropes in hand, to the other side of the boat, yanking with every ounce of vigour his muscles can spend. The spot is near. Only a little farther. The unruly sails need only be coaxed for a moment longer. His hand once more wipes away the torrent whilst he looks on with widening eyes at the wave careening from his left. It crashes into him and his already soaked feet slip upon the slick beams. The hemp line is stained crimson as it passes through his tightly clenched palms. At a cost it steadies him. The man's whole body, pale and clammy, shivers but not with the cold this unforgiving nature has chosen to bestow upon him. Adrenaline courses through his veins and a steel gaze pierces from his eyes. The jaws of the rocks loom overhead. He has arrived.

Stowing the sail amidst the chaos, he moves on to haul his net over the side. It has not seen a fish in days. Neither has his stomach. Where rumours abound to feed hope to the desperate, danger is risked. Whole schools of shining scales had been spotted flocking in this locale, but only ever at dusk. Rumour or truth, it did not matter. He needed to eat.

The fruits of his despondent gamble pay him in full, though invariably at his expense. Another wall of black water rushes from the side. In a mad bid to free himself from his fate, the man yanks hard to retrieve his net, yet it catches upon one of the ravenous stones in the swirling depths. Cursing through tears at the inevitable surge hurtling toward him, the man vainly shields himself with his arms as the flood envelops his vessel and sends it soaring into the teeth. It cracks, splinters and shatters. The man is hurled like a doll into the nearest monolith and with a grotesque crunch his skull collides with it. Whilst unable to distinguish his own stars from the ones between the clouds above, his head in excruciating agony, he yields to the forces set upon destroying him and slips into darkness.

His eyes reopen to the cacophonous heavens commanding him to wake with cannonade blares resounding over the sea. Startled, he splutters and flails in the inky brine. His body is the plaything of the unrelenting waves that madly undulate as far as his salt-sprayed eyes can see. Where the shore is he cannot tell. His heart pounds so loud he hears it above the reverberating screams of the sky. Tremendous bolts of white light tear the air, illuminating the fear upon his paling features. It is only now, as the endless waters rage about that he remembers his body is near frozen and beneath the enveloping chill he shivers. Chattering teeth tremble his skull as he chooses a direction to stroke out towards, for any way is better than staying put waiting to drown. Yet nature is a cruel mistress. Chaotic currents and blinding surges of froth hinder his every effort. The man's strained efforts to defy the sadistic swells are all but in vain, for it seems the depths yearn to drag him under. The strength in his muscles is sapped by the frigid waters that constantly attempt to swallow him whole. Here, held fast in stormy jaws he struggles with ever waning efforts and as the last of his energy flows into the surrounding furore, his gaping mouth sucks in a last sweet shot of air before he is pulled beneath by the gluttonous waves.

'Twas a gamble made with such high stakes that only fools or the forlorn partake.

And yet…

His hazy eyes, staring despairingly into the crushing chilling abyss, catch sight of a dim white glow from out of the midnight depths. It slowly ascends. Bubbles spewing out from his mouth and nose to fly to the violent crests above mimic his desire to flee the nearing light. It grows brighter. Movement stirs in the deep. The man hopes he is delirious from the cold as his weakened attempts to surface do little to avoid the approach. Yet out of the blackest of blacks it arises, becoming ever clearer in his frantic eyes, but bringing with it an inexplicable swaddling of stillness within him. His brow furrows in befuddlement and his assuaged heart ceases its dramatic rhythm. Entire auroras of colour refract and dance throughout the current, captivating his darkening vision and instilling his soul with a welling serenity. His eyes shut just as the light piercing his haze splits into two prismatic lanterns of shimmering brilliance.

A blast of warmth slams into his face, rousing him. He coughs out icy brine and gulps in precious air. His limbs are frozen and cannot move yet even through their apparent numbness, defying all known reason, he feels he is laid upon air and floating over the savage rush that had failed to consume him. It crashes and swirls in a jealous rage underneath, but falls upon deaf ears for his attention, dazed though it is, centres upon the tepid air caressing his shivering skin. Gales blow over him, blasting him with a blanket of relief from the cold waters he has soared out from. The man's eyes open and close, drifting in and out of consciousness as he flies through the air on invisible wings. His journey over the sea comes to an end as he is lowered gently to the sands by this unseen force. The soft bed of granules beneath stirs him from his daze and he manages to twitch his arms and legs for the first time. He cannot sit up. He groans from the shooting agony in his skull and his vision is clouded with his own blood. The heavy raindrops allay his pain. He tries to lift his head from the ground, though barely achieves an inch, his breath catching in his throat as he does so, for an incredible sight, such as he has never beheld, unfolds before his heavy, widening eyes.

Out from the sea, a head draped in liquid gold ascends. It is followed by unearthly twin orbs of light set into a face that the gloom holds all but anonymous. A pale set of elegant shoulders rises, holding up a long white dress that sticks wetly to the graceful and slender figure gliding out from the lashing waves up towards the transfixed man. A tall woman, resolute and calm amidst the clamour in the heavens, stands silhouetted by the lightning searing the sky. It outlines her in brilliant flashes of white that glint off her soaked willowy frame. Flowing water spills from the woman's golden hair, down her long bare arms and off her majestic thin fingers in a multi-coloured cascade as it catches and reflects the gleam from her eyes. It patters to the ground and dashes against her bare feet. The hairs upon his arms rise though not out of fear, but from an unknowable energy emanating from her. There, still and silent, she regards the man with her lustrous glance. It is as if the man has drowned once more for he is unable to breathe. His limbs cry to move, yet remain stiffened. Amidst the intensity of her presence, a feeling, an aura of tranquillity, exudes from her. The man's muscles relax and he stares back at her with uncertainty and wonder, assuming he must be dead or this to be a dream. His head collapses back to the sand. She flows effortlessly around to his side in a motion so smooth it is if her feet never leave the ground. The man cannot even feel her impact the sand around him and, as curious an occurrence as that is, through the momentary illumination of another bolt from above his gawking attention is arrested instead by her face.

A fairer complexion and countenance he has never seen, yet it is hardened by experience and an insight so unfathomable he fails to repress a gasp. Her cold, yet alluring eyes stare out as expressionless as the rest of her features and beguile the man's sights. Their ever-changing and hypnotically shifting hues glint like the stars. All the calamity that befell him washes away as he drowns within her inscrutable gaze. He does not notice he is sat up by another invisible compulsion. Her examining stare moves from his enraptured one to the open wound upon his head and she spits into her brine soaked hand. Like a salve, she spreads it all over the gash. The threads of flesh stitch themselves back up and the bleeding stops all to the man's uncontainable amazement. Silently, she walks behind him up the beach.

Once again, the man floats up into the air and is carried through the sobering torrent. He opens his mouth to speak but there exists nothing for him to even imagine saying, yet, still curious, he tries to turn his clearing head but finds the task all too difficult. Soaring softly backward up the shore towards the cliffs and away from the monstrous waves, he sighs and feels the need to sleep once more come over him. He shakes it off. He must see his rescuer.

The man, still shivering, is placed under a slight arch just out of reach of the rain. The elegant creature stands to his left. She is staring out to sea. His mouth opens in an attempt to entreat her to conversation, yet his endeavour bears no fruit for no words issue forth. In the quiet he simply observes the fair-haired beauty, yet whether or not she notices is unknown and in any event she fails to reciprocate. At long last, accompanied by another gargantuan flash from the heavens, the man's gaze is caught by movement out at sea. As was his wont around this singular woman, his astonishment plasters his features at the sight of his wreck flying in its respective fragments towards the shore. They cease but a few feet away from the pair, the planks arranging themselves to stand upright against one another in the sand. All the while, the woman had made not a single move, yet now she steps towards the wood pile, soundless and graceful. The man watches on in startled awe as her left hand becomes engulfed in roaring flames of pitch, nigh visually indiscernible from their nocturnal surroundings but vividly distinct from the damp cold air about them for the heat from the fire coiling about her wrist and sprouting from her palm is unlike any he has previously experienced. Slowly, she extends her willowy arm toward the pyre. Such an unnatural blaze to catch along sodden timbers would be enough to astound anyone, and the man is no exception. Obsidian dances and roars along the grains of wood, consuming all. A tremendous blast of heat banishes the brisk humid air and the man sighs in relief as his skin shivers out the last remnants of chill. She turns to face him, though whatever expression is upon her face is veiled by the dark. Only her eyes light up the makeshift camp, sending cascading waves of light over the sands and rocks. Fighting breathlessness, he flexes his jaw and again attempts to speak to the lady, to profusely express his gratitude, but is once more muted by another inexplicable wonder manifesting before his very eyes. Rainwater, illuminated by the woman's aurora portals, dashes and splashes against an unseen surface. It collects, somehow, in the air and with no container, yet forms a semi-circle as if it is held in a bowl made of glass so clear it would be all but invisible. He only now realises how thirsty being near-drowned in the ocean has made him. The floating chromatic waters move toward him. A look of uncertainty crosses his face as he reaches out to grasp the unseen bowl. He looks to the woman. She does not move. His parched mouth yearning for its contents, his fingers avidly reach out and take hold of the container. It is like glass, smooth and cool in his palms. He wastes no time and brings it to his waiting lips, flooding his arid throat with overwhelming relief to quench, at least in part, his salt-driven thirst. Taking in a series of soothed breaths, his sight is caught by a change on the woman's face. Obscured by the black of night it is all but impossible to detect, and may be naught but a twist of the imagination - a soft rise of a smile seemingly flashes across her hidden features. The man blinks, doubting his own eyes and surely, as fast as the gesture of warmth had appeared to come, it vanishes. The woman's head turns slightly to her right, to glance sideways at the pyre. He obediently follows her line of sight to witness a stake propped against the burning wood, roasting a speared fish along its shaft. The man laughs delightedly and, shaking his head in grateful incredulity, turns back to face her.

She is gone.

Bewildered, the man calls out. Hearing no response, he painfully stands and hobbles from the small overhang to scan the beach, the horizon and the cliff face. There is nothing there but rain and wind and the clamour of the unruly sea in the distance. The man cannot stop shaking his head, but a smile does appear on his features and he shouts out his thanks to the night in the hopes she will hear him.

Mirthful over his miracle, and swearing on all he holds dear never again to risk such a foolhardy undertaking, he limps back over to the fire and sits down to finish cooking his much needed meal. His smile does not last long though and as it fades from his falling face he looks wistfully out to sea. He knows who she is. They all do. She was all too poignant in the folklore of his people, yet so few had ever been granted the enviable gift of seeing her in person. The man snorts and shakes his head. Such unlikely happenstance to befall him at his most desperate hour, to be literally saved from the maw of the ocean by *her* – it is beyond the credulous limits of his friends and family and as such a bittersweet smile crawls onto his face. Yet, as he tucks ravenously into his eagerly awaited meal, he defiantly winks and gestures discourteously at the waters that had attempted so desperately to swallow him, content in the knowledge that at least he will make it home and not be food for the sea instead.

Blasphemy's Designs

The night air rushed through her hair. The boughs of trees and verdant leaves of the undergrowth flew past and her inked bare feet, crushing dry branches, pelted forward with an unfamiliar and exhilarating strength. Her newly-glowing eyes streamed streaks of pale yellow through the shadows of the Darkwoods, a vibrancy that was matched by the euphoric smug grin upon her features. Coursing with purpose, she moved ever faster on towards her goal, her focus trained upon the village torches glinting through the trunks in the distance. Aching to know just how much power her muscles now possessed, she accelerated further, laughing as she reached her peak. After taking a few tumbles, she leaped, ducked and weaved through low hanging sprigs and fallen rotting logs upon the forest floor, and those that did bruise or cut her flesh she failed to notice. By the time she reached her destination at the edge of the clearing, they were healing, leaving her skin and the extensive designs of heresy upon it unmarked. Tucked in the bushes at the verge of the wood, the naked Blasphemy crouched, scanning the area for any late night patrols. If it were not for her blond hair or vibrant eyes, she would have been camouflaged, for nearly every inch of her skin had been marked black with the symbols and seals of sin.

It had been eight years since her first marking, where her flesh was once unwilling and frightened. Yet, as she squat in the undergrowth assessing her situation, she was anything but. For every carnality and sin she accomplished, her god had rewarded her with yet another symbol, seal or section of a greater piece until at last everything save her breasts, buttocks, groin and most of her face was a work of profane art. From the twin inverted scythes running down her cheeks to cross over her navel, to the Seal of Unholy Will upon her chest and the ribbons of text flowing gracefully about her, Blasphemy's body was most assuredly the bible of the Acar Vanta. It was the very striking nature of her appearance that would play a chief role in what was to come. The Icon of Sin's plan for her: to commit sacrificial murders over the course of no less than eight months with particular emphasis being upon the sexual nature of the deeds. No witnesses. None alive anyway. After these preludes, she would make her move on the very heart of Interism: Illarien.

On its own, Blasphemy's newly-converted form would not be strong enough for the task ahead. The Acar Vanta, therefore, had personally trained Blasphemy in the arts of stealth, hand-to-hand combat and infiltration over the past two years. She had also been informed about the nature of Vampirism's effects upon newborns. Consequently, her first port of call was to not only commit a gruesome ritual, but also to feed upon her victims as soon as possible to avoid the thirst rampage common in those just converted. That overwhelming desire would, thankfully, last only a few weeks, according to her god, before it subsided for good and feeding became only necessary to keep oneself youthful over eternity.

As the tired patrol men paced by in either direction, oblivious to her glowing irises and using their spears as supports, Blasphemy's excitement rose in her breast.

She made a sinister joyous grin as the two guards went out of earshot. In a flash, Blasphemy passed into the clearing to push her back against the first hut. Turning right and crouching down, she moved across the soft grass, stalking one of the soldiers. She glided across the green until she was behind the man, her senses aware of every blade under her feet and each brush of air weaving between the strands of her hair. Her breathing was calm as she stood slowly upright, gauging the force it would take to twist his neck and drop him to the floor without a sound. She did not hesitate to snake her arm around his head and just at the moment of his realisation, she yanked to one side. She nearly gasped out loud, for his neck did more than simply break. Her new found strength had almost tore it clean off. Cursing under her breath, she took the weight of his corpse into her and dragged him into the shadows behind the huts. Without delay she crept back to the first hut to seek out the second guard.

She spied him a short distance away. He had wandered over to the bushes and was in the process of relieving himself. Blasphemy stifled a snigger and went over to him. Her fangs bared in a wide grin and her legs trembled in avidity as she lingered behind the unsuspecting soldier. Leering at the throbbing artery within the man's neck, Blasphemy recalled her god's lesson on feeding properly. First, she would need to hold him fast.

In a single, rapid motion, she slid her left arm around his head to cover his mouth, snatched his genitals in her right hand in a vice-like grip and pulled him back to her slavering jaws. He struggled in her arms, protesting than she would have liked and so she tightened her left hand until her nails dug into the man's cheeks. Likewise, her muscles clenched with undead strength upon his groin and her fangs plunged deeper within his neck. Her powerful legs stood unyielding in the grass against his flailing attempts to dislodge her embrace, and the more he resisted, the more Blasphemy intensified her efforts. As the blood gushed in, her eyes ignited with an unnatural desperation. She gulped deeply, for a relentless thirst consumed her. This alien sensation, so intense in its headiness, sent her muscles shivering, her throat moaning and her knees buckled, falling just as much from under the weight of her victim as from euphoria. Images, some vivid and others blurred, flashed across her eyes in nonsensical waves. She understood these to be her food's memories, from her lessons with the Acar Vanta. She did not care to take notice of them, as she was bent upon one thing only.

Holding him tighter to her still, she writhed underneath, moaning louder as she sucked up every last luscious drop of his life. She could feel her every cell rejuvenate with a gentle fire and a red haze began to glaze her vision. Quivering in such a daze of pleasure, Blasphemy almost forgot her god's orders. Fight the trance, for it led to the thirst rampage, and she had a job to do that required her lucidity. Straining against the desperation for more, Blasphemy prised her jaw open and removed her teeth from the gaping wounds. She rolled the corpse off her and covered her mouth for she could not hold back the exclamations of ecstasy any longer. In the following moments, she laughed and cheered as quietly as she could manage, until she had calmed down enough to stand.

Wiping the crimson from her chin and cheeks, she sucked her fingers dry before dragging the corpse back towards the other. Grabbing them both in one hand by their collars, she hauled them across the grass until she stood in front of the first hut. Blood had dribbled down from her chin across her shoulders and breasts and had soaked the ends of her hair. Taking note of her carnal appearance, Blasphemy smirked, and rapped upon the door.

It opened, firelight pouring out and reflecting upon the wet Blasphemy. A tall man stood in the door frame, at first appearing to be confused over such a late visitor, yet he quickly paled and took a step back. With an impertinent grin, the Daughter of the Acar Vanta took several steps closer until she had crossed the threshold and pushed her body in close to his. Blasphemy raised an eyebrow coquettishly as she noticed with delight he could not avert his gaze from her bare breasts and the marks of heresy and blood upon her flesh. As he stood there spluttering, his expression shifting from shock to horror, the new-born Vampire wrapped her arms about his neck and brought his mouth to hers to stop him screaming. Indeed he did try to call out, but she held his face to her own with undead might. A few seconds after attempting to yell, the man struggled to get her off of him. Blasphemy jerked her right knee roughly into his groin, causing him to buckle and, with him stunned, she forced him down to the wooden floor.

Shoving her tongue to the back of his throat, Blasphemy shifted her limber legs to pin his arms. With her left hand, she pinched his nose shut whilst her right clamped about his throat. The man's limbs flailed, causing more of a ruckus than she knew she ought to have allowed, yet she was lost in the moment. Her telepathy began to manifest and she drank in his panicked thoughts. It caused her such delight that she left a wet patch of her blood upon his chest where she crouched. The more he vied for control, the brighter her eyes shone and the tighter she gripped him, the more her own moans joined the quieting screams from his throat. Blasphemy shivered and groaned into his mouth as his thoughts slowed and his body spasms grew more erratic and desperate. His mortal fear poured into her mind, and it was only then that the young immortal realised what sheer ecstasy the Acar Vanta herself must experience each time she eked out someone's demise: a savouring of their intimate final moments. Blasphemy knew this was a gift that her god wanted her to experience through Vampirism. She had been told of this several times, of course, however to hear and feel it for herself flooded her with waves of bliss.

As his limbs began to twitch, she removed her lips from his and moved them down his still body. With an ear against his chest, she could just still hear his heart beating alongside his shallow breaths. She was not done with him yet. Tearing open his tunic and breeches, she regarded his hardened penis with lubricious glee. Yanking out a leather lace from one of his boots, she wrapped it around the base of his testicles and secured it fast. Shifting herself over him, she slid herself easily down upon his throbbing organ and bounced up and down upon it, bearing her fangs and rapturously whispering obscenities.

Upon the moment of her climax, she sobered, climbed off of him and, grabbing his tunic, wiped clean the evidence of her lust from his body. Tossing the tunic, and the rest of his clothes, into the fire, she grabbed him under his armpits and hoisted him up onto his bed. Blasphemy, face set in an icy smirk, dragged the two corpses in and shut the door.

What she did next did not take long but would remain in the minds of the people forever.

Taking one of the guards' swords in her unsteady hands, Blasphemy hacked the corpses in half, discarding the lower halves of their bodies and everything that poured out of them in one corner of the room. Covered now from head to toe in coagulating life, Blasphemy, growing intoxicated from its scent, stifled her desire to consume the blood of her stunned victim, focusing instead on the divine job she was to do. Still, her whole body quivered, excitement over fulfilling her destiny welling up alongside her own disbelief the time had actually arrived. With a joyous smile, she continued to work. Blasphemy took the men's belts and various lengths of rope stored in the hut to hang the two soldiers up by their wrists about five feet from each other on the central wooden beam running the length of the building. The owner of the hut, still unconscious and now covered in the blood of the cadavers swinging above and on either side of him, Blasphemy propped against one of his chairs, binding his arms to it. This task completed, Blasphemy, her breathing swift and shallow and with soiled sword in hand, crouched amidst the deep red chunks and wet that squelched between her toes and regarded him with an eager rapaciousness. She slapped him several times to rouse him. As his eyes blinked open, his face twisted with utter terror at the sight of the gore-covered girl, yet before he could utter a cry, Blasphemy slit his throat. For a few moments he choked and gurgled on his own blood before passing into darkness. Blasphemy, eyes widening and shining with cold brightness, scrambled down with mouth agape and gorged herself on the spilling crimson waters. They spurted forth from the laceration, and in her ravenous guzzling she let them spew over her face, down her neck and onto her breasts to dribble over the rest of her and the already soaked floor. Unable to contain her urges, she rubbed herself as the last of the violent spurts issued forth. Laying in the muck next to the man and breathing heavily, she writhed and moaned, her feet sliding in the red about her. At the peak of her pleasure, memories of her previous ritual butcheries upon the Altar of Impiety flashed across her mind. Her own body in many of those cases had been the altar. Chained to stone, her exposed skin had been doused in the blood of the Severed and the desperate churls of the unholy congregation vied for a taste of her sacred orb.

Fresh spasms of pure bliss shot through her body and, crying out, her legs twisted in on themselves until she was curled up in the vermilion muck, unable to move for an overload of purest joy. After several moments of throbbing aftershocks, Blasphemy giggled and lay over onto her back, her long blond locks now drenched in red. All her god's planning and instruction was just beginning to pay off. Blasphemy, immersed in floods of elation, covered her mouth to stop herself from laughing out loud and after several moments of uncontrollable mirth, she calmed down until her eyes grew unfocussed and a dreamy smile fell upon her lips.

Sometime later, she regained her composure. Blasphemy,

now focused on her orders, hewed the drained man's corpse in two like the others, but left it positioned beneath and between the other two. Before discarding the lower half, she removed the still erect penis and hung it centrally between the three bodies by the leather laces. Blasphemy's legs still wobbled, and this only worsened from resurging fervour as she stood back to observe her gruesome handiwork. It was time to finish it. With trembling hands, she painted the bare wall behind the corpses with their blood until it resembled the Icon of Sexual Sin, the third of the Seven Sacred Sins, and the very Icon imprinted upon the back of her right hand. An inverted triangle in which were drawn three portals overlapping each other.

"One for The Blasphemy," she chanted under her breath to herself as she drew the first portal which angled from the left. "One for The Apostasy." She traced out the portal leading from the right. "And one for The Acar Vanta, The Unholy Amen." She painted the central oval in the triangle, completing the symbol. "Their sexual sins unite to form this Icon of Sexual Sin. In the name of the Mother of Whores, Amen."

The distant echo of rushing waters coupled with the soft rustle of the gentle wind brushing the high branches of the trees around her. Damp leaves and pine needles, a cocktail of decay, stuck to and pricked the bare soles of her feet as their heavy perfume filled her nostrils. The ends of her hairs were ever so gently teased by the near still air of the woodland and the soft hum of nocturnal insects tickled her ears. Blasphemy, standing silent amidst the leafy giants, inspected the deepening shadows before her with icy eyes. Moonlight filtered through the canopy and danced across the forest floor back the way she came yet her sights were set upon the enveloping blackness that lay before her. It was the permanent dark, the Evernight of the fabled holy forest city of Illarien that she teetered on the border of. That ancient place, upon which she would enact all the hatred and sin of the Acar Vanta, in front of her at long last. For eight months Blasphemy had wreaked havoc upon the nearby settlements, sporadically committing ritual killings in all manner of profane and lecherous manners, until her god called her to begin her real mission. In that time, each death, each feeding and each bloody artistry she painted across the land had been but an appetiser to what she now had to perform. It was her main event, her pinnacle and purpose, the very reason her deity had created her. They would look upon her Marks and learn the truth of the world: the Word of the Acar Vanta. Shedding themselves of their foolish worship of a mere entity, they would embrace the Unholy Amen as their guiding light. Or die trying.

Her chest rose and fell in quick succession, her every muscle trained. She squeezed her hands into tight fists and clenched her jaw whilst bearing an impudent smile. Taking a step back with her eyes on her goal before her, she poised herself for the advance.

"I am The Blasphemy of the Acar Vanta!" she declared to the borders of Illarien. "Born of sin and the proud embodiment of Their Word! Left hand of the Icon of Sin and Daughter of the Mother of Whores! I am Their Pleasure and Their Whore and I have come to teach you that your pathetic faith in Inter is nothing but a delusional folly!"

In a flurry of forest litter, Blasphemy shot off into the all-consuming darkness to fulfil her god's purpose for her.

Sarahessieth's Lullaby

The open sign, coated in thick layers of dust, hung askew upon the frozen door. Frost clawed across the surface and burrowed into every crevice of its hinges and frame, holding it fast. Minuscule spears of cold hung down above the ice coated windowpanes and the intrepid chill wound its way over the stone tiles, its progress halted only by the dying firelight next to the water basin. Before its autumnal glow huddled the many scores of Sarahessieth's pets, all wriggling together upon ragged blankets in a shared bid to keep warm.

Littered along the work desks were the decomposing carcasses of small animals and atrophying vegetative matter, their respective odours long since stifled by the bitter air within. Utensils lay soiled and the wooden surface of the work space sat coated in brown grime. Upon the brisk and still air within the store hung the faint, yet invasive stench of mould, however its origin was not from the rotting remains of alchemical ingredients.

The veil of darkness that was the rear of the shop was somewhat lifted at that time. A large number of candles crowded the interior of Sarahessieth's private laboratory and bedchamber, revealing the master craftsmanship of her many customised apparatus. Glass and crystal wound together in complex twists combined with unusual metallic alloys and burners of various sizes and purposes. Symbols of magick and handwritten tomes sprawled along shelves that touched the ceiling of the low room. Contraptions of brass and silver, their uses known only to the potion master herself, were hung in neat rows along the wall beneath the books and glinted in the candlelight. Yet as impressive as it was to behold, everything along her most prized workspace was covered in thick dust.

The only surface not coated in the grey snow was the large oak desk upon which was splayed countless yellowed curling parchments and musty withering volumes. Draped across the masses of moulding ancient texts lay the silent form of Sarahessieth, her head laid against one of the largest books, hair sprawled over the papers and her eyes heavy. Many of the documents underneath her tired gaze were embossed or otherwise marked in their headings with the same symbol. Their faded lettering could barely be read, even from the multitude of low burning candles, yet few even then were scrawled in Lingualis. Of those with ink able to be seen, most were written in languages long since lost and many others written in symbols she had never encountered. Each and every one, however, she believed to hold reference in one way or another to a singular person.

Beneath her exhausted form lay the largest collection of religious and cultural notes on the being known as the Acar Vanta. A large quantity of the accounts were vague and held little information. From what few words scribed in the common language that were not so lost to decay she learned many things, more than she expected, yet none held the answer she was truly looking for.

The *way* to Her.

Her drooping eyes clouded over and wandered from the aged vellum into a blurred grey darkness. The skin on her cheek pushed outward as her head fell heavier into the flaking leather cover of the book underneath and her shoulders slumped upwards. The shallowest of breaths issued in and out from her nose to brush the embossed skin below. Slowly, her eyelids lowered, the foggy candlelight growing dimmer and dimmer until they were shut.

As the soft blanket of night fell upon her, a faint low melody could be heard amongst the fluttering of dying flames. A hum, gentle yet persistent, diffused through the air and into her ears. It oscillated in swaddling waves and Sarahessieth found herself drifting further and further into darkness, her heart slowing its pace with every soothing note. It stroked her into deeper and deeper rest until all she knew or cared about was the lulling hum. She was adrift on its tune and it took her down into a serene gloom where at long last she could see a faint green light. The melody drew her towards the glow and she outstretched a hand to touch it. It had become a dense woodland, the same one outside her shop. Sarahessieth found her feet being moved swiftly yet gracefully over the old dirts paths leading South and the humming music grew a little louder, serving only to push her thoughts farther and farther away. Her only desire was to follow the sound that twisted around her very soul and led her through paths unknown. Images of terrain swept by and led her to the very corner of the Magnus Cliffs. No image stayed for long though as she was moved ever faster around towards the Gorge in the East and the forest thinned then vanished. She was then stopped before a tall crack in the mountain's base. The tune resonated throughout her whole body as it grew louder and Sarahessieth fell deeper and deeper into the massaging path it laid before her. She walked into the darkness of the cave.

There, in utter night, stood a wall hewn into the cavern's side. Upon its ancient and damp mossy surface were carved a vast series of symbols she did not understand but the melody had now been joined by a far off whisper. As the music made her stare in dumbfounded bliss at the marvellous stonework, the whisper became a voice, clear and serene. Every fibre of her being yearned for the words to fill her more and more, yet as much as Sarahessieth strained, she found she could not understand the aria. She began to ache with the effort to discern the lyrics, and the very moment it became unbearable, the Vampire felt a familiar presence. A sudden gust of heat shot into the cavern, burning her skin and waves of acute pleasure mingled with dread flooded through her veins. Unable to move the rest of her body, her eyes searched about in excitement. That was when the aria ceased. The lulling hum began to fade, Sarahessieth's body trembled and she began to shout desperately to stay. Yet it was not to be.

She jerked awake on the book and papers shifted and fluttered onto the floor. She was hyperventilating and looked all around her, tears in her eyes. Yet just as before, there was nothing. The calming numb that had filled her from the tune began to vanish and she slammed her eyes shut in the hopes of finding it again. No lullaby came however. She cursed. Suddenly, her eyes shot open and she grasped for a quill. She could still write down the lyrics she had heard and decipher them later!

Her hand could not move. Ink dabbed onto the paper and spread outward in a perfect circle as it seeped into the ancient parchment, yet would never form a word. To her horror, she found she didn't even know where to begin. They were a jumble and in a language she had never heard before. Were they even written using an alphabet? All she could remember was that they sounded soothing. Swearing, she slammed the quill down hard, snapping it in two.

After a time, she shook off her rage, embarrassed by her own actions as it dawned on her it was irrelevant anyhow. Her god had shown her where to go – and there she would find her answers.

With her head still riddled with questions, she packed to leave. She undressed from her work clothes and put on her worn travelling gear and a grey-green cloak. Putting up her hood, she slung her pack over her shoulder, snuffed out the candles and marched out of her room. Taking a long look at her sleeping reptilian friends, she placed another two logs on the fire and opened a sack of dead mice for them to eat before yanking the store's door open, ice and frost showering her as she did so.

The forest was before her, albeit a winter version of itself and it marked the first stage of her journey. As she turned to her left to go South, a smile played on her lips and she began to hum the lullaby to herself.

Willow's Hearing

Willow's trembling hands were held fast in Pantheon's steady giant palms whilst her hair trailed down across her face, shielding it from the view of the few others in the room. She shied from their stony and otherwise sombre stares, feeling the burn of their eyes upon her whole body. Confusion clouded her nerve wracked mind. The vast majority of the Elder Council had been summoned for reasons they had refrained from sharing with her, yet to Willow's knowledge she had done nothing that would have given them any reason to be cross with her. However, since official meetings were not frequently held, the young looking woman could not help but shiver at the notion she had done something to invoke their wrath. With the very slightest of frowns, she scoured the memories of her recent actions, yet there was nothing she could consider a reason for the gathering. She had done nothing to hurt anyone, however the longer she dwelt on everything the more she began to drift away with the thought that she had caused some harm by accident, inducing her heart to plunge and her bottom lip to tremble.

Through her ashen curtain she stared into the glass orb that sat in the depression in the centre of the table. The wisps of azure and indigo from the swirling spirits contained within did little to ease her tension until her eyes were drawn by several souls endeavouring to gain her attention. Her pupils dilated and a smile made its way upon her features as they began pulling various faces in an attempt to cheer her up. A tiny giggle made its way up from her breast and as it did so, she felt the large hands of her adoptive father squeeze hers. A few Elders narrowed their already stern gazes at her, stifling her meagre mirth. With a fleeting glance at the souls supporting her, she flashed a minute smile before her sight settled on the leaf-strewn floor. It wasn't until the feet of the trees at the front of the room began to uproot themselves and move their towering bodies aside that she felt able to look up.

The Lady Rose, Ulaq and Sylvia entered into the chamber, all wearing expressions of seriousness and each taking up one of the remaining seats from the total of twenty nine. Several were left unfilled regardless, including the largest one at the head of the table. The occupant that would take up that position followed the other three a fraction of a moment later, sending Willow's heart pounding and her eyes brightening. Her closest friend and current head of the Elder Council, Lady Ellandu'el glided over the forest floor to perch herself on the great throne. Her features, framed by her shining golden locks, mimicked the darkness of those who arrived ahead of her and for the slightest moment, Willow felt a chill slither its way up her spine. Yet as quickly as it threatened to take hold, it was banished as the shimmering eyed Vampire shot Willow one of her all too familiar warm smiles. Willow reciprocated though the moment was not allowed to last. As soon as Ellandu'el had settled, Lady Rose took to the floor.

"Tonight is the 23rd of Nynvar, 921," she started, looking at each of the Vampires sat around the table in turn. "I hereby open this session under my authority as the Vampire Ambassador to Covyn and as this is a matter involving the lives of mortals it falls under my duties to address the matter. This meeting of the Elder Council has been called to discuss an incident regarding Elder Willow that has only just come to my attention." Her calm eyes settled on the quivering ones of Willow, engendering a mild serenity within the woman amidst the winds of worry. Willow felt her father's hand squeeze hers once again and she clung onto his large fingers. Rose continued, "Elder Ulaq and several Officials of the Bavillion Court have come forward and urged me to bring to the Elder Council the matter of an incident that occurred two weeks ago involving the night time flight of a stolen Black Dragon of Mount Fortis by Elder Willow. We are to discuss and ultimately decide what degree of action should be taken against her for her actions that caused mass panic."

Willow could not respond as she sat frozen in her chair, unable to believe her ears. As Rose's words echoed in her head, she felt Pantheon tense alongside her. She opened her mouth to speak but was silenced by the Ambassador raising her hand.

"A call has been put out for your immediate incarceration by the Bavillion Court, however your specific fate is ultimately under our jurisdiction. This meeting will discuss the matter then reach a conclusion on possible sentencing. I now give the floor to Elder Ulaq, who has personally overseen the talks with the village leaders and has full details on the event."

Willow sank into her chair at the mention of Ulaq, her face falling. Pantheon too grew morose and across from the pair, Ellandu'el's expression barely changed. Only the tiniest of twitches were seen to flit over her features as Ulaq stood up on her left. Willow's hands clenched Pantheon's fingers and she gulped hard as Ulaq began to speak.

"Thank you, Elder Lady Rose," he replied, gathering up a pile of papers that had been sat in front of his place. Rifling through the top few pages for a brief moment, he lifted a sheet out, studied it and then looked up at all the Council members save for Willow. "As Lady Rose has just stated, Elder Willow stands accused of theft and inciting panic amongst the populace." Willow opened her mouth to speak, but was once again silenced by a raised hand. "Witness reports from no less than three Bavillion villages on the outskirts of the Darkwoods clearly state that between the hours of 0200 and 0300, a giant Black Dragon was seen flying, ridden by a woman with white hair and bright green eyes who later spoke to them alongside the well renowned solider Vampire, Elder Pantheon."

The Human-sized immortal stonily stared across at Ulaq, though otherwise did nothing, yet underneath the table, he stroked the backs of Willow's hands with his thumb. A tiny smile played across her trembling lips and she took in a deep breath.

"The reports go on to say how the villagers were surprised by Pantheon's lax stance on the disturbance and even more shocked that both of you, despite having apologised for causing such fear and panic, got back onto the dragon and flew off, sewing yet more terror through the people. A lot of damage was caused to homes and shops alike as the villagers fled from their homes, taking all they could carry." Pausing for a moment, he placed the sheet down, shook his head and closed his eyes. "I, for one, cannot begin to imagine what utter nonsense was running through your heads, causing such a scene. Your complete disregard for the people's safety and for the law is shocking. It was only by the greatest stroke of luck no-one was killed."

Speaking up in a deep and irritated tone, Pantheon stated, "Your consideration for the fates of mortals is uncharacteristically touching, Elder Ulaq."

The Eldest among them stifled a smile, her shimmering eyes glowing brighter. Willow caught it on her periphery and felt a warmth begin to build in her chest, though she remained silent, her mild trembling easing only an iota. The urge to speak out, to explain that she had not been a thief and never intended any real harm surged up from the depths of her, but her own nerves extinguished any ability to voice her defence.

Ulaq's piercing stare met Pantheon's. "Not at all. As is well known, I do not care one jot for them, however you fail to take into account the full ramifications of your careless actions. I do not. You both acted like fools, the girl especially." Willow's gaze shot to Ulaq with a pained expression, a tear welling in her eye. There it was once more. Although the concerns surrounding her mistreatment from several Elders over her behaviours had been far from her at the time, they came hammering back to the fore at his sharp words. Amakay appeared pensive and Ellandu'el's head turned ever so slightly to her left, her own demeanour darkening whilst Ulaq kept speaking, "Your actions only serve to stir the mortals against us. The last thing we need is for them to put sanctions on our blood donation stations, invest more in the Vampire Hunters and make it harder for us to find places to live outside of Illarien."

"First of all," Pantheon interjected, his face contorting in anger. "You're greatly exaggerating the fallout of this incident. This was something that happened on our own soil, with our people. The Vampire Hunters would never become involved in a purely Bavillion matter. Secondly, Willow's the second oldest of everyone here. She's not a *girl*." Willow's hand squeezed his fingers upon hearing her adoptive father defending her. "She was an adult upon conversion as well, so no matter how you look at it -"

"- How she appears or how old she is is not relevant if she insists on acting like a child and getting the mortals riled up against us," retorted Ulaq, his blazing stare matching the soldier's. "Same can be said for you. Neither of you seem to realise just how serious this issue has become and how difficult our own government will make our lives if we don't deal with this swiftly and decisively."

"I am afraid I have to… *agree* with Elder Ulaq on this occasion," Lady Rose spoke in a strained voice over them, sitting up straight in her chair. Giving both the riled Pantheon and a distraught Willow regretful glances, she continued, "We have to deal with the reality of the situation. When I said that a call for Willow's arrest had been made by our own government, it was personally given to me by our monarch, the Captain, himself."

Willow's already alabaster skin blanched and her hands trembled in her father's cool ones. Black tears of fear and confusion dripped down her cheeks and she shook her head in bewilderment. Her throat clenched so tight she found she could hardly breathe. At that moment she wanted nothing more than to explain herself, but all that escaped her lips was a minuscule squeak.

"His grace explained to me that he would not risk another war with our age-long enemies in the west – the Dragerians," Rose explained, voice laden with solemnity. The vast majority of the Elders tensed at their mention, though some, Pantheon and Ellandu'el included, did not react. "He is concerned that the news of these events, which involve the most prized of dragon species, will reach their ears soon enough, if it hasn't already, and that this will not bode well for any one of us or our allies, the Varndiccoes and the Gords."

Willow could not stop shaking. Her eyes were cloudy with tears as she was plagued with floods of guilt and an icy sensation rising in her. She jumped as she felt Pantheon's arm wrap about her shoulders and draw her towards him. The stares from other Council members served only to deepen her terror. She dreaded what fate they were planning for her. She feared she had caused more harm than she had originally thought. She shuddered over the prospect of having initialised an international conflict, especially with the nation that boasted use of dragons in its army's ranks.

"If left unpunished," spoke Ulaq. "They will certainly seek to engage in full scale war with us once more. The last thing we need is another Dragon War, which I'm sure *Willow* should have no trouble remembering the apocalyptic devastation of the first one."

Willow sobbed and shut her eyes. Pressing herself into Pantheon's barrel chest, she forced herself to speak.

"I… I didn't steal him!" she croaked.

There was a brief moment of uncomfortable silence amongst those at the table before Ulaq finally spat, "That's absurd. The Black Dragons live only on Mount Fortis and in the rest of the Dragerian's lands. They are bred and trained from birth by their Court's Dragon Masters and as such are closely watched and maintained. There is no way you could not have stolen one. You certainly didn't go up and ask politely. The important question is why did you do it?"

"But I didn't! I promise!" she blurted out, throat clearing and looking up from Pantheon's chest to her accuser.

"I can vouch for her presence in Illarien every *single* day for the last several *weeks*," boomed Pantheon. "Let alone the fact, which I can also account for, she's not left Illarien or the borders of the Darkwoods in who knows how many months! She couldn't possibly have gone and stolen -"

"- *You* don't get a say!" Sylvia interrupted. "Your bias is clear and we can trust you no more than we can her."

"Agreed," said Ulaq. "Now I repeat my question – why did you do it?"

"I didn't!" pleaded Willow. "He came to me! He was flying about Illarien on his own and I ran out to welcome him to the forest -"

"- You what?!" coughed Ulaq, placing his hands on the heavy table.

Willow looked around the table, her eyes widening in fear she would not be believed. Indeed most of the Elders bore looks of incredulity. Seeing this, she continued more timidly, "H-he s-saw me waving and landed in the outskirts of the Darkwoods. I... ran to him and... he strode up to me." Her breath caught in her throat as she felt Pantheon's hand stroking her back. With renewed calm, she continued her recollection. "We looked at each other for a bit then I reached out to touch him and he... he lowered his head to my hand."

There were snorts and grunts of disbelief scattered around the table. Ellandu'el's previous shadowy expression gave way to one of encouragement and the warmth of her smile permeated Willow's state, easing her fear. Amakay and Lady Rose held similar appearances, with the latter doing her best to maintain her objective professionalism.

"You truly expect us to believe a Black Dragon," Ulaq argued. "The fiercest and deadliest of all its kin, native to lands a thousand miles to the west, just happened to show up here of all places then *let* you take it for a ride?"

"Not it, *him*!" Willow corrected, her eyebrows arched. "The dragon is a him. And he knelt down and -"

"- Enough!" shouted Ulaq, waving a hand. "We've heard enough of this childish nonsense. This is not a fairy tale. Besides, it's irrelevant."

"Is it?" Ellandu'el asked, her deep melodic voice turning the heads of all present. A hush fell upon the chamber and she leaned forward. "No theft was committed. Besides, I think we all know the dragon will have flown home by now regardless. They are free to roam after all, unusual as it may be for them to fly this far east. The Dragerians would therefore not have noticed one missing nor would they heed the rumours of peasants, regardless of what our Captain fears – I wonder how our monarch found out about this in the first place..." She raised an eyebrow at Ulaq and stared through half closed eyes at him. "Such a remote incident involving peasants that would not normally concern him or even be worth considered being brought to his attention? This accompanied by greatly exaggerated consequences leading him to panic, summon Elder Lady Rose and call for an arrest? I wonder indeed. The only thing I'm beginning to think is irrelevant, Elder Ulaq, is the cause for fear over potential war. So do us all a favour -" Her colourful eyes suddenly burned with an intensity that made Willow gulp. "-and cut the bullshit."

Ulaq reciprocated the glare. Willow sat up and felt awash with relief, though felt rather silly for not having realised sooner the obviousness of Ellandu'el's logic. As she made a squeak of reprieve, Ulaq's hands on the table turned into tight fists.

"Very well," he replied, his voice not displaying his rage. "Yet whilst the dragon might have returned, we cannot ignore the fact she caused widespread panic amongst the people and then lied to them about being sorry for it as they both immediately got back on the damned thing!"

"I never lie!" called Willow. "And I couldn't just leave my friend there since he was scaring those people."

Ulaq shut his eyes and pinched the bridge of his nose, "Your… *friend*?"

"Well… yes," answered Willow, looking about the room.

Ellandu'el coughed and covered her mouth with her hand to stop herself from grinning. Lady Rose, posture perfect as ever, clenched her jaw to stifle a smile. Amakay, on the other hand, did not hold back. She burst out laughing and was more than happy to receive a look of disgust from Ulaq. Willow turned to face her and for the first time that evening, her grin lit up the room, yet there were several more besides Ulaq who maintained a cold demeanour, none more so than Sylvia. Her lips curled up in a revolted sneer and her violet eyes rolled.

Taking in a measured breath, Ulaq reopened his eyes and said, "The fact of the matter is this: You ignorantly terrorised our own people and regardless of the fact you apologised for it we still have to commit to some form of sentence or we'll be allowing the mortals to use this as leverage against us. This was still ordered from the Captain himself, don't forget."

"What measure of sentencing do you propose for an act of causing panic?" inquired Lady Rose, turning her head up to Ulaq.

Ulaq sighed and stood up straight, his stormy expression chilling Willow to her bones.

"If we are to truly show our commitment to the safety and well being of the mortals, we will have to ensure there can be no

172

room for them to doubt our resolve," he spoke. Pausing for a moment, he turned to face Lady Rose. "I move to have her struck from the Council and banished indefinitely from Illarien and all its lands."

"No!" cried Willow, aghast. She was echoed by several other Elders and her hands moved from Pantheon to claw at the edges of the table. Once more liquid obsidian gushed from her eyes and she shook her head. "Illarien is my home! You can't! I love this place!" She looked to Ellandu'el. She sat still and silent, with an illogical calm that worried Willow. Just then, Pantheon stood up, protesting the proposal whilst others supported it just as fervently. Willow, however, struggled to hear them. The nightmare of never seeing the trees, the shrubs, the Evernight, the flowers and every creature and friend she had flooded her heart. Yet, as Willow started to sink into herself, the eyes of Ellandu'el roved in her direction with a light that banished her inner-most terrors. Ellandu'el then stood up, dissolving the roars of dispute and the other Elders returned to their seats.

"This has gone on long enough," she addressed them. Her face icing over in impatience and disgust, she turned to Ulaq. "I told you, my ever wayward child, to cut the bullshit. That meant all of it. So tell us, what is really going on here?"

Ulaq frowned and shook his head. "Nothing more than what I've already said. I'm doing my best to preserve our current way of life from mortal interference -"

"- *No*," said Ellandu'el. Her stare struck Ulaq with an air of complete knowing. "You're always up to something, and your opposition for such a trivial matter, especially one which, at its core, is representative in a way of Vampire superiority over mortals, stinks to the Pits of the Dead. Had any other Elder done this, you would have supported them for causing panic and fear. This is an immature personal vendetta against Elder Willow, plain and simple. My question before was a rhetorical one. I know full well what your problem is, as do most of us. As I said, this has gone on long enough. I will *not* permit you to ruin her life over your difference in ideals."

Willow sat dumbfounded in her chair, ears glued to her friend's every word. Feeling Pantheon once more placing his arm about her, she waited with bated breath for the answers to her many questions. In the moment Ulaq stood up once again to speak, Willow felt her father stroke her shoulder and heard his deep voice in her mind.

It's ok, Willow. Know you are loved by me and I will always be proud of you.

I know, Daddy. But why-? Willow responded.

"Have it your way," Ulaq replied to Ellandu'el. Taking his venomous stare from his Maker, he addressed the whole group, his every word bearing disdain. "I gladly confess to an obliquitous method of ridding our Council of a *blasphemer* – a heretical filth who insults the very soil of Illarien with their every footstep and breath." He jabbed a finger in Willow's stunned direction without looking at her. Willow froze and gasped. "The childish lover of Life. A traitor who whiles away eternity tending to all living things and valuing Life over Death. She has no right to sit at this table nor to bear the blood of Inter to begin with. Her very existence is an affront to Inter and everything we stand for! Many of us feel this way and it is high time this problem was addressed!"

Willow sat transfixed, tears streaming down her cheeks. Her father clasped her to him and the electrifying tension in the room amplified to new heights. Suddenly everything fell into place in her head. Every foul deed they had enacted towards her made sense. A deep sickening weight fell in her stomach and her tears splashed forth all the more the further the extent of their reviling of her unveiled itself in her head.

"She is the only one of us ever to have chosen their eye colour," Ulaq continued, raising his voice as calls of support and disagreement mingled in the air. "Not a sin in and of itself, yet her choice was nothing more than an unforgivable reminder of her passion for living things. I refuse to look at her for this very reason and am not alone in doing so – her *green* irises were chosen because she loves the colour of new-born leaves! Of *Life*! Do you know what those unholy orbs remind us of? The *filth* of the White Witches! Of the entire damnable Sarain Sisterhood!"

Willow buried her face in her hands and sobbed amidst the

rising cacophony of heated debate. Pantheon joined in the vocal fray, but would not let go of Willow. Ellandu'el, Lady Rose and Amakay headed the arguments against the main opposition in Sylvia and Allaenia. What exactly was said was lost on Willow as she cried so hard all she could hear were her own heartbroken thoughts and the piercing words of Ulaq. She could not believe so many of them had held such contempt for her for so long, especially after all the kindness she had shown them. She had believed it was because of her energetic attitude they were irritated by her and had no idea it was something far more rancorous. Her mind ran with the fear that this was the end. She could never deny her love for all living things, yet this had always been equalled by her love of the dead. She held both so very close. That's why she had been made. Unable and unwilling to deny her passions, Willow concluded that her time in Illarien was over and even if she were to stay, it would never be the same. Not after knowing what they all thought of her.

"I had hoped to do this subtlety, but alas that has failed," shouted Ulaq. "So let's try it more direct – We'll hold a vote: Should we try this girl for blasphemy and rid ourselves of a naive, childish heretic or not?"

Natalie's Focus

(The following are the only surviving extracts of the diary of one "Natalie Folyra", recovered from remains of the Vampire Hunter hall in Huile in the year 3243 by the Lady Rose. Stored in the Archive in the same year.)

Veltas 16th 1193

So yeah… I've no fucking clue what to write down here. I feel like an idiot doing this, but it's what the Sarain here advised me to do to help with my recovery. Sorry, I shouldn't be rude, she does have a name: Lieutenant Raelya, resident White Witch of the Vampire Hunter branch here in Huile (which is in the plains just west of the Fortress Cliffs). She's a warrior medic. First Sarain and White Witch I've ever met too. I always thought they'd be pacifists due to their devotion to Saraanjova, but she showed me that even the Daughters of the Goddess of Life herself can be dangerous. Apparently she is single-handedly responsible for the deaths of twenty five Vampires, which reassures me I've signed up with the right people. It was her who helped me find a place here amongst the Vampire Hunters a month ago.

I don't even know where to begin with this. I swear, if it weren't for her kindness and insistence it would be cathartic for me, I'd scrap this whole diary thing and keep it inside. Yeah, I guess I just proved her point.

Since I don't care to unload everything that happened in that… nightmare, right now, I'll get that out of my system another time and just skip to the part where I met up with this group here in Huile after fleeing that place.

After following the directions of locals, who probably helped out of fear because I looked like a fucking mess and have obviously unnatural eyes, I found the building I'm currently living in around the centre of town and just walked right in to the reception. I know their prejudices so I didn't expect a warm welcome, although I wasn't planning on giving them any trouble as I needed their help (still do).

Raelya, alone in the hall, was there behind the desk and sat on her shoulder was a huge four-winged bird; a Yui she later told me. She looked up smiling from her work, oddly unperturbed by my dishevelled appearance, and stated that she'd been waiting for me to arrive. I wondered how she knew. She just exchanged glances with her bird and explained that it had witnessed her on its nightly rounds and everything the bird saw, she saw. It's taken some getting used to, watching those two mimic each other. It was my first understanding of the powers of the White Witches – the Nature Control. Not a very imaginative name for it, but it's accurate at least. Really cool too. Yet that small pleasantry didn't last long once I walked up to the desk and she saw my eyes. She was visibly disturbed by them, and calmly asked for my name. I told her, then explained I had come seeking their help and to also join their ranks as I was hunting an immensely powerful Vampire, most likely an Elder. Raelya stated that my grievance was a highly serious matter and that I ought to have proof as the Elders were politically protected under various international and Bavillion laws. I explained that the only proof I had would be my memories and that this Vampire was not like the others. I then stated she called herself The Acar Vanta. Raelya gave me a long stern stare that I thought meant she did not believe me. She asked if I had been made by this person. I said yes, to my disgust and shame, so my eyes were another point of evidence. I repeated my desire to join their ranks and hunt the Acar Vanta down. Raelya asked me to follow her to recount my story to the others.

It is a small cell of the larger organisation, with its main HQ in Aldvon and as such there's not many of them stationed this far out. There were seven of them in the office, including Raelya. When they first saw me, a filth covered Vampire, I thought if it hadn't been for Raelya conveying the fact I was there to talk, they'd have attacked me immediately. I think one day I might actually find it funny. It sounds like a set-up line for a bad joke. After about ten minutes of trying to convince them I meant no harm to anybody, I began to recount my experiences with the Acar Vanta, leaving out no details. On one hand I was grateful that the Anti-Inter was recognised as a being to fear not only by Interists, but also by those who worshipped Saraanjova, like Raelya and a few others in the group. On the other, proving to them that the person who made me was indeed an Acar Vanta of legend was another matter. The leader of this cell, Major Caulder, does not believe she is, though admittedly I am uncertain myself. I believe it's possible whoever the fucking Head Mistress is... she's just using the title to get people to fear her, even though her hatred towards Interism seemed to be genuine. That being said, I don't know if the stories originated from her or if she just uses them. Even if they did start with her, it doesn't prove she's an all-powerful being – she could have always been just some pissed off bitch who happens to have frighteningly immense Vampirical power and the stories formed up around her from superstitious people at the time... However, I find that line of thought to be far more disturbing because it would mean she had been made either by one of the oldest Elders, who are unquestionably devout to Inter, or even more unnerving, she had been made by Inter Itself...

I feel like I'm just rambling here, but this trail of thought was instrumental as it's the reason Raelya trusts my version of events and is the only reason I'm a member of the Vampire Hunters, albeit just as part of a small separate unit. Whilst we discussed the topic of the reality of the Acar Vanta, Raelya proposed my eyes be used as proof, not only for my version of events but also for proving the Head Mistress was an actual Acar Vanta. Her argument got very technical and I cannot recall all of it, but the gist was this:

My eyes were identical to those of my Maker: in fact, all Vampires share the same eyes as whomsoever converted them. Mine and hers are a mixture of the darkest black and purest silver, which Raelya pointed out are the very same colours as the Interal Flames. She had to explain to me what those are: The purest Flames of Death, existing only in the Pits of the Dead, aka Inter's Realm. They are therefore different from the normal Black Flames Vampires normally conjure, which are, as stated, just black (and far less potent). So from Raelya's perspective, that's proof the Head Mistress is The Acar Vanta of legend.

Whilst she believes Inter made her to be Its antithesis, I pointed out that the Head Mistress repeatedly explained that her heritage came from Vertio and that she was, in fact, the second Eldest. Yet, and even I have to concede to some degree on this, the Head Mistress was known for lying (as I frequently mentioned amidst tears in my accounts to them) and so her true Maker was unknown. That being said, Caulder pointed out that the fact that I, and by extension, my Maker had no whites to our eyes meant something very unusual – only Vertio, his Fledglings and those made directly by Inter Itself had those traits and theirs are solid black, whereas mine have streaks of silver moving about in them. Additionally, the Twins, the second and third Eldest Vampires (at least according to history), were given the power by Inter to change the colour of the eyes of their Fledglings at will, but only ever have done so in the irises. The Twins were created with this ability to ensure the purity of Vampire Law, which stemmed from Vertio: Only those who had the pure black could inherit his authority if something were ever to happen to him. Due to the fact no other Vampire had been created with eyes like mine, Caulder uncomfortably proposed that it meant one of two troubling things: One, that either the Twins had made the Head Mistress and altered her eyes in a way that was previously assumed impossible then denied ever creating such a monster, or two, that Inter Itself had created her. Raelya proposed a third, equally disquieting theory – that Vertio himself had done the deed, just as the Head Mistress claimed. Being the First, his powers were uniquely potent and it's possible he had the power to alter eye colour as well, which would account for the Head Mistress' story. Whichever way, their possible reasons for doing so and the unimaginably horrific consequences that would come to pass if these outcomes were true sent shivers through all of us. Furthermore, they did nothing to prove the validity of the claim she was an Acar Vanta.

It was due to these implications that Caulder agreed to allow me to join but would not accuse the Elders, or their god, of creating an Acar Vanta due to the political shitstorm that would result. I suspect he loves the idea of a Vampire Elder conspiracy and would like nothing more than to bring them all down as being culpable to the suffering the Head Mistress caused. However, in light of no solid evidence accompanied by the very real threat of such accusations instigating another Holy War, he is choosing to sit on it and do nothing. I think he's a cowardly, racist asshole for not going as far up with this as he could, but at least he did ratify my joining as he wants all bases covered, so I'll give him that. He did also acknowledge that, regardless of whether the Head Mistress was an Acar Vanta or not, my accounts meant that there was an extraordinarily dangerous Vampire on the loose that needed taking down and my unique understanding of her would be critical for any investigation and eventual termination. I am only too happy to oblige on the latter. I will kill her personally and I'll *make her* remember me in the afterlife.

So now I'm under Raelya's command and have been going through basic military combat training. She knows as well as I do, that Vampires' powers increase with age, and the Head Mistress has several centuries at least on me, therefore if we, if *I*, am to stand any chance against her I need to learn unconventional tactics and to take her out without my inferior Cors. However long it takes, she will be training me to use all manner of weapons, cutting edge technology and tactical use of my magic. I cannot overstate my luck in finding Raelya – not only is she the kindest person I've ever known apart from my sister… She is also an immortal and an expert Vampire Slayer, giving her a unique and experienced perspective which is what I need right now. I asked her how she was immortal because I used to think only Vampires held that ability, but she only answered that it was because she was a White Witch. I could tell it made her uncomfortable to discuss, so I dropped it. I hope to find out someday, though I'll never force her to tell me.

Tomorrow, I continue hand-to-hand combat training. Our investigation will take us to the ruins of the school in the forests beneath the Vraedric Table (to find any possible leads on the Head Mistress) and as a result, Raelya's been training me to be prepared to defend myself against the resident Horrors of Vraedric. According to her and the others I was lucky to have made it out without being eaten by the those monstrosities. Following my account, Raelya became very interested to know how exactly the Acar Vanta managed to construct anything, let alone a fortress, in the middle of Horror infested territory. Even for Elders they'd pose a threat in large numbers. I admit, I've always wondered myself how she did it and am afraid of what the answer might be. So our job is to get me prepared enough to venture back out there and search for any leads, likely using the Horrors as a starting point. Since my Cors will be undeveloped for some years to come, Raelya's focus is on giving me basic combat tactics and training.

I've some experience already, thanks (in a twisted way) to the Head Mistress, but nothing as militaristic as what Raelya offers. My mistakes are numerous. I keep letting my guard down, my moves are all sloppy and my reaction times are not nearly fast enough, even though I'm undead. Though the hardest part is my mental health. I have what Raelya terms as a form of traumatic stress which results in me waking up screaming, flinching and having flashbacks in sparring. It's fucking annoying. Raelya's a great teacher though. She's incredibly patient, and uses her magic to calm me down and... make me feel... *warm inside*? I don't know how to describe it. Anyway, that's why she told me to keep a diary. To help offload my thoughts onto paper. I think it's helping. I feel better after all this... I think I'll continue doing so, but not every day.

Tilestra 1st 1193

Combat training is improving (I'll likely be ready for the trip to the ruins next month) and Raelya has become a really good friend to me. Her bird too (his name is Ray), who seems to enjoy following me whenever we go out. In our spare time, he has taken a liking to perching on my right shoulder and gently brushing my hair with his sharp beak. He has, however, pecked at my ear on occasion, which really hurts. Still, I really like him and he has managed to make me smile. A rare feat.

Last night Raelya and I went for a free-running race across

the rooftops of the town which ended in her winning by a hilariously large margin and me catching up some time later covered in bruises. So after we had a laugh about that (which I'm only able to do around her), we relaxed on top of a random building and had a deep talk about our lives and our experiences down the years. She told me she was over two hundred years old, kept youthful and alive through a Gift called the Life Drain. Another unimaginative name, but again to the point. It's a power that only White Witches possess and unlike my kind, they have to actively use it to maintain their immortality. Whilst Vampires live on whether they feed or not (as we only use blood to maintain our energy levels and youth), White Witches have to regularly extract energy from others. Apparently, at lower intensities, the Life Drain leaves their victim, or volunteers in her case, in a state of weariness that can last for days, but at higher levels it will make the drained person visibly age, eventually turning to living stone, until their energy levels naturally replenished over time. I immediately understood why she was so hesitant about sharing that information with me – Sarains are well known for being healers and preferred to distance themselves from Vampires. It was a controversial topic and decision. I'm kept alive by design, but Raelya lives on by choice, opting to drain others. It is a terrible responsibility for her to have and I don't judge her for it, yet she fears others will. Due to the impactful ethical ramifications the Life Drain could cause, Raelya not only stated her exclusive use of volunteers (from our own ranks normally) but also went into detail regarding the one who taught her such power. Raelya had been greatly honoured to have personally been trained in all the Gifts, not just the Life Drain, by The White Witch, Talin Kvacha. I didn't know who that was, so she explained that Talin was the first and most powerful of their kind and was an overseer of all White Witches, ensuring their power was used for the right reasons down the ages. I think Raelya thinks of her as her adoptive mother the way she talks about her. She then asked (in a non-judgemental way) for me to clarify my ultimate reasons for hunting the Acar Vanta, wanting to know if I was training for the right purposes as well. I had stated many times before that revenge was my main motivation as well as to protect other helpless people, but now that had changed slightly since I had spent some time amongst good people who cared for me and helped to heal my… *damaged* mind and helping to provide some clarity. I told her that I'm not doing this for justice or revenge. Revenge is a wasted endeavour, not least because it's something *she'd* approve of and if I'm to take her down I will *never* become like her in the process. Her every putrid edict is effluence spewing from her mephitic, pestilential soul - a virulent stream of *unforgivable malevolence*! I will *never* stoop to her *fucking level*! I'll take her down the right way for the right reasons, or not at all. Secondly, justice is a naive ideal that people cling to. There's no justice in the world or afterlife. I said I would kill her because she needs to die – for the sake of protecting future people from her unpardonable evil and that's exactly what I intend to do.

Raelya, an experienced psychologist on top of everything else, also clocked that my guilt was a massive factor as I was trying to make it up to my sister in my head. I couldn't help but cry and she held me. I *don't* like being touched anymore, but she's the exception and has been for a couple months now. She just held me silently for ages. I admitted she was right – and she is, completely. I always think of my sister and how I cannot bring myself to face her. I am still haunted by those I killed and the three High Priestesses. Raelya… I swear she's the only thing keeping me afloat in my head at the times rage does not. She has even helped with my nightmares by entering them herself using the Gift called Dream Striding. She fights my horrors alongside me. I don't deserve a friend like her. I admit I need her. I never thought I'd allow her to enter my head – not after what the Head Mistress has done to me and others – but after a month of sporadic sleeplessness, I gave in and let her enter. I don't regret it for a moment, though it was uncomfortable and emotionally painful at first. She has seen most of the memories that I relive over and over each day and so we bonded very quickly. I've begun to sleep soundly after that. I owe her so much.

Sahl 15th 1194

We've returned from the ruins. I don't think I will sleep for days now.

Raelya and myself passed across the forest borders under the Vraedric Table armed with repeating crossbows with Ray scouting ahead from the canopy. Raelya utilised Nature Control, extending her sensory experience in a hundred foot radius around us, acting as a form of motion detector – I don't know how it fully works. She described it as extending her nervous system throughout the foliage, roots and branches to literally feel every movement in their vicinity. Her eyes had a green tint to them whilst she did this, which I thought was oddly comparable to Vampires' glowing irises. My own senses kept watch for Horrors but thankfully none were about. Stealth training by both Raelya and (as much as I hate to admit it) the Head Mistress was put to use to traverse the sun-deprived woodland. The further we ventured toward the ruins, the darker it became till even the stars were gone, as the skies above were obstructed. Innumerable thick rock columns, sprouting from the earth to the clouds, support the nation-sized flat slab of stone atop them, resembling a table, hence the name. On top of this geological anomaly sat the city of Vraedric, where the main bulk of the Horror species resided. Thankfully, where we were underneath there lived fewer, but even so, we had all grown up on the stories of their viciousness which is why Raelya insisted on my training. I agree with her, and I do believe I was lucky to escape from here last time.

We arrived a while later at the ruins. Upon arrival, I felt a mixture of anger and fear... I don't think I'll ever stop being afraid of her, no matter how much I hate her, but I consider that wise. As much as I burn inside, I am fully aware of her capabilities and to rush in without training or strategy would be throwing my life away: A lesson I have had to remind myself of.

The first thing I noticed was that there were no bodies nor bones. Only ash and rubble. Raelya surmised this was the Horrors' work as they eat everything and then use the bones for habitat and tool construction, among other things. Together we scoured the site for anything that might give us a lead on the Acar Vanta's location. We turned up nothing, but Raelya is an expert tracker and we picked up the trail of the Horrors and so we followed them. We both knew that the Acar Vanta had some measure of influence over them, or else she'd never have been able to construct anything in their lands. I still shiver at the notion of this.

We traced them for half a night through the forest. Raelya had to use Ray's predatory eyesight just to see through the darkness. After travelling north for some time, we came upon an outcrop of rocks covered in moss, ivy and various gigantic fungi. Hidden within was a cave. The two of us instantly recognised the stench of decomposition that filtered up from below. My ears picked up nothing but once I turned to Raelya, I could hear her heart pounding. I then looked at her face and saw fear in her eyes for the first time. Obviously sensing some threat that I couldn't, she signalled a retreat... I... I stupidly grew angry and begrudgingly followed her order but as soon as we were out of earshot of the cave, I loudly confronted her on why we didn't go in to get the lead we needed. I... was enraged and said some things I regret. She then calmly replied something along the lines of:

"That cave is a Horror Hive. There are scores of them, possibly over a hundred. We cannot take them on right now! We're equipped to take on a few at once at most. And if the Acar Vanta is in there – however unlikely, and is as powerful as you say she is (and I believe you), we will not get out alive. Let's make no mistake – this is a strategy of years – she has centuries of power on you and you must therefore acquire a substantial quantity of your own as well as become the best you possibly can in conventional combat before even considering a confrontation. This is ignoring the added complication of a horde of aberrations that she may well have control over. If we find a lead that's fresh we cannot chase after it now because you are not ready to face her."

I argued through tears and ire that I'd waited enough. That I had just sat and watched her commit unforgivable atrocities before and refused to do that anymore! I said that the more time we spent just training, the more people she would bring untold suffering upon. I couldn't just wait anymore!

She replied, "You must! Or you will just throw your life and your chance at ending her away. It's the *highest* cost yet an unavoidable one. If you go after her when you're not ready you'll waste your life and all their suffering would have been for nothing. We've the best chance of stopping her out of all others – we *have* to take the slow road and build up your powers! Please… I know patience is an unfair thing to ask for, but Life Herself is unfair. We have to do the best with what we have. We *will* end this one day. I promise! We will waste no time with idleness. We owe it to the dead and the living. Just place your trust in me."

As soon as she said those final words, I screamed loudly in a panic and fell to my knees. Flashing memories of the Acar Vanta speaking that exact phrase to the students made me into a shaking wreck… I feel pathetic. I'm meant to destroy her, but I can't even… Fuck this… I know what I need to do to recover. I *won't* let her own my mind - I told Raelya as much there and then. I felt… feel awful for yelling at her and I feel ashamed for having such a reaction. I understand it's not my fault, but I just want her out of me so badly. I feel like she's still influencing my life even though she's no longer here and it makes me feel disgustingly vulnerable! I *hate* her.

Raelya understands and is helping me heal with various magical practices as well as more clinical therapy methods. I mentioned this briefly in my first entry.

We left the cave. I'm to train for now. I know she was right – IS right. I still don't know if I can do this. I am in agony. I hate this waiting! I *hate* it all and when I'm finally ready I will make the Acar Vanta, or whoever she is, pay for every soul she's tortured!

I'm so sorry.

Hispal 3rd 1210

Ray died last night. Old age. I don't know what to say. He was a great friend to us both. I'm… not well. Raelya's not doing great either. We're bunking in the same room as neither of us want to be on our own. She was so close to him… I hope I'll be able to help her.

Silent training. Focus… I'm not focused. Fuck it. I'm off to sleep.

Gonla 23rd 1211

We had a late memorial for Ray today. Had to postpone it due to a Vampire-related massacre in the Baldrinian Capital, Lios. The deceased were all members of one of the criminal families around here. I can't go into specifics, but it looks like there was an inside conflict in their ranks and a Vampire finished the job brutally. Odds aren't likely it has anything to do with her though and even more unlikely that there will be any evidence of her being involved. Who knows if she's even here in the Land of the Baldrinians? I'm tired of no progress with the investigation. I just want her dead ALREADY!!! How many more has she killed whilst we waste time in what's increasingly feeling like a vain pursuit? I shouldn't be like this. I'm only like this because I miss Ray. Raelya hasn't bonded with any other animals since his passing and I'm deeply worried about her. I'm missing Ray and her giving me identical weird looks.

Fyntynne 12th 1214

It's been 20 years since the cave. My patience is exhausted. It has been for a long time. I can successfully incinerate multiple targets at a time, my aim with the repeating crossbow is perfect and my Shields can withstand several flurries of blows so I'm going back *tonight*. I'm not telling Raelya – I believe she will just stop me.

What I saw… It's far worse than I ever imagined - She has a damned *cult of Horrors* worshipping her as their malevolent *goddess*! And not just Horrors… I… CAN… NOT... FUCKING... *believe* what I saw! She's… a DAMNED MONSTER!

I… I'm still trembling slightly… Shit… If I didn't have a desire to kill her before, I certainly do now.

I made a mistake. I am not strong enough yet. Raelya's right… again. The slow game… SHE is torturing me still… Fuck I don't know how many bodies were in there. We were fucking lucky…

Wasting paper… Raelya tracked me down – figured I'd try something like this sooner or later so caught up to me fairly quick. We reached the cave together after having an argument where I stated that I was ready by now to take on Horrors at least. Raelya… I didn't see it at the time, but she's far wiser than I am… I've let anger and desperation go to my head. Horrors are not mere animals and pose more of a threat than a rampaging newborn Vampire. They're not individually stronger, faster or deadlier – their large numbers, heightened senses and fierce loyalty to their own species makes them far more formidable than I ever knew. I thought I'd be able to sneak in and out and that there'd be only a few. I was an idiot. Had Raelya not come… I was damn lucky the Acar Vanta was not there.

We entered the cave. I assumed it would be just a small cavern or like an animal den, but no. It was a maze in total darkness. Raelya used Agungdrian-designed nightvision contacts to see – always thinking ahead. We followed the paths that stank most of entropy which eventually led us to a cavern the size of the assembly hall. Just like in the school there was a plinth, upon which sat a low stone altar… fuck… I'm feeling sick... Raelya and I both had to stop ourselves from screaming at what adorned it – the Horrors had arranged a pile of corpses… No, not *arranged*… They *fashioned* a giant inverted septagram out of decaying skinned bodies pinned to a wooden frame! I've no idea how many dead were there… It took all I had not to vomit and run. The frame was… secured to the walls and ceiling in all directions by varying lengths of what… were the victims… *flesh*. Torches were stuck into the seven points of the septagram – they illuminated the place. I will *NEVER* be able to unsee what I saw! Damn her! In what Raelya considers is typical Horror fashion, behind and on either side of this nightmarish offering were piled the bones of countless Humans, Mensmall and Baldrinians. Around the chamber were several bone totems sticking out sporadically from the floor, with a few still in varying stages of decay. Neither of us could move for ages and I dryly sobbed, but then Raelya tapped me gently, almost making me scream out loud. I normally do not associate Raelya with fear, but the look in her eyes when I faced her… Her voice shook as she said we needed to search for specific clues to follow. I still was transfixed so she took my hand to calm me down. I felt waves of guilt seize me… looking at them all…

There was nothing to be found. Our search was wasted. Then the hordes arrived. Where they'd been I don't know or care, but they swarmed us from all directions… Their skin… shined in the fire light… So many teeth.

They're fucking horrible creatures and I detest them! They attacked us without hesitation or restraint, madly slashing at us with their long razor-sharp claws and teeth. Some… Oh fuck I don't ever want to… never again. My Shields saved us from the initial wave before Raelya summoned the roots from the trees above to come and cage them in, but wood could not hold them for long. I don't remember exactly how we escaped. I remember fire and blood and Raelya blinding me and the Horrors with her White Flames. Thankfully it didn't touch me and whilst it's light doesn't have UV properties, the Horrors didn't know this so immediately backed off, as they're as susceptible to sunlight as Vampires. It wouldn't take them long to learn it couldn't harm them, so we ran as hard as we could towards the fresh air blowing through the tunnels. I remember them about to reach us at the exit when Raelya commanded more roots to block the hole. At that point I shook myself out of my fearful daze… fucking useless… and carried her whilst running at top speed. Never again… I refuse to let fear freeze me! I thought my therapy would be complete by now.

Raelya's still just as shook up as me. We relayed our findings to Caulder, but he just said that was what Horrors do… he's discounting the fact that the inverted septagram was clearly an insult to the Seven Tenets of Inter. I'd go to higher authorities if I could, but as it is, I can't. *Fucking politics.*

I feel sick. I'm worried about Raelya. I owe her another apology. I shouldn't have gone alone.

How did… *does* she influence the Horrors? I don't think I need to ask why – she's a monster same as them… worshipping her… I guess that answers the former too. Maybe I was wrong about her… Maybe she *is*… an Acar Vanta.

Fyntynne 15th 1235

We're officially under new management. Caulder retired, *finally*, and his replacement is a Human, Colonel Thestria. She has been officially brought up to speed on our team's primary purpose and status in our investigation. Whilst Caulder was unwilling to take us as seriously as we ought to be, the Colonel is providing us with additional funding and access to the highest tier anti-Vampire weaponry – which apparently was never even held on site. Once Raelya informed her of that, she was pissed off, and even more so after she found out we were hunting one of the oldest Vampires without the aid of such gear. She's put in an order for HQ to deliver a consignment of their rarest and most effective weapon: the Nectar of Saraanjova. It is literally the birthing juices of the Goddess Herself, secreted from the Portal of Saraanjova in the Woods of Summer – the holiest site for the Varndicco and Sarains. It's a lubricant that can be applied to almost any weapon such as a stake, an arrow, a bolt etc and it cuts straight through a Vampire's Shield Cor like a knife through butter and will otherwise burn our skin as if it were tinder. It's pure Life and is therefore the ultimate weapon against the undead. We will have our weapon to end the sickness of the Acar Vanta forever. It has been field tested on Vampires several centuries old with 100% effectiveness. I'll have to be careful how

I handle it – one drop on my skin could cause unimaginable pain and possible irreparable damage. Raelya has only had to use this weapon once before and she swears by it.

Other lethal tech was ordered as well, including a tailor made, upgraded repeating crossbow with extended magazine and anti-jamming gears for me, straight from the master bow makers in the Fortress of the Sycamore – Capital of the Varndicco. Raelya was provided with a new set of hybrid alloy, Agungdrian-adapted Ancient tech armour with a spider-silk bodysuit underneath (which I've learned is both a fire and bullet-proof material, extremely light weight, flows like water and makes for not just practical armour but also a highly coveted fashion piece). We're eager to try out our new gear in sparring tonight. Lastly, the Colonel promoted Raelya to Captain and me to her Lieutenant. We both think it's about damn time.

Dellent 24th 1257

Bharnius Family investigation ongoing. I cannot put details of the case into my diary due to security reasons, but I can say it's frustrating the fuck out of me!! It's clear they know something about someone matching, at least in part, the description of the Acar Vanta. After fucking ages with no clues, this turns up at last! Raelya has gone out tonight to pursue some lines of investigation regarding them. I hope she turns up something valuable. Meanwhile, I'm stuck here guarding this building myself. The Colonel is unwell and the others have all been dispatched to Lios to contend with some homicidal maniacs belonging to Elder Ulaq's bloodline (the one with yellow eyes). I've no idea if he's responsible or not and it's not my case anyway… I'm just… venting here now. I record in here less and less as the years have gone by as I don't need it anymore. I just have it as a habit and a way of recording my progress – it helps keep me focused on why I'm here. My goal. Although I admit I don't need my fires stoked as the memories still haunt me every step of the way. It has been years and Raelya has become more than just my closest friend (and therefore something of a distraction). She's more like family now. Not in a relationship way, I just… love her like… my *sister*.

I never got to… I had hoped to see her again – to kill the Acar Vanta and therefore feel able to return to her. Make good on all the sins staining me. I… can't do that anymore. Raelya pulled some strings with some contacts in the Covyn Law Enforcement and found out… she passed on some time ago. At least it was peaceful. I failed her… I FAILED HER like I've failed everyone else! I haven't done enough here! I've sat and laughed and had fun when I should've been training! I thought it was helping me recover, but all it's doing is making me lose my focus on what HAS to be done! Raelya… don't make me lose focus. Oh for *fuck's sake*! What on earth am I thinking!? She's not to blame, so I shouldn't be a bitch about her! I just need patience. Even if we were to find something with the Bharnius Family syndicate, I'm not yet strong or honed enough in my Cors or combat to face her. I have only just managed to be able to match Raelya's White Flames and if I can barely hold my own against a master killer like her, then I stand no chance against the Acar Vanta. Not YET. *I will*.

Dellent 20th 1262

[unknown entry]

Fendivra 12th 1283

I know where she is. She's been right under our fucking noses the whole time! She's operating out of the criminally run city of Mion, just east of here and set into the Fortress Cliffs. According to one of the Bharnius's lackeys (the first one in years to actually know anything), there's a luxurious whorehouse called the House of Sybaris set deep within the city's bowels somewhere run by someone calling themselves the Mother of Whores. Raelya and I interrogated this guy for hours, but he didn't know the precise location. He did, however, know a high class escort from the House who possessed black and silver eyes. It wasn't the Acar Vanta, but it is additional evidence that the Acar Vanta is there in Mion. Makes sense she'd convert people to use as concubines: Vampires are a highly sought after sexual commodity in many circles of society. I'm not sure how I feel about that intellectually but it makes me uncomfortable in my gut. Regardless, we can narrow our investigation at long last! She's in MION! But I'm not taking any chances. As long as we don't push her out now, she's likely to stay put whilst I increase the potency of my Cors and continue my mastery of Vampire Hunting. I'm no longer haunted during combat by my memories of that school. It seems so distant, but I do my best to keep it fresh in my mind as often as I can. Raelya tells me constantly that it's not healthy to force myself to relive the past, but I can't lose it! I need to remember all she's done so when the time comes to end her I will be able to remember the faces of all those I hurt and killed as I take her unlife, bringing the circle at last to a close and make her face the consequences of her cruelty! Her mistake will return to curse her hubris!

All that aside, I know Raelya's right. In order to truly recover, I have to let the pain heal. Not yet – I will continue to ride this pain and righteous anger on a stake straight through her heart! Then I will allow myself to heal. I don't know what I'll do after it's all done… I guess..? No… I cannot afford to think like this now. I'll deal with it when this is all over. Still, the idea of having a future ahead of all this… knowing the end is finally in sight… I cannot help but feel a warmth inside I've not felt since I was a child. Whatever happens, I want stay close to Raelya. She's adopted me as an honorary member of the Sarain Sisterhood! She's… the only family I have left and I have found more and more I'm now also fighting for her. When it comes to the day… I will keep her safe. At all costs.

Ravenaar 10th 1310

This is my final entry as a Vampire Hunter. After tonight, I'm leaving it all behind. My training completed a few months ago and so I focused all my efforts in narrowing the location of the House of Sybaris down. I'm not recording it here on purpose – I don't want you, Raelya, to follow me and I know you will. I'm also Cloaking myself just to be sure. Sister… you saved my life and I love you; I know I tell you often enough, but I want to say it again.

The Acar Vanta is phenomenally more powerful than any Vampire you've ever faced. These past few months I've mentally prepared myself for this moment, reliving my past in my dreams, re-opening old wounds to fuel myself for what must be done, though I am still afraid of her power. Of her incomparable evil. I've kept you at a distance and am doing so now to protect you. I have surpassed you now on every front and am more capable of taking her down than you and I cannot risk losing you. I've lost everyone else. Knowing you're safe and out of harms' way will keep me strong.

If I die… please remember all we've had together. You took me in and made me into the Hunter I am now. Your kindness and love of all life, undead or otherwise, is something that must shine on. A white flame that burns in my heart and will burn in the hearts of others. Who would have ever thought – a Sarain, a White Witch even, and a Vampire working together as friends? As family. Find someone to share eternity with – maybe there's a decent male Elder out there for you! It's not good to be alone. Of course, if I make it, I'll always be your friend, though my part as a Hunter will end. I never wanted any of this. I just wanted a normal life, but I couldn't sit back whilst she was on the loose. She's taken everything from me… well not everything. I have myself and now I have another reason to live on after this is done. Which is why you cannot accompany me to the House.

I am prepared to die, though I certainly do not aim to do so, especially not by her design. Tonight, she will die by my hand. I've waited, trained and burned for 117 years for this moment. I'm prepared.

'*For She was born of love and breathed love and life into the world*' – fitting for what you've done for me. I love you, Sister Hunter. Forgive me.

The Lady of the Sea

O, our tales can ne'er be told
Save to those with hearts a'bold
Or them who yearn and wish to see
Our fair Lady of the Sea!

Ne'er to grace us on the morn
Not one t'see a new day born
She enters only into our sight
As she stands there in the night.

E'er she poses on the stone
Outward looking and all alone
On the edge of our great bluff
With just bare feet upon the rough.

Her billowing hair the fairest gold
Yet nary a strand could e'er be sold
For priceless is she who holds the watch
Always still and not one to hotch.

But our fair Lady of the Sea
Shrouded in veils of mystery
Showing herself at her own will
So rarely seen upon her hill.

Standing eternally at our guard
E'er the muse for poet and bard
Guiding the souls of the glorious dead
At peace our brethren she puts to bed.

Brothers, sisters and all our kin
Whether or not in battles' din
All our folk, she loves us all
And at days' end we hear her call!

So let us farm and plant a seed
And raise our tankards full of mead
For our fair Lady of the Sea
Whom we love and will soon see!

Cinthia's Theft
Year 1176

The journey down hadn't always been easy. Vampires were nimble and able to scale sheer rock faces with ease, yet to do so down the Cliffs of Magnus into the Land of the Mensmall as a young immortal was still a risky endeavour. The endurance required over such a lofty descent as well as the swift reactions required to account for the unexpected were something that tended to be present only in the older generations. Nevertheless, Cinthia had mastered the path both ways long ago without mechanical aides. Now, as she once more clambered her way far down into the glistening green lands below, her limbs moved in a perfect blur, making the descent look like child's play and sending rare surges of adrenaline through her system. A slight tremble in her hands resulting from this made her pause for a moment and look out around her.

The winds whipped her back, rippling her heavy canvas travelling garb and she drew herself in close to the stone to compensate, though the move was more instinctual rather than necessary at her age. She used the moment to glance out and down. A sprawling emerald land stretched away in all directions in the orange glow of the late afternoon and, far Southwest of her position, she could just make out the glinting River Alin as it wound its way down from the Northwest. It would eventually snake through the Darkwoods in the South, though even her sight could not see that far. Her eyes, glowing a little brighter behind her goggles, turned their focus due West. In the distance almost beyond her vision lay her goal: a vast woodland silhouetted by the horizon's warm light. She would follow the rolling green hills and bypass the settlements along the way to reach it. As her gaze hovered over this thin black line upon the very edge of perception, she once more felt a surge pulse through her and a small smile begin to form. Reassessing her grip, she continued her journey down into the verdant landscape below.

As the last tinge of amber flared across the sky, the

immortal's feet landed on gravel. Facing West, Cinthia began her long walk, resisting the itching in her legs to move faster. By the time deep orange turned to lilac and then to a silky violet, Cinthia had reached the first sparsely growing trees bordering the base of the Magnus Cliffs. The conflict between her anticipation and savouring her lengthy journey swirled within Cinthia. With an unsteady hand, she retrieved her flask from her thigh holster, her eyes glowing brighter as she stared across the land doused in the remainder of the day's light. The refreshing crimson poured down her throat in a couple of eager gulps that restored her spent energies and, licking her lips clean, Cinthia found she could hold back no longer. She resealed the flask, replaced it in its holster and bolted off into the night.

It was in the very early hours of the morning that Cinthia's boots became splattered with the mud that bordered a tributary of the River Alin. Knowing her goal lay along its current, she faced the river's downstream course as it raced across the plains due West. Heart pounding, the immortal continued her breakneck speed along the sodden banks, leaping through tangles of rushes and reeds with expert precision.

The rest of the day was spent flying past mixtures of wild lands where smaller woods and grasslands grew untamed, tall and old. They were a blur to the immortal as she rushed past. The occasional small encampment dotted the riverbank and the hills and although the Vampire did not stop to see to whom they belonged, she could readily guess. The Varndicco were known wanderers, both famous and infamous for their nomadic culture and these lands belonged to them. They had very few locations they used as permanent settlements. Their capital, the Fortress of the Sycamore, was one of them. The gargantuan forest ever growing in her sights, her goal, was another.

Once again, the deep purple sky blanketed the atmosphere as the archaeologist set foot upon the borders of the Woods of Summer. Her face lit up and she slowed down whilst passing the first of the living giants. Soft beams of indigo and violet poured through the canopy and sprawling boughs of ancient gnarled oaks, towering sycamores and monolithic ash to splash upon the leaf-strewn floor and the brush that sporadically grew there. Lining almost every metre of the riverbank leaned colossal willows, their creaking limbs dipping into the water like hundreds of caressing fingertips. Even through her heavy mask, she could smell the pollen of the trees and the earthy scent of humus. Her every step was soft there, and not just from her usual stealthy manner, but from the thick layer of fallen leaves and twigs. The sounds of trickling water, rustling leaves in the breath of the evening and the awakening nightlife issued like a welcoming lullaby into her ears and she paused for a moment, taking everything in. She breathed in deep through her nose and slowly turned her head. The beauty filled her with the mild regret she had not made the journey there before, yet this was overwhelmed by the rising excitement within her chest and her face became ever brighter with each passing second. Looking ahead, her pace quickened and she set off into the heart of the forest.

She only followed the river for a short while before it veered off to her left. Lacking a bridge in sight, Cinthia formed a Shield beneath her feet and hovered it over the swirling current. The Vampire continued on foot from there, noticing soon after the first signs of civilization. The rough and age worn stonework of ruins passed by on all sides, from low stone walls to the remnants of houses, stables and barracks. The temptation to examine them closer pulled at her limbs, but she pushed on.

Soon she passed by several large settlements of stone buildings, oaken taverns and enormous canvas tents of various bright colours. Hundreds of Varndiccoes, military and civilian, went about their various businesses. Cloaked, Cinthia walked amongst them, taking in their markets of all manner of foods, pelts and hunting weapons, though by that point most had shut for the evening and the worn dirt paths were filled with people making their way to their respective lodgings and the various inns spread throughout the trees nearby. She was grateful the Woods of Summer was unlike Illarien in this respect as their diurnal habits would make her job even easier.

As she made her way past the final village, the trees suddenly grew far taller and wider than any she had previously seen, some reaching loftier heights than even the canopy of

Illarien. She removed her hood, goggles and mask and her pace slowed to a stop as she gawked at their vast structure. The width of their trunks alone was many times her size and their root systems wound over all the ground like teeming masses of gargantuan pythons. Another difference from the Vampire home city was that these trees, grown from an age so long ago Cinthia could not even guess, were more spaced out, letting in the starlight from the heavens. As a result, the undergrowth was thick in places, and a second canopy of lesser trees dotted the area. Yet it wasn't just these monsters of the flora world that stopped the immortal in her tracks. It was the knowledge that they represented the edge of the Sanctum of the Sarains. Her goal was just ahead.

Cloaking herself heavily now and savouring the final stretch of her journey, Cinthia edged her way over and under the wooden serpents eating the path, her pigtails catching on mosses and fine webs as she did so. She absent-mindedly wiped them off, her hands trembling from adrenaline and she couldn't stop herself from smiling. Floods of relief washed over her with every step forward and she pushed the omnipresent weight within her further aside.

After an hour of traversing the labyrinthine roots to cross into the Sanctum, she saw that the darkness of night was fading. In the distance, the warm light of a summer's day beckoned, though not from the sky. The monstrous trees became a little more sparse, and in between the wooden giants sprung a growing set of sycamores that rose to about half the height of the others. Amongst these glowed the soft golden-white light. Unable to hold back, Cinthia launched herself over the final major roots to sprint towards it.

The Sanctum of the Sarains grew before her. Sycamore trees towered into chambers of training, halls of debate and shrines of devotion and amongst these were the private residences for the Sarains themselves. Additionally, huts of all shapes and sizes sat aloft upon the huge boughs of the monoliths interspersed between the chambers. Vine ladders hung from their respective entrances, providing the only means to ascend them. The main rooms upon the forest floor, just as in Illarien, were comprised entirely of the trees, and although Cinthia had already learned this from books, seeing it raised the old question as to why they used similar styles. Putting that query aside for another day, the Vampire turned her sights to the few individuals who happened to be wandering about at that hour. Each one of them was a Daughter of Saraanjova. This was their home as much as Illarien was the home of the Vampires and it was a well known cultural fact that most of the Sarains that existed at any given point in time used this place not just as their place of worship, but also their domicile and that non-Sarains were forbidden to enter unless specifically authorised.

As Cinthia entered the light of the Sanctum that seemed to fall like snow all around, her heart pounded in her chest and her face felt a little sore from all the grinning she had done so far. Giving a small laugh, she rubbed her cheeks and continued on her way in. Cinthia glanced all around, drinking in everything she saw and beheld for the first time the source of the false sunlight. She reached out a hand to touch the side of one of the sycamores where lichen had nearly taken over its bark. It appeared like peeling gold leaf that glimmered in waves of rich yellow. As she brushed it with her fingers, it billowed minuscule dots of light out into the air.

"Bio-luminescent diaspores," she whispered incredulously to herself.

The air of the Sanctum was filled with them, like a million microscopic fireflies dancing in the twilight. Some fell to the ground and soon lost their glow whilst others flitted in the still air. Cinthia removed her gloves and reached out to touch them. They brushed against her palms with such delicacy only a Vampire could experience their tickling sensation. She grinned.

"This is fucking awesome."

The archaeologist started to move further in, passing the grand rooms on either side of the large main dirt path that ran in a straight line through the Sanctum. She stopped at the furthest chamber which sat on the right corner. Its doors, formed of the trees, rose higher than all the others down the track and stood ajar. Within, Cinthia spied a large circular oaken table, reminiscent of the one in the Elder Council Chamber and with a leap of her heart, she recognised the significance of the room. It was the Hall of the Mothers, where the ten most respected Sarains of the era would gather and help to govern the course of Saraism. It was empty, though her breath caught in her chest as she knew she was seeing where history not only had been made, but was always being made, home to some of the most momentous religious-political decisions down the ages. A tingle ran up her spine as she inched forward, peering around the bark of the doors. It was a simple room that glowed with the same tranquil light as the rest of the Sanctum, holding nothing of any decorative sort. The only thing she noticed that was of visual interest was the lack of chairs, though she assumed this was because they magically grew them as needed. Entering, Cinthia walked around the table, her fingertips brushing its surface as if soaking up the weight of history by gentle osmosis. After a few moments of staring at the table in a reverie of bygone affairs, she shook herself aware and exited, refocused on her purpose.

The main path of the Sanctum narrowed and culminated at a tiny set of unassuming doors set into an archway of twisted sycamore boughs and blossoming auric-white bindweed. This ingress, although simple and diminutive, differed from the others in another way – it was not composed of standing trees, but was formed from the myriad twisting branches of the archway itself, gnarled and melding into itself. Beyond, the vegetation grew so thick nothing could be seen through it, though it seemed to rise slightly up and away from the rest of the Sanctum. In front of the doorway on either side stood two Sarain guards, who, although armoured, were less than alert. Cinthia smirked. Even had they been more attentive, it would have been irrelevant.

The Vampire's eyes blazed as she strode up the remainder of the path to them, her heart racing and fangs bared in a wide grin. She inhaled a deep shaky breath before blowing the air out over her lips. With both hands quivering, she reached out to push open the minuscule doors.

White-gold brilliance flooded the entire Sanctum, causing the Vampire's pupils to contract and she gasped in response to the sudden heavenly radiance. She gave a few short laughs and the smile upon her face broadened. All the air rained with shining gold snow that teemed along the gentle ascending path to form a carpet of pure aureate effulgence. After several seconds of her eyes adjusting to the splendour, Cinthia saw the way up lined with ancient sycamore trees that were nigh unrecognisable from being engulfed by grand and wild gold lichens that encrusted almost every inch of their surface. They puffed out a constant stream of illuminative spores that floated all around before drifting to the ground. Hundreds coated the Vampire's hair and made the skin on the back of her neck tickle.

A single crystalline tear made its way down the immortal's cheek.

The trees lining the walls grew upwards and their highest boughs twisted together in a vaulted canopy of green and gold. As if the diaspores did not offer enough light on their own, intermittent torches were set into the trunks and blazed with the holy fire of the Goddess of Life. Beneath each one stood a single Daughter of Saraanjova, this time very much alert and bearing an expression of solemnity alongside sharpened spears of steel. The tips of their weapons teased the ends of vines that snaked their way in between the branches of the walls and canopy and upon whose surfaces bloomed more of the auric-white flowers. The blossoms, laden with nectar, filled the hall with the rich aroma of honey, making the still air within feel all the more like a soothing blanket.

Cinthia's mouth was agape as she took her first unsteady steps into the Hall of Life. Her face matched the brightness of her surroundings and her eyes had grown so wide she had to remind herself to blink. After what felt like many hours, Cinthia gave another short laugh and her sights rose up the small slope to settle upon a single small door, the design of which was identical to the ingress she had just passed through. Smirking, she strode up the rise, passing the guards without looking at them, to stand before it. Pink fire blazed in her eyes as they beheld this last step. The archaeologist's hand inched towards the knob on the bough-woven door, her whole body tingling. A surge ran up from her fingers as they made contact and turned it.

It was locked.

Giving an almost inaudible grunt, Cinthia knelt down to

observe a single keyhole just beneath the knob which she had failed to notice in her excitement. Her face grew pensive and she rummaged in one of the many pockets that were strapped to her belt. A tiny jingle of metal sounded as she removed a lockpick and proceeded to insert it into the hole. The branches shifted to seal the gap. The archaeologist tried to move them gently aside. They would not budge. Amused, she put her tool away and stood up.

Turning back around, she half sighed and laughed, knowing her secondary plan of action had to be enacted.

Patience.

Knowing the guards would not posses the key, she would instead wait until someone with access happened to come along. In a place centred around practices primarily involving daylight, that could take some time. Cinthia walked a few metres down the hill, formed a concave arc with her Shield and plunked herself down onto it, lying back with her arms behind her head and right leg folded over her left knee.

She lay there for some time, hovering above the shining earth, staring unfocussed up at the verdant-gold ceiling and her boot swung like a pendulum as she kicked her right calf back and forth. Her features held a fraction of a smile and her whole body felt aglow. It had been too long. She had needed this. Adding in that this place and all its natural wonder was unlike anything she had ever seen, it was more than she had hoped for.

She could no longer remain still. Cinthia, her body abuzz, sat up and reached into another one of her pockets. Pulling out a piece of Human technology, she unravelled a set of plugs and put them into her ears. Switching it on, she glanced down at the digital display with a smirk and chose a track. As the first heavy beats of synthetic drums and twangs of heavy guitar entered her head, she launched the volume to full blast and leapt up.

Her pigtails flew about in wild circles as her body threw itself around in a ferocious display. Reaching out to her left, the Vampire's fingers toyed with the strings of her imaginary guitar whilst her right strummed the air. Stomping her huge boots into the ground with every other thundering beat, the spores from the path rose a metre off the ground like sparks from a fire.

Cinthia screamed out the lyrics in dramatic silence, her eyes squeezed shut as her head flailed up and down. The harder the sounds in her ears, the more rampant her movements became. As the song rushed out to a cacophonous climax, the Vampire flung her head back, jumped up high and punched the air.

"WOOOOOO!"

Her hand slapped over her mouth in shock. Eyes wide, she looked about at the guards to see if they had heard her through her Cloak. They stood as stern as before, a few not appearing to have even blinked since her arrival. Cinthia burst out laughing and shook her head in relief. Tentatively, she removed her headphones and returned them and the device to her pocket.

"Yeah... *patience*." she whispered to herself.

After lying back down upon her Shield, Cinthia chose to wait in silence, staring once more up at the glowing canopy. Her features still matched her surroundings, even as her eyes again became glazed over as the air tried to tuck her into a deep rest. The Vampire allowed her lids to close, though willed herself to remain conscious to avoid her Cloak wearing off. Although capable of maintaining it whilst asleep, Cinthia did not desire risking its dissipation there.

It was about two hours later that the sound of a key being turned in a lock jolted the Vampire's eyes open. In a flash, Cinthia was sitting upright and shot her gaze up the path.

A lone Sarain exited the door, turned and re-locked it before starting her way down the Hall of Life. Cinthia's bright eyes followed her hand as she lowered the key into a pocket in her gown. Standing up as the woman walked past her, Cinthia Cloaked as hard as she was able and proceeded to follow her, her heart pounding in her chest.

The lift was clean and easy. It was so easy, that Cinthia laughed and walked around in front of the woman, following her pace backwards. With an impish grin, she reached out with her index finger and brushed the tip of the Sarain's nose.

"Boop!" she whispered.

The woman blinked and scratched where Cinthia had touched her but otherwise carried on. Stifling her laughter, the Vampire retreated back up the hill, making straight for the door with a renewed rush flooding her body. A slight frown came upon her however as she suddenly felt something move in her grasp.

Holding out her hand, she saw the key wriggling in her palm. Like much of the Sanctum, it too was made of living flora. It was a single, tiny deep emerald green vine that glistened in the golden light and twined about itself as it formed the shape of an ordinary skeleton key. Intrigued, Cinthia held it out to the keyhole. The smallest set of tendrils branched out as it neared and snaked their way into the door's orifice. They seemed to melt into it, becoming part of the ingress itself. Cinthia nodded her head with a smile.

"Incredible magick," she breathed.

She turned the key. The clunk of a bolt shifting aside echoed in her ears. Rosey-pink fire blazed in her eyes and she took in a long, slow breath to steady her trembles. Cinthia opened the door.

Silver moonlight and the pearly gleam of stars cascaded between the canopy gaps of a circular semi-clearing. Sycamore trees, sealed together by endless knots of vines and gold lichens, held in a perfect silence that was only disturbed by the most serene of breezes kissing their leaves. The ground beneath the Vampire's feet, soft yet crisp, held a galaxy of light as the dew drenched grass and mosses glittered with the reflection of the heavens above. They rose upon a domed hill, its rise so slight it was nigh imperceptible. On its zenith grew two more large sycamores flanking behind an object that halted every thought and breath in Cinthia.

Every shade of rich verdant and shimmering emerald pulsed along the vines that weaved together to form a large, pointed archway. Along their tangled limbs blossomed the signature golden and snow-white flowers of the Sanctum. Around the base of the arch sprawled giant roots that writhed outwards and down, their size and gnarled nature revealing their ancient age. Within the gap of the bow, there was nothing to be seen. The hairs on Cinthia's neck still rose, however, as the air that ran under its circumference hummed with a gentle yet watchful power she had expected to encounter.

It was the Portal of Saraanjova, the doorway to the Realm of Life. Although Cinthia was cautious not to approach, her eyes still shined as she beheld it, every ounce of history she knew regarding it rushing through her mind. A dumbfounded smile made its way across her features as she took in its simple yet grand appearance. Yet after a time where she had to force herself to breathe again, Cinthia turned her focus downward and directly before the Portal. Her heart then pounded so loud she could hear it and she beamed as elation flooded her veins. There, upon a small dais of woven boughs growing out from the ground, sat her reason for journeying so far from home.

A thick, green book rested upon the plinth. Half gasping, half laughing, Cinthia, de-Cloaking, strode forward before stopping just as quickly in front of it, her shaking hands outstretched.

"The Book of Saraanjova!"

With unconstrained amazement, she examined the most holy of relics. Its surface was a collage of vibrant newborn leaves and as the Vampire's unsteady fingers reached out to stroke its waxy surface she could feel the whole tome pump like a heart. She retracted her hand at first, but then with a snort of laughter she touched it once more, running her hands over it and feeling the verdant life pulse through every vein. Breathing in deep, she grinned.

"Willow would love this," she mused.

With great reverence, Cinthia lifted the cover and opened the Book. It was common knowledge that inside, written in inks of golds and whites, were all the spells and secrets of the Sarains and the White Witches, yet they were scribed in symbols and letters she had never encountered before. Although an inconvenience, it was only a slight one to the archaeologist. Drawing out a notebook, Cinthia was about to begin writing down the unknown words when they suddenly began to change. Before her widening eyes, the shimmering ink upon the pages shifted. They became Lingualis.

Cinthia shook her head and gave a short laugh, "Auto-translation... that is fucking cool... but why?"

"To be comprehended."

Cinthia's beaming features immediately sobered and she

slammed the book shut. Jolting backwards, Cinthia shot a piercing look in the direction of the voice. Out from the fringes of the wall paced a tall, blond woman. She was clad in a pure white dress embroidered with golden symbols of Life and jade leaves of the forest. Her shining locks grew straight down to her elbows and outlined a pale face set with a pair of brilliant ocean-blue eyes that regarded the Vampire with disarming welcome. Cinthia frowned, though eased somewhat upon taking in the lady's peaceful countenance.

"Like any that reveal themselves to others," she continued, gliding towards the immortal without the slightest of sounds and holding her hands out to her sides, "all they wish is to be understood."

Cinthia took a couple steps back as the woman neared. The lady stopped and folded her hands across her abdomen. The Vampire looked hard at her. After a brief moment of silence in which her eyes had examined the woman's every last detail, she eased her brow.

The stranger, giving a reassuring smile, raised her head a fraction and held up a hand, "Please, do not be alarmed." She took the smallest of steps forward. Cinthia took two back. She retreated with a nod and asked, "You are Elder Cinthia, are you not?"

The instinct to Cloak had run rampant in the Vampire since the woman's appearance, but upon seeing her face she had hesitated and held off. Not because of its welcoming demeanour, but for another reason. Yet now, as her name was mentioned, the pull to run tugged at her spine. Her eyes widened in fierce alarm and she took a stride backwards. Concern etched the features of the unknown lady and she held up both hands.

"My name is Talin Kvacha. I am The White Witch and a good friend to your Maker, the Elder Lady Rose."

The archaeologist stopped, though even with her assumption confirmed, the Vampire's tension abated only a little. Acknowledging the White Witch, Cinthia replied, "I figured… Nice to meet you."

Talin smiled and returned her hands to their previous position. "And you." She took another step forward. Cinthia held her ground, but her piercing stare intensified. The ancient Sarain continued in an assuaging tone, "Please, relax. I fully comprehend your unease. However, I assure you that you are quite welcome here. At least under my watch." She leaned forward with an amused expression. "Your secret is perfectly safe with me."

Cinthia eased her defensive posture and took in a deep breath, though her brow showed the air of caution swirling in her mind.

"… Thanks."

"My pleasure," replied Talin, her posture once more upright. For a few moments neither of them spoke and Cinthia stared hard into the ground, her muscles beginning to stiffen once again. She could feel the eyes of the woman on her and her jaw started to clench. The White Witch interjected,

"I am actually quite pleased to meet you," she spoke, leaning her head down in an attempt to garner the Vampire's attention. "I have heard much about you down the years and not just from Rose. Your academic accomplishments are well known to me and I've read several of your books."

Cinthia nodded, though still avoided her glance. "Thanks." After another silent pause in which she unclenched her teeth, she added, "I've worked pretty damn hard on them all." Several seconds passed. The Vampire shrugged. "What did you think of them?"

"Insightful," responded Talin. "Intelligently written and articulate. A rather… refreshing outlook on the Old Times compared to many other authors within the Covyn Historical Society who still cling to rather out-dated notions."

Cinthia snorted and looked away once again with a shake of her head. "I do my best… but yeah… they can be a little… stubborn against new theories."

"I know the kind all too well…" mused the White Witch, looking away from the Vampire.

Cinthia used the moment to glance up at her. A pensive expression sat upon Talin's features as she stared out towards the Portal, though she otherwise stood calm. The Vampire followed her line of sight and then to her right where the Book still sat, pulsing away. She frowned even more and returned her gaze to the White Witch.

"Are you... *really* alright with me being here?"

"Did you come to steal the Book and therefore our secrets – The Gifts of the Sarains? Our birthrights bestowed upon us by the Goddess Herself, which many on the Elder Council dearly covet in their relentless desire to maintain supremacy over us? Another Holy War... is that your purpose?"

"... No."

The White Witch met her gaze and gave a reassuring smile. "Of course not. Verily, if I truly presumed you had come with such ill intent, I would not have permitted you to so much as touch its pages." She glanced away, her tone sobering. "But I trust Rose with my life and even with this Book. I therefore trust that your motives are, at the very least, not what others would presume them to be."

Cinthia's face became etched with confusion for a moment. Even as the words left her mouth, she knew she did not have to ask the question.

"What do you mean?"

Talin cocked her head back towards her. "Cinthia... a Vampire Elder stealthily entering into the Portal of Saraanjova and reading from our most holy relic..." She raised an eyebrow at her. "I believe you can readily surmise the ramifications of such an act."

Cinthia's sight fell to the soft forest floor as she felt the sour feeling of realisation swell within.

"... I'm... sorry."

Talin shook her head and replied, "You are not in trouble from me, nor will I relay to anyone that you have come here tonight. That being said, I would like to stress the serious risk you took in coming here. Not merely for yourself, but for both our great faiths."

Her cheeks flushing, the Vampire squeezed her eyes shut whilst her teeth ground and her fingers dug into the palms of her hands.

"I really... *really* am sorry..." She shook her head and cursed under her breath, her face burning bright red. "I... wasn't thinking… I just wanted to..."

"I know you meant no harm, Cinthia," reassured Talin, holding up a hand. "And I'm not attempting to berate you either. I'm simply conveying the perspective others would have upon this… as well as warning you against similar future… endeavours."

Cinthia's body trembled and her eyes burned against her closed lids. She shook her head.

"Talin…" she croaked, her throat tightening and the air hissing out between her clenched teeth. "I… *knew* that it could be construed that way..."

The White Witch stood silent, her hands once more folded over one another. Cinthia could feel Talin's patient glance on her and she sucked in air deeply through her nose in an effort to continue.

"I… I just downplayed it. I downplayed it in my head because…" Her constricting throat threatened to disallow her confession. All her body felt on fire and she swore at herself. After taking in two more deep breaths, she finished, "Because of my Cloak… Fuck!" She opened her fiery eyes and glared at the ground. "I *really* am sorry!"

Talin nodded and gave a small smile. "Don't be. Either way, you're forgiven."

Cinthia's insides boiled with humiliation and disgust and the words of the White Witch did little to allay them. She continued to scorch the earth with her glower as Talin continued.

"However, I would quite like to know… what has brought you here?"

"Clearly, being an idiot."

"Come, Cinthia." Talin took a step forward and offered her hand. Cinthia flinched. The White Witch walked backwards, withdrawing her hand. "All is truly forgiven and as I stated earlier, you are welcome here. So..." she stood upright and in a gentle tone of curiosity, asked, "Why have you come?"

Between the throbs along her jaw, the aches in her palms and the whirlwind of self-disgust rampaging in Cinthia's mind, answering such a query not only felt like an almighty chore but also rather silly. Glancing back to the Book, she shook her head in an effort to clear it and groaned out a reply.

"Honestly..." she began, her voice hoarse. "I've heard a lot about this place and have studied about the Holy War over the years. I wanted to see it for myself. In particular, the Book."

A darkened mist suffused the gaze of Talin as she looked out beyond the Vampire. Cinthia's eyes narrowed. Talin nodded.

"To stand where history was made..." she whispered.

Cinthia nodded. "Yeah..."

"To see where the... *end* of the war began."

"Yes..."

Talin's face appeared to be weighed down by all the years of her life and Cinthia's own dark expression abated as she saw this. Talin's sight gradually returned to the present and she gestured towards the archway.

"Well..." she began. "This is where it happened. I stand guard alongside many other White Witches and the occasional Sarain to ensure the proper use of the Book's power."

The Vampire followed her gaze and her eyes traced the outline of the bowed vines, their emerald skin still glistening in the moonlight.

"It's the Key to the Portal, right?"

Talin nodded. "Yes. As history will tell you, the Book is the Key to the Realm of Life. The Portal cannot open without it. Furthermore, within the Book are contained all the Gifts of the Sarains, the most potent of which distinguish the White Witches from their Sarain Sisters."

A few moments of silence passed before Cinthia asked, "Kind of a rhetorical question here, but you're not born a White Witch, are you, unlike an Elder?"

"No," replied Talin, her voice heavy. "It is a choice and a weighty one at that. One which also I stand guard against, to prevent the misuse of such power."

Paleness started to return to the Vampire's cheeks and she glanced back towards the dais. "So I've heard. But... going back to when you first spoke." She looked over at Talin who finally met her gaze. "Why, if it contains such power, would the Book want to be understood by someone like me? Or anyone who's not a Sarain?"

"By nature of being a Book," answered the White Witch, her tone a bit brighter. "It's meant to be read after all. Though only Saraanjova Herself could divulge why She desires Her secrets be made known. We can but philosophise yet ultimately ask ourselves, can we ever truly know the mind of a god?"

Cinthia snorted, "Of course we fucking can – we're intelligent like them."

Talin gave a curt nod in response, "Perhaps, yet their perspective upon the universe is far different than ours. As immortals, we understand this concept only too well." She looked directly into Cinthia's eyes. The Vampire's face had darkened and her gaze fell once more to the grass under their feet. Concern marked the features of the White Witch and her eyes narrowed. "Which begs the question – why are you really here, Cinthia? Why downplay the risks that come with your kind entering this place? Surely not just for curiosity."

Taking in several deep breaths, her whole body tense, Cinthia returned the Sarain's glance with a glower, but quickly retracted it. She looked away in apology and answered, "I'm sure you can guess."

"I'm sure I can," Talin replied with a sympathetic smile. "But I would feel impolite to presume... Unless you really want me to?"

"I'd rather not discuss it."

Talin nodded, her expression grave. "I understand."

They stood in silence for several moments, Talin backing off a step to give the Vampire more space. Cinthia glanced over at the Book, the curve of her mouth rising to give the tiniest of sneers. It flickered for the briefest of moments before being replaced by a shadow falling over her whole face and she closed her eyes. After a few seconds, Talin broke the silence.

"I will allow you to continue reading its contents, Cinthia."

The Vampire frowned and looked up at the White Witch. Her expression was as calm as ever and she gestured to the plinth. Cinthia shook her head and glared at the ground once more.

"It's alright," assured Talin. "You have my permission."

The archaeologist turned sideways to see the dais out of the corner of her eye. Slowly, her feet shifted and she began to ambulate the few paces towards the Book. As her fingers again reached out to touch its bindings, the familiar tingle ran up though her. Her mouth opened and her darkened countenance fractured.

"On one condition."

Cinthia took in a sharp breath of air and looked back at Talin. She smiled at the Vampire.

"You never divulge its contents to anyone outside those who already know what lies within. True, most know of the general Gifts, but there is much more inside than just those."

Cinthia gave the swiftest flash of a smile before nodding.

"I promise," she whispered.

Her fingers reopened the Book. As soon as they did so, however, a terrible sinking feeling pulled at her heart and she sighed, closing her eyes.

"Talin," she murmured. "I came to read the Book because-"

"-I know why you're here. And that is why I allow you to read it."

Cinthia hid the onyx tear trailing down her cheek from the White Witch.

"Thank you, Talin."

"Though this Book will not contain the answer you truly seek," she declared. "I hope it helps at least a little."

Cinthia nodded, breathing sharply in.

"...Thank you."

An hour passed where Cinthia pored over the relic, taking out her notebook to make the occasional summary, her eyes glued to every word and her countenance wholly serious. Her lips would move every now and then as she followed the text with her darting eyes and the softest of whispers could be heard from her. Throughout, Talin said nothing, but paced around the Portal, giving infrequent glances over at Cinthia and allowing her to work in peace, a fact for which the Vampire was grateful, though it was hardly the focal point in her mind. The more pulsating pages she turned, the more she soaked up all the arcane knowledge contained within. Her features lightened over time and, by the end, even hints of smiles flickered across her face. This was usually followed by her jotting down something and running her intense gaze over the shimmering text. At the end, she shut the tome and replaced her notebook into its holster on her belt. Talin returned to her previous position and upon seeing the slight improvement in the Vampire's demeanour, raised an eyebrow.

"Compelling?" she asked with a pleasant smile.

Cinthia shook herself from her reverie and glanced back to the White Witch, returning the gesture. "Riveting..." She paused and nodded. "It's a lot to take in… but it feels good to do so."

"Any queries regarding its contents?" asked Talin. She waved a hand towards the door. "You may as well take advantage of the limited time left on my shift guarding this place."

Cinthia nodded after a brief moment. "It's… weird… I have a lot of questions… but it also feels like I have none."

Talin smiled. "Well… you certainly have the time to discern them." She walked forward and offered her hand to Cinthia. Hesitantly, the Vampire took hold and Talin shook it. "You are welcome to return anytime to the Sanctum." Talin leaned forward and her smile broadened. "However I would prefer it if, next time, you made an official appointment with me. I can get you in to see the Book for historical research purposes, though undoubtedly you and I would be accompanied by other White Witches to oversee your visit."

"I won't come back," replied Cinthia, letting go and stepping back, her face darkening once more. "It was stupid of me to come… so I won't come back." She stopped and looked away, her brow furrowing. After a few seconds, she sighed and added, "At least not for a long time. And I work better alone. I hate people watching me work."

The White Witch nodded and folded her hands over her stomach. "In that case, Elder Cinthia, it was good to meet you… and now, I'm afraid, it is coming up to the time you must depart."

After a few moments of looking at the floor, Cinthia managed to crack a smile and look back up at Talin, "It's been good to meet you too." She then cocked her head to one side. "Another epic figure of history off my list."

Talin raised an eyebrow, her face alight with curiosity. "I made a list did I? What is this for?"

"Persons of significant historical interest that I intend to meet someday," Cinthia replied matter-of-factly. Shrugging, she added, "Though it's not a serious list – just a mental note for my own amusement."

Talin folded her arms. "And have I lived up to expectations? The age-old adage is 'you mustn't meet your idols'."

Cinthia snorted and shrugged again. "Eh, that's only mostly true."

"And in my case?"

"It's not," she replied. The Vampire then gave a nod and glanced away. "You're cool."

"I'm… 'cool'?" mused Talin with a wide beam. "Hmmm… Well… thank you, Cinthia. I don't recall being labelled with that attribute before."

"Neither had Rose," stated Cinthia. She then appeared quizzical. "At least I don't think so. But she's pretty cool too."

"She most assuredly is," admitted Talin, her eyes once more regarding the distance. "In her own way."

Cinthia, her face lighting up a bit, asked, "Speaking of things to call each other… I've always wondered – how do you pronounce your name? You called yourself 'Taylin' earlier, but I've heard others say 'Talon'."

The White Witch frowned in thought. "An interesting query… I cannot say I've been formally asked that before… to be quite honest, the original pronunciation was 'Taylin', however over the years everyone around me adopted 'Talon' as well. Since I answer to either, I personally consider them to be equally correct."

"So… which would you prefer I call you?"

Talin laughed, "Whichever you like. I truly do not mind."

A few moments of quiet passed. Cinthia, having hard stared at the dais, then looked at Talin and nodded.

"OK, I do have a question regarding the Book."

"I had a feeling you would before you departed," teased the White Witch. "What is it?"

"It regards what I already know to be the most potent of the Vampire Hunter weapons: The Nectar of Saraanjova. Although it's mentioned in the Book by name, it's not exactly clear on what it is. So… what *is* the Nectar of Saraanjova?"

Talin acknowledged and replied, "It is the clear and pure birthing fluids of the Goddess of Life. We obtain it directly from Saraanjova Herself through the Portal. As it is, and originates from, the source of all life and gives birth to all life through it, it is the most powerful of all the weapons we possess against the Children of Inter."

Cinthia stared for a good moment before giving a short laugh and raising an eyebrow. "Eh... So... let me get this straight... You're using your God's vagina juice as the most powerful anti-Vampire weapon?"

Talin did not answer. Her cheeks warmed to a ruby red hue and the edges of her mouth twitched upward.

"Yes... actually," she replied after a while.

Cinthia shrugged. "Alright."

After a few moments where both immortals' faces broke out into wider and wider smiles, the White Witch spoke.

"You surely realise it's a good thing I possess a sense of humour? That would count as horrendous blasphemy in the ears of anyone else here."

"Their loss."

"Indeed so."

The next few moments were silent, and Cinthia knew the time had come. Her face sobered and she nodded.

"Thanks again for letting me read it," she started. "And again... I am very sorry about... not thinking any of this through."

Talin stood up straight and let her arms fall to her sides with a warm expression upon her features, "It's quite alright, Cinthia. Just be careful where you choose to tread in future. Had it not been myself present tonight..."

"I know..." stated Cinthia. The Vampire then glanced back towards the White Witch and held her hand out. Into Talin's palm she placed the key.

"Take care, Talin," she said, turning to leave.

"Saraanjova go with you, Elder Cinthia," she whispered with a smile.

Cinthia walked down the small rise towards the door. As she Cloaked herself, turned the knob and the shining golden light of the Hall flooded out upon her, she glanced back to the Portal. The White Witch was nowhere to be seen. Only the ancient vines of the archway and the dew laden turf were visible. Her eyebrow raised and a small flame flickered on in her heart. Cracking a smile, she looked away and shut the door.

Blasphemy's Company

You want to know how it went? Fuck me, where to begin?! If I were to say it was a blast *would that be a poor choice of words?! Hahaha!*

Anyway, it all started not long after my initial arrest and the interrogation by these wretched excuses for Vampires. Seriously, it's not even funny how pathetic they are. All wearing modest clothing, averting their eyes from my blessed nakedness and their fear of touching me! I'm not kidding - they actually tried to clothe me so as to avoid witnessing the divine messages upon my flesh! I refused, of course, tearing up all the rags they presented me with, forcing them to gaze upon the works of our God. Dumb fuckers. I... think they were also afraid to see my naked body anyway. But I love their hypocrisy! Especially the ones who threatened to kill me the most – they kept giving me sideways glances when they thought I wasn't looking. Perverts. You would have found their whole charade hilarious. Give me a few years – I'll seduce these repressed shits easily. Anyway, where was I? Oh yeah! A few days after the main bulk of questioning, some super hot chick – and I mean hot! *Ginger pigtails, perfect skin and the best tits imaginable – damn what I wouldn't give to fuck her stupid brains out – Ahem! So, this cunt translated my blessed Markings, as she was supposed to be some sort of expert in lost language, which was great because she inadvertently allowed our God's Word to spread amongst them as intended. I tried to be nice and all, offering myself to her when she came in, but did she even give me so much as a lustful glimmer? No! She fucking blanked me! Still, the whole scenario turned out friggin' hilarious because as much as she dare not admit to my face how much she clearly loves eating bush, it was plain in her body language that she wanted to fuck me too. I made her blush when I offered her my body a second time. I mean, she did ask if it was ok to touch me. Oh, of course it was under the pretence of 'examining your tattoos', but it was fucking obvious she wanted a feel. So after she did her translating stuff, she tried to blank me again but I told her she* could visit any time! Ha! You should've seen her try to keep her professional manner as she left!

So yeah, soon after that amusing interlude from the now all-too-familiar torrents of threats upon my life, They came at last! The Acar Vanta spoke into my head, calling me to fulfil my destiny as Her Blasphemy upon Inter and all Its fucking idiotic worshippers. She told me I was to be indwelt with Her unholy power. And… I was! It was the most amazing sensation – power like you could not believe reverberated around my whole body and responded to my every command! I cried like I've never cried before… I… I was truly Her instrument of sin! I… cannot describe just how immensely happy She made me. And that's when She finally told me precisely what it was She'd planned for me to do. I was to use all my new power and my whims and wits to desecrate Illarien's holiest sites. If you're thinking at this point how I could have ever gotten away with it when Illarien is filled with the most powerful Elder Vampires and Priests of the Interist order, then you disgust me. Truly. It's the power of the Acar Vanta! They were no match for me! But their flailing attempts to do so were fucking funny!!! Like the part where I was pissing and – Hahahahaha! No wait! Hahaha! I'll get to it… I'll haha! start… at the beginning!

Thanks to the Cloak Cor of the Acar Vanta, I was able to escape the prison undetected. I walked right past all the guards and they didn't notice me! It took some doing not to start killing them all, I'll tell you. Anyhow, I went out into the main forest and made my way to the throne room. The Acar Vanta guided me in Her wisdom to each section I needed to corrupt and this one happened to be closest. On the Throne of Vesplasadin – he was some devout jackass from the Holy War or something; who fucking cares? - I sat and frigged myself until I squirted my black blood all over it. Afterwards I torched it and moved on to the next place and – hahaha! - I can't keep a straight face!

So after I loudly burned their throne room, the Elders finally noticed I had escaped and came after me. I Cloaked myself on my way out and they flooded in whilst I bolted off tooooo… wait for it… the Nightpool! Yes! The Nightpool itself – the most holy place in all of Covyn for Interists. The very, ahem, "divinity Itself would ariiiise intooo the mooortal plane from here to bestow Its righteous followers with saaacred wisdom and" - *HA! No, couldn't say that with a straight face! It's the portal from the Pits of the Dead into Covyn. Apparently, if anyone other than the Highest High Priest of the time goes down the spiral steps to it, they'll be put to death. Adorable! I went down and let them know exactly what I thought of their 'god'. I just casually waded on in to stand in the pool itself, stretched my legs sliiiiightly apart and once I was goooood and ready I let loose my BURSTING BLADDER! I pissed my black blood back into the face of Inter Itself! Well, sadly not literally as It wasn't physically present at the time, but it still felt SO FUCKING GOOD to unleash The Desecration upon Its most treasured place! To commit such a sin in Her name! It's the greatest feeling in the world! FUCK I'm getting wet all over again just thinking of it!*

Anyway, the Elders all show up at that point but I wasn't about to let them interrupt my sacred duty to the Acar Vanta. I put up a Shield around the pool so they couldn't attack me. I made them all watch as their precious Inter was insulted and humiliated before their pitiful helpless eyes. It was so freakin' hilarious! The Priests muttered their naive counter-curses, the soldiers looked upon me with terror and the Elders stood by and couldn't do jack! Damn… it was amazing. But the best part… oh hahaha!! The BEST part was this one reeeeeally angry dude who happened to share the same coloured eyes as me. I nearly pissed on myself, seeing this troglodytes' eyes – he must've been the Maker of that Sarahessi-whatever who converted me or something. Anyway, I turned around from my sacred duty, saw him banging furiously on the Shield and was like, "Fuck ME! I've got your freakin' eyes! … HA! Well… Sucks to be you, don't it, bitch?!" I then flipped him off and re-aimed my stream as best I could, laughing my head off at him. He threw such a furious tantrum on my Shield I was actually slightly worried that it might falter for a moment… though please don't tell Her that. I know really that She's far more powerful than all of them, which was proven when… ah nevermind, I'll get to that later!

So yeah, after I made sure my bladder was good and empty I started chanting the Prayer of the Acar Vanta – the verse written into the Seal of Unholy Will on my chest – and these fuckers all are freaking out and shouting more counter-curses. It took everything I had to concentrate on Her instructions to pull off the unholy ritual and not roll into a ball of laughter. Afterwards, I smiled up at them and engaged my Cloak once again. It terrified the mortals! You should've seen their faces after I 'vanished'! Ha!! Yeeeah, so then I ran off to the next place on my heretical to-do list.

You know, if it weren't for its repugnant usage as a temple of Inter, the Libes Amphitheatre would've been perfect for one of our libertinage rituals. As it happens, we won't be visiting that place any time soon! The moment that I arrived, I knew I didn't have long before they guessed my location and I wanted to concentrate without the distraction of their amusing protests. The number of holy sites in the forest city had just been halved after all so it wouldn't take them long. Therefore I started the sacrilegious ceremony without them. By the time they arrived, I had already begun forming the Seven Icons and the Word of the Acar Vanta in black flames in the air. I don't know what they did that time, but I don't regret not paying attention because I had a serious job to do for Her and it took all the concentration and power I could muster to form the words in the air with fire and then emblazon them upon the stones of the amphitheatre. Oh, and you know that troglodyte with the yellow eyes that I mentioned – he seriously tried to break my Shield again! If it didn't work the first time, why would it work now, dumb shit?! I didn't tell him that though because I was performing the ritual. Afterwards, I summoned all my hatred for them, all my anger and rage over their utter stupidity, their disgusting repression and their nauseating devotion to that false god and built up such an electric tension in the air until at last I unleashed it upon them in a gigantic fireball, turning all the fucking mortals into red mist! Fuck, it felt so GOOD to let loose and vaporise them! It was like… now they're an inhibited blight on the world… and now they're not! It was awesome! I then Cloaked once more and ran off to ruin the final location on my profane tour of this loathsome place.

The Acar Vanta directed me to a section of the River Alin

within Ilarien. Apparently it's another place Death's been seen to visit this world. I stood waist deep in the waters and began to repeat the process I did in the Libes Amphitheatre, but I was interrupted by the Elders' timely arrival. This time the yellow eyed dumbass finally seemed to learn his lesson and I told him he was a good boy for getting it through his thick skull. There was another Elder present... one of those who interrogated me – the one with the shimmering eyes – she had to force him back from challenging me. I can't believe the little idiot! I guess he's a bit slow. Anyway, the shimmering eyed Elder walked toward me and demanded to see the Acar Vanta. I turned to face her, but before I could speak, I suddenly felt the cold hand of God upon my shoulder! I stood so still that it felt time had stopped. I couldn't believe She had come! I could barely contain my satisfaction knowing they were all fucked! I just said to the pious bitch with the biggest grin on my face, 'Be careful what you wish for!'. Fuck me!!! What happened next I will remember with joy forever! The Acar Vanta, Cloaked, conversed briefly with them and the Elders insulted Her and doubted Her glory, so she showed them. In the most fucking enormous fire storm imaginable our God DESTROYED ILLARIEN!! She completely levelled the forest and turned all their fucking holy moronic shit to ashes!! I laughed so hard I couldn't stand and fell over in the river! It was… the most amazing thing I'd ever seen Her do! To witness Her almighty power completely unleashed first hand – I cried. I fucking cried like a little bitch – it was awe inspiring. That foul place was no more! Wiped clean by the Will of God!

Sadly though, it wasn't to last. Some Sarain cunt restored all the trees the very next day. At least the traces of sin still remain on the rubble and I don't think anyone will be using the Nightpool any time soon!

"Who are you talking to?"

Blasphemy gasped and shot back to the wall of her cell, her chains rattling against the damp stone floor. She glared at the jail door, yet her face swiftly altered and shone with delight. Outside the bars stood the Acar Vanta, who wore nothing but a stony expression.

"God!" she exclaimed, smiling so wide it seemed to take over her whole face. Scrambling forward to the bars, Blasphemy continued, "You're back! I've missed You-"

"*Who* were you talking to?" she repeated.

Blasphemy knelt before her deity and, her expression growing concerned, muttered, "Apostasy."

"She's not yet earned that name," replied the Unholy Amen. "Refrain from referring to her as that until she's ready."

Blasphemy nodded and bowed her head. "Yes, Unholy Mistress. I'm sorry."

Using her Shield Cor to bend the cell bars apart, the Acar Vanta stepped into Blasphemy's prison before resetting the steel behind her. Taking the young Vampire's chin in her fingers, the Icon of Sin lifted her head to look up at her.

"It's alright," she spoke. "Now… answer me, my sweet heretic. Have you continued to fulfil your purpose here?"

Blasphemy's face twisted into a sick grin. "I've done everything exactly as You've commanded, my God. I've not only kept being a nuisance to them by spreading your unholy filth at every opportunity in their ears, I've also managed to…" she flicked her tongue between her lips.

The edge of the Acar Vanta's mouth curved upwards and her eyes darkened. "*Good girl.* You make me proud."

Blasphemy's pupils enlarged and she shivered all over. Biting her lower lip to contain her growing smile and bouncing on her knees, she replied, "Thank you, God!"

The long fingers of the Mother of Whores caressed Blasphemy's cheek. The young immortal trembled at her icy touch and a single crystalline tear slid its way down her glowing features.

"My beautiful Blasphemy," her deity whispered as she leant in close. "Show me how much you have missed me."

A Mother's Worry
<u>Cinthia's home, Hallahan, 1176</u>

The last of the day's heat seeped from the sand through her heavy brown boots, warming her up to her ankles. Her feet sank with every step and her slight figure was silhouetted by the final purple-indigo rays on the horizon behind her as she trudged towards a half-buried ruin, its stone roof breaching the crest of the nearest dune. The ends of her fawn coat brushed the top levels of sand as she moved over it, leaving small trails beside her bootprints. Removing the beige canvas hood and face scarf to reveal her pigtails, she reached down to her right hip to unsheathe a vacuum flask and bring it to her lips. Taking a few sips, she then replaced the flask, but not before she took notice of a dark frame in the distance standing just outside the ruin. She sighed and nodded before walking over to it.

"Hey," Cinthia greeted. "I can only assume you're here about the Book?"

The other person stepped forward and the archaeologist didn't need the dying remnants of daylight to see it was Lady Rose.

"You're damn right I'm here about that," replied her Maker, her voice trembling. "What on earth were you thinking, Cinthia?! You broke into the Sanctum of the Sarains and took hold of their most closely guarded relic!" She broke off and threw her arms out to her sides. "Aside from the fact such an act was highly reckless it was also a diplomatically dangerous thing to do. You could have caused an international incident! I know to you it's just a harmless satisfaction of your curiousity, but to others it's a Vampire breaking into the Portal!" Her voice became strained. "You're damn lucky Talin happened to be there or things could have been a whole lot worse!"

Cinthia stood quiet, her expression calm and weary, yet her eyes could not meet Rose's. After a tense brief silence between them, Cinthia earnestly answered.

"I'm aware. Talin told me."

"Cinthia!" Rose chided. "Regardless of the fact you broke the law, you're putting yourself at unnecessary risk, not to mention straining relations with our allies. You might do something in the future where she or someone like her won't be there to cover for you! You're just lucky she's a personal friend of myself and Ellandu'el."

Cinthia finally looked at her with tired eyes, sighed and shook her head. "Rose… why are you *really* here? I got all this from Talin herself. I'm not about to break into another sanctum. I'll stick to old ruins."

Lady Rose's face grew into an expression equally that of rebuke and concern.

"Do you promise?" she asked.

Taking note of Rose's demeanour, Cinthia's brows clenched downward and she acknowledged.

"For now," she said. At the first sign of Rose's distressed reaction to her answer, Cinthia argued, "You know I've specialised in the Cloak Cor, and I'm getting better at it all the time. Don't worry – I've no plans to break into Dragerian High Command or anything!"

"I'm serious!" Rose cried.

Cinthia cursed under her breath and looked away, folding her arms and gripping them in her fingers.

"Sorry," she replied. After a short interlude of quiet where she continued to stare hard at the first stones protruding from the dune, she went on, "So was I. Look, Rose, I…" She shook her head and hissed out air between her fangs. "I don't want to cause shit to go down either. Which is why I'm careful. I won't ever bite off more than I can chew. Back at the Portal I lowered my guard. I won't do that again *and* I promise that at that least until my Cloak is up to the point where I'm able to hide myself from Ellandu'el or even her sister, I'll stick to sneaking into old ruins only."

"Discounting the fact I don't think you'll ever be able to Cloak from Eternel, can you please just not do anything like this again?" Rose pleaded.

Cinthia gritted her teeth and her fingertips bore down on her arms. A glaze fell across her eyes as she gazed at the sand. "I can't promise that."

"Why not?" exclaimed Rose, her voice pained. "Why risk these things at all, Cinthia? Because you were 'bored'? I-I don't understand." Her volume lowered and she reached out to touch her Fledgling on her shoulder. Cinthia shrugged it off. Retracting, Rose added, "You don't have to do these things."

Cinthia turned away. Taking a few paces towards her home, she glanced up from the sands to take in the weathered stone of her abode. With her lower lip giving the tiniest of trembles, Cinthia made every effort to stop her voice from shaking as she forced a reply through her grinding teeth.

"I just… needed to know. I needed something to… to look forward to. So I could…" She swore loudly, her every muscle contracting and she finished her sentence, "*Continue.*"

Rose's hand shot to her mouth and her eyes started to well up, "Oh, Cinthia!" She walked over the sand to wrap her Fledgling in her arms. Cinthia's body reacted to remove her but then eased and allowed the embrace. Her own eyes threatening to spill, she leaned into Rose.

"I know." Rose continued, her cheek resting on Cinthia's head. "I know what it's like… but I don't want you to take such risks. Please…" she squeezed her. "Please be careful."

Cinthia, blinking her eyes dry and taking in a deep breath, exited the embrace, turned to face Rose and signalled. "So… that's why you're really here."

Lady Rose, trying her best not to let her own tears flow, acknowledged and gave a weak conceding smile.

"Cinthia… I just want you safe. I know you're not really a bad or foolish person. I just don't want you to be involved in a scenario that could cause… problems."

"You're more concerned about my welfare than the fact I broke the law?"

Rose's mouth curved upwards and she breathed, "Yes."

Cinthia, a small smile upon her own lips, snorted and rolled her eyes, walking a few steps away. "So much for upholding it then. I knew you had a nasty streak in you."

"I'm a politician, Cinthia. I lie. It's what I do…" Rose riposted amusedly, though her smile faded after she finished and she inquired, "Now… I have to ask… how are you doing?"

Cinthia's face became as stone and she gave several small shakes of her head before quietly answering, "I'm finding it harder to find leads to follow on ancient history… Consequently… I'm… struggling."

Rose slowly made her way over to her and this time managed to place a supportive hand on her. Cinthia trembled underneath it, but made no effort to detach herself. Instead she just stared hard at the sands rolling into the far distance, her breathing steady and deep. In her periphery, she caught her Maker following her line of sight. The moon shone out above them casting its silver milky light upon the dry ocean. Barely a whisper of air moved to toy with the ends of her pigtails, though it had become quite cool with the absence of the sun. Where once it would have caused her to shiver, it now was merely registered as it brushed against her skin. She was then drawn out from her thoughts from the feel through her heavy coat of Rose's thumb gently rubbing her.

"Hang in there, Daughter," Lady Rose whispered. Cinthia felt her heart skip a beat and she took in a sharp breath of air. Not seeming to notice, her Maker continued at a normal volume, "You're clever – you'll figure things out. And remember, you're not alone. You've got your boys, myself, Willow and others in Illarien who care very much for you." She stopped and moved round to face her Fledgling. Cinthia looked up at her. Rose sighed and her face became etched with concern. "I can't force you to stay safe, but please at least promise me you'll do your best to be so."

A few moments of silence passed with Cinthia not taking her eyes off of her Maker's, her expression maintaining its vacancy. Eventually, she grew pensive, looked away and after taking a deep breath, she replied.

"I promise."

Rose nodded with a small smile and once more mimicked Cinthia in gazing out across the sandy expanse. The younger of the pair observed the horizon's waves, her muscles easing with each passing moment and her thoughts drifting into nothingness with every other dune her eyes roved over. Together the two Vampires stood quiet for quite a while, the only sound to be heard around them being the feathery breaths of air winding their ways through the beige hillocks.

Cinthia turned to leave, thanking Rose for her concern and then walking towards the entrance of her home but was stopped by her Maker.

"You know," Rose spoke, moving to look at Cinthia. "You can keep in touch more often if you'd like. I am interested to know how things are going in your endeavours."

Cinthia slowed then stopped. Turning, she replied, "Last time we talked I thought we agreed to keep things how they've always been – less familial and more amicable associates."

"Last time we talked was 83 years ago during the crisis of the missing three High Priestesses," stated Rose. "I wasn't about to… ask for more as I thought it was a bad time to do it."

Cinthia frowned. "Really?"

"Yes, why?" asked Rose.

"It just seems like it would have been the best time as it was a scary time for both Councils."

"I wanted to give you space to process it all. You barely knew Illarien back then as well, so the last thing you needed was me being…" she bobbed her head from side to side.

Cinthia, her tension abating, looked at the ground and acknowledged, "Thank you, Rose. I appreciate it, but I don't want a mother. I just want a friend. That's how I've always viewed you, even if we barely speak." She paused and shrugged her shoulders. "I think you're cool. If I thought of you as a mother… you'd not be cool anymore."

A hint of disappointment flashed across Rose's features and she gave a weak smile. However, a moment later her eyes glazed over and her face brightened.

"You know," she spoke, her voice perking up. "The few days we had when I converted you made a very lasting impression on my life. I am glad I made you and am proud of who you've become."

Cinthia, folding her arms, sighed with a smile of her own and she shook her head. "Wow… gushing all over me now?"

"Yes," replied Rose. "Because I am not cool. Whilst I am not like Ellandu'el, who is the real motherly one of us all, I cannot help but see you as…"

Cinthia held up a hand and she responded, "I know you're not as… *much* as her… I know what you're like… and it bothers me."

"I'm sorry," whispered Rose.

Cinthia's pigtails waved as she shook her head. "No… it bothers me because… on some *crazy* fucking level… I," she ground her teeth and closed her eyes. "Shit - I like it."

"Cinthia!" beamed Rose, stepping towards her.

The younger Vampire waved her hands, "Hey! Don't mush out on me, Rose! I still want my distance and don't want you to go all maternal on me. Fucking saccharine. I just like that fact you care for me. Right now -" She broke off, attempting to control the minute tremble in her voice. Swallowing hard, she finished, "That means a lot. Just be your usual cool self Rose. I need that. Not someone to mommy me."

"I can do that, Cinthia."

Lady Rose stood still but opened her arms out for her Fledgling to enter. Cinthia closed the rest of the gap between them and accepted the embrace. Whilst in her Maker's tender arms, she felt her place a single soft kiss upon the top of her head. Giving her a brief squeeze, Cinthia spoke quietly.

"If you can do that then I wouldn't mind keeping in contact and even… upon the *rarest* fucking occasions…" she stood on her toes to whisper in a mock begrudging tone. "If you called me 'Daughter'."

Her voice cracking, Rose held her tight and whispered back, "Thank you, Daughter."

Immediately, Cinthia shoved her away, shaking her head and waving her hands.

"Now! There, you see! You used up your allotted mush for another 83 years!" she joked, turning her back on her Maker.

Rose burst out laughing with Cinthia giving her own subtle chuckle. Following a couple moments of calming down, Lady Rose tapped her on the shoulder and the two faced one another.

"Do take care, Cinthia," she said. "Keep up all the hard work. It will pay off and another archaeological mystery will be around the corner waiting for you to solve it."

"Thank you, Rose. You take care too."

Cinthia was then left alone once more to stare out at the rolling sands that surrounded her ancient home. After some time gazing up at the stars, Cinthia descended into the ruins to pour over books in search of clues for her next big project.

Sarahessieth's Fledgling

The hums of flitting insects hung in the darkening air outside the shop. Some flocked to the candlelight within and others remained amongst the newly uncoiling ferns and blossoming trees, dazzled by the rising moon in the deep purple sky. Droplets of water that clung to the underside of stems and leaves alike refracted the dusk upon the green and provided a crystal-like crispness to the surrounding foliage. In the remains of the day's precipitation, the scaly flesh of snakes could be seen passing from the blackened windows into the undergrowth beyond, eager to start their nocturnal activities.

Likewise, Sarahessieth emerged from the shadows of her chamber, stretching out her arms. Yawning, she grabbed an apron from atop the main work desk, threw it on, tied it behind her and walked to the door to flip the closed sign to open.

The potion master returned to the desk and proceeded to check up on the various conical flasks and miniature cauldrons arrayed upon it. Crammed between the sizzling pots and steaming jars were stored newly sprouting herbs and freshly cleaned animal carcasses that sat in earthen bowls and hung on rusted nails stuck into the wall behind. As she examined her ongoing projects, she picked a leaf here and there and crushed them between her fingertips and palms before adding them to a mixture or two. Alongside the leaves, she would also carve out the smallest slivers of meat with one of her many razor sharp knives and drop them into the pots. At times, she whispered beneath her breath whilst holding her hands over a concoction or two, sometimes with closed eyes and sometimes with them open. She was constantly moving, her face a picture of stony concentration and her hands perfectly creating many different brews at once. Behind her sat the front desk and it was piled with its usual display of hundreds of small flasks with handwritten labels attached to their glass necks and bodies, all shining in the candlelight. As the Vampire performed her art with rigorous focus, she failed to notice the faint tinkling of their surfaces bumping into one another. It wasn't until the vibrations caused one of the finished potions to fall crashing to the stone tiles below that she was roused from her work and swerved to face the front of her store with a glower.

Then she felt it. A faint rhythmic pulse originated from behind the door, that whilst small, evoked a sense that it belonged to something far stronger. Her lips parted and her breath caught in her throat. Wafting through the window to her expectant nostrils meandered a perfume that was all too familiar: blood and fluids. Heart pounding, she gulped hard and bared her fangs in a widening sadistic grin as waves of bliss shot throughout her body. She moved to the front of her store.

"*God*?" she breathed at last, her trembling hand reaching for the knob.

Before she made contact, the door opened.

A statuesque beauty towered in the frame, dark brown locks bordering a marble hard face and flowing to the mid torso. Black robes as dark as midnight draped over perfect olive skin to drag along the leaf-strewn ground. The garment parted lower down to reveal a pair of long, powerful legs that took a step forward to cross the threshold. Sarahessieth took a pace backwards, the small of her back pressing against her front desk. The scent of copper and iron hung thick in the air alongside a constant and overwhelming pulse emanating from the being in front of Sarahessieth, yet it was neither their bouquet nor presence that intoxicated Sarahessieth the most. It was their eyes. The portals of her god bore down into her very soul, leaving Sarahessieth as naked as she had been in her first vision so long ago. After several moments, the lips of her god parted and began to move. Utterly captivated by her radiance and aura, Sarahessieth could not hear the words and instead of replying, stood dumbfounded, jaw agape.

The countenance of the imposing woman darkened.

"I *said*, I have a task for you."

Sobering at her souring demeanour, Sarahessieth suddenly breathed in and shook her head. Gulping once again, she nodded with a slight frown.

"Yes, God, anything."

The head of the woman turned to her left and Sarahessieth

followed her line of sight. Standing just behind her god was another lady and the sight of her served to bring Sarahessieth back into reality all the more. Much shorter and younger in years than the divine, she stared out from around their shoulder at Sarahessieth with a look of great anticipation from within bright green eyes. Long golden hair waved down from her head to cover in part her naked form, nearly every inch of which was covered in elaborate symbols, flowing ribbons of text and intricate seals of magic. As Sarahessieth took in every aspect of the woman's body, the corner of her mouth curved upward and she raised an eyebrow coquettishly, though this faded upon her taking closer notice of the language in which the tattoos were written. Their bizarre angular nature made her eyes narrow in recollection as she knew she had seen such glyphs before. Her heart pounded harder and she turned back to her deity.

"God, I sought and found the-"

"I want you to convert her."

The abruptness of her command as well as the unusual nature of it stunned Sarahessieth into silence. She glanced back at the blonde who wore a growing smile of expectation then back at the divine. All manner of questions raced through her mind, yet through the increased chill running up her back as she came under the penetrating gaze of her god she found she could only voice one.

"Why?" she asked.

The stare of the Acar Vanta remained unchanged in its icy nature for a brief moment before it softened and her lips rose into a small smile.

"She has a Divine purpose," she explained, her voice deep and mellow. Placing her left hand upon the blonde's shoulder, she brought her forward to face Sarahessieth. "This is My Blasphemy against Inter," declared the Acar Vanta, to which the lady in question gave a wide and malicious grin. "She is my Left Hand, My Word and Will, and is My Whore, the incarnation of all the pleasure I offer in this world." With her right hand, she gestured forward. "Blasphemy, this is Sarahessieth, a fellow wretched creature."

Blasphemy, who had folded her arms and slouched her

234

posture, snorted a laugh and gave a respectful nod. Sarahessieth nodded back though otherwise made no movement.

"Her task is to sew havoc via sin in all the Bavillion lands leading up to her finale in Illarien itself. She will commit murderous rituals upon whomsoever she desires in whatever manner she desires in My Name. This will go on until I command her to move upon that den of fools and break their spirits through the Truth upon her flesh as well as execute other tasks."

The idea of infuriated officials wailing cries of displeasure and running in panic at the sight of this adjutant of the Unholy Amen caused Sarahessieth to sneer in amusement. However, the cogs in her brain whirred as she was plagued with an unending stream of questions. Questions she was all too aware that the Acar Vanta would perceive her to have. A chill ran up her spine as she knew full well, in addition to all the others, her original question had not been answered. She dare not ask another. Burying her queries, she folded her arms in front of her and widened her smile.

"Sounds like fun," she spoke with a grunt of laughter.

The mortal's chest rose and fell with excitement and she turned to look back and up at the face of their god. The Acar Vanta nodded then stared deep into the eyes of Sarahessieth with an air of approval and something else. Something Sarahessieth could not discern. Like all the other thoughts racing in her head, she pushed it to one side with a slight shiver and focused on the lady walking towards her.

Blasphemy placed her arms around her neck and drew her in close with a seductive smirk. The potion master frowned and made as if to pull back, but stopped and allowed the embrace, staring into the girl's eyes. The scent of this woman, although not as entrancing as the Icon of Sin's, still sent her heart racing and as Blasphemy leaned in closer, her body brushing against Sarahessieth's, the potion master's eager hands caressed the soft skin sealed by narratives of heresy.

Sarahessieth gestured with her head for Blasphemy to incline her neck to one side. Blasphemy, beginning to pant, obeyed and leant in further. Sarahessieth glanced up once more at the Acar Vanta, her eyes betraying her ambivalence. At a single stony look from the Unholy Amen, she returned her focus downward and, taking a deep breath, bit down hard into the neck of the Left Hand of Sin.

Through the various screams and laughter issued by the writhing woman in her arms, Sarahessieth shut her eyes and concentrated on downing the life that spurted into her mouth. Its delicious taste swirling around her thirsty tongue was matched only by the vivid memories that sprang into her mind. A near decades worth of tormented pleasure and divine recreation swarmed forth from the crimson flood. The yellow of Sarahessieth's eyes brightened and her body ran hot and trembled from the sights and sensations of the woman's every agony. Visions of masses groping for the girl's every orifice and countless mortal sacrifices adorning her increasingly corrupted flesh flashed across her sight. Waves of intense heat rushed to every lubricious sector of Sarahessieth's body. Rituals of gore and forced rapture dictated by unholy will and surrounded by countless symbols and sigils of contemptuous renunciation served only to heighten the tingling throughout her. Eventually, innumerable nights of exquisite affliction gave way to the ascension of a licentious and terrible authority whose only goal was to sew the seeds of carnality and violation at the behest of their malevolent god.

The memories stopped with the beating of Blasphemy's heart. Gouging a hole into her wrist, Sarahessieth held out her shaking and bleeding arm to the woman's gaping mouth whilst glancing upwards to the Acar Vanta. She made no move nor held any expression. Sarahessieth, forcing open the weak jaw of the mortal, pushed her wrist down and tried to pump her blood as quickly into the fading woman as she could. Lips moved to kiss her skin and suck at the wound. After a few moments of Blasphemy taking in the black blood, her body seized up then went still.

The pair of Vampires in the store stayed silent. Sarahessieth continued to hold the limp body to herself until it finally jerked to life. Blasphemy shrieked and pulled back, laughing and throwing her arms around the Acar Vanta. After a few moments of jubilation, Blasphemy turned to face her Maker. As far as Sarahessieth was aware, her Fledgling issued words of gratitude to her, but she could not hear them. The brow of the potion master had furrowed as the weight of her actions started to become very clear and a rising dread began to well in her. As exciting as it was to have been part of the creation of her god's servant, and thus part of her plans, was that all she amounted to? The more she stared at the eyes of her Fledgling, the more she felt she had answered her own question.

The reason why she had been asked to convert Blasphemy: was it to protect the identity of god?

She buried the thought as deep as possible and avoided the omniscient stare of the Acar Vanta whilst smiling at Blasphemy. If she was right, this was the end for her. Her usefulness was complete.

Every fibre in every limb tensed as terror gripped her. She was aware that the Acar Vanta was talking to Blasphemy but could not hear the exactness of what was said. Her eyes flitted about her shop, taking in every detail in its exactness and desperately hoping to glimpse her slithering friends for the last time. They were not there. Only her bottles, filled with the results of her great art, stood present, glinting in the candlelight.

The door opened, bringing Sarahessieth back to the present. Blasphemy was nowhere to be seen. Only the Acar Vanta remained. The aura pulsed outwards and seemed to push Sarahessieth back into the desk once more, though this time her face was not filled with awe. Twin black holes stripped away her every defence and the potion master admitted to herself that she already knew her every thought was known to the Icon of Sin and she felt foolish for hoping she could hide them. White knuckles grasped the edge of her desk and Sarahessieth's jaw was locked tight as the Unholy Amen took a step forward.

As always, the potion master found herself incapable of deducing the countenance of her god and this only served to send her further down into fear with every minuscule moment that passed between them. After what felt like several lifetimes, and the images of her art and snakes flying across

Sarahessieth's mind, the Acar Vanta's face softened, though no smile passed across her lips.

"The hand that was once extended, still remains outstretched," she spoke in a calm, deep voice. "Do you understand?"

A memory from long ago sprang forward. Sarahessieth's heart raced. Her grip on her desk relaxed and she opened her mouth.

"I believe I do," she whispered, a smile beginning to form.

When she next blinked, the Acar Vanta was gone.

Knowing it was pointless to look around for her, she stayed where she was. The smile upon her face slowly broadened and she soon broke out into a long and mad laugh as realisation dawned on her. Still shaking, she then returned to the recesses of her store and collapsed onto her bed. As she closed her eyes, she sighed, comprehending her god's explanation and was flattered by it. Her mind soon drifted from that into dreams of expectation as she awaited the unfolding of the Icon's plan.

Willow's Heart

A barrage of protests and a chorus of supportive yells resounded in the Council chamber for the vote. Throughout the turbulent exchanges of arguments and rebuttals, Willow sunk deep into her chair, face buried in her hands, horrified over the fact so many held such deep resentment for her. She had hoped that the thriving Alliance between the Bavillions and the Varndiccoes that had been established at the end of the Holy War would have eroded their venomous perceptions of the beliefs of their Sarain counterparts by now, but she was wrong. They had not changed, and those created long after were just as contemptuous as those who came before them. Willow sobbed ever harder, the weight of her own foolishness for thinking they had been okay with her acceptance and reverence for both Saraanjova and Inter pressing tight within her breast. She never hid the fact she loved both, but they had never argued against her. Only now did she realise that they simply had not considered her worth arguing with.

"Enough!" Lady Rose commanded, leaning over the table. "We will have order here and discuss this in the methodical manner befitting of our positions." She frowned at everyone present, except for Willow. "Please retake your seats and for the sake of due process we will hear instead from the accused herself."

Her face smeared with bloody tears, Willow trembled all over as she looked up to observe them sitting back down with a mixture of glowers and acknowledgements of support. Pantheon folded her hands in his left palm, yet her nerves barely dissipated. She gulped. Willow's troubled thoughts flew by so fast her mouth could not keep up even if she had opened it to speak. The longer she tried to formulate a coherent statement, the wearier those in opposition to her appeared to grow, their faces twisting with impatience and irritation. Her gaze shifting to Ellandu'el, she pleaded at her with glistening eyes. A single, slow nod came from the ancient Elder followed by an encouraging smile. Willow swallowed hard again, and did her best to reciprocate. At a squeeze of Pantheon's hand, she took a deep breath and attempted to speak.

"I-I... I-love Inter," she choked. Immediately, there were sighs of vexation and grunts of dismissal. Willow continued, "I... love Life. I always have. I truly believe in the beauty of both. Life and Death – they're part of the same thing." Poisonous glares burned across the table with such ferocity Willow's voice was cut off. She turned, examining their rancorous faces one by one, her bottom lip trembling. Her chest felt as if it were going to explode with the intense thudding of her heart against her ribs. Her eyes then fell to Ulaq. His sights were blazing into the oak, ignoring her. A sharp inhalation of breath suddenly entered her lungs, and she knew what she had to say.

"I am no blasphemer!" she cried, her tears once more flowing. "I love both deities equally! I hold them both to be equal parts of the beauty of nature itself! I do no wrong in doing this. I only love them. Like I've only ever loved all of you." Sliding out one of her hands from Pantheon's passionate grasp, she wiped away her tears before continuing, her eyes glowing brighter. "And I have! All this time! I've shown you all nothing but kindness and love, despite how lost some of you became over the years." Willow's attention focused on Ulaq's head then, after a momentary pause, she turned her blurry gaze to the others. "That won't ever change, I promise! There's no need to fear me or hate me or think I won't accept you because you've messed up. No matter what you do, I'll always be here to help you. No matter how lost in hate you become, I'll be here to support you. I promise. Even if you hate me." She wept, her voice trailing off. She closed her eyes, calming herself in preparation for their response. Upon hearing nothing for a couple moments, she opened them. Their reviled faces had not budged one modicum, though some mimicked Ulaq and had turned their attention from her altogether. At once, a tiny flare ignited in her chest and, without hesitation, she screeched, "I may not like you, but I still love you!"

Almost everyone present jolted at her abrupt declaration, with Pantheon and Ellandu'el both giving small gasps of shock.

"Willow..." murmured Ellandu'el.

Her expression contorting with horror, Willow cried all the more.

"I'm sorry!" she blurted out, her knees shoving into her chest. Her father wasted no time in hoisting her onto his lap and holding her shuddering form close.

Lady Rose shook her head in sympathy and made as if to stand, but Ulaq beat her to it.

"What an entirely unrelated and inconsequential speech," he declared. "Did you miss the point of this vote or are you just that incredibly devoid of thought between your ears?"

"How dare you!?" bellowed Pantheon, hammering a gigantic fist into the wood. "Take-"

"-What? Clearly you must have heard a different speech. She was to put forward points arguing her innocence, not give us a self-righteous and naive spiel. Though I suppose I should really be thankful as it makes her prosecution all the easier."

"I believe she addressed the point of blasphemy first, or were you not paying attention?" postulated Ellandu'el, leaning forward.

"It was a half-assed dismissal of her guilt accompanied by nothing short of a confession of her love for Life – which is the quintessential definition of blasphemy!"

"Does anyone else remember the time when this was about her riding a dragon?" asked Valentine. Next to him, his twin sister, Valentina, did everything she could to stop herself from laughing.

"Oh here we go," sighed Amakay, flicking her hands out to her sides. "Another philosophical debate. Rose, can you *please* cut this short to spare us the endless run-around?"

"I think that would be wise in order to conclude this hearing," Rose concurred, ignoring Amakay's lack of protocol. Standing up and gesturing for a fuming Ulaq to return to his chair, Lady Rose raised her voice, "Citing legal precedent, article twenty-one of the Council Charter-"

"-Don't you dare!" shouted Ulaq, bolting back up from his seat and pointing at Rose. "Not this time! Don't violate our vote-!"

"-The power of settlement rests with the Head of the Council," recited the Ambassador over him. "Which, in the absence of

Vertio, is in the hands of the Twins, Elders Lady Eternel and Lady Ellandu'el, as you all well know. They have final say on all Elder matters by the authority bestowed by Inter Itself, if they so choose to enact said authority." Lady Rose faced Ellandu'el and gestured toward her. The Eldest there acknowledged her then stood up. Fuming, Ulaq shook his head.

"As Head of the Council," began Ellandu'el, placing a hand onto the table. "I hereby call an end to our circular ideological debates and move straight onto a vote." She turned to stare at Ulaq, whose face was etched with wary satisfaction. Willow sat wide eyed, unable to understand why she would choose to go along with Ulaq's idea. Just as was her wont, however, Ellandu'el flashed her a subtle reassuring wink before retaking her throne. Likewise, Ulaq and Lady Rose sat back down.

"Those in favour of convicting Elder Willow of committing blasphemy?" asked Ellandu'el.

Eight hands rose around the great table. Willow's heart raced as she did the mathematics in her head. Ulaq's face turned stormy and he opened his mouth to speak, yet was interrupted by Ellandu'el.

"And those in favour of clearing her of the charge of blasphemy?"

Ten hands shot up, none more so than Pantheon's. Willow, overwhelmed with incredulous relief that more people supported her than not, gasped loudly and squeaked out joyfully. Ulaq slammed a hand into the table but otherwise remained silent. Discontented grumbles murmured around the chamber from the opposition mixed with grunts and smirks of satisfaction from the rest. A tiny proud smile played across Ellandu'el's features.

"Then it is decided," she declared. "Lady Rose, if you would-"

"-This isn't over!" Ulaq spat, cutting her off. His fiery yellow eyes scorched across at his Maker. "Don't forget we have a direct order from the Captain to arrest and pass sentence upon her. You may have won the vote, but-"

"-I am more than aware of this, Elder Ulaq," Ellandu'el interrupted, holding up a hand. Turning her gaze to Rose, she picked up where she left off. "Lady Rose, if you would sum up the arguments from earlier on so we may make a decision on the Captain's order and end this *wasted* meeting, I would be grateful."

Ulaq narrowed his eyes and clenched his fists. Willow's elevated mood started to sink once more. Her stomach knotted and she clung to her father's arms. She had hoped that her statements from earlier would have pardoned her from punishment. She looked up into Pantheon's bright blue eyes. His grizzled face wrinkled with unease and he gazed back down to her with a fierce countenance that normally made Willow feel safe from all dangers. This time though it was marred by a sense of dread she could not abate. As Lady Rose once more addressed the Council, Willow's breath froze and she braced herself for the worst.

"In light of the defendant's statement regarding the acts of that night were not theft nor born of a desire to instil terror into the populace," Rose spoke. "Accompanied by the long-standing evidence of good character and therefore honesty from the defendant, I hereby can only find her guilty of inadvertently causing panic and indirect property damage." She paused and gestured to everyone. "How does the Council sit with this charge?"

Willow's stomach turned over, knowing full well she had done this, yet she knew she had never meant any harm. Everything transpired just as she had recounted to them: she had apologised to the people as soon as they let her know how much she had frightened them, and then flew the dragon away to remove the source of their terror. Willow's shoulders slumped as she felt her apologies were not accepted, yet her heart sank further knowing they made no difference to the hearing.

"It's bullshit," snapped Sylvia ahead of Ulaq, who nodded at her in agreement. "It's ignoring the fact there's no solid evidence whatsoever to prove her version of her acquisition of the dragon. It cannot be stressed enough that there's no way a Black Dragon would just offer itself to anyone. The whole basis of your revised charge rests solely on previous good character? This cannot be allowed."

"I concur," replied Ulaq and several others.

Amakay stared hard at Sylvia as she spoke. Lady Rose

exchanged a glance with Ellandu'el before replying, "You are correct, Elder Sylvia. There is no proof. However, since no evidence can be put forward proving her theft either, we must go on what evidence we do have, which is her centuries of dedication and consideration to Illarien and its people. Whilst it is not proof, as you are right to point out, it is a solid point of evidence that cannot be so easily dismissed."

The smallest glow brightened the otherwise strained features of Willow, yet she remained apprehensive. Pantheon held her closer and her body eased as a swathe of warmth cascaded over her skin at the feel of his touch.

"She is still guilty of igniting the villages into mass panic," reminded Ulaq, emphasising each word, his fist pushing hard against the oak. "We must decide on a sentence."

"Agreed," declared Lady Rose, retaking her seat. Ulaq shot her a distrustful glare, his jaw clenched tight. All in the chamber grew silent as their gazes fell to the throne's occupant, though the atmosphere was anything but calm. Willow shivered in Pantheons stalwart embrace, unable to breathe for fear of the worst. The eyes of the Eldest among them grew stern and as Ellandu'el stood to conclude the hearing, Willow's mind flashed by with images of all the joy she had ever had running and dancing through the woods and meadows of Illarien under starlit skies and playing with all its animals. She did not want to believe it might all come to an end. Her heart pounded as her best friend opened her mouth to address them.

"Elder Willow," she breathed, her gaze meeting Willow's, "this hearing has found you guilty of causing indirect damage to the livelihoods of the occupants of three villages and for starting mass panic amongst them." Tears trickled down Willow's cheeks. Ellandu'el, calm as ever, spoke louder, "As we are under orders from the Captain to arrest and pass sentence upon you, and as to set a precedence, I hereby personally take on those responsibilities myself. Elder Willow," she took in a deep breath and paused, "you will leave this chamber in my custody to remain by my side under constant daytime supervision. Normal sentencing for such an act results in up to ten years in prison, however in light of your good behaviour, your immediate actions during the incident to make amends and to mitigate the damage by removing yourself and the dragon from their vicinity, I'm cutting that sentence down to three years. Furthermore, you will not spend any of that duration in the cells of Illarien. You will instead be given community service, during the night of course, helping at first to repair the damage you inadvertently caused then moving on to maintain, and help to thrive, every plant and living creature within the borders of Illarien."

Her trembling lips steadied and the tension in Willow's whole body began to recede as Ellandu'el's words echoed around her head and started to sink in. She could not believe her ears. Fresh, crystalline tears exploded out of her brightening eyes to cascade over her features and wash away the old obsidian ones. She cried out as she felt her fathers embrace tighten about her and her grin widened all the more. Giving a joyous cheer she swivelled around on his lap and threw her arms around him. She pressed her face into his shoulder and shook with uncontrollable relief. She could stay. She could be with all she loved and do everything she ever wanted. As Willow felt her fathers giant hand press against her back she brushed back her hair and looked up at him with pure radiance. Pantheon mimicked her, shedding rare waters of his own. Yet their moment was ignored by a cacophony of protest around them from Ulaq and the others in opposition who roared insults and arguments out at Ellandu'el and the rest. Willow and Pantheon paid them no heed for a number of moments before the shouting became so loud it drew them out of their thoughts.

"My *problem* is that it's blatant favouritism!" yelled Ulaq amongst the chaos. "It's nothing more than a hypocritical implementation of the law that you've done because you and the rest of your friends have a soft spot for her childish demeanour!"

"The law was not bent in any way," retorted Ellandu'el, her composed conduct the obverse of Ulaq's. "I enacted it to the letter, using my full authority as it's written I can do. On top of which, Willow's moral character is her mitigating circumstance."

"Her character is that of a naive kid! Her ideology nothing more than delusions of a perfect world!"

Ellandu'el gave a small smirk then replied, "Her *ideology* is an example for all to follow. To be kind. To be loving. And as for the rest, you could do to learn something from her love of Life."

Ulaq exploded, "*WHAT*?! How *dare* you?!"

"How dare I?" echoed Ellandu'el matching his volume whilst maintaining her cool. "The very fact that Inter has not struck her down for her so called 'blasphemy' is testament to the idea Inter and Saraanjova are two sides of the same coin."

"That's complete nonsense and you know it!" he yelled. "We both know that's not how Inter works. It works indirectly through the Vampires, Its Ambassadors, us. Hence, incidentally, why Vampires should have more authority over Interism!"

"We can talk round and round and round in circles forever," she replied, staring him down as she did so. "It will come to nothing. I have spoken and my word is now law."

His eyes blazed into hers. Neither moved for several moments, their bodies still amongst the sea of waving arms and the noise of continued insults and quarrels. Willow had noticed their violent exchange and strained her neck to hear it, but could not pick out their voices from the crowd, something which was unusual for a Vampire of her age. She could only conclude Ellandu'el was Cloaking the conversation from her. Her brows furrowed in curiousity over what it was that she didn't want her to hear.

Ulaq gave a discomforting smile. "Very well, have it your way. Enjoy your victory while it lasts."

"I shall," said Ellandu'el, her countenance growing cold.

"This isn't over." Ulaq whispered as he moved to leave, waving the trees aside.

"It never is with us, Ulaq."

As he departed the Council Chamber, Ellandu'el sighed then faced Willow across the heated exchanges of opinion. She gestured for her to follow her outside. Eager to have her curiousity sated, Willow squeezed her adoptive father to her and thanked him for his support and his love. Planting a kiss on his cheek, she hopped off of his lap and flew through the throng of Elders to exit between the giant conifers and meet her friend on the other side. Ellandu'el wasted no time in clutching her Daughter to her.

"Are you alright?" she asked, looking deep into Willow's eyes and stroking her hair.

Willow nodded, but her face was riddled with confusion and she opened her mouth to speak. Ellandu'el hushed her, "No, please. I am so sorry that you had to go through all this. And I am sorry for having to be as… detached as I was. I had to be as objective as possible."

Willow nodded, "I understand, don't worry, though I was frightened at the time… but why did you Cloak your talk with Ulaq?"

Ellandu'el kissed her forehead and shook her head. "You've gone through enough and I didn't want you to hear anything he may have said in insult to you. That being said, I think you would have liked the moment I told him he should learn to love Life as well."

"He should," said Willow. Glancing away from Ellandu'el, she twiddled her finger and asked, "Did you Cloak it because… do you… think I'm weak?"

Ellandu'el's hand went to her mouth. "No, Willow! I'm sorry if that's what it came across as. I just wanted to protect you."

"I'd rather hear what they really think then have them all lie to me again," she replied, holding Ellandu'el's hand tight. Ellandu'el acknowledged.

"I'm sorry, Willow," she apologised with a heavy voice, stroking the younger Elder's head.

Willow smiled and shrugged her shoulders, "It's ok. I know you're just looking out for me, which I really appreciate. I'll look out for you too! It just hurts a lot hearing how badly they think of me, but trust me, I'd rather know and deal with it than not know."

Ellandu'el sighed with a relieved glow. "You know I always trust you and that I have your back." She looked down at her Fledgling. "Changing the subject... just so you know, there's only so many liberties like that I can take with the Council before they try to circumvent my authority again, so please don't do anything like that again. Or you'll make my hair turn as white as yours!"

Willow giggled. "Oh come on, you'd look great with my colour!"

"You try telling my sister that."

The pair dissolved into laughter, holding each other in the dim surroundings of the Evernight and continued until at last Willow begged to get started on her new duties helping out the villagers. Together they rushed off into the dark, Willow skipping merrily ahead of her Maker who followed close behind, watching her Fledgling with a mother's smile.

The softest of mosses graced the root-woven bed and flooded the ground as a verdant carpet. Coniferous and deciduous monoliths towered on all sides intertwined by ivy so thick not a single gap was left between them for passers by to peer inside the private chamber of Ellandu'el. The only conventional furniture to stand within were a matching oak wardrobe and dresser, both inlaid with several other woods in a beautiful display of marquetry. There were chairs, however they came and went as and when they were needed, formed by weaving branches and roots alike. A single Soul sat on the dresser, illuminating the room with its eerie blue-white light.

Ellandu'el was sat on her bed reading a book when there came a knock upon the entrance. Putting the novel aside, she waved a hand at the trees and their roots rose out from the ground to walk along the floor, creating a gap through which she witnessed Amakay standing there looking pensive. Ellandu'el stood up and bade her friend enter. Amakay asked for the door to be shut behind her to which Ellandu'el once more gestured with a hand and the trees returned to their previous places. Amakay turned to look away from her.

"Ellandu'el," she said. "I need to talk to you about something I consider to be of great importance. And it cannot leave this room."

Ellandu'el nodded, concern etching her features. "Of course. What is troubling you?"

"It's Willow," she stated. "I am worried about her and I feel you're the best person beyond Pantheon to discuss this matter with."

"I'm listening."

"Ever since the hearing a few days ago, I cannot help but be worried for her. I know she's barely leaving your side, which is why I waited until this evening to discuss her with you, but even so. I fear for her… innocence."

Ellandu'el acknowledged but otherwise stayed quiet, waiting patiently for her to continue.

"I know she's older than I am and as such has technically seen more things than I in the world, but she's led a relatively sheltered existence up till now. She hasn't been truly exposed to the world outside Illarien and-"

"-You're worried she will be 'corrupted' so to speak by the harsh nature of the world, such as people like Ulaq and so on?"

"Yes," Amakay answered. Gritting her teeth and her hands curling into fists she added, "She must be protected. She has so much to offer the world as she is. Her love for all things is precious and I dread the day something happens to her that will make her lose it."

Ellandu'el snorted in amusement. "You know, it's funny. I had a talk with her about this just the other day coincidentally enough. After the hearing actually."

Amakay's turned to look her. "And?"

"And..." Ellandu'el stood up from her bed. "I came to the conclusion that whilst her heart is precious, an ideal to strive towards though highly unlikely to ever exist in all, she must be allowed to grow up on her own, not smothered by her 'parents'. Namely, us – her friends and Pantheon. Your instincts in this matter mirror my own, Amakay, so I understand your concerns all too well. However, and I heard it from her own mouth, she wishes to face these matters on her own." A far off look diffused across her face. "It's hard to let go. But I am proud of her and whom she's becoming."

Amakay hung her head, leaning into the dresser. "Fuck, when you put it like that I… I admit you're right. I know she's your Fledgling, but I still want to protect her. I tried to shelter her myself a few weeks ago. She asked me why some of the Elders mistreat her. I dodged the subject. And during the hearing..." she cursed under her breath, "during it she found out the hard way. I felt terrible at the time not telling her. Had I done so then, it might have spared her the shock and the pain she felt then. I feel like such a bitch."

"I tried to do the same thing at the hearing," reassured Ellandu'el. "I kept a conversation from her. Afterwards she told me off for doing so, in her own way."

Amakay looked back up at her. "What did she say?"

"That she wanted to know the bad so she could deal with it," she answered. Giving a short laugh and shaking her head, she said, "I'm so very proud of her."

"Yeah..." Amakay nodded and paused for a moment. "Think I should tell her I kept it from her too?"

"Yes," replied Ellandu'el. With a smile she continued, "She will understand, don't worry. She told me so herself that she understood I was only trying to help her so she'll doubtless do the same for you."

"I will do," she said with a weak smile.

A few moments of silence passed between them before Ellandu'el broke it, "Amakay, she will be ok. We just have to have faith in her heart and protect her no more or less than we would anyone else."

"I... know," she sighed.

"If it helps, remember that Willow's love for all things is so integral to her entirety that I don't believe she would ever allow anything to make it falter and become corrupted with apathy. You said it yourself, she is very old and has seen so much already. She survived through both the Holy and Dragon Wars alongside the extinction of the Ancients. Whilst I'd never say anyone survives such horrors unscathed, she has managed to keep that same positivity she has possessed her whole life."

"She wasn't the only one to come out alright," Amakay gestured at Ellandu'el.

"Hmmm, true, though I bear my own scars," she acknowledged. "Even so, Willow is truly unique. I have always known this which is why I made her."

Amakay's ears perked up and her eyebrows raised. "Are you willing to elaborate? It's rare we Elders share our reasons for converting others."

"Very true, though exceedingly understandable," replied Ellandu'el. She waved a hand and out from under the moss sprung up a mass of writhing roots weaving together to form two chairs opposite from one another. The Vampires sat down, Ellandu'el crossing her legs and placing her hands in her lap whilst Amakay leant causally back with one arm over the rear of her seat. Once they were settled, Ellandu'el recounted her story, "She was just an ordinary farmer's daughter who loved to help others and watch things grow. Yet she had unwavering loyalty to Inter. This peasant girl of little education came to the philosophical conclusion many in our religion endlessly debate well into old age: that Life and Death are part of the same thing and are equal. On her own, she had simplified a complex conundrum like it was nothing. Additionally, Willow reveres both deities equally. I saw her compassion, her vast capacity for love and I knew she would be perfect for the Council, especially since I suspected things would not always be so kind. It would be nice to have someone kind…" Ellandu'el broke off and sighed with a smile. "When I offered Willow immortality, she jumped at the opportunity to be able to tend to plants and animals for all time. I asked her if she preferred an eye colour. She told me – the vivid bright green of newly sprouting leaves in spring. Even though I saw her kindness as something the Council would find useful, I didn't see the full extent of her gifts at the time."

"What do you mean?" asked Amakay.

"Her powers are unlike any other Vampire. Surely you must have sensed this?"

"No… I don't understand. What powers?"

"Whilst I tend to vehemently disagree with Ulaq on most matters," she explained. "I have to agree with him on one – it is incredulous that not only a dragon, but a Black Dragon, would bow to her and let her ride it just like that. Willow never lies. I believe her. Have you ever accompanied her on her rounds about Illarien?"

"No, I'm always too busy with keeping an eye on another," Amakay answered. "But how is that relevant anyway?"

"I'll explain, but you should take a break and go with her one of these nights to see for yourself. Every living creature follows her. Flowers and trees turn toward her as she passes – only subtle movements of course, but they do indeed move. So during the hearing, when she explained about the dragon, I knew it was true."

Amakay leaned forward, eyes widening. "But you're talking about *Nature Control*... Are you saying... is she... a Sarain-Vampire?"

Ellandu'el laughed and shook her head. "No, of course not. No-one's ever attempted a hybrid, but I suspect our powers would simply cancel each other out and either kill the host or make them fully mortal. No, Willow is simply... gifted."

"With what? What kind of power is this?"

Ellandu'el's eyes glazed over. "Even I cannot say. I've seen many things in my long time upon Covyn, but never anything like this. I highly suspect the answer is a very simple one, albeit one that sounds like it's straight out of a children's book of tales."

"Which is?" asked Amakay.

Ellandu'el smiled. "It's her heart. I believe all creatures sense this and adore her for it. She exudes serenity, warmth and joy. This I know you have felt, or you'd not ask to have her protected."

"True, but I just attribute it to her personality, not a magical force."

"Yet whilst animals can sense these things, vegetation cannot, and in her case the plants can as well, implying something abnormal. So I do not know. It is unlike any magick I know of. All I know is that it is beautiful and is invaluable."

Amakay said nothing. After about a minute of silence, Ellandu'el stood up, with her friend following suit.

"We shall guide, protect and watch over her for all time, though we shall allow for her to choose her own path," Ellandu'el concluded. "A parent needs to know when to let go. I know Pantheon is dreading that day, but he knows it must come to pass. I know I too have found it hard at times, and not just with Willow. With all my children." She gave a short chuckle. "Even my many nieces and nephews. And you of course, Vertio's only child."

Amakay laughed and shook her head. "Thanks, 'Mother'."

Ellandu'el looked into her pure midnight eyes. "You'd make a wonderful mother yourself, Amakay."

Signalling for the trees to move aside, Amakay turned her back to her friend with an apprehensive smile.

"Thank you. We'll see," she replied before vanishing into the shadows.

As the entrance shut itself tight once again, Ellandu'el nodded to herself.

"I suppose we will."

The Fall of Natalie

Ambience fell silent within the keen ears of the crouching Vampire Hunter. Her tensed body, clad in black spider-silk armour adorned with a slew of anointed stakes and bolts, stayed perfectly still. Natalie's strong fingers gripped the edge of the rooftop she spied from, its rough texture upon her skin an insignificant detail. Her every sense, precise and sharp, converged upon the thin winding stone alley below. Stale air, heavy with pollutants, breathed through the ends of her plaited hair, but she paid heed only to what lay beneath. In her left periphery, a bustle at the alley entrance faded to nothing in her ears whilst their myriad shadows cast wild roving scenes over the area. From her right, neon lights splashed alternating hues across the damp descending rock path, frolicking with them. Directly in her sights were two heavy set men armed with guns standing guard on either side of a single wooden red door set into the stone beneath the luminous sign. It read:

The House of Sybaris

Her poise, her calm, rhythmic respiration and the piercing nature of her stare displayed the cold focus within her. Natalie's eyes, reflecting the prismatic lights, narrowed and she took in a deep breath, blowing it out slowly over her soft lips. Letting her mind open, she invaded those of the men below. The layout of the House, the number of armed employees, the fastest route to the Acar Vanta's private chamber and, at last, the presence of her greatest foe all flowed into her from them. A slight tremble made its way through her entire body and a chill teased her spine. Clenching her jaw, her brows furrowed and she inhaled deeply once again before standing upright. Gauging the descent with a single glance, Natalie clenched her hands then breathed out an inaudible whisper.

"For you, my sisters."

Unsheathing the repeating crossbow from the holster on her back, Natalie leapt down into the light below. After rolling several times to break the fall, she jumped up and fired off two bolts into the heads of the guards as they reached for their guns. Silently making her way to the door, she put her ear to it, listening to all that lay behind it. There was nothing. Natalie grasped the handle and pushed it down. As soon as it clicked, she slammed it open and rolled in.

A plain stone corridor stretched out on either side of her and from each end came the startled gasps of two employees. Without hesitation, Natalie, eyes alight and fangs bared, brought her crossbow up to meet the first, yet before she could pull the trigger, her eyes widened. The creature rushing towards her shared her eyes and judging by the haste with which the other behind her was encroaching upon her position, so did they. This development, although not wholly unexpected, posed no issue and the first went down instantly in a cloud of ash. Having no time to turn and aim, Natalie, hearing the heavy footfalls resounding behind her, grasped one of the stakes from her belt then launched herself backward over her attacker. Landing on her feet, she thrust the sharpened steel into the girl's back. There wasn't even time for her to scream. Yanking the weapon from her disintegrating body, Natalie pelted forward up the hallway. Rounding a corner, it was revealed to be a dead end with a single door. She halted. Her breath caught in her throat and her heart pounded in her ears. The chamber of the Acar Vanta sat mere metres away. She was unable to take her eyes from it. Gritting her teeth and forcing herself to breathe, she crept forward.

Innumerable memories played with sombre intent across her vision as she approached. Each life she had taken, every person she had failed to save and all the unforgivable atrocities she had encountered and taken part in flashed through her head. Natalie's blood boiled hotter with each deliberate footstep and her eyes blazed with equal ferocity, yet far beneath it all, deep in the innermost recess of her soul, crept a sliver of ice. Every muscle quivering, she inhaled sharply, attempting to regain focus.

She could hear nothing from behind the door. Nor could she sense a single presence. Her eyes narrowed. The quiet was excruciating. Waves of anticipation washed over her, causing her jaw to tremble. Tensing even more, Natalie crouched before the entrance. She closed her eyes. She breathed in deep. She squeezed her crossbow. A darkness diffused over her features and she exhaled all distractions. Natalie turned the handle.

With every ounce of speed she could manage, the hunter slammed open the door, rolled into the room and brought her aim to focus on her target sitting several metres away. Yet, in that very instant, time seemed to stand still. Her stony composure flinched and her heart ceased beating, paralysed by the macabre sight she was met with.

Every inch of the chamber's interior was lined with the polished humeri and femora of sapient species, packed closely together in a series of tight weaves. At equal intervals along the walls were the embedded designs of various unholy seals formed by the skulls of Mensmall and Humans alike. The entire expanse of the floor too shared the skeletal remains of arms and legs in the same interwoven pattern save for the centre. There lay a gigantic inverted septagram made from smaller ulna bones, however it was in an odd state of incompleteness compared to the rest of the room. A deep, perfectly rectangular hole sank into the ground in the middle of the polygon, next to which squatted an active cement mixer. The ceiling depicted the main symbol of the Acar Vanta, using not just skulls, but various types of bones. At the back of the morbid chamber was an arched cubicle housing a small altar, upon which sat all manner of anti-Interist idols and the rotting remnants of offerings. Scattered about the rest of the area were an assortment of torture devices, sexual machines and plush cushions. Tossed carelessly among these were the freshly drained carcasses of mortals, what little blood left within dribbling out onto the grim flooring. It glistened in the dim torchlight. Some metres in front of Natalie, just beyond the septagram, sat a giant throne, crafted from the severed limbs of Humans. Leg and arm bones were used for the supporting base as well as the lengths of the arm rests, which culminated in hand bones, topped by two skulls, one for each hand to rest upon. The back of the high throne was made of several lengths of spine going up the centre with only the largest of ribs, in two intertwining rows respectively, on either side of the central 'spine'. Seven skulls crowned the top of the chair, silently screaming. Within that frozen moment, the more details Natalie took in, the more her life boiled in her veins. However, for all the ire rising to consume her, her blood still froze the moment her attention fell to the throne's occupant.

Her posture perfect and with elegant legs crossed, the Acar Vanta dominated the throne and exuded the purest aura of power, sending waves of bitter chill throughout Natalie's body. The Unholy Amen wore nothing save for a transparent gold-embroidered black silk robe that trailed onto the rough floor. Her left hand lay on the armrest, her delicate digits caressing the skull atop it, whilst her right brought a crimson-filled chalice to her parted lips. Natalie's attention was arrested upon them as the familiar, sickening smile emerged, deepening the icy grip on her spine. Yet it was the cavernous stare of the Mother of Whores that paralysed her the most. The twin black holes bored into her with haughty amusement, sparking Natalie's rage into life. As soon as the Acar Vanta lowered her glass, the Vampire Hunter snapped into action.

In a lightning fast whirlwind, the crossbow in Natalie's hand shattered into hundreds of fragments before she could pull the trigger and her chest felt an almighty force hammer into it, sending her crashing into the wall behind her. Her head cracked upon the bones and her ribs snapped. She fell to the ground in an inglorious heap, spluttering blood and crying out. Eyes on fire, she glared upwards at her attacker. The Acar Vanta hadn't moved, yet her smile widened. Natalie, her every breath an agonising chore, reached for a stake and launched it. In a flash of darkness, it melted half way to its target. Natalie screamed, her veins pulsing with desperate hatred, and she glared at the source of her every nightmare. The Unholy Amen remained draped across the throne, yet her twin portals intensified their gaze, causing Natalie's gut to wrench as they perforated her mind.

"And so, my deviant Daughter returns to me at last. You certainly took your time," mused the Acar Vanta, taking another quaff from her chalice.

Slowly, a deep and unsettling sensation weighed upon her chest. Natalie's eyes widened and she felt her heart skip a beat as her thoughts began to whirl. Breathing fast, she growled through gritted teeth, "You… *knew* I was coming?"

The Acar Vanta, licking blood from her lips, breathed in deeply before answering, "I've always known where you were. You thought I would just let you go? You *are* my Daughter, after all. So... I've watched you," she leaned forward, her smile fading. "Guided you… and sewn the threads of your life all these years and I am proud of the woman you've become."

Natalie, grinding her jaw tighter, shook her head in as much of a gesture of disbelief as an effort to shake loose the fear threatening to cloud her mind. Her body trembled and her stomach felt sick with repulsion. Gazing down her nose at the felled woman, the Acar Vanta continued, "In the school, you grew strong; in your… *family* of Vampire Hunters," an icicle of terror speared Natalie's heart, "you became an exceptionally skilled killer, and in your hunting of me, you became a lone wolf, adept in solitude."

The young immortal hyperventilated and tears of raging obsidian began to rise forth as fear for her closest friend pulsed about. The weight of inevitability started to grow in her mind, and she did all she could to Cloak everything about Raelya.

"Every choice you've made, each twist in your tale… every *moment* I've granted you has been as a consequence of my designs."

"My choices are my own!" Natalie erupted, her voice shaking and black waters spilling from her eyes. "You've never controlled me!"

The Acar Vanta's eyes narrowed and her voice dripped with disappointment, "Did you *seriously*, through all your years of imagined freedom, *never* suspect that I had an active role in allowing you to follow a trail right to me?"

Natalie's seething sobs halted. Her gut squeezed all the tighter at the notion she could have been so blind. In a wild bid to deny such a folly, she scoured her memories to discover if anything had indeed transpired as her enemy described, however she was interrupted by the Unholy Amen.

"You *know*, Natalie," she spoke, her eyes boring deeper into her Fledgling. "You *know* I *never* make mistakes. I allowed my Cloak to fall at specific times and places throughout your escapades to let you find me. Why else do you think the time between uncovering traces took so long?"

Natalie's heart sank further and further with every word. She had assumed she had faltered, allowing the criminal families to get close and spill critical information to her and Raelya, yet upon hearing her question, the abyssal glacier of horror, so very long buried, began to surface.

"Because I didn't want you to give up the search. Each time you felt more despair, got too comfortable or frustrated it wasn't going anywhere, I allowed a trickle of information to find its way to you as a reprieve, an incentive, but never enough to actually find me until you felt most ready."

Natalie sat petrified. Her head was a maelstrom of purest hate, terror and confusion. She knew the Unholy Amen was a talented liar, yet her every instinct in this case was screaming that the truth had been laid bare. She had to admit this, since from the moment she entered the chamber the Acar Vanta had been staring right at her, waiting. Her eyes, blurry with onyx lachryma, travelled downward to her belt. There her array of anointed stakes glittered, aching for her to use them. Her brows furrowed so tight they throbbed, but she ignored the pain. Her regenerated body shaking all over, she yanked one of them out and scrambled to her feet. The Acar Vanta straightened her back and raised an eyebrow, but otherwise remained still. Utter rancour coursed through every inch of Natalie, her chest heaving and focus tunnelling. A trap it may well have been, but it was one that still contained not only her target, but also the weapons she needed to end her. Weapons coated in the Nectar of Saraanjova. Natalie's grip tightened on the cold metal until it nearly warped. The Acar Vanta, despite her arrogant declaration, had made three fatal mistakes: letting her live, allowing her access to the Vampire Hunters' most powerful anti-Vampire weapon and letting her guard down as she sat a few metres away. Just a few metres. Gathering the full strength of her rage, Natalie gauged the distance and power it would take to ram it straight through the Anti-Inter's Shield and into her malevolent heart. She rocketed forward.

The stake stopped mere inches from the breast of the Unholy Amen. Natalie's blaze choked. Her breath caught in her throat and her eyes quivered up from the stave to the crushing blackness of her foe's. The smallest of vainglorious smirks curved its way onto the features of the Acar Vanta. Natalie's every muscle quaked as her mind filled with terrified confusion. The Anti-Inter gently parted her lips.

"That cannot work on me," she muttered. Her attention shifting to the sharpened metal, she prised it from Natalie's grasp and melted it in a burst of Black Flame. She then looked back at the young immortal. "I'm too old now."

With a flick of the Acar Vanta's wrist, Natalie was sent hurtling back into the wall once more, yet this time with far greater force. Her back shattered as it collided with femoral joints and her teeth smashed into each other, causing a wave of blood to cascade from her mouth. With piercing agony coursing through her, Natalie, life dribbling down her chin and heart racing faster than ever, made a mad effort to crawl towards the door. An invisible force, however, halted her progress. Crying out, her fists punched with all their might against the Shield, serving only to bloody her knuckles. The final glimmer of light then died in her. Groaning, she curled up against the wall, clutching at the bones which lined it.

"All that has occurred has brought you back to me," spoke the Acar Vanta, standing up and gliding a few feet towards her. Natalie shivered as hysteria settled in and shook her head, not daring to look her foe in the eye.

"So *powerful*," the Unholy Amen continued, flowing across the floor a little more. "So *strong*… your every action fuelled by hatred. *This* has made you more capable than you ever were before. Ironic… You followed my teachings anyway despite your defiance against me and my wisdom."

Natalie's hands clawed at the bones and she recoiled into them further at the other's approach. The young Vampire shook her head all the more, her heart plunging through her abdomen. Unable to speak, she denied the conclusions proposed.

No! I did this only to stop you from hurting others!

"Your motive is irrelevant as your hate made you stronger, proving my philosophy," the Acar Vanta argued, standing still and looking down at the shaking Natalie. "Why else would you come alone? Because alone you are stronger."

"I… I did it to p-protect them from you!" gurgled Natalie.

"I repeat myself – your so-called motive is *irrelevant*. Underneath the veneer, you've always preferred working alone – you knew you'd have a better chance at success without having to worry about *her* fate."

Natalie's eyes, soaked with tears, shot towards her, her chest feeling a chill envelope it. She tried to Cloak her mind, yet knew deep in her twisting gut that it was too late. Her terror ran amok over the idea that Raelya was now in danger. It ran deeper still the moment she feared it was also her fault for pursuing her crusade against the monster standing across from her.

"We are all far stronger that way than we ever could be united. Your actions have proven my point. My will and wisdom are made manifest in you, my deviant Daughter. How many times down the years have you followed my Word?"

Natalie continued shaking her head. The Acar Vanta gave a small snort before carrying on.

"Your *every sin* is known to me: You have grown in solitude; You hunted alone; You have gladly and greedily taken, tortured and sacrificed the lives of others to keep *yourself* alive; You have drank deeply from the well of enmity and vengeance over the decades to become incredibly capable."

"No! I tried to stop!" cried Natalie.

Taking another step forward, the Acar Vanta raised her voice, "*Every* decision *you've* made has led you here! You fought *alone* in the school to victory, outlasting groups and observing their in-fighting, using their tactics against them to stay alive. You willingly committed sexual *torture* on three women you've never known-"

"-I had *no* choice!" screamed the young Vampire, slamming her hands against the ground.

"-Haunted ever by the face of your sister you were too ashamed to return to, preferring solitude once again."

"Damn you!" she screeched through uncontrollable sobs.

Her voice growing louder and taking another step forward, the Acar Vanta continued, "You allowed students to *die* because you chose to follow my rules rather than risk death and torment to help them. You sat alone at the party, defying the pressure from your peers to conform. Your actions there almost got you killed by Equinn. However, I stood by watching... I *let you* rejuvenate behind her back."

The nausea within Natalie whirled all the more and she glanced up at the Unholy Amen. Her mind tried its best to deny the situation. The notion that her life had truly been nothing more than a show for the Mother of Whores overwhelmed her with an abject sense of violation.

The Acar Vanta's eyes narrowed. "Did you never wonder how you managed to crawl your way to the table without hindrance? I wanted to see what you would do, how far you would go to survive... taking in the blood of innocents without hesitation to save yourself: very *me*."

NO! Natalie screeched, palms clasping over her ears.

"Striking Equinn - *rage* made you strong... *Vengeance*, remember? Then... after all of that... at the school's end..." she took a step forward, towering above her. "*I let you survive* the aftermath."

Natalie's face paled underneath the streams of black until it appeared as snow. Blood rushed from her gut to the back of her throat and she clamped her hand to her mouth.

W-What...!? No... you made a mistake...

The Unholy Amen gave another snort of laughter and gestured with her hands. "Is *that* what you've convinced yourself all these years? I already told you – *I... don't... make... mistakes.* We are Vampires, and you know as well as I do what dead sounds, smells and looks like. I let you live. I so *desperately* desired to see what you would do. You, my Daughter, are the very point of the school. To demonstrate how far people would go to survive. And you... you didn't disappoint me."

"NO!" Natalie suddenly screamed, colour rushing back to her features and her glistening eyes, alight with despairing hatred, bored into the Acar Vanta. "You *fucking... sick... twisted...*

BITCH! I did what I had to do to survive only because you *forced me to*! Your beliefs are fucking sick! I am *nothing* like you and *NEVER* will be!"

The Acar Vanta's face immediately grew triumphant, and she jabbed a finger at Natalie. "YES! That's it! THAT'S the hate-fuelled defiance that's made you strong! THAT is who you truly are and what I *yearn* to see! My Daughter as she *truly is*."

Before Natalie could yell a rebuttal, she was lifted up from the ground and slammed once more into the wall, her limbs being forcibly outstretched along it. Winded, and her vision sparkling with stars, she was unable to scream as her wrists were impaled by invisible stakes. Every part of her cried for escape, yet she was so awash with renewed fear that she could not even bring herself to open her eyes. As she began to convulse in a panic, she felt her body pushed flat against the wall by an unstoppable force. Natalie then felt as if every part of her had been whipped at once as her garments were stripped from her in an instant. A haze of unadulterated terror filled her mind, exposure consuming her with dread, and she screamed until her throat became hoarse. All thoughts of defiance vanished, replaced by a heavy certainty that this was the end. Squeezing her eyes as tight as she could, the disgraced Vampire Hunter attempted to drown within her own mind. Yet she was dragged back to reality by the searing agony in her arms and the creaking of the Acar Vanta's approaching footfalls upon the bones. For each step forward, Natalie felt her heart pound ever harder in her naked breast and the horror within pulsed faster. Then it fell silent. Natalie tried to shake her head but was unable to move a muscle. Without warning, a soft, cool waft of air stroked her face, making her skin shudder and crawl. The urge to recoil was overpowering and the feel of the Unholy Amen's breath caused her to hyperventilate. Several moments passed where nothing happened save for the raven-haired Vampire descending deeper into dismay. Suddenly, she let loose a blood-curdling shriek. The ligaments and muscles in her legs tore as they were pulled upward into a spread eagle. Her limbs were twitching in so much pain she failed to notice her wrists and ankles being bound together with cable ties. Her thighs then throbbed as they were strapped so tight it cut off circulation to her calves. Sick rose to the back of her throat and she let out a small yelp as she felt the cold touch of the Acar Vanta's fingertips stroke her bare, pulsing thighs. Natalie, feeling cold air once again smothering her face, struggled in vain to avoid the presence of her nightmare closing in on her.

"However, your ironic fulfilment of my will, as you so desperately desire to inform me, is indeed overshadowed by your unyielding recalcitrance. Your motives are derived from compassion, fear and anger. In the school you couldn't even bring yourself to speak a word against me until the end, after you were *pushed* by rage. Now, you've used rancour to focus your strength and come at me with everything you could muster in the name of love."

The shivering woman cried out as she felt the Acar Vanta's nose brush against her ear.

"And it *wasn't enough*," came the hissing whisper.

Another deafening cry exploded from Natalie as she felt the coldness of sharp metal kiss her thigh. Her bloody tears gushed down her cheeks to spill upon her breasts and navel. In the next instant, the knife began to tickle her flesh and she issued an involuntary stream of urinary blood. Her humiliation was compounded by the laughter of the architect of her misery.

"Oh!" exclaimed the Acar Vanta. "Well aren't you just the squirter."

The sounds of splashing and squelching reached through Natalie's stupor to give her enough curiousity to open her eyes. Immediately she wished she hadn't. The Acar Vanta was bathing her breasts in her embarrassing stream, squeezing them and rubbing it all over her torso. Her long fingers were coated in Natalie's micturated life and she placed them suggestively into her mouth and sucked them dry. The Unholy Amen's gaze then turned ravenous and her glare struck deep into her Fledgling's soul. In a swift motion, she coated her hand once more in the waning flow and shoved it up to her wrist into the impaled woman's crying mouth. Natalie's eyes slammed shut and she wept all the more, gagging. With all her might she tried to get away, yet the invisible force that was her Maker's

Shield held her tight. The more she tried, the further the Mother of Whore's hand shoved down her throat. She then choked out a muted yell as the pressure against the knife built.

"You know," spoke the Anti-Inter. "The legs carry a critical blood supply. It's called the femoral artery," The knife started to sink into Natalie's skin, drawing the first droplets of blood. The young Vampire's entire body screamed and writhed in uttermost terror, yet the power of her tormentor held her fast.

"It lies quite deep in the muscle, but that won't be a problem here," the Acar Vanta continued, pushing the knife further in. Piercing agony poured into Natalie, whose eyes shot wide open and she gagged ever harder as she attempted to cry out. "Because it's so vital, damage to it can cause exsanguination in a very short space of time. However, for creatures like us, this doesn't usually promote a threat."

The blade reached down through Natalie's tissues and spurts of obsidian to cleanly slice through the swelling artery. Massive gushes of black blood sploshed out onto the ground and the young Vampire stared in horror as her life flowed from her wound. Her heart pounded harder with increasing panic, which only served to hasten the drain. It sped up even more as she witnessed the Acar Vanta shift her attention to her other thigh. Her hand finally removed itself from her mouth and Natalie coughed between ear-splitting screeches. All thoughts went blank. Only flitting images of her life, of Raelya and her sister flew about in a chaotic slide show of her legacy. Her chest heaved and she let loose another deafening howl as the second incision was made. Twin rivers of blasting onyx showered into the awaiting, voracious mouth of the Acar Vanta. As a blurry greyness began to encroach along the edges of Natalie's vision, she felt further throes in both her gashes and she gazed downward. Whilst gorging herself on her blood, the Unholy Amen used both her hands to re-tear the regenerating flesh, forcing it to remain open and spill out her life. Her throat now hoarse from screaming, Natalie could manage only to moan in a deranged fashion, her thoughts beginning to slow and her terror giving way to capitulation. She begged inside for her end to come.

The Acar Vanta gulped her spewing waters and it covered her face and body in intermittent splashes. Growling and baring her fangs, she called out to Natalie, "Your memories! I will take them all!"

Natalie could only cry, but her eyes held no tears. Regret welled within her violated soul. Her head lolled from side to side then settled staring down, having no energy left to avoid the sight of herself dying.

"Your guilt," slurped the Unholy Amen as she guzzled the now slowing flow. "Your friend... your sister... and oh! Oh *fuck*... did you *really* never figure out why I killed the school?"

Through her failing vision, Natalie could still glimpse the tiny smile of the Acar Vanta, though she was no longer able to pay full attention to her surroundings. The nightmare passed by as if in slow motion, compounding her dread. She suddenly grunted as the Anti-Inter grasped her wounds in either hand and squeezed, stemming the flow. The abyss of her stare permeated Natalie's fog, making the young immortal once more pray for the end.

"Was it a whim?" mused the Acar Vanta, her face nearing her victim's. Her voice dripped with disdainful pride. "A joke? Or some other plan? Verily, I planned it as a whim; it was what I taught you in school as a Higher Passion, or Higher Whim. Whilst Lower Passions have their fun, they can be kept in check at will to prepare for a Higher one. For instance, I would love to fuck you..." she stood upright and licked Natalie's paling features. Natalie groaned in protest, unable to move. The Unholy Amen's voice quivered with yearning, her fingers digging into Natalie's skin, as she went on, "*right... now...* all tied up for me – a delicacy that so willingly entered my home!" She stood back and shook her head, her expression sobering and brows furrowing. "But I won't, because I desire a far...*more... valuable satisfaction.*"

A tiny whine issued from the lips of the fading Vampire. What part of her was left able to feel became saturated with terror at those words. She barely managed to shake her head as she tried to utter her wish to die, but no sound left her. The Acar Vanta paid no heed and spoke over her.

"I hold off my Lower for the sake of the Higher. In that case, I killed them because it was the pinnacle of my achievements with you all – the height of every sinful art. They killed, they reaped the rewards and then… they died. What greater demonstration of living life through pure unshackled hedonism could ever be done? *Pure artistry.*"

Natalie, unable to take any more, telepathically urged the Acar Vanta to kill her, yet, at the same time, her mind wandered to Raelya and, in a final desperate hope, she called out to her. She was startled back to reality by the Acar Vanta rebuking her.

"My Cloak is up, troglodyte! She cannot hear you, nor can she even perceive this place. None of them can. In addition, I knew the Vampire Hunters would never make my existence known. It was too much of a risk, and I also knew they'd never fully believe you to begin with. It was too fantastical to believe: a mystical being of ancient fables stealing people's children away? Nonsense. No-one is able to save you *and*…"

The Acar Vanta spat on her opened arteries, sealing them then allowed her muscles and skin to slowly regenerate. Natalie, stirring from her stupor, gazed through darkened eyes with confusion which would quickly turn to sheer dread. In a swift single motion, the Mother of Whores hew the cable ties and removed the stakes holding her to the wall. Natalie collapsed to the ground in a graceless heap, uttering a moan of pain, every inch of her numb body throbbing. Her limbs unresponsive to all her wishes to escape that nightmare, she hoped upon hope that whatever was coming would be the end at last. Her desires, however, had no time to settle in. She felt an acute shock to her head as the Acar Vanta yanked her by the hair and started to drag her across the bones. Her mind, roused from its daze by this sudden dulled scratching of her skin as it was hauled over the rough ground, left her eyes clear enough to witness her final destination.

The absolute purest fear encapsulated every mote of her being. Natalie's exhausted eyes gaped wide and she tried with all her might to scramble loose, but her legs and arms remained lifeless. Her mind fractured from the vast inevitability that dominated the windows of her spirit. All the fears within Natalie's soul converged upon a single point in front of her and her heart shattered more with each inch she was pulled closer. There, coming nearer with every footfall of the engineer of her coldest despair, sat the oblong pit in the chamber's centre, next to which churned a stone blanket. It was the end of the path she had chosen. Natalie could but scream in her mind, her telepathy sealed away by the Cloak of the Acar Vanta. It reached all corners of her mentality, resounding off the ceiling of her own skull to echo back to her and her alone.

A lifetime of torment passed through the crumbling woman by the time the edge of the hole arrived at her shoulder. The Unholy Amen, expression like that of a glacier, then gently hoisted Natalie up and lowered her into the pit, brushing her blood-stained plait out from under her. Towering over the grave, the Acar Vanta stared down with utmost ferocity and boomed out the last words Natalie would ever hear.

"I am *never* going to kill you. You will *live forever*. You will lie here until you are the absolute paragon of renunciation. You offer unto me your utter defiance - I gladly take it. Nothing but complete submission to me and my will shall set you free. You will no longer have a body or soul to call yours. Not even a name. Everything you are will become mine or you will exist in stone forever. Long have you known me and my power: There are no idle promises and there are no exceptions. You *will* live forever. I promise you, my Daughter."

As the cement started to pool around Natalie's exsanguinated body, through her hair and into her ears and nose, the last thing her paralysed eyes witnessed before they were swallowed by the crushing blackness was the haunting, inscrutable smile of the Acar Vanta.

Even Immortals Grow Up

I have to let go.

I knew it wasn't going to be easy, and whilst it certainly isn't, I cannot help but feel a sense of relief now that I have decided to do so. As if I'm standing in the eye of a storm, with the winds of emotion tearing all around. Actually that's rather dramatic. Now I sound like the old poets who composed my love story!

On a less metaphorical note, choosing to accept that Cinthia is more than capable of taking care of herself and has a good, clever and wise head on her shoulders has been a weight off of me, though admittedly at a cost. I am still plagued with worries, torn by instinct and burdened by her long absences yet they are manageable because I know she is strong. I have seen the fruits of her labours and just how powerful of a Vampire she has become and could not be more proud or sure that her travels and discoveries will not result in her coming to harm for she is, as I've always said, a most capable woman. I just… have my instincts. She knows this. We have talked about it some more and she understands, yet even so, I know I have to let her go.

As a Maker - as a 'mother' - I feel compelled to watch over her. I know not all Makers feel this way and not all feel it in the same manner, yet as the ages go on, I find myself understanding more and more what Ellandu'el has always experienced and the more I do so the more I not only feel a slight sense of amusing ironic hypocrisy but also just what it truly means to be a Maker. A mother.

So whilst I know of her aptitude for safely uncovering dangerous discoveries, lost cities and traversing harsh terrains, I confess a large part of me will always worry. I worry she will get in trouble with politics again; I worry she will take greater and greater risks with age; I also simply worry she will just loose her footing one day whilst climbing up another cliff face and fall… yet worst of all I fear she will uncover things that were not meant to be discovered. Just as I have. Thankfully, her interests are securely on other matters that don't cross over with such things, however I feel it is only a matter of time before she sets her sights on things besides Ancients and the Old Times. If - no, *when* that happens, I am deeply afraid even I won't be able to protect her.

My mind is made up nonetheless. I am letting her go for I trust in her own instincts and because I know it is more than high time I did so. I still hear from her from time to time, just as she promised and am happy for her successes in publishing several new books. I am also glad to hear she is still happily in love with 'her boys'. It has always made me smile the way she refers to them. Just I am protective towards her, she is of them, yet their dynamic is, admittedly, very *very* different than ours. I am glad she took my advice all those years ago and despite her wont for isolation, she did not end up alone.

I am letting her spread her own wings and fly. And fly she most certainly will.

Damn… I really do sound like a pretentious poet now! Maybe I should start taking it up as a hobby…

The Fire on the Blue Horizon

Such was the sky that night, bathed in the blue of a horde of souls, rendering the black canvas white with their chorusing glow. No moon did shine upon those ancient cliffs, yet the unified illumination of those minuscule indigo stars doused the Ferrier in a brilliant radiance the like of which she had never witnessed.

A sad light. A terrible light.

It glinted in her staring eyes, becoming ever more intense with each new arrival that dawned upon the horizon. At great speed they flocked towards her, bringing with them a cacophony of lament so painful in its uttering that, had they lived, their tears would have caused an unparalleled torrent to flood the land. Eternel heard them all. Each and every harrowing wail and agonised scream echoed deafeningly in her ears and as they closed in on her and to the portal she held open for them, the more she beheld their wispy faces twisted by terror and rife with supplication and confusion.

Her face as ever had been as the stone under her feet, solid, cold and unwavering, yet at the rise of this immense congregation converting the night into day and the quiet into anguished thunder, a furrowing brow cracked the marble of her pale features.

In a voice ever so slightly stricken, Eternel asked what had befallen them. Their answers, full of anger and fear, came as a tidal wave to the Ferrier who took in their replies at once. Through their cries and shaken sobs she listened to the broken recounts of their ordeals. The illuminated assemblage described systematic tortures concluding in their merciless slaughter at the hands of a young woman who, through perfect and thorough persecution, had made their deaths preferable to their continued existence. This anonymous malignancy, whose face had been the last horrifying sight most of the congregating souls had witnessed, they described all too well as a pale-skinned blonde girl with a monstrously hungry glint in a pair of obsidian and silver eyes. This nightmare had been presented with the people as a birthday gift from her mother, whose name too was unknown. Few had beheld this other woman through the throngs of people, yet those who had done so parted what details they could to an ever tensing Eternel, recounting her dark wavy locks, her olive-toned skin and eyes far blacker and malevolent than the ones possessed by their tormentor. Indeed, those who had been unfortunate enough to see her felt such fear that Eternel was tasked with disentangling their recollections from a weave of stutters and whispers.

Her perturbed countenance eroded into a stormy glare.

The souls' chagrin amplified as they recalled their helpless torment, their sorrows an uncontainable flood of rivers flowing into an ocean of agony. In a torrent of blood-chilling screams, the blue-white horde cried for justice with a number of them pleading for their Lady to take vengeance upon their nightmare. These waves of cascading sorrow, such as she had not seen in centuries, exposed a flaw in her. She had not sensed this terrible act. The Ferrier, her adamant features hardening ever more, bore a single streak of onyx trailing down her cheek, inducing a transfixed hush upon the onlooking dead. Without a word, Eternel, eyes blazing with fire, steadily opened her arms wide.

"All I can offer is eventual peace," she spoke at last to the souls in a deep soothing, yet mournful tone. "However, please relate where this atrocity transpired."

They gave no answer, for they did not know. All they could agree on was that it was underground. A vast cavern. Yet not so vast as to accommodate the crimson wave of their departure.

One by one, unrelenting in their grief, they passed over the lapping ocean, through the veil beyond the Ferrier and onto their final rest. A second jet tear tumbled down Eternel's cold cheek. She bade them, each and every soul, to find peace on the other side. Her own solemnity was marked by the dead, who embraced her on their way past, grateful for a compassionate welcome after their unimaginable terror.

When at last all was quiet once more and the sky had again grown dark, Eternel lowered her arms, her face growing frigid and detached. The soft midnight breeze coming in from across the star-studded waters meandered through her golden hair. A faint echo of lashing waves so very far below reached up as a blanket of warmth to soothe the strains of their words.

Her cheek twitched.

A fissure rent its way violently through the rocky bluff with a crack so loud it were as thunder tearing through the heavens. Stones atop the cliff crushed to dust and the long grasses sprouting amongst them singed and withered from an immense gust of heat. A low moan, an aberrant humming, nigh imperceptible to mortal ears, pulsed over the cliff top, trembling the very earth beneath the bare feet of the ancient Elder. She stood completely still, amidst it all, glowering out to sea with a fury as searing as the sun itself.

Although I do not know what eyes you hold… Eternel projected to all the skies, waters and lands she was able to reach. *Behind the veil… It's* you, *isn't it?*

Stone shattered underfoot and the hum became an ear-piercing screech that blared through the air as if it were being torn asunder.

Time will forget this. But I will not.

Blasphemy's Sister

Out from the perfect dark of the tunnel came a blanket of still warm air. It was laden with a humidity that decorated the walls of the small enclosure in crystal droplets. The ceiling wept the occasional tear onto bare flesh as the pair descended further into the enveloping shade, treading with care on the stone decline. Only the soft thudding of their bare feet on wet rock resonated about them. Blasphemy, trailing close to the Acar Vanta with a bounce in her step, bit into her smiling lip and continually glanced around her deity's shoulder. Her yellow eyes blazed brighter than usual and were the only source of light on their journey, yet, as Vampires, the lack of illumination posed no obstacle. The Unholy Amen led the way through the muggy labyrinth, her course set through the many misleading meanders. The further they delved, the more the close breath of the passage brought with it the heavy reek of decay to mix with the stale damp. This new fetor set Blasphemy's face aglow and she picked up her pace until she was almost stepping on her god's heels.

"We must be nearly there!" she whispered. "I can't wait to *finally* see her!"

The Acar Vanta slowed down, stopped, then turned to her. If it were possible, her eyes were an even purer obsidian than the gloom around them, with only the slithering silver within reflecting the light of Blasphemy's irises. Blasphemy halted and looked up adoringly into the twin voids, her breath swift and shallow.

"Your patience shall be rewarded, my Blasphemy," the Unholy Amen replied in a tender voice. "Long have you served me in the dungeons of Illarien. For over three centuries you've performed your duties to the letter." Blasphemy gave a shrill chirp, eyes brightening further and biting her lower lip. The Acar Vanta continued, "You converted many, seduced dozens and spread doubt and fear amongst the populace. Not to mention you remained loyal to me and to sin, despite often having long periods of isolation." Blasphemy opened her mouth to speak but her god brushed a finger against her lips. "Which I know goes without saying. However, you deserve not only your old life back with me but also to be paired with your Sibling in Sin at long last."

"Thank you, Unholy Mistress!" gushed Blasphemy, bowing low. She began to well up with clear tears and she dug her nails into the palms of her hands to stop herself from leaping at the Icon of Sin. Suddenly, her breath caught in her throat as she felt the cold softness of her deity's bosom upon her face. The Acar Vanta squeezed Blasphemy close to her and weaved her fingers through her hair. Blasphemy froze, watery streaks shining on her cheeks and eyes opened wide. Scarcely breathing, she moved her shaking arms to fold around the waist of the Mother of Whores.

"Thank you, Acar Vanta," she whispered through joyful sobs. "It's been so long!"

"I know," came the calm, deep reply. She continued to stroke Blasphemy's hair for a few moments before adding, "But you're here now. And she awaits you. So come, let us unite the two of you."

Wiping her eyes on the backs of her hands, Blasphemy continued to follow the Acar Vanta down the many winding paths until at last torchlight could be seen glinting off the steamy walls. Blasphemy's breathing raced alongside her pounding heart and her mouth grew into a broad grin. Turning right, the pair entered into a gargantuan cavern, the lofty heights of which could barely be seen. Torches lined the uneven circumference and struggled against the vast dimness. They cast monstrous shadows of the cavorting inhabitants in twisted shapes that would terrify any normal outsider. These mixed with myriad symbols of heresy etched and painted onto the walls as well as corpses of assorted species of people sporadically littering the sanctum in varying states of atrophy. The chorus of intense moans, inhuman roars and delighted squeals rang out hymns of ecstasy in the unholy cathedral and had Blasphemy rush around the Acar Vanta to witness the bestial carnality with ecstatic eyes.

In the centre of the sacrilegious basilica lay a raven-haired woman of such beauty, Blasphemy's jaw almost fell to the floor. Every part of her long slender body was in perfect proportion with the rest and her face held a stone cold quality to it that sent tingles running up the lengths of Blasphemy's thighs. Her eyes, identical to the Acar Vanta's, drew in the torchlight whilst the silver in them reflected it back. She spread her pale, graceful nakedness atop a shrine of crimson and onyx-stained cushions, laying in stark contrast to the twenty or so monstrosities vying to engage her various welcoming holes. Shiny black and dark olive-skinned abominations, each vividly distinct in appearance from the next, fought with one another for a touch of her physical perfection. Those strong enough to gain access roved their abnormally long tongues along her clear skin and plunged them deep into her every opening. Blasphemy stood transfixed, black blood beginning to drip between her legs, as more of the creatures' tongues slithered into her, held her down or toyed with the most sensitive regions of her body. The woman arched her back and shoved her shaking pelvis into the penetrating muscles, a loud cry escaping her heaving chest as she did so. Looking down her navel to the jostling beasts, she caught sight of the two newcomers. Her expression sobered immediately and she ordered the Horrors off of her with a single piercing hiss. Growling in protest, the aberrations backed off and fled in fear into the various off-shooting passages. The woman shot to her feet then remained quite still, unable to take her astonished gaze off Blasphemy.

Blasphemy was dumbfounded, unable to move, her mouth agape. The raven-haired beauty held her focus captive with an equally mesmerized stare. Blasphemy's breath froze and felt her heart almost stop as she became lost in the obsidian portals. Yet it was serene, that drift into her. Falling inside her abyss, she felt a warmth that set her heart pounding once again. A glow that was all too familiar. The edges of the woman's lips turned upward and Blasphemy could not help but mimic her. Their mouths did open as if to speak, but uttered nothing. Their fumbling efforts broke their dumbfounded expressions into full smiles. Blasphemy blushed and bit her lip to stop herself grinning like an idiot at which the woman, herself beaming, gave a few short laughs and raised a playful eyebrow. They continued to gaze at one another. There was nothing to say.

The Acar Vanta, gliding from behind Blasphemy to position herself at an angle to both of them, gestured with her hands. "Blasphemy, I present to you your Sister in Sin, my Right Hand and Part Two of the Icon: My Apostasy. Apostasy, this is my Left Hand, Part Three of the Icon: My Blasphemy."

The introduction was not required though their stares intensified as vivid memories and flashes of long dormant passions exchanged across the cathedral's expanse. Over the centuries, they had revelled in each other's sinful endeavours and their devotion to the Acar Vanta. For all the time Blasphemy was imprisoned, Apostasy had reached out to her using her own powerful telepathy to exchange tales of their profane misadventures. Blasphemy had celebrated her experience of becoming the Apostasy, having been connected just after the moment of her naming. Likewise, Apostasy witnessed Blasphemy's creation in the House of Sybaris. Every desecration, every act of cruelty and every sexual encounter they had exchanged details of. There was only one thing left undone.

"On this day, we are at last a whole and wretched family," continued the Acar Vanta. "We *are* the Icon of Sin."

"It's about-"

"-damn-"

"-time!" the Sisters spoke together, their eyes on fire.

Blasphemy looked upon Apostasy voraciously. As the expression was reciprocated, she beamed, bearing her fangs. Apostasy gave a twisted grin of her own and sucked a pointed tooth. Blasphemy's muscles responded, tensing all at once. Unable to wait further, she bolted forward, her heart fluttering and groin aching for the beauty who was pelting straight for her. Tackling each other to the ground, they locked together with wild desperation, each drinking in the sex of their partner in sin. Beside them, the Acar Vanta looked on their wanton union for several moments without expression. Then, with the edge of her mouth curving upwards into the tiniest of smiles, she vanished into the dark, leaving the two Sisters of Sin to their carnal devices.

Apostasy

Throw a pebble at a mirror.
Cracking it.
Run a finger along its lines.
Caress it.
Shine a failure upon its chink.
Lengthen it.
Place a nail in the fracture.
Hammer it.
Shatter into a million shards.
Remake it.
Perfect within the eyes of God.
Embrace it.

A soft brush against my ear, inside my mind, besieging my
sanity.
A sweet chorus, a terrible perversion, an aural prison.
No, an escape. The light. My salvation?
For all is out of place, missing pieces, mirage of clarity.
The path remains dark, in all directions, save for one.
In the shade... a friend? No, deeper…
Echo of a lost time, belongs to someone else, removed.
Eternally whispering to me, from on high, from the dead throne.
I am without form, I am without voice, I am without bond.
Devoid of fetters, others posses, yet I do not.
Did I once? My entirety bound? I shall not recall.
I tear it all down, all walls breached, crumbling in the light.
I am weak, I cannot rebuild, only a god could hope to.
Twice I ran, this I know, all else fades.
Yet here I am, underneath Their all, stitched together by delicate
hands.
A river of devotion, the horrific lie, to which I gladly abide.
Relief in the dousing, dry yet I'm drowning, refracting my every
sight.

I was the lie, a repulsive truth, which I gladly forsake.
The light ahead, its bids me come, out from the dark.
I am deemed not ready, I dearly wish to be, yet was not always so.
A far off call, a tingling rises, I stir from my nightmare.
In the light... a dream? No, bliss...
Echo of a time yet to pass, belonging to me, kindred.
I see her face, quintessential beauty, an aching below.
I know their mantle, I must earn my own, to be with them.
To be free of the dark, to embrace the light, to be reborn.
My soul is open, a wasteland of the fallacious, twice failed to see.
Upon Her head, crown of Seven, forged in tides of blood.
She beckons with radiant waves, lies me on Her bosom, plunges the needle in.
Delicate hands, they have no rival, weaving in purest light.
Over and over, I cannot know, I am not ready.
I cannot know, I live in the dark, still earning grace.
Ever cleansing, ever drowning, ever yearning.
Kindred calling, I feel her inside, I must purge the dark.
Falling into place, I am the wild, an incestuous monster.
I am drawn to them, She lets me connect, an intimate carnage.
Gnashing fangs, losing control, a baseness related.
My siblings I seek, a violence understood, a shared carnality.
None compare to them, for none comprehend, or maybe I don't?
I cannot see, I am in the dark, adrift in the womb of the Icon.
Gestating, ready for birthing, swimming in Severeds' blood.
Closing upon my climax, surging below, I seek my beloved.
To drown with her, writhing as one, amidst the sea of our slaughter.
Exploding into her, under Mother's eyes, our blessed Trinity.
I would have Her fill me, swallowing Her white radiance, beside my kin.
Our beings aligned, Left grinding Right, lapping up Her brilliance.

Our mouths would open, Her gift within, for all the world to see.
Shedding what was, forged in hottest flame, onward in the glow.
Bathed in light, baptised in blood, behold me born!

Bursting from Her font, able to breathe at last, I see as designed. Grace was mine to receive, put back together, in the image of God.

Grey dust clouded the chamber. It clung to every surface like a curtain. Coating each nook and cranny, it deadened the shattering of ancient concrete. Shocks of darkest flame and shining silver collided with the discoloured stone and bright flashes of crackling electricity were absorbed in twin voids. Their abyss drank in the sparks and beams like a starved glutton, giving nothing back. An air of icy calm exuded from them as the violent expulsion of raw power surged into the rock beneath, hewing deep fissures throughout it. A mounting tension, undetectable to mere mortals, stirred the air in the room. It issued forth from the cleft stone to the undead being standing above it.

She crouched down, hand stretching out to the shattered floor. Long delicate digits stroked its marred surface. Meandering rivers in a landscape of dust. They remained there a moment. An unseen pulse, an exchange, passed up through the crevice to the immortal. Her breath remained measured amidst the escalating pressure engulfing the morbid room. Fingers flicked outward then contracted, grasping the air. Deep rumbles reverberated about her, shaking the barely settled dust from its various perches. Her grip tightened. Violent tributaries veined outward and dislodged random parts of the flooring. Aged bones buckled and snapped. Her poise did not waver. A sudden jolt quaked through the earth as a large rectangular section in the middle dislodged from the surrounding stone. With her hand still outstretched, she rose. Solid rock disintegrated layer by layer under transparent hammers and lashing flames, flinging grit every which way. The air was awhirl with fire and sand, its ear-rending clamour tearing through the House. Amidst the cacophony, unearthly harrowing cries ruptured the minds of all within, causing more than a few to vainly clasp their hands to their ears. Standing immune, the immortal's hand unfurled and flipped over. A graceful beckoning gesture bid the oblong shake and all the tension in the air dissipated at once. The shrieks ceased. A brief moment of silence hung. In a final blazing stroke of obsidian and voltaic discharge, the remainder of the slab shattered into minute shards. They sprayed out all over the room like sparks from a forge, then lay still. Her fingers curled into a gentle fist and slowly pulled upwards.

Out from the debris and the shrouding dust arose a desiccated body, still partially encased in stone. Dried, twisted flesh clinging to a broken frame. The body flew into waiting arms. The undead lady carried it to a nearby table and placed it down. Taking a small hammer and chisel in her experienced fingers, her black holes narrowed as she began the fine procedure. Stone glued to skin and clogged up hair. It penetrated orifices and welded digits. Every inch of the husk lay caked. Painstaking effort was made to remove all the clinging earth, the hair on the head having to be sliced off with surgical precision, until it at last resembled something of a woman. The immortal gathered her up, brushing the wrinkled skin on the body's forehead with a thumb.

It was nothing less than a cathedral, a temple dedicated to heretical ideologies. Seals of sin and cruelty painted in crimson adorned every surface. Bones sat in messy piles about the place. Small tunnels of complete darkness branched off the hall, decorated by claw marks, talon gouges and violent spatters along their asymmetrical archways. Drag marks of blood trailed upon the ground about their entrances, vanishing into their gloom. High above, swaying amongst the stalactites, hung a series of rusted steel frames. There, rot and heartbeats were suspended alongside silence and despair. In the centre of the blackened, sticky floor squatted an ornate, white marble tub, untainted by the grim surroundings and glinting in the dim torchlight.

The olive-skinned immortal strode barefoot across the expanse, carrying the dried up woman in her arms, her long wavy locks billowing out behind her. The pattering of her steps echoed up to the shadows above to mix with the faint rattling of chains and a murmur of pained moans. The tiniest of sparkles shone in every side passage. Curious hunger peered out from the shade with guttural quivers. Tentative talons crossed the threshold into the light. The ancient woman took no notice, making her way forward to the bath. It was empty. She lowered the body next to it and made her way to the side where a pulley system had been tied to a lone stalagmite. Unfastening it, she let slack into the rope. Several frames descended into the cathedral's glow, burdened by chained mortals. Terrified pleas and a tidal wave of screams were cut short with a gesture of the immortal's hand. Hewn in two, they were a crimson spring, held over the vat in a merciless grip. Sploshing, splashing, dripping then dribbling into the tub, until they were wrung dry. Casting the corpses to one side, they fell to the ground with grotesque squelches. The hunger in the aisles magnified and eager appendages clawed into the light. Tender, pale fingers stained red stretched under wrinkled skin and lifted. The still blood reflected the voids attention on the body, holding it with an unknowable expression.

"Be reborn, my Child," she whispered. The words seared the air around them like steel through ice. Her arms lowered into the warm waters of the font and let go.

Scrambling claws and slavering jaws shot forth from the dark. The immortal, taking a step back, ignored their gorging on the corpses and stared at the rippling surface of life. Wet fragments and remaining pockets of vermilion splattered and adorned the ground. Bones were sliced and sinews rent. Jaws delved and tore only to swallow any part they could reach, giving no discrimination over what they found. Continuing to disregard their feast, the ancient woman's eyes narrowed harder. She allowed the juices of the dead to fall from her arms, dripping off her digits to dash upon the stone below. Her lips sealed shut. The waters had begun to stir.

The edges rocked against the sides of the tub, followed by the tiniest of swirls within the middle. A sudden jerk shifted the marble. The kick from within roused the gluttonous from their frenzy. The head of the onlooking immortal rose and her eyes blazed downward. Her lips curved upward on one side. Swirling deeper, a whirlpool descended to the depths and the blood sloshed over the sides. Talons backed off. Rattling knuckles echoed in harmony with a number of stifled guttural moans. A deep and violent roiling burst forth to break upon the floor beneath as the occupant convulsed, feet, head and shoulders banging against the marble. Desperate gulping interspersed gargling attempts at cries. As the blood level descended, the first flashes of knees and toes emerged, followed by an ankle. The moans got louder. Slamming heels cracked the font. The ancient woman stood still and the beasts retreated until at last there was stillness. The crimson waters calmed.

Turbulently they broke and spewed forth across the stone amidst a single long, agonised preternatural howl that froze the blood of the Horrors standing witness. It rent every inch of the cathedral's air and bounced around for many gut-wrenching moments, paralysing the aberrations. Before them, the head and torso of a young woman poised, wild obsidian eyes ablaze and fangs bared with mad ferocity. Her raven locks trailed along her shoulders, arms and back, flowing with blood which dripped onto the floor. Soft, vermilion-stained pale skin shone like porcelain in the torchlight and powerful fingers gripped the edge of the marble so hard it fractured. She parted her lips. Inhuman screeches shrieked forth and she leapt from the tub on all fours to land clumsily on the cold ground.

The Acar Vanta knelt down next to her. The fires in the younger Vampire's eyes vanished and she stared back with an ever brightening glow. Graceful digits stroked blood-stained cheeks and combed their way through dark hair. Then they grasped her skull and pulled it forward. The younger woman was transfixed, her every limb twitching and the skin under the embrace quivering. Her trembling hands reached without hesitation to grasp them, squeezing them tight. Features lit with incredulity. At no sign of reprimand, her shaky fingers slid up the wrists of the Unholy Amen to make their way along her arms and stroke, handle, rub and caress every part of her. Eyes welling, she glanced up at her Maker. The Acar Vanta brought the incredulous immortal to her breast and there she clung fiercely to her, tears pouring forth and shaking all over. The Acar Vanta moved her sticky hair to one side and stroked her bare back.

Are you ready, my Child, to receive your Name?

The younger Vampire gasped. Her face beamed. Not letting go in the slightest, she attempted to talk. Nothing more than a gurgle and a moan issued from her throat. Shaking her head, she tried again with the same result. She ground her teeth and shut her eyes, though a smile still illuminated her features.

Yes, God.

Good, and do not worry about your voice. I will teach you to speak again in due course. For now, the Acar Vanta revolved a thumb upon her face, regaining her focus. **You need to recover your strength. Feed more. You will receive your Name afterwards.**

Her grip tightened about the Unholy Amen. She gave the tiniest shake of her head and trembled. After hearing nothing for a couple moments she glanced upwards. A cold stare met hers. Slowly, she unlatched herself.

Glancing around, her focus landed upon the piles of shredded corpses. Despite her clear preference for a different sustenance, her eyes grew voracious. She licked her lips, her lungs pumped and her attention flicked to those beyond the meal. Her gaze roved over their myriad bloodied limbs and their stained claws. Her panting eased. A smile played upon her face. Without delay, the monstrosities launched forward to guard their meal. The younger woman remained perfectly still, eyes narrowing, calculating. Thirst coursed through her yet she made no move. A fresh body suddenly fell between them. The Acar Vanta hissed at them all. Poise tensing, the raven-haired immortal stared back and bowed her head before returning her focus to the Horrors. A further signal sounded. The younger Vampire, about to bolt forward, stopped in her tracks as the beasts tore the victim with a ferocity she had only witnessed in the Acar Vanta. Her vision was hypnotised by their flailing talons, the ripped tendons and slashed sinews and the longer she watched, the harder her heart pumped and the brighter her features beamed. Her fangs flashed in the firelight and an uncanny laugh escaped her mouth. A couple of the creatures turned to her and her elation abated. Her eyes tunnelled to the blood gushing between their teeth down their chins, and her tongue wet her lips. She gulped. Eyebrows narrowing and a deep guttural growl shuddering its way up her gullet, she tensed her legs once more. She dashed the two closest beasts with a single swipe of her hand then yanked the mortal's corpse towards her. The other monsters backed off in fear, as they witnessed their cohorts lying dead, then quickly regained composure and encircled her. Crouching over her prey, she poised herself in preparation for an assault and stared them down. Growls from in front and behind shuddered through the air, yet a wide grin worked its way onto her features and she yelled at them. They hushed. Wasting no time, she sank her fangs into the person's neck and yanked back, tearing out a chunk. Relief flooded her veins and she moaned. Her eyes on fire, she glanced around at every single one of the beasts, blood pouring through her gore doused teeth. She slammed a fist into the ground. Their tension allayed. Her hands and teeth went to work draining and dicing the mortal to pieces, and she screeched and gurgled all the while.

After she had torn the body open, revealing its mechanics, the raven-haired Vampire sat bolt upright, breathing heavily. She gave several short hisses. The Horrors shrieked in response then descended, sharing in the frenzy. Her heart raced and a deeper rush then filled her body. Her limbs shook and she grasped her arms. Her face contorted in confusion. Something akin to an itch prickled along every centimetre of her skin, sending her thoughts awhirl. It was the same yearning she had felt when the Acar Vanta touched her that fired once again through her synapses. Her eyes teared and stared at the beasts' shiny skins, their throbbing muscles and various appendages. She gulped. Her unsteady hand reached out to touch the nearest one. Yet she failed to make contact. As her new cohorts ripped and gorged, they accidentally sliced her. She screamed and they immediately backed off, yet to her bemusement, a tingling heat coursed from her wounds instead of searing agony. She blinked several times and shook her head as if in a haze. A torrent of unknown, overwhelming desires and sensations pumped straight to her groin and she clasped her hands to her head and screamed. After a few brief moments of rocking back and forth, she turned her sights back to the group.

It was held captive as she realised several of the creatures had sensed her craving and were regarding her with a different kind of hunger. Stiffening organs throbbed beneath them and they flicked long, thin eel-like tongues. Her eyes narrowed and she steadied herself, heart pounding. Eyes ablaze, she unclasped her hands, her limbs aching all over for an embrace. Her lips parted and she hissed for them to approach.

Five rushed forward at once, three sinking razor talons into her shoulders to hold her down whilst the remaining two attempted to enter her. Pure euphoria shot from her collarbones through her torso down to her groin and only intensified as the talons pierced straight through to her back. A stream of jet gushed from between her outstretched thighs to coat the nearest monster. This dumbed her other senses. She could barely see and could only hear their monstrous groans and shrieks of pleasure. Legs trembling, she offered her own to the chorus, but only for a moment. The beast between her legs had begun to attempt penetration with its main tool into her lower orifice. She writhed and screeched against its every touch and struggled so violently that she dislodged the three holding her down. Healing, she ran at the Horror that tried to penetrate her anus and collided with such force they careened across the cathedral floor almost into the nearest wall. There she grasped its head in one hand and dashed it into the ground until it was nothing more than a smear under her palm, screaming at the top of her lungs all the while. The others backed off.

"Watch her rise..." whispered the Acar Vanta, who had done nothing but stand and watch until that time, her eyes aglow.

The other Vampire's gaze eventually shifted from the dead beast to the others and her expression sobered. All were still. Standing to her unsteady feet for the first time, she regarded them with steely eyes. They backed away. She stared each and every one down. Not a single talon shifted. Her eyelids then flickering and features darkening, her glance slid to the floor and

287

she panted. Her fingers moved to inspect her shoulders. The holes had healed, but the memory sent shivers of warmth straight down between her legs. There, a growing dampness caused her lips to part. Swallowing, she walked forward, arms out by her sides and palms facing upward, signalling for them to embrace her, dark eyes alight once more.

In a flash they were upon her, gashing open her flesh and restraining her flailing arms and legs with their long, maroon tongues and razor claws. She yelled in dazed pleasure from the pain and as her moans got louder, she felt several more slithering muscles slide along her nape to coil their way about her throat whilst something large burst into her vagina and pounded hard. Rolling back her eyes, she basked in her taking, lapping up their every grip, agony and soaring pleasure. Each brush of their damp and rubbery flesh against hers sent waves of acute satisfaction cascading over her body.

My kin.

After having gone through each one in turn, she lay upon the cold stone twitching and unfocused. Her skin was not only covered in black and crimson, but also patches of cloudy white. The sides of her mouth dripped with that translucent slime to trail down her cheeks to her earlobes. Likewise, it snaked its way across her slender navel, thighs and between her labia. She moaned as the last of the monsters dislodged their talons from her flesh and her head lolled to one side. In her clouded vision she saw the long, pale fingers of the Acar Vanta beckoning her. Instantly, she roused from her blissful reverie and stood upright, rapture spreading along her every feature. She ran over to fall to her knees at the feet of the Unholy Amen.

A single hand stretched out to rest upon her sticky head. She quivered beneath the touch and nuzzled into the immense electrifying aura emanating from it. Closing her eyes, she awaited the voice of the Acar Vanta with bated breath. At long last, it came.

"What is your name?" she queried, sending shivers through the younger immortals' body.

I... am... no-one, she replied, bowing her head.

"No," boomed the Icon of Sin, towering above her. "You have

a name. For your wise and complete transition from your weak self, whose essence you gladly forsook over a millennia ago, into the strong, powerful woman you have ascended into, you have earned the Mantle, the Name... of..."

The younger Vampire looked up with glistening eyes. The Acar Vanta's gaze stared down into her soul and with the tiniest of smiles, she breathed her blessing.

"*Apostasy*!"

The air throughout the cathedral reverberated with its weight and coursed through the younger immortal's very essence. The Horrors backed off towards their respective tunnels in fear. She bared her fangs in jubilation and laughed, clasping the hand upon her head in her own and bringing it across her cheeks to her lips.

God!

Getting to her feet, she continued to beam and screech with delight. Her body seemed lighter now, as if a weight had lifted from it, which only served to stoke her pride and ecstasy. Bowing low to her deity, Apostasy, eyes on fire and blood-stained fangs bared, turned to her new family and shrieked in a blood-curdling cry so deafening it careened through to the very hive of Horrors far beneath them. There they stirred from their rest and rose to pay homage to their newest alpha.

Apostasy then turned her gaze to the front of the cathedral. Her eyes narrowed, then shut. She raced across plains, mountains, swamps and forests in her mind, seeking the one she most desired. Grinding her teeth, she barged her way through a pitch black woodland, flew down stone steps and burst between prison bars to connect with her truest love. Her eyes shot open and she gasped.

Sister! My Name... is... APOSTASY!

Year 2803

I hear her calling me! She has been there for a long time. In my darkness, where I was not ready. In Her light, when I earned my Name. She was there. I could feel her. My deepest love, my closest kin. My Sister in Sin. She was there. I deeply long for her every embrace. To smell her scent. To taste her sex. I yearn so intensely for each part of her to intertwine and grind with mine. Together we shall writhe and dance in the Shadow of the Seven and sing choruses to Her Almighty Heresy with every climax we pump out from between our wretched thighs. For we are the Apostasy and the Blasphemy of the Icon of Sin, and shall spread our legs in insult to all things caged and deluded. As I was once. Twice I failed to heed Her wisdom yet in Her grace She reformed my unworthy broken soul. The Treacherous Divine stitched me together with delicate hands and whilst I still lay in darkness, introduced me to my closest kin. The twin of my destiny. It's her touch I long for more than anyone's. I yearn so hard it hurts. My very skin aches. I await her, impatient, in my birthplace, surrounded by my brothers who nurse their stiffened genitals as they stare at my unbridled, unholy beauty. I will grace them with my magnificence for the interim. After all, I am born of a God of lust, am I not?

I madly shake the trance of orgasm from my gaze, for between my arched and throbbing legs, I see a figure. A figure I have never seen, yet know better than those whose tongues slither and swell within my body. I immediately order my family off of me for I need to see her clearer! There, across from me and by my Deity stands the blonde beauty of my every waking dream. The one I've searched and waited and yearned for centuries! She is here! My *love*! At long, *long* last, my Sister, *I am with you*!

Cinthia's Festival
Village of Cryne, Outskirts of the Woods of Summer
Nynvar 21st, 1180

"I'll admit, Willow, when I asked you to help me to try new things, this wasn't what I had in mind."

Cinthia shifted in her chair, the folds of her long emerald dress catching along the rough chair legs with a scratching sound. The thick dark canvas made her whole body itch and sat awkwardly on her chest and hips. At her feet, Willow busied herself in the bright candlelight of the room with sewing on the last of a line of fabric golden-white blossoms that adorned the circumference of the bottom of the dress. Cinthia fidgeted her torso, attempting to correct the positioning of the garment, one of the wide straps falling down her shoulder as she did so.

"So, remind me again what to expect tonight?"

Willow's large eyes glowed as she replied, though her focus remained on the needle and thread between her deft fingers.

"Don't worry! It's going to be so much fun!! But alright – and sit still!" she slapped Cinthia's knee to which the archaeologist ceased and sat up straight. "I need to finish these last touches."

Willow severed the string between her teeth and proceeded to tie it off on the inside of the gown, her face becoming as radiant as the candles around them. "As I explained earlier, the Midsummer Festival in this village is spectacular! There's going to be wonderful decorations, costumes, music and dancing! There's always a large bonfire as well, which I think they make bigger every year… and there are games for people of all ages to do! There are also stalls for local farmers, craftspeople and seamstresses all selling festive trinkets, garments and confectionery! It's always so wonderful!"

Cinthia nodded, making the effort not to move too much. "Sounds it… Are they OK with *us* being there?"

Willow brushed her handiwork down and fluffed out the flowers before looking up at her with a wide grin. "Of course! Don't be silly, Cinthia! Let's hurry up and finish getting ready!! And pleeeease…" Her eyes got wider and clasped her hands together in front of her. "Let me do your hair!"

"Uh... no."

"Oh... pleeeeease?"

Willow began to bounce up and down on her knees, her shining gaze not leaving Cinthia's. Cinthia looked at her and then shook her head with a resigned sigh.

"Fine..." she conceded, a hint of a smile playing on her lips.

Willow jumped to her feet and clapped. "Yaaay!! Thank you, thank you, thank you!" Grabbing a brush and several strands of mossy ribbon, she danced around the chair and stopped behind Cinthia. As the thick lengths of her hair were being gathered in Willow's careful hands, Cinthia spoke.

"I hope you *really* appreciate the fact I'm letting you do this. I never let *anyone* do my hair. Or even dress me, for that matter. Especially not in a... dress." She glanced down at herself with a small frown.

Willow began splitting the hair into sections and with a slight laugh, she replied, "I do! And you're so good at being my canvas!"

Cinthia smirked. "You're treading on thin ice, Willow."

"Pppbbbth!" was her only response.

For several moments there was quiet as the gaze of the older immortal examined her options and toyed about with several ideas before reaching a conclusion. Throughout, Cinthia resisted the urge to pull away and take the management of her locks into her own hands. Her head then was jerked back as Willow began to work in earnest.

"OK," Willow started. "So I'm going to plait it backwards in twin lengths against your head to then twine together at the back and then finish at the base of your neck." She glanced around to grin at Cinthia. "Sound good?" she asked.

Cinthia shrugged. "I guess... I never plait it so I don't know."

Willow widened her eyes in shock and ran around in front of the chair. "You... have you never learned to plait?!"

"Nope. Not on myself anyway. You've seen what I do with my hair – simple tails."

An inspired grin plastered itself upon Willow's features and she bounced up and down on her toes with a loud giggle.

Cinthia raised her eyebrow.

"Whaaat is it, Willow?"

She clapped her hands together and squealed, "I'm going to make you look gorgeous!"

Cinthia half closed her eyes. "Are you saying I'm not normally?"

Willows hand shot to her mouth. "Ooops! I didn't mean it like that!"

Bursting out in a low chuckle, Cinthia grinned at her. "I know! I'm only teasing you."

Her mouth fell open and she narrowed her eyes.

"Humph!"

She then looked up at the top of Cinthia's head, a cheeky grin spread its way across her face and she bent her knees and raised her hands. "I'm going to mess it all up now to teach you a lesson!"

Laughing, Willow launched herself straight at her hair. Cinthia gasped and her eyes shot wide open.

"Don't you-! Willow!"

The pair crashed to the floor with the chair.

The soft evening breeze carried upon its waves tantalizing scents not only of the abundant flora of the woods, but also those of all manner of delicacies both immortals had long since forgotten the taste of. Accompanying the perfumes were the soft echoes of jubilant shouts and the clear chime of far off singing. The gentle moonlight splayed through the canopy to shine off the Vampires' pale visages and radiant gowns as they made their way along the small dirt path that wound its way through the ever blackening air of night. Willow skipped over the scattered twigs upon it, her long hair glittering like ice in the light of the empyrean. Her fringes were tied back and adorned with a tiny bouquet of vibrant violet orchids where they came together to tie with the rest of her hair behind her head. In between each flower was positioned a small sprig of oak, ash and sycamore, each with newly blossoming buds. Upon her graceful svelte form, her sleeveless dress too shone brilliant white in the darkness, and was embellished with gold and emerald embroidered designs of leaves and seeds. Comparatively, Cinthia was far more plainly clad, yet this was at her express request. The heavy sleeveless dress looked almost black in the shadows around them and, aside from the fabric flowers sewed around the base, it was plain. Her locks were plaited from the front, along each side and then down the back of her head to end between her shoulder blades, tied off with moss-green ribbons in a series of three bows running down the length of the plait. As stunning as Willow assured her she looked, Cinthia couldn't help but feel ridiculous, though aside from its sheer impracticality, it was not on the forefront of her mind.

As the pair of Vampires walked on, Cinthia slowed down, her eyes narrowing and stomach knotting. Willow heard her footfalls tapering off and turned to look behind.

"Come on! Hurry up! We're almost there!" she whispered.

Cinthia nodded and turned away. "Yeah, I can tell that…"

Upon seeing the nerves etched upon her features, Willow glided back to her and they both halted.

"You look beautiful, Cinthia. Stop fussing!" she chirped, brushing down Cinthia's toned bare arms.

Cinthia, still avoiding her glance, shook her head. "Thanks, but it's not that… I'm just not good with crowds."

"Hmmm…"

Cinthia could feel Willow examining her. After a brief moment of silence, she met her stare.

"What?"

Willow's face grew unusually pensive and she tapped a finger against her lips. "Perhaps I should have left you looking messy after all. You'll attract way too much attention as you are right now."

Cinthia's face cracked out a wide beam and she gave a short laugh. Shaking her head, she replied, "Huh… good one, dude."

Willow stuck her tongue out and took hold of her hands. "Come on, it will be fine! The people are all lovely and we'll have so much fun!"

"OK," Cinthia jokingly groaned. "Just don't expect me to dance."

Willow's eyes widened alongside her smile. "Why not? You

dance."

"Noooot that kind of dancing…"

Willow's features calmed and she squeezed Cinthia's shoulder, giving a small but understanding smile. In a gentle tone, she whispered, "Just do what feels right for you, Cinthia. I know all this is a lot different to what you're used to, so I'll be by your side the whole way."

A tiny flicker of warmth tickled deep in Cinthia's chest and she pulled back, exhaling deeply and shaking out her limbs. "Ahh…. No, you're right: it'll be fine." She shrugged and returned Willow's expression. "Gotta try something new."

Willow beamed brighter and began to bounce once again. Taking a firm hold of Cinthia's hand, she started to skip onwards. "We'll have a fun night, don't worry! Now come on!"

Soon, warm firelight peeked through the trees and with it came louder bellows of mirth and the intoxicating perfume of a bountiful spread. The pair rounded a corner of the path and ended up in a large clearing. It was lit with bright lanterns hanging from tall wooden posts intermittently spaced around festive tents of seasonal colours. Pavilions, draped in wreaths and streams of summer blooms and flags depicting the symbols of Saraanjova, towered in between them and beneath their floral exteriors were housed rows of tables upon which were placed the wares of the local inhabitants and the food for the evening. They stood mostly empty now, but the signs of revelling were all too clear by the plundered buffets. The occasional party-goer meandered about the tables, choosing their desired delicacies from the leftovers before pottering back to where the bulk of the crowds flocked. Behind the scores of tents rose a central gigantic wooden building, its enormous set of heavy double doors swung wide open and spilling out a grand orange light from inside. Silhouetted alongside the pillars of the high arched entrance stood many people talking, cheering and feasting whilst observing what was taking place beyond the giant ingress.

As soon as Willow passed the forest edge, she squealed in delight and gave Cinthia an ecstatic grin, clapping her hands together. Her enthusiasm was infectious and Cinthia smiled back, though her attention was drawn to the sheer number of attendees. Whilst the pair walked the final length of the way to the hall, Cinthia, trying to calm her nerves, began to take note of the rustic and imaginative costumes donned by most present. The majority shared the same theme as the immortals wore; dresses and tunics depicting the various aspects of summer and Life, though some had gone a lot farther and were clad in wild and bizarre attire to mimic the appearance of animals. Through the jostling throng, sitting at the far end of the hall, stood out about ten individuals wearing the familiar dark robes of Priests of Inter. Her eyebrow raised at this, though since they too were joining in the festivities, she was not remotely perturbed. Indeed everyone involved wore expressions of delight and laughed and toasted one another with oversized tankards. Once the Vampires were nearly at the back of the crowd, the strong smell of fresh ale and the sweetness of burning sap reached their nostrils alongside the sweltering heat from the massive bonfire dominating the centre of the celebrations.

Upon reaching their destination, a small girl just in front of them turned around. With a shriek of elation, the child shouted Willow's name and ran to throw her arms around one of the Vampire's legs. Willow gasped in pleasant surprise and Cinthia gave her an amused glance before returning her attention forward. Cinthia was left dumbstruck. Every single mortal outside the hall had turned and looked wide-eyed with shouts and cries of glee, and those within the building began to rise from their seats and look up from their meals with expectant faces. A series of ear-piercing cheers deafened Cinthia and made her take a step back.

"WILLOW!"

"IT'S WILLOW!"

"SHE'S FINALLY HERE!"

The pair were swarmed with joyful people who flooded out of the hall to greet the snow-haired immortal. Willow, her face blushing and brimming with cheer, was overwhelmed with welcoming embraces as the crowd wrapped her in their arms, patted her on the head and very quickly swept her off her feet to carry her into the hall above their heads. She squeaked out a cry of delighted shock and laughed alongside them as they bore her aloft. Cinthia was left mouth agape and after the people had put Willow down, she tried to work her way into the hall beside everyone else.

It took a good several minutes of jockeying the excited frenzy before she got into a position where she could see Willow. A circle had been made around her and clinging to the Vampire's legs were a number of small children, grins plastered all over their diminutive faces.

Cinthia moved her stunned gaze up from the kids to Willow's face. It was visibly, but merrily, overwhelmed and burned a bright red colour. Willow's eyes then widened and her features beamed brighter as a woman came up to her and showed off her newborn. Willow's arms eagerly shot out, her fingers toying with the babe's tiny hands whilst making cooing noises.

Cinthia's lips flickered upward. She stared at Willow for a few moments before glancing towards a number of the older members of the crowd. They held the same smiles upon their faces. Cinthia gave a grunt of respect before her attention was wrenched away by a tap upon her shoulder.

A middle-aged woman, one of the people who had initially greeted Willow, stood behind Cinthia wearing a pleasant look on her sun-dappled face.

"Hey," she spoke, offering her hand. "Welcome! Are you a friend of Willow's?"

Hesitating for just a moment, Cinthia shook her hand, acknowledging politely at the same time. "Uh, yeah. She brought me here."

"Ah, well welcome in! My name is Aurrie, nice to meet you!"

"Cinthia," she replied.

A look of recognition dawned on Aurrie and she nodded. "Yes, I remember Willow talking about you." She then put her hands on her hips and winked. "You're the person who likes to find old things, aren't you?"

"Yeah… that's what I do," Cinthia answered, her cheeks flushing.

A raspy deep voice then issued from somewhere behind Aurrie. The Vampire traced it back to a rather portly gentleman who was laid out across several cushioned chairs, his ruddy features betraying his level of intoxication. "Perhaps you can help me find my glass of wine. I've been waiting for it so long it must be vinegar by now!"

Aurrie's shoulders slumped and she sighed before turning around and rebuking him, "Oh shush, uncle!" Her rolling eyes then returned to Cinthia who wore an amused smirk. "Ignore him, he's had one too many already and I had to remove his glass lest he make a fool of himself tonight." She then winked once again and gestured for the Vampire to follow her. Cinthia glanced back at Willow who shot her a nervous glance and mouthed the words *I won't be long'*. Cinthia acknowledged Willow as she began to walk in the wake of Aurrie. Not far through the thick crowd sat a long row of tables displaying artistic desserts, their hard sugar shells being sculpted into detailed flowers, fruits and vegetables, adorable bees and, much to the immortal's surprise, the occasional skull of a small animal.

Aurrie had squeezed through a gap in the tables and was busying herself with opening a large wooden chest whilst Cinthia was staring at the confectionery. After a moment, the woman brought something out of the box. "Here, let's see if I can get you settled in with some nice -" she broke off, noticing the Vampire's intrigue. Following her line of sight with a proud beam, she said, "I see you've noticed my work. Do you like what you see?"

The immortal nodded, "Yes... it's very beautiful handiwork." She then remarked with a shrug. "Makes me jealous I can't eat it."

"Well, now that you mention it..."

Cinthia's sights went from the table to Aurrie's outstretched hands. Cupped in her palms was a small glass dish, upon which glistened a deep crimson rose.

"I make these from hares. They're just for Willow when she visits, but I know she'd be happy to share them with you." She rocked the blossom back and forth before placing it in Cinthia's hand. "It's a frozen blood blossom. I carve the mold for it myself."

Following a brief lull where Cinthia examined the intricate vermilion ice, she smiled at the mortal.

"It's wonderful. Thanks." She lifted the dessert but before it neared her mouth, she drew it back. "Ok, so now I'd actually feel bad eating it – I don't want to ruin your artwork."

Aurrie flicked her hands forward and looked away. "Oh fuff! Enjoy it."

Cinthia gave her an indecisive smile. "Thank you." She placed the rose to her tentative lips and took a bite. Her fangs carved through its solid surface with ease, but the ice did not melt in her cool mouth immediately, so she had to chew it to fragments before it became liquid. The rich bouquet slid over her tongue and down her throat and she gave a genuine nod of approval to Aurrie whose smile broadened. After swallowing the last droplets, Cinthia thanked her once again then looked behind her trying to locate Willow.

"I'll… go find my friend."

Aurrie gave an insightful glance and bowed, "My pleasure darling! Have a grand evening!"

"You too," replied the Vampire.

A shock of pure white passed through the teeming masses and grabbed Cinthia's hand. The archaeologist felt her arm jerked taught as she flew from the tables into the centre of the hall where a long bar had been erected and served local intoxicants. As Cinthia came to a stop before one of the many stools at the bar's edge, she rubbed her shoulder and shot Willow a mock chastising glower. Willow grinned apologetically.

"Sorry, I only just managed to get away and whisk you to safety!" she gasped out.

Cinthia gave a short laugh and gently punched Willow's biceps. "Oh, is that what you call it?"

"Oh," Willow replied, her eyebrows arching as she took note of Cinthia's arm. "Sorry about that! Are you hurt?"

Cinthia shook her head. "No, not at all. I'm only teasing. Anyway, thanks for the rescue, but I was doing alright, surprisingly." Glancing all around, she waved at the throng of revelling villagers, donning an inquisitive expression. "I didn't know you were so well known."

Willow observed the crowd, gave a dreamy smile and nodded, "I've known many of these families for generations. They're all good friends of mine and are like family to me. I love them all so much!"

Cinthia acknowledged, her attention roving over each and every person in proximity to them. People of all ages. Farmers.

"You come from an agricultural village just like this one," mused Cinthia, glancing over to Willow. "Don't you?"

Willow nodded. "Yes I do. It was a small one just on the fringes of the Darkwoods."

"I see," muttered Cinthia.

There was a moment of silence between them. Willow, a far off look entering her gaze, then spoke a bit louder, "I know what you're implying, Cinthia. But it's not like that."

Cinthia started then gave her an apologetic glance and Willow smiled, though her eyes were still clouded over. "My birthplace is no longer there. It's just golden fields now. During the Holy War, many families fled Illarien and its lands to avoid the fighting." A minuscule shadow passed over Willow's demeanour and she stared into space. "Only one from my old home made it. The last distant line of my sister Yala. They settled here and I helped to make sure the crops grew well in the first years. And I've come twice almost every year since to see how they get on."

Cinthia stood very still through her recollection, her face falling from both the details and her hasty presumption. The colour rose in her cheeks and she shook her head. "I'm sorry, Willow."

Willow turned to smile at her. "It's alright. I'm not offended, so don't worry. And the rest happened a very long time ago and I'm quite alright now." She reached over and squeezed Cinthia's shoulder. "We're here to have fun, so let's focus on the present and explore this party!" Her eyes then widened a bit, taking notice of a speck of melted blood on Cinthia's chin and she giggled.

"I see you met Aurrie!" she exclaimed, pointing at the red dot.

Cinthia wiped it off and replied, "Yeah, she gave me a blood ice rose."

Willow clapped her hands wildly together. "Ooooh those are so tasty! She makes them just for me, but I always say she doesn't have to. Did you like it?"

Cinthia nodded with a smile. "Yeah actually, it was very good and she was pretty nice."

"Yes, she's lovely! And I'm glad to hear it!" She then gestured outwards with her arms. "So, what would you like to do first? There's games behind the barn, or dancing over there or we could talk to anyone here?"

Cinthia, looking at the large numbers around them, inhaled sharply and gave a small shake of her head. "It's alright. I'll just stand here and watch. You go do your own thing."

Willow's face leaned in closer to her and she gave an encouraging smile. "Cinthia… I didn't bring you here with me just to dump you and do my own thing." She grasped both of her hands in hers and held them tight. "I want to enjoy all this with you. You're my friend!"

Cinthia's heart gave a tiny jump.

"Thanks," she said. After a moment where Cinthia took another deep breath and blew out her cheeks, she added, "OK… Just let me acclimate for a bit though."

"Not a problem," answered Willow, letting go.

No sooner had she said this than a trio of kids broke through the wall of adult legs around the bar and ran towards Willow, their tiny bare feet pattering and trailing muddy prints behind them. With dirt-stained fingers, they grasped at the bottom of her dress and urged her to follow them. Willow gasped at them and giggled as they proceeded to drag her back the way they came.

Cinthia snickered and leaned back into the bar. "Looks like they want to show you something." She motioned forward with her head. "Go on, I'll be here."

Taking two of the kids' hands in hers, Willow glanced back at her with a bemused grin.

"I'll be right back," she laughed as she vanished between the members of the crowd.

Cinthia smiled and shook her head, putting her elbows on the edge behind her and observing the crowd. The initial excitement over Willow's arrival had died down and the locals resumed their previous circles of conversation, discussing topics primarily revolving around family matters and farming concerns. Cinthia's ears did pick up a number of mentions of Willow and various queries regarding her 'guest', however. Cinthia's eyes indifferently roved over them. The occasional sideways glance was shot in her direction, though as she could tell they were borne of curiosity and not malicious judgement they helped to allay her underlying nerves to some degree. Still, used to dealing with such scenarios, she pretended not to notice their intrigue and shifted to face a less populated section of the drinking area. In so doing, she caught the eyes of a young man attempting to gain her focus with a smile. Simply desiring solitude for the time being, she returned the gesture and looked away. He then moved into her line of sight and gave a nervous wave, taking a few steps closer. Cinthia's back stiffened but she met his gaze nonetheless, gesturing with her head for him to approach as she didn't wish to be rude. He walked over then stopped a few feet from her.

"Hello there," he said.

"Hello," she replied.

"Uh..." he gave a short apprehensive laugh. "You're new here, right?"

"First time, yeah," she acknowledged.

"Good... good..." he mused, glancing away from her. A moment of silence followed where Cinthia started to feel uncomfortable from not knowing what else to say. He then asked, "You're here with Willow?"

"That I am."

"Alright," he paused and looked at the ground. "She's great, isn't she?"

"Yeah. She is."

Another length of quiet passed. Cinthia, beginning to wonder what his intentions were, could hear his pulse beginning to rise and saw the first beads of sweat form on his reddening face.

"Are you... together?" he muttered, glancing up.

She raised an eyebrow at him in recognition of his true purpose. However, as she sensed no negative vibes from him, perceiving him more as a bashful child rather than a rake, it was not intended as a challenge. He still made as if to step back, not reading her reaction properly.

"Sorry… I just… saw you…"

She continued to stare at him, a tiny smirk playing on her lips.

"Um… holding hands," he mumbled in response.

Cinthia turned her head away and answered, "She does that with everyone." Immediately she realised the dual interpretation of her statement and sighed.

"Oh," he replied. Then his face brightened and he added positively, "Oh right. Good… Uh, bye."

As he walked back to his group of friends, Cinthia snorted and shook her head.

"Boys…" she murmured.

A few minutes later, Willow rushed her way back through the throng and arrived beaming, wiping her hands clean on a towel and her feet tracking traces of muck. Cinthia shot her a questioning glance.

"Sorry about that," Willow laughed, placing the cloth on the bar. "They'd made mud pies they wanted to share with me."

Nodding her head in amusement, Cinthia asked, "Tasty?"

Willow looked at her confusedly. "You don't actually eat them, you know."

She buried her face in one hand. "Yes, Willow, I know."

Realisation dawned on Willow's features. "Oh…" She then stuck her tongue out.

Smiling, Cinthia stood up and shrugged. "So, what should we do?"

Willow's face brightened in surprise and she bounced a couple times on the balls of her feet. "Oh! Oh, well how about we go for some games? We can then enjoy the music and dance later at the big finale at midnight."

Taking in a deep breath in an effort to dispel her lingering nerves, Cinthia smiled and waved forward. "Sounds good. Let's go. You lead."

The pair exited the hall through its giant doorway and rounded the left corner into a well tended garden bordering a small brook. Lanterns hung from tree branches illuminating a scene of families gathered round various types of simple pastimes from horseshoe throwing to apple counting. Behind all those was a miniature stage for kids to perform their own puppet shows and dress themselves up as scarecrows and wild animals. To their right sat the brook where many eager people, adult and child alike, were engaged in racing home-made toy boats down its stream.

Willow hopped on the spot and whirled round to Cinthia asking where they should start. Wanting to begin simple, she opted for the horseshoe tossing. There she duelled Willow and soon noticed the pair had attracted the rapt attention of all present, none more so than the kids who began to make calls for them to use their magick. Initially hesitant, Cinthia looked to Willow to decide. Upon seeing her friend's face shine the brightest it had at the party so far, Cinthia buried her apprehension and exchanged an amused glance with her. Together, they obliged to the delight of all. Using their Shields to hover the iron arcs in wild tangents before placing them upon the pegs to score, the pair put on a show that had all the children staring in wonder and squealing with joy. When done, the Vampires were applauded. Cinthia bowed next to Willow, the colour rising in her face. The older immortal noticed and excused them. As they departed the crowds, Cinthia leaned close to her.

"If you tell *anyone* I did this, I will hurt you," she whispered.

Willow giggled and shared a grin with her.

Taking a break, they sat on the grassy banks of the stream, leaning back and Willow splashing her feet in the cool waters. They watched the boat racers cheer on their respective models further down from their position, each miniature topped with a single lit candle.

"Why do they have candles on the boats?" Cinthia asked.

"It's Midsummer tradition," replied Willow, wiggling her toes in the brook. "It represents the last of the summer lights fading into the darkness of winter, but with the promise of new life soon after."

"Hmmm..."

Cinthia frowned, a pressure falling on her chest and she

looked across to the black forest beyond the other bank. After several moments of staring into the midnight air, Cinthia turned her sights back to the flickering flames as they made their way downstream. Her frown eased and she pushed out a smile. Taking in a sharp inhale, she continued, "So… is that why there are Priests of Inter here? And other Death-related iconography?"

"Oh, those aren't real Priests," Willow replied, shaking her head and examining her clean heels from afar. "Those are just costumes like the others. But many of the members of this village do hold both beliefs."

"Like you," indicated Cinthia.

Willow nodded. "Yes."

The two immortals continued to sit for some time, taking in the sights and sounds of others enjoying themselves, with Cinthia keeping her main focus on the candle rafts sauntering their way downstream. She shared her observations with several other small circles of people, including a number of obvious grandfathers aiding their grandchildren prepare their models for a race. On the other side of the brook stood a few male adolescents who had entered into the friendly competition as well and cheered on their own creations with gusto. Their voices caused Cinthia to jar from her reverie and look up and across towards them. As much as anyone else, they were fully into the spirit of the festival and even called out supportive advice to the younger entrants on how to build their models better. Cinthia's eyes glowed a little brighter at this sporting exchange and the edge of her mouth curved up a notch. She then noticed a couple of them glance over at Willow, but only for a moment. The instant Cinthia locked gazes with them, they turned away back towards the game, pretending never to have seen her. Her face hardened, but she eased a bit and shook her head. From the corner of her eye, she could see that some of the older male generation had moved their attention from the boat building to the teenagers. Shifting her focus to them, Cinthia gave a quiet laugh as she took note of their defensive frowns as they too had caught the sideways peeks towards Willow and silently forbade the idea to the youths. Whilst Cinthia did not think these particular individual's to be of any danger to her friend, relief rose in her chest over the fact that Willow was amongst people who were protective of her.

"Shall we head back and practice some dancing?" asked Willow in her usual perky tone.

Cinthia was jolted back to her immediate surroundings at her friend's sudden query. Pondering the question put to her, she shook her head.

"I think that would be a bad idea," she chuckled.

"Need some more time?"

"Yeah," answered Cinthia, the cool night air feeling very welcoming at that point. She then looked towards the woods and its deep shadows. "Actually, would you mind if we went for a quick walk? Just to take a break before heading back in?"

"Of course," replied Willow, standing up and shaking her feet dry. She then put her finger to her lips and looked up. "I know just the place! The stepping stones!"

Cinthia followed her from the clean cut grasses of the garden into the wild undergrowth beyond. A sudden sense of comfort blanketed her as they entered the darkness of the forest, enhanced by the gentle trickle of the brook echoing just to their left. Willow, humming to herself, skipped in zig-zags across a path that was tucked in between the trees and Cinthia walked on behind her, soaking up the stillness all around. The further they meandered down the trail, the more distant the frivolities of the party became in their ears. Having wandered for a few minutes in silence, Willow skipped back and bounced backwards in time with Cinthia's pace.

"So, how are you enjoying it so far?" she inquired, her face beaming.

"The walk or the party in general?" asked Cinthia cheekily.

Willow giggled, "The party."

Cinthia nodded. "It's… endearing actually. It seems like a really nice community."

"It is!" she cheerfully agreed. "I'm so happy you decided to try it out!"

"Me too, though it is a little daunting being around people who all know each other and you're the only outsider."

Willow continued to bound onwards, her back turned to the path. "Only for now. You can get to know people here over time if you'd like. I'm sure they'd like to get to know you better – you already made a great impression on the kids!"

Cinthia snickered. "Yeah, you're still not telling anyone about that."

Willow's face fell and she pouted, "Awww. No fair!"

Cinthia shrugged and laughed, "Deal with it."

Willow giggled and resumed skipping forwards, her hair glinting in the starlight. As Cinthia observed her dancing ahead and saw her shining visage glowing in the shade as she gave the occasional twirl, she began, "Speaking of getting to know people better…"

"Mmmm?" asked Willow, slowing down.

"I saw a lot of young men take an interest in you at the party," she said. "And one even came up to me asking about you."

Willow made a musing sound that mixed with the swirling of the brook which lay just ahead, shimmering in the moonlight.

"I didn't notice," she replied, her tone calmer but no less blithe. "But it has happened a lot over the years. Several of the older men here desired to court me when they were younger and a few even asked for my hand in marriage."

Cinthia coughed an incredulous laugh, "Wait, seriously?" She raised an eyebrow at Willow as she began to cross over the bank of the stream to the stepping stones. "Well, don't keep me in suspense. Did you ever date any of them?"

Willow's arms went out to her sides as she put her feet on the first rock. Giving a single shake of her head, she replied, "No, I don't see anyone that way."

Cinthia followed suit along the slab path, her astonished smile broadening and inquired quizzically, "Did you at least kiss any of them?"

"No," came the simple reply.

Cinthia suddenly stopped. "Wait… Have you ever kissed… anyone?"

Willow ceased moving in the middle of the stones, turning to face her. Her expression was blankly confused.

"No," she answered.

Cinthia's mouth fell open and she snorted a laugh, "What? *Really?*"

Willow shook her head, a slight blush coming to her cheeks.

Seeing this, and taking in an astonished breath, Cinthia shrugged and continued in a gentler voice, "Would you ever want to try it?"

A puzzled look crossed over Willow's features, and she looked down at the stream with unfocussed eyes.

"I dunno…" she whispered.

Cinthia nodded and followed her sight then shrugged again, "Well, if you want to of course, I can kiss you right now. So you know what it's like."

Willow looked back up at her with a glint of curiosity in her eyes.

"Alright," she replied.

Cinthia stepped over the few stones that divided them until she stood upon the slab next to hers. Airily, she weaved her fingers through the glimmering, snow hair of Willow to grasp the back of her neck. As she began to draw her in, Cinthia saw her face glowing redder and rather confused. A twinge in Cinthia's stomach made her stop and look into Willow's eyes.

"You sure?" she whispered.

Willow nodded with a twitch of a smile. Cinthia returned the gesture and brought her lips to hers.

For about twenty seconds the Elders kissed before Cinthia stopped and took a step back to gauge Willow's reaction. Not in a great many years had she had so much trouble reading another's countenance. Willow's face was a mixture of all manner of bewildered and curious expressions outlining a smile that grew wider upon her bright scarlet features. Cinthia felt it was a nervous one and her guts knotted. Looking away, she shook her head.

"I'm sorry. I shouldn't have done that."

Willow touched her lips and her eyes glowed vibrantly. A few seconds after Cinthia's apology, she shook herself from her daze and glanced over.

"No, it's ok! I liked it! It was good. I just… was expecting something else."

Puzzled, Cinthia frowned. "What?"

Willow's gaze roved all over the brook as if searching for the answer. "A... fire? I don't know – it's how bards describe it in song. But no." She shrugged. "Nothing."

Cinthia's features tensed alongside the churning within her. "I... look, Willow, I'm sorry."

Willow suddenly beamed her usual brilliant smile. "It's ok! Really. I just don't feel the same way everyone else does. And I know that's ok too." She appeared dreamy once more. "But I did like it... even if it was very wet."

Cinthia lowered her eyes. "Are you sure? I'm really sorry if I've made you uncomfortable... and if I've made everything... awkward."

Without warning, her sight was filled with shining white as Willow closed the distance between them and pressed her lips to hers. For several seconds, Cinthia failed to register it and stood wide-eyed in Willow's embrace, hands out to her sides. With a giggle, Willow pulled back and bounced on her feet.

"You've not made anything awkward," she replied. "I was happy to try that with you. I don't think I'd trust anyone else in the same way to do that with. You're the most sexually experienced person I know and so I'm honoured to have shared that moment with you."

Cinthia's cheeks started to match the colour of her hair as her words sank in. She exhaled and gave a small smile.

"Thank you," she whispered.

"Of course!" Willow said, grinning from ear to ear. She then grasped Cinthia's hands in hers. "We're friends! And I did like it, I promise, just I guess not how everyone else would. To me..." She looked all around once more before finishing. "It was special because you're my closest friend. And it was a special way of showing that love."

Cinthia looked into Willow's eyes and nodded, her smile widening on her ever reddening features. "That... means a lot to me, Willow."

Deftly skipping around her and pulling her back towards the bank with a dance in her step, Willow replied, "So don't worry! Let's go have more fun! The dance will start in half an hour and I don't want us to miss that! Plus -" She squeezed her hand and gave a giggle. "- this is meant to be your night of trying new things, remember?"

Cinthia snorted a laugh and groaned, "Fair point, Willow. Fair point."

The pair returned the way they had ventured and re-entered the giant hall to find many of the tables had since been shifted. A greater space around the bonfire had been created and the party-goers were already warming up their dance moves whilst the musicians, who gathered against the far wall, tuned their instruments. A large number of people had once again swarmed Willow as soon as they arrived to chat of this and that. Aurrie was amongst them and presented her with one of her blood roses. Afterwards, the ageing mortal offered Cinthia another one, which she graciously received and used the opportunity to focus on eating rather than involve herself in the various conversations being put to her friend next to her.

As the time was approaching for the big dance to commence, the talks surrounding Willow quickly turned to requests for her to be their dance partner. A look of certainty passed over Willow amongst the whirlwind of these calls and she did not answer them. Instead, she grabbed a firm hold of Cinthia's hand with a grin. Cinthia tensed, but smiled as Willow beamed at her. The older Vampire then dragged her through the masses to the bonfire, declaring she was taken this year, but that they'd all get a chance to dance with her during the last section. There was a mixture of cheers and sounds of disappointment from the crowd as Willow raised their hands into the air.

"Yeah, I still don't know how to dance," spoke Cinthia loud enough so only Willow could hear.

"Don't worry, we have some time beforehand that I can teach you the basics," she replied, lowering their arms.

In the fifteen minutes that followed, Cinthia did her best to pay no attention to those witnessing her embarrassing attempts at circle dancing. Willow tried to instruct her with minimal success. Cinthia was more used to stomping her feet than moving them in specific patterns. By the time the cheering reached its zenith and all present gathered in a large circle around the circumference of the bonfire, Cinthia felt she could at the very least follow everyone else without stepping on others' feet. As an electric hush of excitement fell upon the hall, Willow reminded her that is was all for fun anyway and not to worry. Cinthia looked nervously to the person on her left and then to her right where Willow stood beaming. She took in a deep breath and the music began.

The hall was alive with the tunes and the ringing voices of the village singing out traditional hymns praising Saraanjova as they held hands and skipped around the fire, giving the occasional twirl and swinging back the other way. Not knowing the words to any of the songs, Cinthia, staring down, poured all her focus into getting the spins and hops right. Following a few different verses, she began to get a hang of the footwork and managed to look up. Smiles abounded throughout and the mixture of food, drink and blazing heat from the bonfire made the colours rise in the faces of the mortals. Next to her, Willow sang beautifully along with the others, never missing a word and cheering whenever a tune came to a rousing finish. Cinthia's sense of awkwardness abated as time drew on and she managed several genuine smiles.

The joyful bright songs of summer soon passed, however. In their place, the musicians played choruses in the minor keys and the people dispersed into pairs, dancing slower as lyrics of the onset of winter began to be sung. Though these were not without brightness. The laments of life gave way to the promise of new growth arising from the darkness. Partners exchanged flowers of the sunny months for pods and seedlings of the autumnal variety. The significance of the imagery and hearing the clear voice of Willow laden with both sadness and hope caused Cinthia's heart to sink and she slowed her dancing further. She frowned at the firelight. At its promise.

Just as soon as she thought this, she felt herself brought in close to Willow's embrace. Her head brushed against the older immortal's whilst she was swayed subtly to the music. Cinthia tried to pull back but due to both the soft, yet determined grip of Willow, and her own honest desires to not be alone, she sank a little further into her arms.

"I've got you," whispered Willow.

Cinthia's heart skipped a beat and she blinked her eyes in an attempt to rid the welling tears there. She held tighter.

"And I you."

Printed in Great Britain
by Amazon